STORIES

ELIZABETH JOLLEY

STORIES

Five Acre Virgin

AND

The Travelling Entertainer

VIKING

VIKING
Published by the Penguin Group
Viking Penguin Inc., 40 West 23rd Street,
New York, New York 10010, U.S.A.
Penguin Books Ltd, 27 Wrights Lane, London W8 5TZ, England
Penguin Books Australia Ltd, Ringwood,
Victoria, Australia
Penguin Books Canada Ltd, 2801 John Street,
Markham, Ontario, Canada L3R 1B4
Penguin Books (N.Z.) Ltd, 182–190 Wairau Road,
Auckland 10, New Zealand

Penguin Books Ltd, Registered Offices: Harmondsworth,
Middlesex, England

First American Edition
Published in 1988 by Viking Penguin Inc.

Copyright © Elizabeth Jolley, 1976, 1979, 1984
All rights reserved

Page vii constitutes an extension of this copyright page.

LIBRARY OF CONGRESS CATALOGING IN PUBLICATION DATA
Jolley, Elizabeth, 1923–
Stories.
Contents: Five acre virgin — The travelling
entertainer.
I. Jolley, Elizabeth, 1923–   . Travelling
entertainer. 1988. II. Title.
PR9619.3.J68A6   1988   823   87-40312
ISBN 0-670-82113-6

Printed in the United States of America by
Arcata Graphics, Fairfield, Pennsylvania
Set in Times Roman

Contents

Acknowledgments

Some of the stories in this book first appeared in *Australian New Writing* (Thomas Nelson Australia Ltd), *Sandgropers* (University of Western Australia Press), *Stories of Her Life* (Outback Press), *Tabloid Story,* and *Westerly.* Some of the stories have also been broadcast in the form of Radio Plays by the Australian Broadcasting Commission and the British Broadcasting Commission's World Service. The self-portrait, 'A Child Went Forth,' was commissioned by the *Australian Book Review* and was first published in that magazine.

The story collections, *Five Acre Virgin* and *The Travelling Entertainer,* were originally published in separate volumes by Fremantle Arts Centre Press.

Five Acre Virgin

Author's Note

I saw Mr Hodgetts when I was five. I peered at his back through his lace curtain. I wrote in a Boots Diary before I knew the alphabet. I loved smooth paper, I still do.

In trying to write I start with one little picture, a few words, an idea so slender it hardly matters and then, suddenly, I am exploring human feelings and reasons. The first story I wrote in Western Australia was 'A Hedge of Rosemary', about 1960. I suppose it contains things I had left behind, like the old man who carefully studied the soles of his boots whenever he took them off, and things which were new to me but known already by people who had always lived here, but it is more a re-enactment of the reality of transplantation and chosen exile experienced vicariously during childhood.

The stories in this collection are taken from that time to the present.

The first six stories come from a collection of twelve in which I have tried to present the human being overcoming the perplexities and difficulties of living. The collection is called 'The Discarders'. The characters appear to inhabit a crazy world. I think it is our world. Perhaps, because of too much shy hope and tenderness and expectation, people discard each other when it might be more satisfactory to discard the complacent acceptance of the values of our society and education and the repeats on television.

'You know, land isn't just for sheep,' Mother said. 'It's for people to enjoy themselves.'

I think she'd say the same about reading.

Elizabeth Jolley
1976

Another Holiday
for the Prince

We're having this dumb play at school Falstaff or something I was supposed to be the Sheriff of London but the bell went before my part came on and as it was the long weekend Hot Legs let us go before the bell stopped. I went down and hung around the Deli for a while with the others and when I got home Mother was already there.

'Don't bang the door,' she said, 'He's still in bed.'

'Sorry!'

'He's sleeping,' she went on, she seemed relieved. 'Sleep's the best thing he can have. I wish *he'd* eat!' She watched me as I took bread and spread the butter thick, she was never mean about butter, when we didn't have other things we always had plenty of butter. I ate my pieces quickly before she could tell me not to spoil my tea.

Mother always called him the Prince, she worried about him all the time. I couldn't think why. He was only my brother and a drop-out at that. Dropped out from school and then dropping in and out of one job after another, sometimes not even staying long enough in one place to get his pay. I could always tell by Mother's face when I came in.

'He's back, was back when I came home,' and she would sit

in a heap at the kitchen table. And after a bit I'd say, 'What's for tea?' and that brightened her.

'What do you think the Prince would like?' and she'd go up the terrace for liverwurst or something tasty to fry up.

My brother smoked and drank and coughed and watched telly with the blinds drawn day in and day out and half the night too.

'He's resting,' Mother comforted herself. 'Boys outgrow their strength. They need extra rest. If only he'd eat and go outdoors in the air, though!'

Saturday mornings I often went with her to her work to get her finished up as quick as possible.

Mother said it was a revelation every time she got off the bus and walked round the corner and saw the wide river below shining so peaceful with the far bank dark with trees and all the lovely homes piled up on this side of the hill. It was like a great big continental post card. The stillness and the blue misty light on the smooth water made her feel rested she said and she felt she was a better person every time she saw it.

We had the house to ourselves, it was all vinyl and bathrooms. She wouldn't ever let me do out the study.

'There's big cigars in there and sex drinks and books with titles,' she said and she sent me to hang out the washing. There was nothing in the *Seducer's Cook Book* to upset her she said and dusting those nude drawings didn't affect her, she was too worn out and faded for that kind of thing.

We seemed to get on really quick with the work and when we sat down to have our cocoa she looked out at the river approving of the calm.

'They'll stay out in their boat the weekend,' she said, sipping gratefully.

'I don't like you going out to work,' I said.

'You don't want to mind about that,' she said. 'Everyone's got to work at some time or other, it's best to like it,' she said. 'Otherwise you'll have to spend most of your life not liking what you've got to do,' she said. 'My Mrs Lady is a lovely woman, such a good mother too, you saw all that nice washing! really sets an example, so clean you could do an operation in any room in this house. And don't you ever forget those nice dresses and jumpers you've had from her.'

'But you're going for your life all the time.'

'Hard work never hurt any one. It's good for me, helps to fight off the menopause.'

'What's that?' Mother used big words. She read too much.

'It's when your life changes, you'll find out later,' she said, and then she said, 'and where else could I have an avocado pear with my cocoa.'

'Ugh! Avocado pear!'

'It's an acquired taste,' and she waltzed off with the broom. Later while I was wiping out the saucepan cupboard I could hear her queer singing above the noise of the floor polisher. She seemed to get quicker and younger as she worked.

As we were about to go home Mother took a little key off a hook in the kitchen.

'I've a very nice surprise for you,' she said, twirling it on her bony finger.

'That why you were singing then?'

'Oh was I singing?' Her cheeks were suddenly bright red and her eyes seemed to be full of tears as if an idea was trying to burst out of them.

'What do you think! Mrs Lady has left me the use of her car and some money so we can go away for the weekend!' Oh I felt an excitement, I hugged Mother.

'It's a wonder you didn't die keeping the secret all morning.' I hugged her again.

'My! Mind my living daylights,' she gasped for breath.

'The Prince,' Mother said. 'We'll get him to that nice motel again right on the sea front. He won't be able to avoid breathing the sea air if he's right in it.'

6

Of course my brother growled. He was in a terrible mood. Mother pleaded with him through the clouds of smoke.

'Only pack up a few things and just come. I have the car. Come and see.'

Grudgingly he looked. It took all the afternoon to persuade him.

'Look at the roo bar, and see, there's a radio,' Mother urged him, she fretted at the waste of time. She promised to let him drive once we got down into the country to try to make him come.

'But what about a license?' I asked.

'Hold your shit Bogfart!' He gave me a shove.

'Now just you watch your language!' Mother was severe. 'Mrs Lady has fixed everything. Only be quick and let's go!' She had had a shower and her wet hair was flat on her head. She urged and pleaded and threatened and we set off very late, about half past five.

Next day he stayed in the motel room watching T.V. and Mother fretted on the beach.

'Come in!' I called her from the water. 'It's beaut in!' And it really was considering the time of the year. But she couldn't get up any enthusiasm, she couldn't bear to see all that lovely sunshine wasted because he wouldn't come out.

Lunch time my brother was still disagreeable. It spoiled the meal and he refused to eat his sweets. But Mother said afterwards not to take any notice when he growled, it was only because he had used his pudding spoon for his soup and she knew it wasn't any use telling him with that snooty waitress looking on.

The motel was really gas! There was so much hot water Mother washed out all our clothes and we both washed our hair again. I got out my social studies. Hot Legs has this idea about a test every Wednesday.

'Shit head!' My brother started picking on me. 'Why don't

7

you get out before they chuck you out. That's all crap,' he said, knocking the book across the floor. 'You'll only fail your exam and they don't want failures, spoils their bloody numbers. They'll ask you to leave, see if they don't.'

I sat there and howled out loud, though I didn't want to, not in front of him.

Mother was furious, her face went bright red.

'Why you son of a bitch!' she screamed, I really thought she was going to go for him, she looked that mad.

And he put on a real idiot's face and turned his eyes up so only the whites showed and he said in a furry thick voice like as if he was drunk, 'Well if I'm the son of a bitch dear lady you must be the bitch,' and what with his daft face and Mother standing there all towelled up there really was a funny side to it and we all laughed our heads off. I wasn't sure if Mother was laughing or crying, anyway she got dressed and went off down into the town, we heard her crash the gears at the corner, it's been a while since she drove anything. She came back quite soon with steakburgers and chips and ice cream and Coke and we had a really good evening watching the T.V.

On the Monday just when we should have been setting off for home, my brother said, 'What's the beach like?'

And Mother couldn't get him there quick enough. Oh he was a scream. He kept sitting backwards into the water just as a wave came and he went under as if he was drowning with only his thin white fingers reaching up out of the water as it swirled back. I thought Mother would kill herself laughing. She was really enjoying herself.

'Halp!' My brother sat back disappearing again into the sea and his wet white fingers grasped the froth of the wave. Mother played in the water like a girl. 'Give you a race!' She swam splashing and choking. She could only do about five strokes of anything.

I don't think I've ever seen her so happy.

We were nearly the last to leave the beach. We saw the sun

8

go, leaving only a long red sky far out over the water which was boiling up dark along the sand.

'Come on!' My brother was nervous and irritable.

'Our Prince is cold and hungry.' Mother hurried me in the change rooms. 'We'll get a chicken and eat it on the way home.'

She seemed anxious suddenly. Her agitation was worse at the Chicken Bar, we had to wait as there'd been a little rush on chickens. She paced up and down the narrow shop and she kept looking anxiously out at the car. My brother was sitting there, we could see his white face through the dark, he was listening to the radio. We were all hungry.

'Smells all right!' He even smiled as we got back into the car. Mother tore up the chicken dividing it on bits of paper between the three of us.

'I'll have to step on it,' she said. 'I don't want to inconvenience Mrs Lady over her car.'

We were just about to start on the food when it seemed we were surrounded by the police. There they were poking their heads in at the windows, I felt a real fool.

'Eat!' Mother commanded, but of course we couldn't and neither could she.

'It was me! I took the bloody car!' I didn't recognize my brother's voice, I couldn't believe the words were really coming from his white face. He lit a cigarette blowing smoke all over his ragged bits of chicken. I could see his hands shaking.

'You filthy bloody liar. You shut up!' Mother screamed. 'Don't listen to that son of a bitch he's . . .'

'If you're not careful Missis,' the cop said, 'I'll have to book you for obscene language too,' and then he seemed to remember something. He looked hard at Mother.

'You don't vary much in your sort of crimes do you Missis. Wasn't it just about here in similar circumstances a few weeks back, if my memory isn't playing tricks.'

'This is the only sort of crime, as you put it, as I need to do,' Mother replied with quiet haughtiness. 'It so happens it was a

9

different car and it was a whole year ago. Time must pass very quick for some people!' she added.

Mother cried when she knew she had to go to gaol, she never could stand unbleached calico next to her skin she said. And she felt so bad about Mrs Lady too. She'd hoped to get the car back before they got in off their boat and of course she'd intended to work off the cheque she'd written for herself. She would have liked to have the chance to explain to Mrs Lady.

After a bit she stopped crying.

'It'll be better for the Prince,' she said. 'A more regular life, and they'll see he eats.' This seemed to comfort her.

'Be a good girl at the Home,' she said to me. 'You won't be so strange as there's sure to be a few you'll know. And everything will all come right,' she said. 'A change is as good as a rest they say.'

It was awful hearing my brother cry later. I didn't know it was him at first, he sounded like a man crying. In his room he'd got this big box of chocolates all wrapped up ready for Mother's Day, it wouldn't go in his case with all his things and he didn't know what to do.

'I'll help you,' I said to him.

'Oh go to hell and get stuffed!' he said and banged his door on me.

In Pottery Class I'm making a jar with a lid. If it comes out all right I think I'll use it for a jewel box as we don't ever eat marmalade.

Five Acre Virgin

'There's a five acre virgin for sale.' Mother scooped up her avocado pear and drank her cocoa quickly. She pushed the country towns and properties into her shopping bag. 'We'll have a look later,' she said. 'Might be just right for Mr Hodgetts.' She looked at the clock. 'We'll have to hurry if we're going to get all the rooms done today.' Some days I helped Mother like today when I had a half day from the toy shop where she had got me this little job to keep me occupied, as she said, during the long summer holidays. I was screaming mad in that shop, it was so quiet in there. Like yesterday I only had two people in all day, just two little boys who looked at everything, opened all the boxes and took things off the shelves, spilled all the marbles and kept asking me, 'What's this?' and 'How much is this?' And then in the end they just bought themselves a plastic dagger each. I preferred to go with Mother on her cleaning jobs. She had all these luxury apartments in South Heights to do. We got a taste of the pleasures of the rich there and it had the advantage that Mother could let people from down our street in at times to enjoy some of the things which rich people take for granted like rubbish chutes and so much hot water that you could have showers and do all your washing and wash your hair every day if you wanted to. Old Mrs Myer was always first in to Baldpate's penthouse to soak her poor painful feet.

Just now Mother was terribly concerned over Mr Hodgetts our lodger. He was a surgeon in the City and District Hospital; he worked such long and odd hours Mother felt sure a piece of land was what he needed to relax him.

'He don't get no pleasure poor man,' Mother said. 'There's nothing like having a piece of land to conquer,' she said. 'It makes a man feel better to clear the scrub and have a good burning off.' All doctors had yachts or horses or farms and it would be quite fitting for Mr Hodgetts to have some acres of his own.

Mr Hodgetts never stopped working. He used to come home clomping his boots across the verandah. Mother said his firm heavy step was Authority walking. She said it was the measured tread of a clever man pondering over an appendix.

His room opened off the end of the verandah so we had to pass it going in and out of our own place. He needed privacy, Mother said, and she put a lace curtain over the glass part of the door and she got my brother to fix up a little plate with his name on. The plate had to be right at the bottom of the door as this was the only part they could make holes in for the screws.

'Who ever heard of a surgeon being a lodger,' my brother said.

'Well anyone might be a lodger temporarily,' Mother said. 'If the Queen came she'd have to stay somewhere till the council got a palace built for her.'

'Not in a crappy place like this.' My brother shoved at the window to open it and the whole thing fell into the yard.

'Well Mr Hodgetts hasn't said he's the Queen, has he.' Mother had to go out to get something for tea then. Thinking what to get Mr Hodgetts and my brother for their tea was a real worry.

'What about lamb's fry and bacon,' I said, but Mother said she thought she had better prepare something elegant like sardines. She was always on about the elegance of sardines and brown bread and butter.

'You'll be giving us celery and yogurt next!' My brother looked disgusted. 'You know I can't stand fish,' he said, 'and tell your surgeon he can take off his cycle clips in the house.' With that he slammed off out. Sometimes he was in a terrible mood, Mother said it was because he couldn't tolerate the false values of society and didn't know how to say so.

'I'll have to hurry,' Mother said. 'It's Mr Hodgetts' ear nose and throat clinic tonight.'

Mother always assisted Mr Hodgetts. He just presumed she would wash and iron his white coat and every night he stood with his arms out waiting for her to help him into it. The first time I saw them dressed in white with bits of cloth tied over their faces I nearly died laughing. I had to lean against the door post it was killing me laughing so much. Mother gave me such a kind look.

'Just you sit down on that chair,' she said to me, 'and you can be first in, Mr Hodgetts will see you first.'

'But I don't want to see Doctor Hodgetts, there's nothing wrong with me.'

'It's *Mr* Hodgetts,' Mother said ever so gently. 'Surgeons is always Mr not Doctor.'

That shut me up I can tell you. So every Friday I had my throat examined and Mr Hodgetts sat there with a little mirror fixed to a band round his head. He peered into my ears too and made notes on a card. Mother fixed up his medical book between the cruet and the tomato sauce on the sideboard. The whole thing was covered with a cloth. Every day we had to bake cloths in the stove to make them sterile for Mr Hodgetts. And Mother made and changed appointments for the people down our street in the back of my old home science note-book.

When Mr Hodgetts went on the night shift Mother took the opportunity to suggest we go to have a look at the five acres.

13

'We can go on the eight o'clock bus,' she said to him, 'and come back on the one o'clock and you can have time for your sleep after that. We could have a nice outing and take Mrs Myer, it's been a while since she was taken anywhere.'

Mr Hodgetts pondered and then said, 'That's right. The lists don't start till eight p.m.'

'The list', Mother explained to us, was the operations.

'Who ever heard of operations being done all night,' my brother was scornful. 'And they don't wear boiler suits in the operating theatre and who ever heard of a surgeon having his own vacuum polisher and taking it on the bus.'

'Well he can't take it on his bike can he,' Mother said.

It was true the wash line was heavy with grey boiler suits; every day Mother had this big wash, white coat and all.

'Just you hush!' Mother said as I was about to ask her something. 'And you mind what you're saying!' she said to my brother. Mr Hodgetts was clomping through the verandah.

'Oh!' I said very loud. 'I could have sworn I saw a cat hunched on the window.' Of course there was no cat there, I said it so Mr Hodgetts wouldn't think we were discussing him.

'Oh that's nothing,' Mother said, 'your Aunty Shovell once saw a black umbrella walk right round the room of itself.'

Just then there was a knock on the kitchen door and who should come in but our Aunty Shovell.

'Oh!' Mother had to sit down. 'Talk of angels!' she said white as a sheet. 'We just this minute said your name and you walk in through that door!'

'Nothing I wouldn't say about myself I hope.' Aunty Shovell dropped her parcels, lemons rolled from her full shopping bag, and she sank, out of breath, on to the kitchen chair. 'Got a kiss for me then?' My brother obediently gave her a little kiss and Aunty Shovell smiled at him lovingly. She had a special place in her heart for my brother, she always said. She even carried a photo of him as a little boy in her handbag. Mother would never look at it. She said there was too much shy hope and tenderness and expectation in his face.

'Who's our gentleman?' Aunty Shovell indicated the verandah with a toss of her head. The firm footstep was on its way back from the wash house.

'Anyways,' she said before Mother could explain, 'a man who walks like that could never be a thief.' She settled herself comfortably and didn't make any attempt to leave till she got Mother to ask her to tea the next day.

In the morning we nearly missed our bus, as my brother wouldn't get out of bed and Mr Hodgetts took so long writing up his kidneys and then old Mrs Myer was late too.

Mother was half under the bus.

'I think there's a big nail drove right into your tyre,' she called up to the impatient driver. 'You better come down and have a look.' Mrs Myer was waddling up the street as fast as she could. Everyone just made it into the front seats of the bus by the time the driver had climbed down and been under to check the tyre which seemed to be all right after all.

We found the piece of land but Mr Hodgetts did not seem very impressed.

'Look here's a few fencing posts, probably thrown in with the price.' Mother pointed out the advantages. 'And over there there's a little flat part where you could put your shed and I'm sure these rocks could be useful for something.' Her face was all flushed from the fresh air and her nose had gone red the way it does if she's excited about things.

'There's no money in wool,' Mr Hodgetts said slowly.

Mother agreed. 'Too right! There's nothing in wool these days and, in any case, if you put sheep here they'd break their necks in no time,' she said. 'And there's nothing for them to eat.'

It was a terrible piece of land, even if it was virgin. There was no shade and it was so steep we had to leave Mrs Myer at the bottom.

15

'Oh it's so fragrant!' Mother said. 'You know, land isn't just for sheep. It's for people to enjoy themselves.' She waved her arms. 'I'm sure there are masses of flowers here in the spring, you must agree it's a wonderful spot!'

Mr Hodgetts stroked his chin thoughtfully.

'I feel this land is very strong,' Mother urged, 'and what's more it's only two hundred dollars deposit.'

'Why pay two hundred dollars to kill yourself,' my brother said, 'when you could do it for nothing,' and he pretended to slip and fall down the steep rock.

'Halp! I'm falling!' he called and his thin white fingers clutched at the fragments of scrub. 'Halp!' His long thin body struggled on the rock face as he went on falling. He put on his idiot's face with his eyes up so only the whites showed. 'Haaalp!'

'Oh Donald be careful!' Mother called. As he fell and rolled we had to see the funny side and we both roared our heads off while Mr Hodgetts stood there in his good clothes and boots.

Suddenly we saw smoke curling up from below.

'Quick!' Mother cried. 'There's a fire down there, Mrs Myer will get burned to death!' She began to scramble down. 'Fire always goes up hill,' she said. 'Hurry! Hurry! We must stop it! Don't be afraid, there's my good girl!' she said to me and we got down that hill much faster than we got up it.

'I am josst boilink my kettle,' Mrs Myer explained from the middle of her fire. 'I sought ve vould all hev tea. I bring everyding in my begs,' she said. 'My leetle cookink is surprise for you!' I don't think I have ever seen Mrs Myer look so happy. My brother was already stamping out the little runs of flame and the rest of us quickly did the same while Mrs Myer busied herself with her teapot.

Mother had a lot on her mind on the way home. It was clear Mr Hodgetts had no feeling for the land.

'And another thing,' she said to me in a low voice. 'There isn't a soul for his outpatients clinic tonight. The street's all been. Wherever am I going to find someone else to come.' She

16

seemed so tired and disappointed. And of course she would have extra to do at South Heights to make up for not being there today.

'What about Aunt Shovell?' I said. 'She's never been examined.' Mother shook her head.

'Shovell's never believed in doctors,' she said. And another burden settled on her. 'Whatever shall I get for *her* tea tonight?'

All through the meal Mr Hodgetts never took his eyes off Aunt Shovell. Mother had asked him into the kitchen as it seemed a shame for him to eat off his tray all alone.

'Mr Hodgetts this is my sister Miss Shovell Hurst, Shovell this is Mr Hodgetts who lodges with us.'

'Pleased to meet you Cheryl.' Mr Hodgetts leaned over the table and shook hands and after that it was all Cheryl. He kept getting up to pass her the plate of brown bread and butter. He kept telling her things too, starting every remark with, 'Cheryl, I must tell you,' and 'Cheryl, have you heard this . . .' And then he asked her a riddle. 'Cheryl, what lies at the bottom of the ocean and shivers?'

'Oh,' she said, 'now let me see, what lies at the bottom of the ocean and shivers? I give up!'

'A nervous wreck,' Mr Hodgetts laughed his head off nearly, so did Aunt Shovell. And then she said, 'Pass your cup, I'll read your tea leaves and tell your fortune,' so we all listened while Aunt Shovell predicted a long life of prosperity and happiness for Mr Hodgetts.

'Romance is to be yours,' she said leaning right across the table. 'Miss Right is nearer to you than you think!' Mr. Hodgetts sat there amazed.

'Is that so, Cheryl,' he said. 'Well I never,' and after tea he asked her if he could take her home before going to his own job.

'We never had the clinic,' I said to Mother when Mr Hodgetts had left for the hospital, walking Aunty Shovell to her bus on the way to his. 'Mr Hodgetts forgot about his clinic.'

'Never mind!' Mother said.

'I never knew Aunty Shovell's name was Cheryl.'

'Yes Shovell, like I said, Shovell,' Mother said.

'Is Aunty Shovell a virgin then?' I asked.

'Nice girls don't ask things like that,' Mother said.

'There's pretty near five acres of her whatever she is,' my brother said.

I thought Mother would go for him for saying that but she only asked him, 'Is my nose red?' as if he cared.

'Just a bit,' he said.

'I expect it's the fresh air,' Mother said and she began to sing,

'How do you feel when you marry your ideal . . .

it's a popular song from my youth,' she explained.

'How do you feel when you marry your ideal,
ever so goosey goosey goosey goosey,'

and she laughed so much we thought she must be really round the bend this time.

A Gentleman's Agreement

In the home science lesson I had to unpick my darts as Mrs Kay said they were all wrong and then I scorched the collar of my dress because I had the iron too hot. And then the sewing machine needle broke and there wasn't a spare and Mrs Kay got really wild and Peril Page cut all the notches off her pattern by mistake and that finished everything.

'I'm not ever going back to that school,' I said to Mother in the evening. 'I'm finished with that place!' So that was my brother and me both leaving school before we should have and my brother kept leaving jobs too, one job after another, sometimes not even staying long enough in one place to wait for his pay.

But Mother was worrying about what to get for my brother's tea.

'What about a bit of lamb's fry and bacon,' I said. She brightened up then and, as she was leaving to go up the terrace for her shopping, she said, 'You can come with me tomorrow then and we'll get through the work quicker.' She didn't seem to mind at all that I had left school.

Mother cleaned in a large block of luxury apartments. She had keys to the flats and she came and went as she pleased and as her work demanded. It was while she was working there that she had the idea of letting the people from down our street taste the pleasures rich people took for granted in their way of living. While these people were away to their offices or on business trips she let our poor neighbours in. We had wedding receptions and parties in the penthouse and the old folk came in to soak their feet and wash their clothes while Mother was doing the cleaning. As she said, she gave a lot of pleasure to people without doing anybody any harm, though it was often a terrible rush for her. She could never refuse anybody anything and, because of this, always had more work than she could manage and more people to be kind to than her time really allowed.

Sometimes at the weekends I went with Mother to look at Grandpa's valley. It was quite a long bus ride. We had to get off at the twenty-nine-mile peg, cross the Medulla brook and walk up a country road with scrub on either side till we came to some cleared acres of pasture which was the beginning of her father's land. She struggled through the wire fence hating the mud. She wept out loud because the old man hung on to his land and all his money was buried, as she put it, in the sodden meadows of cape weed and stuck fast in the outcrops of granite higher up where all the topsoil had washed away. She couldn't sell the land because Grandpa was still alive in a Home for the Aged, and he wanted to keep the farm though he couldn't do anything with it. Even sheep died there. They either starved or got drowned depending on the time of the year. It was either drought there or flood. The weatherboard house was so neglected it was falling apart, the tenants were feckless, and if a calf was born there it couldn't get up, that was the kind of place it was. When we went to see Grandpa he wanted to know about the farm and Mother tried to think of things to please him. She didn't say the fence posts were crumbling away and that the castor oil plants had taken over the yard so you couldn't get through to the barn.

There was an old apricot tree in the middle of the meadow,

it was as big as a house and a terrible burden to us to get the fruit at just the right time. Mother liked to take some to the hospital so that Grandpa could keep up his pride and self-respect a bit.

In the full heat of the day I had to pick with an apron tied round me, it had deep pockets for the fruit. I grabbed at the green fruit when I thought Mother wasn't looking and pulled off whole branches so it wouldn't be there to be picked later.

'Don't take that branch!' Mother screamed from the ground. 'Them's not ready yet. We'll have to come back tomorrow for them.'

I lost my temper and pulled off the apron full of fruit and hurled it down but it stuck on a branch and hung there quite out of reach either from up the tree where I was or from the ground.

'Wait! Just you wait till I get a holt of you!' Mother pranced round the tree and I didn't come down till we had missed our bus and it was getting dark and all the dogs in the little township barked as if they were insane, the way dogs do in the country, as we walked through trying to get a lift home.

One Sunday in the winter it was very cold but Mother thought we should go all the same. We passed some sheep huddled in a natural fold of furze and withered grass all frost sparkling in the morning.

'Quick!' Mother said. 'We'll grab a sheep and take a bit of wool back to Grandpa.'

'But they're not our sheep,' I said.

'Never mind!' And she was in among the sheep before I could stop her. The noise was terrible but she managed to grab a bit of wool.

'It's terrible dirty and shabby,' she complained, pulling at the shreds with her cold fingers. 'I don't think I've ever seen such miserable wool.'

All that evening she was busy with the wool, she did make me laugh.

'How will modom have her hair done?' She put the wool on

the kitchen table and kept walking all round it talking to it. She tried to wash it and comb it but it still looked awful so she put it round one of my curlers for the night.

'I'm really ashamed of the wool,' Mother said next morning.

'But it isn't ours,' I said.

'I know but I'm ashamed all the same,' she said. So when we were in the penthouse at South Heights she cut a tiny piece off the bathroom mat. It was so soft and silky. And later we went to visit Grandpa. He was sitting with his poor paralysed legs under his tartan rug.

'Here's a bit of the wool clip Dad,' Mother said, bending over to kiss him. His whole face lit up.

'That's nice of you to bring it, really nice.' His old fingers stroked the little piece of nylon carpet.

'It's very good, deep and soft.' He smiled at Mother.

'They do wonderful things with sheep these days Dad,' she said.

'They do indeed,' he said, and all the time he was feeling the bit of carpet.

'Are you pleased Dad?' Mother asked him anxiously. 'You are pleased aren't you?'

'Oh yes I am,' he assured her.

I thought I saw a moment of disappointment in his eyes, but the eyes of old people often look full of tears.

On the way home I tripped on the steps.

'Ugh! I felt your bones!' Really Mother was so thin it hurt to fall against her.

'Well what d'you expect me to be, a boneless wonder?'

Really Mother had such a hard life and we lived in such a cramped and squalid place. She longed for better things and she needed a good rest. I wished more than anything the old man would agree to selling his land. Because he wouldn't sell I found myself wishing he would die and whoever really wants to wish someone to die! It was only that it would sort things out a bit for us.

In the supermarket Mother thought and thought what she could get for my brother for his tea. In the end all she could come up with was fish fingers and a packet of jelly beans.

'You know I never eat fish! And I haven't eaten sweets in years.' My brother looked so tall in the kitchen. He lit a cigarette and slammed out and Mother was too tired and too upset to eat her own tea.

Grandpa was an old man and though his death was expected it was unexpected really and it was a shock to Mother to find she suddenly had eighty-seven acres to sell. And there was the house too. She had a terrible lot to do as she decided to sell the property herself and, at the same time, she did not want to let down the people at South Heights. There was a man interested to buy the land, Mother had kept him up her sleeve for years, ever since he had stopped once by the bottom paddock to ask if it was for sale. At the time Mother would have given her right arm to be able to sell it and she promised he should have first refusal if it ever came on the market.

We all three, Mother and myself and my brother, went out at the weekend to tidy things up. We lost my brother and then we suddenly saw him running and running and shouting, his voice lifting up in the wind as he raced up the slope of the valley.

'I do believe he's laughing! He's happy!' Mother just stared at him and she looked so happy too.

I don't think I ever saw the country look so lovely before.

The tenant was standing by the shed. The big tractor had crawled to the doorway like a sick animal and had stopped there, but in no time my brother had it going.

It seemed there was nothing my brother couldn't do. Suddenly after doing nothing in his life he was driving the tractor and making fire breaks, he started to paint the sheds and he told Mother what fencing posts and wire to order. All these things had to be done before the sale could go through. We all had a wonderful time in the country. I kept wishing we could

23

live in the house, all at once it seemed lovely there at the top of the sunlit meadow. But I knew that however many acres you have, they aren't any use unless you have money too. I think we were all thinking this but no one said anything though Mother kept looking at my brother and the change in him.

There was no problem about the price of the land, this man, he was a doctor, really wanted it and Mother really needed the money.

'You might as well come with me,' Mother said to me on the day of the sale. 'You can learn how business is done.' So we sat in this lawyer's comfortable room and he read out from various papers and the doctor signed things and Mother signed. Suddenly she said to them, 'You know my father really loved his farm but he only managed to have it late in life and then he was never able to live there because of his illness.' The two men looked at her.

'I'm sure you will understand,' she said to the doctor, 'with your own great love of the land, my father's love for his valley. I feel if I could live there just to plant one crop and stay while it matures, my father would rest easier in his grave.'

'Well I don't see why not.' The doctor was really a kind man. The lawyer began to protest, he seemed quite angry.

'It's not in the agreement,' he began to say. But the doctor silenced him, he got up and came round to Mother's side of the table.

'I think you should live there and plant your one crop and stay while it matures,' he said to her. 'It's a gentleman's agreement,' he said.

'That's the best sort.' Mother smiled up at him and they shook hands.

'I wish your crop well,' the doctor said, still shaking her hand.

The doctor made the lawyer write out a special clause which they all signed. And then we left, everyone satisfied. Mother had never had so much money and the doctor had the valley at last but it was the gentleman's agreement which was the best part.

My brother was impatient to get on with improvements.

'There's no rush,' Mother said.

'Well one crop isn't very long,' he said.

'It's long enough,' she said.

So we moved out to the valley and the little weatherboard cottage seemed to come to life very quickly with the pretty things we chose for the rooms.

'It's nice whichever way you look out from these little windows,' Mother was saying and just then her crop arrived. The carter set down the boxes along the edge of the verandah and, when he had gone, my brother began to unfasten the hessian coverings. Inside were hundreds of seedlings in little plastic containers.

'What are they?' he asked.

'Our crop,' Mother said.

'Yes I know, but what is the crop? What are these?'

'Them,' said Mother, she seemed unconcerned, 'oh they're a jarrah forest,' she said.

'But that will take years and years to mature,' he said.

'I know,' Mother said. 'We'll start planting tomorrow. We'll pick the best places and clear and plant as we go along.'

'But what about the doctor?' I said, somehow I could picture him pale and patient by his car out on the lonely road which went through his valley. I seemed to see him looking with longing at his paddocks and his meadows and at his slopes of scrub and bush.

'Well he can come on his land whenever he wants to and have a look at us,' Mother said. 'There's nothing in the gentleman's agreement to say he can't.'

The Wedding of the
Painted Doll

'She's got two sets of collar-bones and a double breast-bone and that's why she's so big,' I explained to Mother.

'How do you know?'

'She was in my class, you remember, every day when she changed for sport she ripped her blouse. Peril Page was just as dumb as the rest of us but she hardly ever got picked on even in home science where she was a real dill. Hot Legs was for ever picking on me, never Peril.'

'Pearl, you mean?'

'Yes, like I said, Peril.'

Mother glanced in the rear mirror, she was shaking her head, pursing her lips and then straightening her mouth and nodding her head vigorously. After a while she stopped her silent conversation with an unknown person and said, 'I can't think what got into Donald . . . of course boys have their lives and mothers can't tell their sons or their daughters what to do. It's what we want really, isn't it, for the children to get absorbed with their own lives and quietly drop their mothers.' She looked at her smart little watch. We all had watches, really good ones, there wasn't a thing more we could have wished for. We had plenty of money now that Grandpa's farm was sold and we had the right to live there under the gentleman's agreement. Mother bought us everything we wanted, nothing cheap or vulgar, all good quality and really nice.

'I'll have to step on it or we'll be late for the wedding.' We were going too fast already down the road through the valley to the small road bridge over the Medulla brook and, at the main road, she hardly paused for caution but swung out and round to the right, the trailer with the little Jersey cow perilously following. Afraid that the trailer might have unhitched itself I looked back but Dora was still there, her pretty head swaying a little and her ears shaped soft and dark against the paddocks as the slopes receded, one after the other, as if running away from us back up the valley.

The white and silver invitation from Mr and Mrs Page to the wedding of their only daughter Pearl to Donald Humphrey Morgan at the Great Saints Church Greatmount and afterwards at the Greatmount Lodge Hotel had surprised Mother.

For a while she seemed out of her wits.

'I'd forgotten we named him Humphrey,' she kept muttering to herself as she was going round the verandah on her knees oiling the boards with linseed oil and turps.

'Who's it after?'

'Your Grandpa's other name, not that he bothered. We thought it would please him and then he said he'd never liked the name Humphrey in any case, there's gratitude for you!'

She rose to the shock of my brother's forthcoming marriage with energy and we kept going to town to buy clothes. Mother bought herself three dresses as she couldn't decide which one was suitable. I had new shoes too as I have this terrible habit of kicking shoes to death almost as soon as I wear them.

'You're terrible hard on shoes,' Mother used to moan but now that we were not short of money she simply bought new shoes and my old ones lay discarded. I think I had more shoes in my room than Royalty.

'Four o'clock, what a time for a wedding,' Mother took the car and the trailer round the hairpin bend like she was in a race. 'What with going from one place to another and then the reception it'll be dead dark for the drive home. Not that I mind that! It's just that it'll be only the two of us from now on.'

I couldn't think why Mother minded so much, we were good company the two of us. Mostly our rows and troubles came because of my brother. All the same, I missed him, the place had seemed empty even before he left. When he had packed his case the room seemed bald as if robbed of everything. I couldn't bear to look at the case standing alone on the edge of the verandah, it was like seeing him standing there alone. His good clothes were already at Peril's place: everything was being done from there and they wanted him there for a few days to learn some etiquette from a book Mrs Page had bought.

It was worse for Mother, she tried not to show how she was feeling. She suddenly had a bit of a scream on the last evening he was with us. I suppose it all came over her all at once. 'What can they teach you that I can't or haven't already? Why can't you be dressed from here? What's so wrong with you, you son of a bitch, that you have to stay with them to be improved?' She went on like this even though we had dropped our language since coming to live in the valley. My brother, the Doll, as his friends always called him, just stood there instead of shouting back and losing his temper. After carrying on she suddenly asked him, 'Is my nose red?' After going for him she would always ask him if her nose was red, as if he would care.

'Just a bit,' he said. Perhaps he realised it was because she couldn't bear for him to go, and, though she never said anything, I suppose she was bothered about that Peril Page. That girl was so big and white somehow she reminded me, at least her legs at the tops reminded me, of that terrible white pudding we had every day at the Remand. I don't know what Mother thought of her.

'Any ten cent bits?' the Doll suddenly asked Mother. 'I want some money! Any ten cent bits?' he said.

'Now let me see . . .' and the pantomime began. 'If I'm not

a liar, there should be one on the mantelpiece . . .' and together they rushed off. He crashed into her in front of the stove, staggering and pretending he had broken ribs, he clutched his chest.

'Oh Donald are you hurt?' And he fell against her again.

'Oops pardon! beg pardon lady, let me see you *are* a lady?' He put on his idiot's face, brushing and dusting her thin body so vigorously that she nearly fell in the fender. He pushed his hands along the high mantelshelf, spilling matches and buttons, candles and pencils and a jar with a bunch of twigs and leaves.

'Mind the pins!'

'Oops pardon dear lady, your pins! So sorry!' Again the idiot's face with his eyes turned up so only the whites showed. He pretended to fall over her. As they bent to pick up the pins they met with a crashing of heads which sent them both reeling, one to each end of the small kitchen.

'Oh! I'll die laughing!' Mother was helpless.

'Halp!' My brother sat backwards into the wood box. He grasped at the air with his thin white fingers. 'Halp! I'm stuck. Haaalp!'

'I might have one by the bed,' Mother managed to gasp through her laughing and, suddenly free from the box, my brother jumped for the door as my mother flew through it first. The cottage really trembled as they plunged across the bed to the table, a whole lot of things fell in confusion down beside the bed, but no money.

'Nothing there? Well, we might try the little drawer in the sideboard,' screamed Mother, her thin face was really flushed. Both of them tugged at the sideboard knobs. Plates and knives and forks shivered. Screws, nails, scissors, aspirins, everything cascaded.

'Listen!' Mother suddenly said, 'what do you want ten cent bits for anyway, you'll not be parking the vehicle from now on.' We were all pretty serious then I can tell you. The Doll was out of breath, so was Mother: they looked at each other.

29

'What's for tea?' he asked her suddenly.

'Oh! the Prince wants his tea!' Mother straight away threw the cloth over the table and pushed a small bunch of knives and forks into my hand. She was still out of breath and her eyes were bright and her cheeks were very red.

'What's for tea?' the Doll asked her again.

'Just you wait and see!' We all got lost then in the smoke as Mother opened the oven door. 'I think it's done,' she lifted the hot dish on to the table.

'Ugh crud!'

'Come along,' Mother said, and with a flourish she began serving out.

The next morning, when I got up, he had already gone away on the early bus with his case. I swept out his room. There were a few bits of paper in his waste tin, they looked like poetry and I took them to read by myself in the toilet. I never thought of my brother as being interested in things like that.

Mother filled in the next few days with a little dispute over the Jersey cow. The cow had been brought over in the first place from a small property nearby but the people refused to pay the grazing fee. For herself Mother would not have minded but the land was not hers so she felt obliged to take the cow back.

We were going to be late for the wedding because of Dora. Before we put on the new dresses and shoes, in our petticoats only, we had coaxed Dora into the trailer.

'We'll take her home on the way to the wedding,' Mother said. We had to go out of our way on a dirt road across from the valley but Mother was sure there was a back road beyond the little farm which would lead to where we wanted to go, but she was mistaken.

No one was at home at the little farm.

'What now!' I stared about the desolate yard. There wasn't even a dog there. The house was almost a ruin with stones to

30

hold down the scabby corrugated iron on the roof. The windows were papered over on the insides and all round was the worst lot of rubbish we'd ever seen in our lives. Cans and cartons and bottles and an old armchair with a terrible hole in the seat. It was the kind of feckless heap feckless people create, Mother said, even the lemon tree was covered with poor fruit, rotting lemons lay on the ground, the air was heavy with the sharp smell of them. The place was quite uncherished but beyond was a most lovely stretch of country spreading for miles. For as far as the eye could see large peaceful pastures unfolded in gentle curves decorated here and there with the scattered groups of eucalypts which made tranquil patches of welcome shade.

'We can't leave her,' Mother said. 'What'll she do if no one comes.' There wasn't time to take her back to our place. Mother still had the impression then that the dirt road went on through to a miraculous short cut. We looked around the yard and the sheds once more. It really was a terrible place, it looked as if the people who lived there must be both ill and poor. Mother wondered out loud if they found it intolerable there or if they quietly got used to it. 'You can get used to anything if you try,' she said. 'We'll have to take Dora to the wedding,' she went on. 'I know! I'll give her to them as a wedding present.'

'But you've already given them their present.'

'Yes I know but I'll give the cow too.'

'But she's not ours.'

'Never mind!' So there we were on our way with Dora swaying in the trailer all the way down to the Medulla brook and on, once Mother had discovered that the track didn't go through but ended in an old quarry where there was an even worse rubbish heap.

I couldn't think how a cow would fit as a wedding present in that garden suburb home where the Pages had folded back the folding doors between the dining room and the lounge to make spaces to welcome and accommodate the presents. I could picture the jugs and glasses and salad bowls, the percolator, the fondue set and the mixer and the coffee mugs and dessert plates together with table cloths and sheets spread out on every available flat space. Mother had already given a substantial present. She had chosen to give cutlery, rushing rather to go and choose.

'Elegant cutlery,' she used the word 'elegant' more and more. 'We'll give a canteen of cutlery, a very elegant gift.' She said she liked to use the word canteen as it seemed such a lot to give. She couldn't help thinking, she said, of tea and coffee steaming in lovely white round cups and of waitresses and plates of sandwiches made from soft fresh bread with fillings like egg and parsley, fish and asparagus, all that sort of thing.

'Canteen's just the box. It's just the name of the box, that's all it is.' I nudged her. I was afraid the sales girl would hear her going on, the girl had such grumpy eyes and moved the things on the counter so impatiently it really spoiled the shopping when we should have been enjoying it.

'Yes yes I know,' Mother said in a low voice. 'It's just that it suggests so much.'

'I don't like that shop,' I said after.

'It was the girl,' Mother said. 'Poor girl she's not happy there and she seems to spread her unhappiness all round her.'

As we reached the metropolitan area Mother was forced to slow down.

'What'll we do with Dora?'

'Well, she'll have to come straight to the church as there isn't time to go to the house first.' She swung into the churchyard and drove right between the people who were standing in little groups, all of them wearing new clothes. She stopped the car on the drive on the other side so that we were pointing out to another road. She knew she couldn't back the trailer anywhere and I was glad she had thought of doing this.

'The first thing I'll need is the toilet,' she said, and as we made our way to the church she could see, as I could see, that something was wrong. First I thought we were too late but no one was taking any notice of us, not even of Dora who was an unusual guest. There seemed consternation on all sides of us, the wedding was not over, late though it was. The wedding, it appeared, had not taken place. The people were all talking among themselves: some voices were raised in anger and surprise. There was no sign of Mr and Mrs Page and Pearl and there was no sign of my brother, only these crowds of strange people clean and dressed up for the Doll's wedding. Mother gave a little wave but no one took any notice and we hurried into the little church.

'The "Ladies" is sure to be unlocked,' she whispered.

'Excuse me! Excuse me please!' Mother elbowed her way through a little group of wedding guests.

'I've never heard of anything like it!' a lady with a big hat was saying, she had a deep voice, big, so like a man's I looked back at her to make sure but her green dress was filled up with a woman all right, no mistake.

'Has she known this young man long?' Two faded but very clean dollies were hung up close to Big Voice. 'We are Pearl's two aunties from Sydney so we know very little.'

'It's a disgrace! Letting down that lovely girl like that. Why I've known her since she was in the cradle! No one knows where *he* is.' Big Voice attracted more people.

'Where's dear Pearl?' someone else joined in.

'That poor lovely girl's with her mother and daddy, the Reverend's taken them into a little private room. She's crying her heart out. The boy's a country fellow, he must be a heartless beast. Never did trust country people! You can imagine what the family are like. Lazy as hell y'know.'

'Yes we heard he was a dropout all along the line.'

'Whatever did Pearl see in him. Such a lovely girl!'

'The Pages, lovely people, good family y'know, were going to make something of him. Nice-looking boy but no prospects. Absolutely none! Mr Page, Howard y'know, you his sisters? Or Myrtle's?'

'Myrtle's.'

'Oh well you won't know Howard then. Howard's a very fine person. Heart of gold. Same with Myrtle. Howard would do anything for Pearl, only child y'know. Howard, I said, you're making a terrible mistake to let Pearly go and stay with those people but all he would say was if Pearly wants to go she goes. I suppose he thought to let her see what that boy's background was and she would see for herself what path to take but she didn't seem to come at any sense so, Pearly, he said, if you want Humphrey, Pearly, you shall have him, Daddy will take him into the business. You know of course Howard's done wonders over the plastic toilet seat . . .'

The aunts nodded together, they really hung on to that Big Voice. Even when we closed the heavy door of the cloakroom we could still hear her going on.

'I warned Howard y'know but would he listen! You may be doing wonders in business now, I told him, but don't spoil yourself now, I said, don't take back all you've put out, I said, and put it over that good-for-nothing young fellow . . .'

'It's raspberry-flavoured toilet paper,' I called out to take Mother's mind off.

'Mary where d'you think he is?' Mother was white-faced. 'I suppose he's where he feels best off,' she answered for me, pulling her clothes straight. She gave herself a stiff look in the shabby mirror and went back out into all the guests. As I followed her it came over me how all these people were strangers, there wasn't one person there for us except my brother and he hadn't turned up. Had he been there we would have been the only ones there for him.

'Not turned up for his wedding! His own wedding!' the little groups merged into larger groups. Voices were loud with indignation.

'What kind of a young fellow is it who runs away from his own wedding!'

I wondered which were the Pages' relatives from England. People had come from all over the place for this no wedding.

And all the presents too had come from such a lot of different people.

Somewhere a choir boy was practising with the organist, softly the music and the young voice came out from the church. I have often wondered if Mother was sad because her children couldn't play or sing or act or swim in races or run fast or get high marks. Peril Page was a stupid girl, nearly as dumb as me at school. Once I got a mark more than she did because she had forgotten to put her name and the date on her test and lost her mark. But the Pages and their friends did do things like going out in their boat or having musical evenings round the piano. Peril played the flute so she could do something even though it sounded terrible when she played.

'Perhaps we better go to Dora.' I pulled at Mother's new coat. I was afraid she might go to war with all these people and there was only me to help her. 'I think I can hear Dora,' I said. The voice of the young cow was welcome in all that spiteful crowd of wedding guests. It seemed like I could smell the valley then. Mother gave a little smile. Perhaps Dora reminded her of the magpies filling the stillness, attacking the morning with their voices tumbling; perhaps Dora brought the comfort of remembering the jarrah seedlings.

'The boy ran away from school,' the new man was saying.

'Stands to bloody reason . . .'

'Stanley please! It's the churchyard . . . !'

'Stands to bloody reason, begging your pardon, he'll run away from his wedding and his work and his wife ha ha ha! All Ws . . . get it? . . . Work Wedding Wife ha ha ha!'

'I'll just say g'day to Moneybags and Flossypants,' Mother said to me. And she went right into the group.

'The boy you're talking about happens to be my son,' she said. I could hear her voice give a little shake, I did wish she would come away.

'Dora's crying,' I pulled at her again.

'It so happens,' she went on, 'that he did make a protest

about the education system and since then he has made his own protest about working conditions in various warehouses and factories. Some might call it dropping out . . .'

I kept on pulling her coat. 'Dora's hungry, I think Dora's hungry.'

'Yes, I must take my cow home,' Mother said with haughtiness and she stalked off looking as though she was holding up her underwear with her elbows.

It was a relief Mother had put the car and the trailer the way she had otherwise we should never have got away. Cars were all round the cemetery and down the street. Imagine being bogged in that place, stuck, with the trailer wrapped round a grave. People were beginning to move. Apparently the Pages wanted everyone to go to the reception in any case, all that food couldn't be wasted now. And, with all the travelling and the waiting, people were bound to be hungry. Even if Mother had been starving to death she would never have gone to eat anything with that lot. Never.

'Humphrey!' Mother crashed her gears. 'I never gave that name a thought, fancy we called him Humphrey! Fancy him getting mixed up with all those pastel nylon pleats and the pale pink and blue spectacles, they've all got them! So many clean women and showered men with nothing to them except clothing bills and excess water. A marriage of accessories. Accessories! Poor Pearl, all the same,' she muttered away to herself. 'That poor girl suffocating in gift wrapping and sponge fingers.'

After a bit she said, 'What did you say Pearl was doing?'

'Oh you remember, she went in for nursing and you know what? she's nearly as dumb as me.'

'She is dumb,' Mother seemed calmer, driving brought her voice back to normal. 'But then . . .' she went on, 'a lot of people are stupid, especially nurses, only they manage partly because life and death come from somewhere out of our reach and partly because it is a profession where stupidity can be hidden behind the intelligence of some of the other nurses and, of course, a good many patients are pretty bright!'

As we turned off at the twenty-nine-mile peg to cross the Medulla brook I suddenly thought how silly my brother was not to have gone to his wedding. It was better to be married than not married because of having your home and little children and neighbours. Being married brought friends and furniture and possessions, boxes of groceries, Christmas and having a job and holidays. And then I couldn't help wondering if I would ever get married. Whoever was there in the world who would want to be married to me! And suddenly there seemed no one at all and the night seemed black all around us. The country is so dark at night and the loneliness of it all really got hold of me and I began to howl my head off. There I was bawling like a little child in the car.

'OH!' Mother was upset. 'Oh!' she said. 'You're tired and hungry. I should have got you something to eat. There . . .' she went on. 'Don't cry! there's a good girl. We'll be home soon and I'll make you something nice. You'll see. Just hush your noise there's a good girl.'

We had not been living out in the valley long, it was when the jarrah forest was still seedlings. We had just about finished the planting when my brother said he wanted to invite Pearl Page for the weekend.

'You mean Peril Page from my school?'

'Correct,' he said.

'Well of course!' Mother was surprised. It was the first time he had ever wanted to have someone come to stay. But she fixed the room so my brother could sleep on the couch in the kitchen and Pearl had his bed. She was a big girl with very white thighs and a lot of fair hair. Her screamy voice was the same as it was and her stomach bulged just the same as it always did. She was always grabbing handfuls of herself to show you she couldn't pass the pinch test.

That weekend, cherishing her, the Doll took her to town, Mother let him have the car, and he bought her a ring and they bought a jumper, sometimes he wore it and sometimes she did. She was still at school then but I didn't ask her anything, what Hot Legs was up to and things like that. I didn't ask and she didn't tell. Of course she only wanted my brother. They washed each other's hair and lay on the bed listening to the radio till it was time to switch on the telly.

Slap!

Laugh

'Donald don't!'

Laugh laugh

Slap slap laugh

Laugh slap

'Donald don't!'

My correspondence lesson had fallen through so I hadn't anything much to do, but I kept out of the way and dusted all the new shelf papers in the kitchen. All that weekend Mother had a sore throat, it hurt so much she said she could have ripped it out. She got a bit depressed as it was taking so long to go off. All the same, she said, it was nice and peaceful for once and she rested up. It was lovely us all being together, she said, and the house was clean and full of sun so that the polished boards looked dark and rich and the red and purple bed rugs seemed to glow with comfortable life.

'I really feel well off!' Mother said in her funny furry voice, it was all rough with whatever was wrong with her throat.

'What are you doing?' I asked her, sitting on the edge of the bed.

'Oh. Just copying something from this very good story by a man called Leo Tolstoi.' She showed me the page covered in her long black sloping handwriting. She loved copying wisdom, as she called it, from books. 'It's a story called "What men live by",' she said. 'You should read it, it is so deep I wish I could have written it myself.'

'Tell me what you copied then.'

'Well what I copied was this,' she said, and she read,

I have learnt that all men live not by care for themselves, but by love.

And then this,

It was not given to the Mother to know what her children needed for their life.

'Well what does it mean then?'

'Well you know this. I've read the story over and over again and I have to keep reading it because I still don't know it all and I keep forgetting just what it is that men live by!' And then Peril came in to show Mother the ring, all pleased, while my brother looked on smiling.

'That's very nice. Is it an engagement ring?' Mother asked.

'Aw!' my brother laughed. 'People don't get engaged these days.'

'It's in very good taste,' Mother said to Pearl. It was a plain little ring, the Doll didn't have money of his own so he had to be careful borrowing from Mother all the time.

Mother let my brother have the car to take Pearl back early on the Monday morning and we all sat round the table a bit gloomy and no one saying anything and Pearl all washed with her face red in her school dress and stockings.

'Have an egg?' Mother asked her.

'No thank you Mrs Morgan.'

'Shall I fix you some bread and butter?'

'No thank you Mrs Morgan.'

'Well, just a cup of tea then?'

'No thank you, nothing, thank you.'

Pearl came a few times and then she left school and practically lived with us till Mother had to put her foot down and then for weeks and weeks she didn't come and we never thought to ask after her. We thought it must be all over between them so, as I said, the wedding invitation had been a real surprise.

At last we were turning off the road on to the track to our place.

'What's for tea?' I asked.

'Would you like bacon and egg?' Mother said, trying to guide the car between the pot-holes, the trailer jumping about behind us.

'Can I make a cake?'

'It's a bit late but if you really want to I suppose it's all right,' she sighed. I suppose it came over her all over again, the house dark and empty and us not knowing where the Doll was. 'We'll have to get Dora into the shed first,' she said.

I suppose we hardly said two words to each other. Mother lit the stove and sat down with the tea pot and I mixed my cake. We sat the long evening by the stove and both of us were scared stiff when my brother suddenly came in: it was his sudden appearance in the lonely evening, just coming in from nowhere. 'The return of the prodigal son,' he said in his idiot's voice. 'I thought I could smell burned cake.' He stood there just inside the door, he was very white and I noticed his hands shaking as he lit a cigarette. 'Any crud left?'

While he ate Mother raved and swore about letting down the girl Page. 'You irresponsible son of a bitch!' she screamed, 'what kind of a son are you!' His ears went red while he was eating. Perhaps Mother noticed them for suddenly she said, 'Ah well! I suppose it's better to break now instead of a bit later on.' Her voice softened. 'Will you have a cup of tea?'

He nodded.

'I'll give you this,' Mother said. 'It takes courage to do as you've done. But I'll say this too, you should have had the courage sooner. I suppose you didn't realise till old Page began telling you how to hold your knife and fork . . .'

The Doll gave a terrible double-barrelled burp, he could bring them up from right down inside himself and he could even say 'hallo' in the middle of one. 'Ber hallo erp!'

'Dear lady,' the Doll said, getting up and putting his plate in the sink, 'those reasons are mere chicken feed! Let me tell *you*, *They* had their toilet seat varnished and forgot to tell me. What about that for a reason?'

Mother stared at him and then she burst out laughing. 'The painted Doll!'

'Correct,' my brother said. 'Framed.'

'Oh!' Mother said, 'I'll die laughing.' She began to sing,

'It's a holiday today! Today's the wedding of the painted doll . . .

It's a popular song from my youth,' she explained.

She put one hand on her hair, flattening it down over her forehead. With the other she twirled imaginary beads, strings of them, and she danced kicking out her feet to the sides, heels up, toes down and in. She was all over the kitchen, singing in a crooning sort of voice,

'It's a holiday today! Today's the
Wedding of the painted doll
It's a jolly day
The news is spreading round the halls
Red Ridin' Hood and Buster Brown
The jumping jacks jump into town
From far and near they're coming here
Church bells ringing, ringing
All the little dollies
From the follies
With their painted cheeks
Little Momma Doll
Has fussed around

For weeks and weeks
Shoo the blues!
No time to lose
Rice and shoes
Will spread the news
That it's a holiday
Today's the wedding of the painted doll.'

Together Mother and my brother danced across the kitchen, my brother kept bending his knees and tapping his head and his knees and his elbows and all the time he had on his idiot's face, his eyes turned up so that only the whites showed. I was still trying to figure out why he hadn't married Peril Page. They were laughing so much I knew it must be all right.

Suddenly Mother screamed, 'You son of a bitch! You goddam liar! They don't varnish plastic seats!'

'If I'm the son of a bitch, dear lady,' my brother said in a thick voice as if he'd been drinking, 'if I'm the son of a bitch, dear lady, then you must be that bitch!' He put on such a face.

He really did look ridiculous. We all roared our heads off. Mother laughed till she cried and so did my brother.

'You're really crying!' I said to him.

'Aw! Shut your face!' and he slammed off outside into the night.

For the wedding Mother and I both had new handbags. Mine is white with gold studs and little fur handles, it really is ever so pretty.

Several times I have looked at the bits of paper with my brother's poem, it isn't a real poem, it doesn't even rhyme, but I suppose him writing, *Till I met you there were no seasons*, and then him having to be with the Pages and their ways. *Till I met you there were no seasons* is a daft thing to try to tell Peril Page and maybe he found out about all her extra bones as well.

Mother's handbag, the one she got for the wedding, is nice, but for me I like mine best.

One Bite for Christmas

'I'll tell you something about Christmas, something terrible, when we're not eating.' Fingertips kicked his dog gently.

'Don't talk about Christmas!' My brother pushed his plate away. 'That animal will live longer than I will,' he said, 'and I'll starve to death with disgust.' He kicked the dog too. He wanted to sell the piano. He'd seen an advertisement, a girl wanting piano lessons.

'But if we sell the piano,' I said, 'where'd I put my chinese vase and what about Mother's photo?'

'Aw! Come on Maise. Don't get sloppy. We need some money. We need a day at the races. As for that vase!' My brother or the Doll, as he was called, swept it off the piano and it broke in a little heap against the wall.

'There, that's tidier, isn't it.'

I said nothing. I was tired out cleaning other people's homes all day and trying to think, on the way home, what to get my brother and his friend, Fingertips, for their tea. All I could come up with was polony and mashed potatoes. Of course they didn't like the polony so I told them about Missis Butterworth. She's the lady where I work.

'Morgan, Missis Butterworth says to me, she always calls me

43

Morgan. Would you like a piece of this fruit cake she says, thank you Missis Butterworth I don't mind if I do I says and then she says Morgan do you think this cake would keep till next year? And I says yes Missis Butterworth I think it will and there I am with my stomick rumbling and her putting the cake back into the tin—'

'Aw! I'm dying laughing!' The Doll was sulky about the piano and the polony. Christmas wouldn't touch it either. We all sat there, gloomy, staring at the piano. It was ringed with cup marks and yellow and split down one side.

The piano was all I had left. When I looked at it I thought about Mother and how she had changed over the years and I could hardly bear it. She had always worked so hard to keep my brother healthy when he was smoking and drinking his life away and watching telly day in and day out with no fresh air. She said he'd dropped out of living because he couldn't explain what it was about people and their attitudes he couldn't stand.

Mother was with Betsy now in a very solid suburb. Betsy's my older sister. Years ago when we first came out from the Black Country Betsy married the wheatbelt and we never saw her till recently when she had to go to the valley to fetch Mother. After the Doll and I left the valley Mother went queer out there all alone. Because of the gentleman's agreement Mother made with this very kind man, who bought the farm after Grandpa died, Mother was allowed to stay on the land till her one crop matured and, with her having chosen to plant a jarrah forest, she had all the time in the world to be there.

When Betsy found Mother she was sitting alone staring at the grey weatherboards of the old barn talking to herself in a very posh voice saying, 'This inhuman life into which so much human emotion has been projected is so completely indifferent to human life,' she was just sitting there saying it over and over again. 'This inhuman life into which so much human emotion has been projected is so completely indifferent to human life.'

So now Mother lived with Betsy, each putting up with the presence of the other. Betsy with the more patience.

When I went to see Mother she insisted on taking me round the garden to show me Betsy's boring plants wrapped up in bits of old blanket. Though she knew I was in a hurry she'd try to keep me.

'Wait a bit! I'll give you some lemons,' she tried to grab a few off the tree with her old hands. Whatever would Fingertips and the Doll do with a lemon!

'Mary,' she always called me Mary. 'Mary, I can't ever see my tin box,' she complained, poking in the shed with her stick. 'It's in here somewhere, it's got my name on it. They're always hiding it.'

I didn't try to hide my impatience. I couldn't think what the old goat would have in her trunk anyway. Probably only dockets from the sale of sour fruit years ago.

'Oh you'll stay and see Betsy,' the old woman was hopeful. 'She'll be in directly.' I felt I couldn't stand Betsy and all this wasn't helping me with something tasty to cook for Doll and Fingertips.

'Tell Donald I'm askin' after him and be sure to smell the honeysuckle as you go out the gate,' I could hear the old crab shrieking her head off but I didn't bother to look back and wave. I knew she would already have forgotten I'd been there and would just go on poking and muttering in the shed.

Mother refused to leave the valley after my brother, bored and disillusioned with the country, took up with this Fingertips. He, Fingertips, appeared in our lives all of a sudden. The two of them burned out the clutch and tore up the tyres on two cars driving them round and round the dirt roads skidding with screaming brakes and hidden in clouds of grit and dust.

'You're not going with that lazy good-for-nothing creature!' Mother screamed at my brother when he came in all dressed to go out.

'I want some money to put on a hoss,' my brother said, 'and hurry up and cough up you old cow.'

She screamed at him but gave him the money. She couldn't bear to disappoint him.

'Get off out of here!' Mother screamed and then she asked him if her nose was red as if he cared.

It broke her heart all the same and she couldn't stand Fingertips waiting there and grinning all over his face, quick with a politeness which had no meaning.

'Smile and smile and be a villain,' Mother said emptying her purse into the Doll's open hands. 'That's from *Hamlet* but you wouldn't know, the words not the money,' she added. Mother came from a household where they wept over poetry and music one minute and tore up pictures of politicians the next.

The piano was the only thing I had. Betsy had a whole houseful of furniture, trees, flowers and lemons, four children, a husband with a good job and a shed.

'I'm not selling the piano,' I said.

My brother was a great discarder. We had nothing left. Even at the holiday cottage where we went once he cleared everything out, even the lucky horseshoe. He had it off the door lintel the first evening, he said it made the place look untidy.

Fingertips was as bad. They threw everything away including their shoes, they never had them repaired. They had crafty methods, the two of them together, to get what they needed.

'Orl right,' said the Doll, 'orl right Maise, calm down. Fair enough. We'll just have to get on to another job. And that means you too Maise.'

'My very word it does!' Fingertips said.

'Oh Donald!' I said to my brother, 'Mother is asking after you.'

'Thanks for nothing,' the Doll said.

'And!' I said to them. 'Get this! I'm not lying tied up at the bottom of no lift shaft ever again to oblige the two of youse. Never again! You can think of some other method. Talk about the horrors! I still can't sleep of a night.'

46

'Orl right Maise old duck!' the Doll soothed. 'We've got a better idea. It's all worked out, just you listen carefully.'

It was when I was working I missed Mother most. She used to clown through a morning's work making up her face, trying on other people's posh hats and wigs and eating their avocado pears with her cups of cocoa. She was a real scream then. So full of energy.

I felt I was being invaded when the Doll and Fingertips were suddenly there in the Butterworths' big clean House. They seemed ugly and out of place in the white and gold bedroom. Both of them were stuck all over with grass seeds and bits of Prickly Moses because of hiding down on the cliff just below the wide windows of the house.

'Missis Butterhips gone off safely to her hoss?' the Doll asked. He started at once to search along the dressing table and then poked his head into the wardrobe.

'I'm starving, where's the kitchen,' Fingertips went off to look.

'Mind my clean floors!' I called out, my voice shaky and nervous.

'Mind my clean floors!' the Doll mocked me.

I wished straight away I hadn't let them in. I started the ironing, pretending I didn't know what they were doing. I could hear them though, muttering and ransacking all over the house.

'There's nutting to eat at all!' Fingertips was the first to come. 'There's no food!' he said.

'There's chicken soup in the fridge,' I said. I didn't tell him Missis Butterworth had been trying to get me to finish it up for the last three weeks.

'That!' said Fingertips. 'That stuff would turn me stomick!' In the end he opened a tin of cat food and ate it on a piece of bread. And then the Doll came all flushed up and angry.

'There's no money!' he roared. 'There's no money, not even your pay. She's not even left your pay to get pinched.'

'I know,' I said. 'She always forgets to leave it. I can't help that!'

'Two transistors without batteries, two piggy banks and only a kid's camera,' Fingertips reappeared. 'It's disgusting!' he said. 'What a place! You can't take anything, even the telly's fixed, built in and there's nutting to eat. All this posh big house and nutting at all to eat.'

'There's good clothes, shirts and—' I began. I didn't like them being disappointed. But they weren't listening to me, a terrible mood had come on them. I could hear them in the kitchen throwing tomato sauce and jam at each other.

'Have a avocado pear!' The Doll threw them all down the hall and into the rooms.

And then the Doll's mood changed again. Suddenly they were laughing. I could hear water pouring.

'Boys!' I was anxious. I never called them boys, it was because I was so frightened that someone might come home unexpectedly. Whatever would I do if Mr Butterworth came home early from the office.

'Just a little water fight,' my brother called out an explanation.

'Hurry up and go. Do!' I really was afraid. I wanted them to go. It was like being at the bottom of the lift shaft again. At that time I was working in a block of luxury apartments. After I'd let them in they left me all tied up waiting to be found by the night watchman. That was real fear that night and I felt it now.

'Anyone for tennis?' The two of them were in the doorway done up in the white bedspreads.

The Doll slided across to the record player. 'Do you dance?' he asked Fingertips. Oh he was elegant! 'Shall we?' And when they began to dance up the room and back it was so ridiculous we nearly killed ourselves laughing, especially when the Doll closed his eyes and began to sing and they both fell over the coffee table and broke it.

I was an hour and a half late leaving work on account of having to clear up their terrible mess. I'd only just finished when Missis Butterworth came in, and as usual, she hadn't any change to pay me.

So we didn't get to the races. We didn't get anywhere. We just had some left-over polony and potato for tea.

'This towel's soaking,' my brother shouted at me. 'How d'you expect me to dry my hands on something wetter than I am!' He sat down, gloomy, staring at the piano.

To pass the time the Doll and Fingertips had an argument. 'Don't you ever tell me anything about Christmas,' the Doll growled. 'I don't ever want to hear about that dog. It's bad enough having to see him. You oughta get him put away.'

'I gotta tell you about him,' Fingertips persisted. 'I gotta tell you he bit this man. You know that big feller down the street, you know him, he's got teeth like elephants' trusks—'

'Tusks, you mean.'

'Yes trusk like I said, well this man says Christmas bit him, really bit him bad.' Fingertips poked the dog gently with his foot. 'He says his leg's poisoned.'

The Doll glared at Christmas. 'I told you. I keep telling you. Have him put away! That dog'll get us into real trouble. Get rid of him!'

'Christmas is allowed one bite by law,' Fingertips said.

'No he's not!'

'Yes he is! Dogs is allowed one bite. Christmas can have one bite.'

'Well he's had it, now have him put away!'

Their voices went back and forth across our empty room. And, as none of us felt like going to sleep I dusted the piano and Mother's photo and, just after nine o'clock, we all went out to try to sell Christmas.

'Surprise! Surprise!' from Matron

We are all ready in the dinette, waiting for the ambulance. Lt Col Shroud, Reggie we call him, keeps going to the front door.

DOCTORS AND VISITORS ENTRANCE ONLY
Signed Matron A. Shroud

'Mind the step!' Matron bawls after him.

'It's all right Amy,' he calls back. 'I'm not going outside.'

She's afraid he'll fall on the broken step out there, it keeps crumbling away a bit more because of the milkman being such a heavy build. Matron says he's ruining the hospital falling all over it every night the way he does.

Mother is one hundred years old today, she had her picture in the paper and a Royal telegram and we are going to have a birthday tea for her off Matron's best white cloth, the one she keeps for Holy Communion. I only hope Mother will realise. Matron has made a birthday cake and has a surprise for Mother but she won't say to any of us what it is.

Mother is being brought over specially in the ambulance from the City and District Hospital where she has been getting better from a broken hip. She would keep getting out of bed and then, one day, down she went in her bed socks on the slippery floor even though Matron kept saying patients were not to get out of bed in their wooly socks.

We couldn't have the party at the City and District but here at The Ferns Hospital for the Aged we can do as we like as the place belongs to the Doll and Fingertips, they won it from Matron's brother, the Lt Col, playing poker. It was hilarious.

'You can still be Matron,' they told her, 'as we'll need one.'

Reggie, the Lt Col, misses Mother dreadfully so I hope they let her stay once she gets back. He goes all over the place looking for her under beds and in the cupboards.

'I say old sport,' he says, 'when *is* she coming back? I do sort of miss her you know what?'

The Doll says he's so dumb you can't help liking him. I'm on the day shift now and I don't feel nearly so tired, you really need your beauty sleep, it's the time before midnight that really rests you. Mind you, I usually got a couple of hours on the sofa before the wild life started up in room three. But once the poker was on every night there was no sleep for any of us. It was amazing how my brother and Fingertips were so full of life at their age and Betsy, too, suddenly living it up, painting the terrace red after all those solid years with that good solid husband she had and living that healthy suburban life bringing up her four girls. I got so tired long before they did but of course I was the only one working.

When Mother gets into bed now she gets in like a little girl, climbing in between her sheets with all her treasures filling up the bed and, when she goes to sleep, she lies all curled up with her things, her handbag and the clock and her photographs and her old tin box all round her, and you could think she was just a child there in her bed except that her hair is white and she is all wrinkled and shrivelled up and these treasures aren't what you might call toys.

When I don't see Mother I forget how she is now and my mind goes back to when we were in the valley all those years ago. Once on her birthday she was waiting and waiting for my brother to come. After dreading his visits and always wishing that he would keep away and not keep turning up with Fingertips to get more money from her, there she was watching the empty road, wishing more than anything in the world to see him coming along, passing the gap by the clump of trees and coming on towards the property. After he had taken up with Fingertips he lost interest in the farm and the jarrah forest he had been so keen to grow. I daresay some of it's still there between the new houses which seemed to spring up as soon as the land was subdivided.

'You can't clean up nature,' Mother kept telling my brother. He tried to clean out the creek bed and he was always hacking and cutting and burning off but all the time the castor oil plants and the wild radish and cape weed came back invading and taking over. Trees and branches blew down, wrecking the barn and the fence in places, and every time it rained the top soil washed down the slopes and then the meadow and the bottom paddock were so wet even the cows got bogged. He lost heart and wanted to go back to town, so he went off and only came to see her when he wanted money and then he never came at all. Like on her birthday.

'If only he'd be early!' Mother stood up beside the logs where we'd been sitting waiting all the afternoon. There was a pile of them up a bit from the weatherboard house, they must have been pushed there years ago. From these logs we could see the road. She shaded her eyes with her hand.

'Nature has her own ways,' Mother always tried to comfort my brother as everything filled in so quickly when he cleared. Mother worked hard even though the place was not hers and she was only on it by this gentleman's agreement. She stood by when the owner, Dr Harvey, was having trouble with the bore he had put down. The engineer had come and Mother was out there right on top of them telling them what to do. You could see the doctor felt uneasy to be on his land with us being there,

52

and though he was quiet and very polite while the engineer was trying to get the siphon going, it was clear he was really wishing Mother miles away. There was a great long black plastic pipe all down the slope to the small three-cornered water hole we called the dam, its banks were muddy and trodden down by the few cows left behind from Grandpa's time.

'It's like a stomick washout,' Mother explained at the top of her voice. 'You must get the whole hose full of water before you let it start to run. Fill the hose, pinch it while it fills and then let it go into the dam and it'll start to siphon. Just imagine!' she shouted at them, 'water coming up from all that way down under the earth, no trouble at all!' I don't think either of the two men paid any attention to Mother. In a well-bred sort of way they ignored her. Later on that same day Mrs Harvey and her two children, a boy and a girl, both of them tall grown-up children, came out to the valley. I watched them from behind the barn, they hardly ever came so I wanted to see them close up. They were pale and uneasy walking together round the fence line, the boy and the girl, one each side of their mother, pressed close up to her as if they were needed to help her along with their own bodies. Their eyes looked sad, I thought, and very unfriendly.

'Why do we have to have them on our land?' I heard the boy ask his mother as they passed near where I was standing staring at them. But Mrs Harvey just went on walking, looking straight ahead as if she had two stones in her head instead of eyes. They all three looked so unhappy, it was because of them looking so unhappy Mother wanted to advise them about everything but they didn't want Mother.

Well my brother never came on that birthday though she was so sure he would, and by that time she was really longing for him to come after wishing for years to be rid of his disagreeable presence. An empty road where you keep expecting to see someone you want to see seems terribly desolate when they don't come. There was a triangle of red gravel over there going steeply off the road where a track went up to some unknown person's place. Mother said the gravel patch was a symbol of complete loneliness and she couldn't bear to look at it any longer and, in the end, we left the log pile and went back down in the dusk to the weatherboard house. The sun had gone from the top of the meadow and that place, usually so bright, seemed desolate too. My brother the Doll never came and soon after that I left too to go wherever the Doll wanted to go.

There is a commotion in the hall, we all sit up a little more thinking it is Mother coming but it is more like the crash of a bucket and a fall.

'Where's my nurse?' It's Matron, she's just come down. 'Who put this pail in such a silly place!' Someone has fallen over the pail. It sounds like Mrs Hailey moaning, 'Oh my leg! Oh my poor leg!'

'There dear,' Matron comforts her, 'just sit down on this chair and vomit.' And we can hear Matron clearing away the pail and then all of a sudden Mother is here with us. There she is, very thin and old and very clean straight from the City and District. The noise of the pail stopped us hearing the ambulance.

'They always discharge patients so clean from there,' Matron approves, and then she bawls down the passage for the kitchen girl, Jeanette this new one is called, to make the tea.

'Now dears give Mrs Morgan a hip hip hooray!' Matron squeezes into the dinette beside Mother's wheel chair and Matron sings, 'Happy birthday to you!' She wants everyone to join in but no one does, so Matron sings it all the way to the end by herself.

'Happy birthday to *you* . . . Happy Birthday to *you* . . . Happy Birthday dear Mrs Morgan. Happy birthday to *you*,' and she gives Mother a kiss and we all go to kiss Mother and the Doll takes hold of Mother's handbag.

'Just you let go of that!' Mother says sharply.

54

'I was just goin' to hold it for you,' he says.

'I can hold my own thank you,' she says.

'Now dears what about some lovely cake. Isn't this a lovely party dears, give Matron a lovely smile,' she says to Mother. But Mother looks round the dinette.

'Where's Betsy?' she says. 'Why isn't Betsy here, she is my eldest. Betsy ought to be here.'

'Now dear,' Matron says in her most sensible voice, 'now dear, don't you remember that beautiful funeral. You remember dear, don't you, I'm sure every one of us here remembers Mrs Thompson's beautiful funeral.'

So we all have some cake, Fingertips is to hand it round but Mother won't have any from him and she eats my brother's piece. She is hungry after the polony and mashed potatoes every day in the City and District and she eats nearly all the cake. Reggie can't take his eyes off her.

'We'll just save a teeny piece.' Matron puts the plate up on top of the linen cupboard and then there is a ring at the front door.

'Surprise! Surprise!' Matron goes to answer the door and, to our great surprise, she comes back with a very thin old man in a wheel chair, he also is clean as if scrubbed by authority for years. With him are two orderlies in clean, badly-ironed overalls.

'Can we come in?' Matron coyly parts the curtains of the dinette. 'Is it all right if we come in?'

'O' course it's all right,' Mother says. 'I've got my knickers on.' Between Mother and the old man there is a moment of recognition. Then is an uneasy pause.

'I thought you was doing life,' Mother suddenly says.

'He's very deaf,' the orderly eases the chair round.

'I thought you was doing life!' Mother roars at him.

'Yes he was,' the orderly begins to explain.

'Well so are we all in a manner of speaking,' Matron says. 'We are all doing "life" dears aren't we,' she smiles all round the dinette. 'Now Mrs Morgan, give Mr Morgan a nice birthday smile. Remember dear his birthday is the same as yours and you are both one hundred years old. Just think of it, two one hundred birthdays! Hip hip hooray!'

We all sit there staring and clap a bit with our hands but no one cheers with Matron except the Lt Col who has to be hushed up because of getting too excited. 'Oh I say HOORAY!'

'I thought you was dead,' Mother says to Dad. 'I thought you was dead,' she says really loud but he just sits there with that faint little faraway laugh deaf people have. Dad really looks as if his skin has never got dirty, tied to his wheel chair are a cup and plate made of aluminium and a knife, fork and spoon made of the same stuff.

'Why has he got them tied to him?' Mother wants to know.

'He's got used to them so he has them with him now,' the orderly explained. 'He takes them everywhere.'

'Happy birthday!' Matron roars into his ear. Dad just smiles, no teeth, just clean gums, and smiles. 'We saved you some birthday cake.' Matron reaches up to get it. All this time the Doll and Fingertips have been looking very uneasy: I couldn't help noticing and wondering if it was the toilet they wanted. They half get to their feet and make as if to leave the dinette.

'Sister,' Matron says in her most posh voice, 'take Mr Morgan and Mr Shady to the toilet please.' So I get up, and out in the passage Doll says, 'Maise we got to get out from here. Quick! We got to!'

'Whatever for, Dad's simple, he can't hurt you.'

'It's not that.'

I try to reason with my brother.

'Well Mother's not in a bad mood or anything, she'll get over Matron's Surprise and everthing'll settle down.' We edge down the passage all three together.

'It's not that, it's them! the two men with Dad.' The Doll is really agitated, so is Fingertips.

'The big one, that's Bluey he's dumb but is he strong!' Doll

56

says. 'And the little one he's little but he's strong too. I never forget a face,' Doll says, 'not theirs anyhow and I've an idea they won't have forgotten ours! I expect we're still wanted.'

'Too right.' Fingertips is opening the back door.

'Quick Maise,' Doll says, 'get us Matron's car key.'

'You're not taking her car!'

'For a little while only and it's ours really in a way . . . '

'Too right!' Fingertips is prancing on the brick path outside the laundry and along by the chicken pen.

'Get us the key.' The Doll looks ten years younger in his agitation. 'We'll just go off till those cops have took Dad back.'

'You're not taking that car,' but I go for the key all the same, Matron keeps it on the back of the bathroom door.

In the dinette there is a terrible commotion as Mother has mislaid her handbag. Lt Col Reggie is on his hands and knees under the table.

'I'm stuck Amy! Yoohoo Amy I'm stuck, can you move the table?'

But how can Matron move the table with Mrs Hailey and Mrs Renfrew and Mother and Dad and the two orderlies who were once exercise-yard cops wedged all round it. Matron herself is stuck as there is hardly room in the dinette for the table and chairs let alone people.

Mother is really carrying on.

'He's pinched my bag,' she accuses the old man, she makes a dive at him. 'He's pinched my bag and he's sitting on it, look my bag's gone!'

Dad just sits there, he doesn't understand and he's smiling. Mother goes for his legs and the orderlies pull his chair back.

'Now Mrs Morgan dear,' Matron bends over Mother, 'Mr Morgan wouldn't take your bag, would he now, not on your birthday! Remember it's your birthday, lovely old birthday! Happy birthday!'

'I'm telling you he's got my handbag, he thieved it from off

57

me, he'd take anything, you don't do life for nothing,' she screams. 'Doing life don't change a man,' she bawls. 'Look at him, you can see he's a thief and worse!' Matron tries to calm Mother, Mrs Hailey and Mrs Renfrew get a bit hysterical too, and Mrs Hailey begins to take off her clothes.

'Not now dear!' Matron says to her, soothing her as much as she can.

'Pick him up!' Mother screams at the two orderlies, 'and just see if my bag isn't under him!' So the frail clean old man who is my Dad, though I don't remember him at all as I never saw him and Mother never ever spoke about him, is lifted up off his chair, his little thin legs dangling in the grey pyjama trousers, he smiles round at everyone and nods his head from up there.

'Higher!' Mother yells. So the orderlies pick him up again like as if he is a feather but there is nothing under him except an air cushion for his poor thin bottom and a square of plastic.

'Well I think the lovely birthday party has to come to an end,' Matron says and the two orderlies wheel Dad away.

'Poor Dad,' I say out loud. 'Poor old Dad.'

'Why poor?' Mother says. 'He's had a long life same as me, if it's a long life we all want.'

I help Mrs Hailey and Mrs Renfew back to room three and Matron gets her brother, the Lt Col, from under the table. Mother sits muttering to herself and asks Matron for a glass of water and some bicarbonate of soda as the birthday cake has upset her stomach.

'I never could digest bad cooking,' she says.

And then she says can she have a dose of medicinal as she thinks Matron's Surprise has done for her heart.

'Oh my poor heart,' she says clutching herself. So Matron gets the brandy from out of her hiding place under the sofa.

'Did they get away?' Mother whispers to me.

'Just for a little while,' I say.

'That'll be long enough,' Mother says and she sips the medicinal dose slowly.

'Thank you my dear,' she says to Matron. 'Just fancy silly old me making all that trouble,' she says smiling sweetly. 'I had my handbag all the time, I didn't realise I was sitting on it! I don't know how I could have been so stupid!' She tugs at herself and pulls out her terrible old handbag.

'Nurse,' Matron says to me, 'take Mrs Morgan to room three and help her to bed.'

'Thank you for the lovely party,' Mother calls out to Matron, 'and for the lovely surprise. I never thought I would enjoy myself so much!'

Just when I have tucked Mother into bed I hear the scream of brakes and the tyres on the gravel in the hospital yard. It is the Doll and Fingertips back from their little disappearance ride. The Ferns is all surrounded by cape lilacs, they are all in flower just now and they look like big rain clouds piled up in the sky just outside the windows. There were cape lilacs in the township near the valley where we lived for the last crop, and in those times, when Mother was busy with the sky waiting for rain, she often thought rain was coming but it was only the cape lilacs in clouds of flowers making the sky look as if it was going to pour with rain.

'One of them trees is sure to be a honey tree,' Mother says as I arrange her pillow. She suddenly seems old and frail, withered up and small. Years ago when we walked about over the land she would look at the old trees, there were so many bees about. 'One of them trees is sure to be filled with honey,' she used to say, and she would knock on the bark or press her ear against the trunk to hear the honey dripping slowly, filling the tree.

She was always hoping to find the honey tree, a tree unknown to any human being which over the years the bees had filled with honey. All the years we lived in the country she hoped to find a hollow tree full of honey.

'Mind you don't get stung!' she says trying to sit up in her bed. 'All those bees Mary, just you mind!'

'There's no bees here,' I say. 'There's no bees and no trees so be quiet do!'

'Where's all my things then?'

'Here,' and I stuff them into her bed, the old handbag and the clock and the photographs.

'Where's my tin box?' she asks me. 'They're always hiding my tin box.'

I get her box, it's probably only full of old dockets from the sale of sour fruit all those years ago. I push the box beside her.

'Thank you my dear,' she says and though she calls me Mary I don't know whether she knows I am her daughter or not. And then she says, 'I really must pretty myself up a bit in case my son comes,' and she fidgets in her bag for her old comb. She wants me to tidy her hair, she says.

'Tell Donald I'm askin' after him? Was that him I heard on the gravel just now?' she asks.

'Yes,' I say, 'he's back.' I push her down under the covers. And she says, poking her head up at me, 'The glory of the young men is their strength; and the beauty of old men is the grey head.'

'I didn't know you knew the Bible.'

'I don't, it's the text for today, Proverbs 20, verse 29, look for yourself, it's in the paper, bottom of the page.'

And then she starts to laugh and laugh.

'The only thing is,' she says, 'he don't have glory and o'course no beauty because he's got a boiled head.'

'Bald head you mean.'

'Yes like I said a boiled head.' And after that she lies down.

When I go out to the backyard with a sheet to put on the clothes line, there is no sign of the Doll and Fingertips and no sign of Matron's car. It must have been another car I heard. I hang out the sheet dripping wet all into my shoes and I can't help wondering when I'll see the Doll again, but more than this, I can't help thinking and thinking will I ever see him again.

The Shepherd
on the Roof

How sweet is the Shepherd's sweet lot!
From the morn to the evening he strays;
He shall follow his sheep all the day,
And his tongue shall be filled with praise.

For he hears the lamb's innocent call,
And he hears the ewe's tender reply;
He is watchful while they are in peace,
For they know when their Shepherd is nigh.
'The Shepherd' from *Songs of Innocence* by William Blake

Yes. There's been an accident.

No, I wasn't trespassing. I've never dared to trespass, that's why I've never found out something I've always wanted to know. I want to know if my house is like my neighbour's house. They have a kind of secret blessing on their house. Yes they have, you can see it quite clearly. But I can tell you something I do know. I can tell you there is one thing which one human being can't deny another. I do know this.

What a long drive it was with those two hostile young people. Yes I must have hit the trees. What a relief! How dark it is and wet! They've put sheep out here as well as cattle. Is there anyone there? If the Lord keep not the city, whatever comes after that, If. Yes. If the Lord is my shepherd . . . oh yes I've had some sort of accident. Someone always comes along when there's been an accident.

I suppose you are here to look after the sheep? Could you wait a bit? Will you just give me more time? Please? I'll explain everything.

I know the road so well, you see I drive this road several times a week. I know this clump of trees too. Honey trees. Some years they're covered with creamy white flowers, the valley seems to be dripping with honey then. You can smell it. During the day the flowers light up the countryside and in the moonlight they look like snow.

The road curves so often in an engineered repetition that I think I've driven round one certain curve and then find I'm coming to it again. I have come to understand this repetition.

I know the two long paddocks so well too. I think of them as mine just from looking along them with so much pleasure. Because of this, it gave me a shock to see sheep in the first paddock. There were calves there too, sturdy and curly, such innocent baby cattle.

'They've put stock in there!' I said to my husband. And he said, 'Well, what of it, it's not our land.'

How could we own such land. The second long paddock is better than the first, it curves flowing back between the fringes of the jarrah forest like a wide green river. I often think how I'd like to stop the car on the gravel just off the road, by the honey trees. I've often wanted to stop here and feel the rough red-gum darkened bark of these trees and to be in the grassy freshness of the air, and I've been wanting to walk the whole length of the second paddock to see what's at the other end of it. I know both paddocks are said to be over a mile long.

'You can't go in there,' my husband says every time.

'Why not?' I ask him. But I know that on all the gates there are warning notices, *Department of Correction. Keep Out.*

There's no money in beef just now. When these calves are ready for the market, prices will change. There's good beef running and fattening on the pastures of the Crown.

Are you here with the sheep?

I'll try and keep to the point of my explanation. It's like this. A man died in my ward last night. He had cancer all over him. He'd been to Germany for this new vitamin treatment and then to the Philippines for faith healing and he came to us in such a deteriorated state, he was only forty-three. By rights I should have died before him. His wife cried so much she had to be given the Valium written up for him. That's why I looked forward to this evening so much.

There are other reasons too. I'll tell you. Five years ago we bought a few acres of land in the hills. We cleared the bush and planted fruit trees, plums and almonds. We have pigs and poultry. Whenever we have the chance, we go up there. That's how I know this road so well, it's the road to our place. The weatherboard cottage is just a room and a kitchen. Visitors like to come because it's clean and pretty, it's restful too. We hardly ever have it to ourselves.

Sometimes I long for the peace there would be if I never said another word to anyone again. Perhaps I'll have this peace when I have explained? You see, I seem to be the only means of communication between the members of my family. If I never speak again I wonder if this absence will be noticed. I wonder if they will think of me in my long silence.

What a Saturday! If only I could stand on the edge of the verandah and call out, 'Come back wasted hours! Come back spoiled day!' You simply can't have time, any of it, over again.

I looked forward so much to this Saturday, to the journey up to the country and then everything went wrong while we were having the midday meal.

'Mr Stannard wants a shed,' I said. My husband didn't take

any notice at first. He was watching television and eating his pudding.

'Mr Stannard wants a shed,' I said again.

'We've got a shed already.'

'Yes, but it's not Mr Stannard's.'

'I know it isn't his, it's mine.'

'Ours.'

'All right, ours.'

'Well, he'd like a shed of his own.'

'But he doesn't live here.'

'If he doesn't live here, where does he live then?'

'Look! Mr Stannard doesn't own this place. Who does he think he is! He's only the lodger. I own the place. I'm the owner of the property.'

'Yes I know but Mr Stannard's lodged here for nine years, nearly ten, don't you forget that. If we hadn't had him lodging here all this time we'd never have been able to buy the farm.'

'That's more than a bit of an exaggeration!'

'Well, he wants a shed.'

'We've got a shed.'

'Yes, he wants a shed, of his own, a second shed.'

'Whatever for!'

'To work in I suppose.'

And then I had to ask my husband to be quiet. His chair grated back from the table and he began shouting all the reasons why Mr Stannard couldn't have a shed.

'Keep your voice down,' I said. 'You don't want him to hear you, do you.' And that was the end of the peace I'd looked forward to so much.

When Mr Stannard came all those years ago to take the room I could see he was a quiet man, very refined and clean. He said he didn't want much, just a room to himself and three good meals a day and he was prepared to pay well if he could have what he needed.

He has the room off the end of the verandah. To make it

64

more private I put up some curtains. 'Thank you for the curtains,' he said the first evening when I took in his dinner on a tray.

He seemed so appreciative I got him a white table-cloth and he put his own cruet in the middle of the table and his own sauce bottle too, nicely wiped, next to the cruet.

He sits with his back to the glass door eating his food and reading the paper; he often goes on sitting after he's finished his meal, reading and picking his teeth with a sharpened match. I like to think he's happy with us.

Some time ago, when Mr Stannard asked me about the shed, I said, 'Why of course Mr Stannard, what a good idea.' And he said, 'I'll price the materials, the timber and the slabs and I'll do all the work, you know, all the work of putting it up. I'll do that,' he seemed really pleased.

I know he's very low these days, he really needs a holiday. Everyone needs a holiday sometimes. There's three weeks owing to him but he daren't take it. He's afraid the firm will find they can manage without him and pay him off. That's what happens these days, they simply find people redundant. It doesn't matter how long they've been with a firm, they can be paid off with a week's notice.

The thought of the shed made him look so happy.

'I'll do everything,' he said.

'And we'll pay for it,' I said.

'Of course it'll be your shed really,' he said, and I agreed. In that way it seemed we would avoid all problems.

My husband doesn't use his own shed much, it's crammed with empty kerosene tins and old bicycle frames. One side of it is filled with a work bench all piled up with empty boxes and jars and broken tools.

I was down the garden with Mr Stannard while he searched out the survey pegs. The next door garden goes up a steep bank from ours and he thought he would dig into the bank as far as he could to save garden space.

We could hear the neighbours. They are elderly and pink, washed in the afternoons when they've had their rest. On Sundays, freshly showered, the neighbour man is so happy in the garden calling to their little dog. His voice breaks tenderly with emotion, an imitation of youth, because of his being married again and having the Sunday morning caresses and then looking forward to Sunday afternoon, sedate lovemaking with his new treasure. Both have been someone's treasure before but have found happiness all over again. A repetition of confined, safe domestic harmony, it's enviable, their pulling up of weeds together, their safe suburban scraping and tidying. The antics of the little dog delight them both, it's a little white pig dog with golden brown patches. They like to shout at her with playful authority and, while we looked for the pegs, we could hear them together at the end of their garden.

'Tootsey Wootsie Wootsie?'

'Lovey Dovey Dovey!" discussing in well-bred serious voices where to put their new incinerator.

I can't hear the sheep. I suppose you'll look for them? I can hear the stream, it pours steadily over the rocks not far away and the frogs keep on with their lives and their noise quite unconcerned that I am out here by the trees. I've always tried to put as much as possible of myself into living, in all sorts of ways, but in return there seems to be nothing.

We had white cups at school with thick rims. I liked to let my cup overflow before I drank. When I was thirsty I let the cup fill and run over, it was nice like that. Water. I'd like some water. I remember the school yard and the picket fence and the dirt path. There were Moreton Bay fig trees all along the side of the school yard. I had to take all grade one to the toilets before the bell went. I pulled down their knickers for them and I pulled them up again. I looked after them in the playground and on the road going home.

I don't suppose Mr Stannard has changed much since he was

a boy. Thinking of the colourless middle-aged man as an eager little boy with jam and bread crumbs stuck to his cheeks, made it hard for me to tell him he couldn't have the shed.

'Who does he think he is!' my husband shouted. My husband often says he'd like a divorce. He likes the idea of a family law plan where everything's sold and the money divided. He says we only meet each other in a world of family cares. We live in a constant rush and tension, so the arranging of the house and the furniture means a great deal to me. It comforts me. The children too, they've made flower beds and planted trees and built hen houses. They have their own rooms which they look after. If everything is sold and we have half the money each, I shall have nothing left because half the money wouldn't buy half the things I have now. You can't buy back a garden path made by your son when he was nine. Sometimes I'm really afraid my husband is just waiting to get his share of the money. It seems as if money, what a man is worth in coins of the realm, is all that really matters to him. What does a man do, he always wants to know, what does he earn and where.

What does he live on? is the question he always asks.

It comes and goes, this divorce thing. Sometimes it's ridiculous and we laugh about it together and at other times it's serious and frightening. Like jealousy and revenge it has no reason but is there, like some kind of fate, and it's because of this I can't say to my husband that Mr Stannard must have his shed. You see, the little farm means a lot to me too.

Arms on desks the teacher said at school. Heads on desks. I'd like to sit like that now with my head down resting.

Can you help me rest? I'd like to withdraw from the community of families. I don't even want to look at them through the window as they pass in the street. No one in my family has anything to say. They go off to their own rooms to stare at their own faces in the mirrors or to watch their own television. No opinions and no ideas. If only someone would question something. No one even wants to be a vegetarian.

'Fold arms!'

'Fold arms on desks, heads on arms. Rest!'

At my table I thought I'd try it. My arms, not accustomed, ached at once and it was awkward and then suddenly I was resting. I heard the noises of the house and my feet began to get cold.

That was this afternoon. I'm telling you my feet are cold now. I suppose you want my explanation. Never mind about my feet.

All the afternoon I heard the different television programmes through the walls of the house, the noisy voices of sport and football.

It's quiet here except for the noise of the girl crying. Is that Janice crying still? I'll explain about her. She's Tessa's daughter. Tessa is a friend of mine. She was a special friend but I can't keep up with her. She's a woman's liberation person always putting up notices to protest about things and always wanting five dollars from me for some cause of which she is to be the leader. I'll tell you about her later.

Thinking about Tessa made me wonder whether to get into bed with the electric blanket and perform all the things of a lonely weekend depression.

It's the weekend I kept thinking, and Mr Stannard can't go on with his shed. And, because I'm in the bedroom with my head on the table, we aren't on our way to the farm.

Yesterday Mr Stannard showed me the wood and today I've had to tell him, 'I'm afraid, Mr Stannard, you can't put the shed here.'

'Why?'

'It's the noise,' I said. 'My husband is worried about the noise.'

'What about on the other side then? It's farther from the house.'

'But you've done all the digging now, on this side.'

'Yes, I have, that's true! I'd need it this side too, so that the

68

cables for my drill, you know the power tools, would reach from the verandah power point. I really couldn't put it anywhere else.'

'Well, I'll go in and ask him again.'

'Oh no, don't do that. Don't you see, it's no use. I couldn't even hammer a nail let alone use the power drill if I felt all the time I had to be careful about noise. I just couldn't do anything.'

We both stood there looking at the black place where he'd worked so hard digging out and carting away so much earth. He'd made a great hole in the bank and gone down deep enough for a grave.

If that is Janice still crying, tell her to hush her noise. I'll be over directly I can get up. I hope she isn't hurt too much. Tell her to stop crying, tell her I'll be over directly. First I want to explain it all.

You can see why we needed the peace together today, just on our own. People need this peace very much and hardly ever get it.

As soon as we set off, the rain started. Instead of the western sun lighting up the jarrah forest, lightning flashed and the dark heavy clouds seemed to be pressing down on to the tops of the dark trees. Flooded streams poured over the road bridges and the evening was noisy with the rattling of frogs.

'You've got coleslaw in your beard,' I told my husband after supper. He wiped it off before he kissed me.

'I do love you very much,' he said. 'Even though you're such a nasty piece of work.' He held me close to him.

'I don't know!' I said. 'Whatever keeps us together!'

'Mutual contempts,' he said and kissed me again.

I lay beside him listening to him snoring. I thought of the children and how there seemed no place in the world for them. My husband often says he can't understand why they won't pretend to study, like Tessa's children, and get a government grant. But I think, like me, he does understand. And then I

69

thought of Mr Stannard wanting his shed and not being able to have it. The kitchen tap dripped and I could hear the stream rushing and the unchanging noises of the frogs and I wanted to wake my husband and talk to him. I wanted to say, 'Let's not quarrel and argue any more.'

Then suddenly, I heard voices outside the cottage and someone stumbled in the porch and knocked at the door. Knock! Knock! Knock! Oh I felt afraid. 'I'm coming!' I called. 'I'm coming!' Whoever could have come to our lonely place. Something terrible must have happened. I lit the candle and opened the door and there, all soaking wet and white-faced, was Janice, Tessa's girl, and her boyfriend.

I opened the door wider to them.

'Mrs Clark,' Janice said. 'This is Paul.'

They stepped close together, arms round each other as if unable to be parted, into the kitchen.

'Whatever's happened! What's wrong!'

Janice made no attempt to answer me and Paul, putting his arm tightly round her, caressed the nipple of her breast. He brushed his red lips over her hair, closing his eyes, and they kissed each other as if they couldn't stop.

I stepped back into the dark bedroom. My husband was sitting on the edge of the bed.

'Get them out of here!' Anger made it hard for him to whisper.

'But I can't send them away. I can't turn them out in the dark.'

'Of course you can. This isn't a hotel. The girl can go home.'

'But it's forty miles.'

'Well, it's only one mile to the 'phone box. She can 'phone her mother to fetch her. Do the old bag good to see what her daughter's up to, high-minded old faggot! She can drive out for them.'

'But it's one o'clock in the morning.'

70

'All the better! Get them out of here. How did they get here in the first place? And why?'

'I suppose they want to be together.'

'Yes and her mother, your friend Tessa, doesn't want them to have their togetherness in her house. The girl's a bulldozer like her mother. They bulldoze their way into having what they want. You ought to know Tessa by now. Well, this is Tessa's offspring. Get them out!'

'I'll drive them to Roseville to the train.'

'You're mad!'

'Well they can't stay here, you don't want them here.'

'Quite right. I'm not having them here. Be honest for once. You don't want them here either.'

'It's a responsibility.'

'Whose! Not ours. We've enough of our own. Just drive them to the 'phone box if you must drive them somewhere.'

'But I can't leave them down there at the crossroads in the cold and the dark, it's pouring again too.'

'Why ever not. They must have come here somehow. They shouldn't have come. They're old enough to know. They can't stay here. Get them away!'

In the kitchen they were still kissing, clasped together as if nothing could ever separate them.

'I'm sorry,' I said, 'I haven't room for you.' They turned to me. The boy was sturdy and curly with a youthful innocence. A small metal cross hung round his rosy throat, it reminded me of the brands punched into the ears of cattle. The cross might have been there against his will, but just accepted, as the calves accept their branding.

'Oh it's all right Mrs Clark,' Janice said. 'We'll sleep on the floor, if you've just got a blanket to spare. We don't mind the floor.'

'I'm sorry Janice, you can't stay here. Your mother wouldn't like it . . . I'm sorry you can't stop in the cottage.'

71

'Mother doesn't know, and in any case, it's not her business.'

They sat in the back of the car, close together. Janice sobbed and the boy was sulky. I was afraid of him. I had to get the car up the track between the trees. It seemed a long way to the road. I told them there was a train through in about an hour and it would only be a short walk then to Tessa's house.

'I don't want to go home Mrs Clark,' Janice said after a while.

'Janice,' I said, 'I have to think what your mother would want.'

The road curves so often in a kind of engineered repetition. I know the clump of trees by the second long paddock, it's the place where I've always wanted to stop. These trees represent years of growing. When the road was made they were left undisturbed. The sun wraps colour round their bark and they glow with the friendliness of a familiar landmark, a place to get back to. I have always had the feeling that if I could stop here by these trees no more harm could ever come to me. It's like this, you must try to understand. How could I have left these two children at the crossroads in the middle of the night.

I know the road so well, I was afraid I might fall asleep. It's a long drive.

I feel envious of our pink washed neighbours. There's a kind of blessing on their house. There's a shepherd on their roof. I suppose he's there all the time but they don't know. I want to tell them that I see the shepherd there every afternoon.

I'd like to have a shepherd on the roof too but I'm afraid to find out that we haven't got this secret blessing. Our children have been out of work for over a year. I can't stand this unemployment and the children not wanting their dinners yet being hungry for something unexplainable. I can't stand my husband not letting Mr Stannard have a shed.

I know if I tell anyone about the shepherd on the roof they'll laugh, they'll say it's easily explained, it's the chimney shadow, and what looks like the rod and staff of the Good Shepherd is the thin shadow of the long pipe ventilating the drains. I'm trying to be quick to explain. My feet are cold, really cold. I went to get some boots the other day.

'I'd like a pair of boots please.' I was a bit shy, asking.

'Yes certainly Madam, what saddle do you ride?'

'Saddle? No it's boots I want.'

'Yes but what saddle do you ride? English? or stock?'

'Oh, which kind do you keep?'

'All kinds Madam all-purpose, spring-tree, rigid-tree, poley, stock and show.'

'Ah yes! Well it's just a pair of boots I'd like today.'

'For what kind of saddle?'

'Oh just around the farm.'

'These boots would be very suitable for feeding the pigs and poultry Madam.'

'Oh! I suppose they would keep my feet warm.'

'Certainly they would do that Madam.'

'I'll take these then.'

How could I tell him a saddle of mutton is the only kind of saddle I know. The boots were too big really and didn't come far enough up the leg. 'Puss in Boots' my husband said as soon as he saw them, and I thought he'd never stop laughing. I have to agree. The boots are brown like milk chocolate, ugly with suede tops turned over and decorated with leather thongs. I dress like a cowboy to feed the hens.

It was a terrible drive the day I went to see about the other boots. I get so tired driving especially if I'm not sure where a place is.

Am I all alone out here? There don't seem to be any sheep and where's Janice? I don't hear her crying any more. I'll watch the night slowly changing into morning. I can see the sky turning pale. There's been a star just up there for some time, just one. I'll look at the star, it reminds me that there is something more beyond this clump of trees.

The bootmaker's shop when I found it was only half-made. There were pieces of plain wood for partitions, unvarnished, carpet squares still loose in the dust and unvarnished shelves along the walls. There was an unfinished display shelf, unvarnished, and two shabby chairs.

I had to stand and wait while the fragile man made telephone calls in Italian. They made the boots there, half-sewn boots were everywhere.

'I'm not used to high heels.'

'Madam the boots are all made with high heels. The boots will not be comfortable as the shoes you have on.'

'These are twenty years old.'

'I can see that Madam.'

'Will you measure me please?

'Madam kindly stand, without your shoes, please, on these two pieces of white cardboard, excuse please while I measure, please to lift your hem, while I measure, the small bones, the length, the narrowness, very long and very narrow. I do not know if we can make anything to these measurements, too long and too narrow.'

'I don't see how you can refuse!'

I suppose there is only one length and narrowness we can have made to measure. About these measurements there is never any doubt. Human beings deny each other so many things but this is the one thing one person cannot deny another.

It's getting colder.

The walls of the place where I work are shining green on the lower part and a glossy freshly painted yellow above and the corridor reflects this polished mixture of colour. If I could just get to the bench in that corridor I would be warmer. The Gideons put bibles there. Little raffia crosses fall from between the pages leaving their faint marks on the thin paper. There might be something there to tell me if there's a shepherd on every roof.

74

Somewhere I've seen another cross. Oh yes, the boyfriend has a tiny metal one on a chain round his shining wet neck. It sparkles and shines in the headlamps against the red background of his blood.

I wonder if they are all right, the two young people. Janice has not stopped her crying after all.

Yes, there's been an accident. Just give me time to explain. It's a long drive, I think it's my fault though I gave my husband the responsibility. . . .

I've always wanted to stop at this place to touch and feel the rough red-gum darkened bark of these trees and be out here in the grassy freshness of the air.

I can smell the soft grass of the long paddock. I never dared to trespass and that's why I've never discovered if we had a secret blessing on our roof too.

'You can't go in there,' my husband said when I wanted to walk in the long paddock. But I am going now. Are you there shepherd? I want to walk now and go on walking right to the far end. I've never seen what's at the other end of the long paddock. Are you there shepherd? Come down off the roof shepherd. Are you there my Good Shepherd?

Outink to Uncle's Place

'How can a man get tired of his food,' Uncle Bernard said at the evening meal. Because of the draught he wore his hat indoors, his white hair showing like a bandage beneath the brim.

Every evening we ate a plateful of macaroni. Uncle Bernard sorted out the packets in his sales case and used a soiled or damaged one. He cooked it in boiling salty water. Already I disliked the macaroni, it bored me and I sighed as I took up my fork, and I could not help complaining.

'Spik English please,' Uncle Bernard said. 'Eat!' he said. 'Is good!'

'I gotta get a job,' I said and sighed again.

'Yes,' he said, 'you gotta. But eat all the same!'

'I try everything and there is notting, always notting.'

For a time Bernard did not speak, he just sat there eating. I felt again the bleakness of the ugly room as I had been feeling it for days. It seemed as if I had not had a good night's sleep since I arrived. I had not expected it to be so cold. Cold air seeped through the thin walls and cold fingers of damp stroked my face all night and I lay uneasily on the edge of sleep. And somehow in the noise of the rain on the roof I seemed to hear my mother's voice talking up and down.

When I lay in bed, long ago at home, I could hear my mother's voice like a stream running as she talked up and down to my father. And every now and then my father's voice was like a boulder in the way of the stream, and for a moment the water swirled and paused and waited and then rushed on round the boulder and I heard my mother talking on, up and down.

In these nights of cold and pouring rain and the half-remembered voices I experienced painfully the bitterness of homesickness.

'Back home in Holland . . .' I began. Uncle Bernard raised his fork in warning.

'We got nice room here,' he interrupted, 'beds, stove, cupboard.' He waved his fork in a generous movement. 'And food,' he said. 'Eat!'

'Every place I go for job,' I said, 'is gone!' I snapped my fingers to show how quickly prospects disappeared.

'We got nice room,' Uncle Bernard said. 'You find job. So!' and he snapped his fingers showing me how easily I would find work. 'Is always hard at first,' he comforted.

Sometimes when Uncle Bernard spoke, his voice reminded me of the smell of the bakehouse back home and I longed to be there. I wondered why ever I had come to the New Country. Though I expected a wonderful new life to open before me, I wished all the time for the streets and houses and for the people of my homeland. When I saw how Uncle Bernard lived, I couldn't, at first, believe it. The room was so cold and ugly, and straight opposite the door was a noisy cistern. And all the time the landlady screeched at him.

'Mr Oons—your room, look at your dirty room!' and 'Mr Oons you owe me! You owe me! When you pay?' She had a shrill voice and it annoyed me that she did not bother to pronounce our names correctly. And always, of course, the macaroni.

I could not think how Uncle Bernard could have written the joyful things he wrote to his wife and family. These letters, like little ships of thin blue paper crossing all those thousands of miles of land and sea, were passed from house to house and all of them were read several times.

Bernard is getting on spendidly, everyone said, the climate is wonderful and the people so kind. A good life over there! They nodded their heads, plenty of everything, especially for the young people. I read Uncle Bernard's letters too and could hardly wait to make arrangements to join him.

In the morning we had no milk. The milkman never left us any. Uncle said to take the landlady's bottle.

'No troubles,' he said. 'She won't come out for it a long time. You have time to fetch for her, later.' He put ten cents on the table for her milk. He brushed his coat carefully and took up his cases to go.

'Idle bodies only busybodies,' he said. 'Time is money.'

'What about my job?' I asked him.

'Yes,' he said. 'Your job?' He put down the cases. 'Tell you what,' he said, 'I'll give you half my macaroni round.'

'But how you bring out your wife and children on half a job!' I pushed him to the door.

'I denk for you,' he said. 'All day I am denking for you.'

'Tanks.'

I took the ten cents and bought myself an air letter and wrote the most poetical phrases I could think of so my mother also could wave a thin blue slip of paper at the neighbours and say, 'Claus is doing all right out there. Very nice place.' It hadn't taken me long to know why Uncle Bernard had sent those letters.

'No troubles,' Uncle said in the evening. 'I gotta job for you. Chocolates!' he said, and he lent me his other jacket. He brushed the worn cloth.

'Remember, you must ask to put the case on the table— so—,' and he gave a little demonstration and then he made me practise, I had to pretend to sell him chocolates.

'Good!' he said. 'We sell and sell, everyding, and then I take you to my place.'

78

'Your place Uncle?'

'Yes, we make little outink, you will see, very nice.'

I did not know anything before about Uncle's place, it was a very nice surprise. The thought of him having property comforted me. I felt quite cheerful. First the job and now the property. I wanted to talk about it to Uncle Bernard, but he was already busy with his studying, and was not to be disturbed.

Every night, after the macaroni, Uncle sat reading. He borrowed innumerable books from the library and he read and copied whole pages into an exercise book. He was studying about the growing of grapes and about wine making. He read aloud to me.

'Listen to the soil!' he said, and he read, 'The latitude is thirty-two degrees south, the height above sea level below a hundred feet and the rainfall about thirty-five inches per annum, temperature ranges well into the high nineties during the summer. The soil is a deep alluvial sandy loam.' His voice was deep with the pleasure of the soil. He wrote out the names of the grape families.

'Is like a poem,' he said and he read them aloud, 'Tokay, Shiraz, Grenache, Pedro, Muscat and Frontignac.' He made me repeat the names, correcting my accent which was hardly much worse than his own.

He designed wine labels too. He had another exercise book for these and fondly he turned the small smeared pages showing me the designs which, in red and blue ink, described wonderful growing conditions, rare vintages and exclusive private bins. All were lavishly embellished with inky maidens entwined with grape vines and marked with improbable dates. Some of the names were familiar. I recognized them easily—Claret Bernard, Bernard Burgundy and Bernard Rosé Sec. There were others, aunts and cousins, whose names took on a delightfully new meaning when thus attached to Uncle Bernard's wines.

My uncle closed his books, snap, study time was over.

'Is bed now,' he said. 'Then work. Then . . .' and his voice deepened with the promise of a treat, 'then the outink to my place.' I could hardly wait to see Uncle's place. The thought of it dispersed all the dreariness and bitterness of homesickness. I slept well.

'So Claus has chob at last.' Mrs Schultz, the landlady, rose early the next morning for the occasion or else it was to be sure of getting her milk.

'Vait!' she said on the verandah, and she fetched her nail scissors and trimmed my cuffs.

'Gut lock!' she said.

'She denks of the money you bring home,' Uncle Bernard said as we walked together to the bus with our cases, he with his macaroni and I with the chocolates.

My area was a narrow strip between the railway line and the sea. In spite of the fragrance of fresh-cut grass it was a crumbling and depressing suburb. I was supposed to find the shops, exhibit my samples and fill the page of my fat notebook with orders.

As I approached the first shop I prayed no one would be there.

'How you get order then?' I could almost hear Uncle Bernard's exasperation though he was by now on the other side of the town fondly describing his macaroni. I stood on the pavement hesitating. I was afraid someone was peering through the lace curtain at me so I walked on and round the corner where I rested under a tree. The morning was light and cool and the doves were laughing softly to and fro to one another. I thought I would go back to the shop, but after a while I walked on. I envied people who were on their way to work, they seemed so certain about what they had to do.

Across the road in among some tamarisks and eucalyptus trees there was a small shop. In front was a crazy verandah on tottering posts and the name *Sam's Deli Store* in faded paint on the sun-blistered board. The cathedral of trees made a trellis of light and shade and relived the spiritual wilderness of the street.

I opened the flywire door and pushed in awkwardly with my two cases, already my shoulders were torn apart.

'Gut mornink,' a quiet voice spoke from the darkness. 'I am dealer in second-hand froots and vechetables.'

I supposed it was Sam.

'May I rest my case on your table?' I asked, my voice cracked with embarrassment. I seemed to fill up the whole shop with my cases and my request.

'Most certainly,' he replied with courtesy. As there was no table I opened the cases on the floor and Sam bent over them and admired everything and said, 'Perhaps next time . . . Business is good you understand,' he made a sad movement of apology with his hands, 'but not so good.' His whole body seemed to take part in the apology.

The next place was a milk bar, *Pam's Pantry*.

'May I rest my case on your . . .'

'Listen!' she said, smoothing back her blue rinsed hair. 'I'm up to my eyes in egg and lettuce rolls,' she said. 'Don't come chocolates at me,' she said. 'Don't, DO NOT bring chocolates here. Look at this lot . . .' she pointed at her shelves. 'I can't afford to keep the air conditioner going and when the hot weather comes chocolates don't keep, they go off. Money down the drain as far as I'm concerned. Get me? And who around here wants chocolates anyway. Icecream, yes, cool drinks, milk shakes, yes, but chocolates, no. No I'm sorry, like I said I'm up to here,' she raised her hand to her forehead, 'in egg and lettuce, I'm that rushed! I'm sorry. On your way. If you please!' She drew breath.

Everywhere was the same, all day.

The children were coming from school already. I sat exhausted on the grass at the edge of the road. All day I had not eaten. I opened a case and took a chocolate and ate it. The children were passing with their little bags.

'Chocolates?' I said to them and opened the second case.

'Chocolates,' I said. 'Take!' But they only stared at me with their school eyes and crossed the road to walk home on the other side.

Uncle Bernard was waiting for me in our ugly room.

'Chocolates,' I said. 'No good.' I sat on my bed, I felt bruised as if I had been fighting, and so tired.

'Same with macaroni,' he said. 'No good.'

It was Uncle Bernard's idea to have a party. Mrs Schultz was delighted with the idea, her bulging eyes shone behind her thick lensed spectacles.

'A partly!' she screeched. 'I go tell the girls and Mr Hubbard. We never had a partly in years!' and she waddled off to the back part of the house where the other lodgers were. We could hear her screaming the invitation over the noises of the cistern.

It improved our room to have people in it. Uncle Bernard was busy at once with the macaroni. And the girls, Maureen and Rose, helped me, with their long painted finger nails, to remove the chocolates from their wrappings and arrange them on the table. We all ate as much as we could.

'I have always . . . how you say . . . sweet teeth,' Mrs Schultz sat back happily. She kicked off her shoes. She turned to me. 'I am not . . . how you say . . . my beast till night then my beast comes out, at midnight! Schultzi always said it. My Schultzi was, how you say, a goof, he buy me presents all the time and I never like.'

The girls were giggling at Mrs Schultz's mispronouncings, they danced together, dreamily, a tango. And Mr Hubbard, in a cordial manner, shook hands with us several times.

Some time later Mrs Schultz seemed suddenly to see reason.

'Mr Oons!' she screeched. 'Mr Oons you owe me, you owe me! How you gonna pay me?'

Uncle Bernard sat picking his teeth with a sharpened match. We all looked at the empty cases.

'Maybe,' Uncle Bernard said thoughtfully, 'maybe we sell. Tomorrow is outink, the day after tomorrow we sell. Suitcase business now.' And once more we all shook hands with Mr Hubbard.

As promised, the next day Uncle Bernard took me out to see his place. We went together by bus to the wide, gently sloping valley where the vineyards lay in neat patterns stretching in peacefulness to the line of low hills beyond. Sand tracks crisscrossed the vineyards like pale ribbons and we walked along the softness of the first one. On either side the vines, just beginning to show little bursts of fresh green leaf, seemed to be kneeling on the earth as if praying quietly, row upon row of little praying vines. And at the edges were narrow orchards of trees trimmed just now with pink and white blossom.

'Almond and plomm,' Uncle Bernard waved his hand. He seemed suddenly much younger as he walked energetically, he breathed deeply and his happiness spread to me. We sang as we walked.

The air was soft and sweetly scented.

'Bean flowers,' Uncle Bernard explained. 'The beans are growing between the vines and when the pods are picked, we dig the bean stalks in to nourish the vines.' He sounded like one of his text books.

'Is not far now,' he said.

The track came out on a road and there was a great fig tree standing in a sandy patch just back off the road. A rough trestle table stood under the tree and some scales hung in one of the lower branches.

'We sell here, muscats,' Uncle Bernard said, 'and melons, in summer of course,' he added. Behind the tree was a small shabby weatherboard house with a deep verandah overhung with corrugated iron. And on all sides the vines came up to the windows of the house. 'How you like?' Uncle Bernard asked, his smile was too big for his face.

'O very very nice,' I said, 'very very nice Uncle.' I was about to ask him when we could move there when I saw a white painted board propped against an old barrel.

'But it's for sale,' I said. 'Why are you selling?'

'Spik Enklisch!' Uncle Bernard said. 'We buy,' he said, 'as soon as possible we buy!' He stood gazing at the place.

I stared at Uncle Bernard standing there in the golden tranquillity which seemed to drop from the tree. Uncle's place wasn't his place at all, it was only a dream he had. I turned in my disappointment and began to walk along the road: soft grey clouds had gathered and it seemed darker. Rain winds rustled. Uncle Bernard hurried to catch up with me. We paused on the bridge. The river was aching and swollen, purple brown.

'All that topsoil washed away,' Uncle Bernard sighed. The tumult of the flood flowed unseen below the smooth spreading surface of the water. On either side the grass and small bushes lay as if combed down by the recent rushing of the river widely overflowing and now receding.

'We find work,' Uncle Bernard consoled softly. 'Everyone here find someding. Sooner or later. You will see,' he said. 'Work, save and we buy place. You will see. No troubles. Is hard at first, but later . . .' He snapped his fingers.

I looked at Uncle Bernard's kind face and I looked down from the road bridge to the river. I looked at the water curving between the banks, on either side quiet trees hung motionless. In the quietness it seemed to me that this must have been what it looked to the first men who came to this place and I felt renewed.

'Yes,' I said to Uncle Bernard. I agreed with him because I knew that he was right.

Bill Sprockett's Land

Every time Bill Sprockett left the wooden verandah of the lodging house, *'ADASTRA' Superior Board Residence for Men*, and went for the bus to go out to the hills he felt a happiness and a sadness which was hard to put into words of any kind. It was a relief to leave the smell of cheap meat stewing and the shrill scolding voice of his landlady.

'I'm like a scalded bat outa hell this morning.' This was her daily hymn. 'I'll never get done in a month of Sundays. All these dishes to do, and just look at your room Mr Sprockett! Mr William Sprockett just take a look at all that dust!'

Symbols of his dreary existence. The room had so little in it that it could hardly be accused of untidiness, but the old floor boards exuded from their splintery cracks indescribable dirt and fluff. It seemed to crawl out all the time, especially at night, and lay in unsightly tufts, guilty and obscene in the slow warm shafts of morning sunshine, the only beautiful thing the room had, and that was gone of course when he came home after a weary futile day at the vegetable processing factory where he worked.

Every weekend when other people were trimming their lawns or watching sport, Bill Sprockett went out to the country to look at his land. He took the bus to the Kalamount Hotel and walked on up the hill from there. The road was newly made, the edges, turned up and heaped aside by some big machine, were like little cliffs of crumbling red earth, stuck all over with the burnt stumps of half-uprooted blackboys and toppling crazy bushes of the prickly moses. Back a bit from the road the wild hovea, growing in clumps, clambered over the undergrowth and hung down in curtains of misty blue flowers.

He left the road and walked in the scrub to the top of the rise to a place where he could look down across the sun-warmed slopes. The tops of the trees caressed the middle distance between the earth and the sky and every time he felt as if he was seeing the land for the first time. Every time he had the feeling that he was the first person to look down this valley, for the first time. Across the stillness the air was soft and fragrant and echoing with the sound of frogs croaking. He had never known before such a stillness and such a peacefulness.

The land was marked off in lots, little wooden stakes with numbers on them were stuck fast in the soil. It was all for sale right down and along this valley. Here and there dead trees held out their broken arms and stood headless, haunting the grey-green growth of the bush with their ghostlike whiteness. The peaceful stillness was unbelievable.

The valley was being sold, some of it could have been his land but he had no money to buy any.

Then his father sent him a cheque. It was the savings of years and the amount seemed unreal.

'Your mother's had a stroke,' his father wrote and went on to say that because of this they would not be able to come out to Western Australia to Bill as they had planned. 'Buy some land Billy,' his father wrote, 'and tell us how you get on.'

Bill Sprockett meant to do as his father said and he went every week, on Saturdays, to look at this valley. And in the evenings, because he was lonely, he went to the trots and he spent just a little of the money. He always lost the money and every week, his face glowing and relaxed after the day in the fresh air, he tried again and again to retrieve what he had lost. But always his luck was bad and the money dwindled hopelessly, and his life went on week after week, dreary and futile and lonely as before.

But he had already written to his father describing the land, the beautiful gentle slope of it and the length of time the sun lay upon this slope and the way the wind blew softly there, gently caressing wind, never a gale. And the creek was never dry, never even in the hottest summer, a waterfall fell down the rocky boundary, and all the year round the rocks shone silver in the sunlight with the streak of precious water.

And his father wrote back to say it sounded all right and he was glad there was water there and he was looking forward to hearing more about it.

So Bill went out as usual on Saturday, on the bus, and walked up and looked down the valley and watched the man, whose land it now was, begin the clearing of it. And on the Sunday he sat in his ugly little room and wrote to his father describing the men working and the machine they had for uprooting the dead trees and tearing up the scrub. It seemed as if the soil was bleeding, he wrote, it showed so red in the late afternoon sunshine. And he wrote about the burning in the evening, the smoke curling up and the hillsides aglow with so many smouldering fires.

After every dreary week in the factory and the boarding house he went out to look at the land and every Sunday he wrote to his father telling him everything that was being done. There were the foundations and then the building of the house and then the outhouses, and the installing of two sparkling galvanised water tanks. Then there was the preparation of the garden and the orchards. Every week there was something else to write about.

There was a brown-haired woman he could see there and he

wrote about her, Peggy he called her, and his father straight away sent a letter back to say how glad he was Bill was settling down at last.

The curtains went up in the little windows.

'The curtains are white,' Bill wrote, 'and the front door is going to be red when it's finished.'

The weeks and months went by and there was a cot, draped in green gauze, on the porch by the back door and Bill wrote to say that the orchards were coming along nicely and the baby was fine.

Soon there was another little baby kicking and crying in the cot and the first one, now a fair-haired little girl, was toddling about all over the garden.

'You should see her on her tricycle!' Bill wrote, sitting in his lonely shabby depressing room. 'You should just see her get up and down the path on it! and the trees are bearing.'

Every time he went up to his quiet place among the trees above the valley to look upon it, he marvelled at the progress he could see. Sadly every week he enjoyed going there.

Being a landowner, even if only in his dreams and in his watching, he found he had worries and difficulties. One year there were very bad brush fires, and his father, reading about them in his English newspaper, wrote anxiously. And Bill was obliged to take a sickie from the factory in the middle of the week to go out there as quickly as he could. There was such a danger from the long grass and dry scrub, tinder in the hot sun, on other people's neglected land, he wrote to his father in the evening, but all was well, the valley fortunately had not been in the path of the fire. And he wrote an extra page describing how everyone worked to prevent the fires from spreading, he wrote about their equipment and how, in the evenings, there was a queue of tired men waiting to have treatment for their scorched, incredibly painful, sore eyes.

And so the years went by and then Bill's mother, paralysed and bedridden this long time in the small front bedroom of the small house in the Black Country, died. And Fred Sprockett, sitting on a box in the damp aromatic warmth of his greenhouse, wrote to Bill in his careful but shaky handwriting. There was nothing to keep him in England now, he wrote, and he had been saving up and he was coming out. He had the fare, every penny of it, and he was coming out to see the realisation of his dream at long last.

At the place of look-out on the rise between the thin eucalypts and the quaint twisted banksias the old man leaned eagerly forward. His eyes were bright with happiness as he looked down the sun-warmed slope where the trees reached their narrow glittering leaves up towards the sky, and beyond these trees to the clearing where the neat brick house stood. The windows sparkled and clean washing flapped lazily on the modern aluminium hoist. He could see the lemon tree by the back door and the white hens down at the end of the garden. There was a rooster too, they could hear him now and then even from this distance. There was such a peacefulness and a quietness and sounds seemed to carry clearly.

'Hark at them pullets talking!' the old man said, not hiding his delight at all.

Bill Sprockett could hardly bear to look at his father. He had forgotten to count the years going by and the old man's aged frailness had shocked him when he went to the ship. He was glad he had hired a car to fetch him. They had come straight out to this place.

The work of all the years lay before them, serene and safe and comfortable, with more than a suggestion of prosperity, in the tranquil sunshine. It was all enhanced by the love shining softly from the old man's eyes.

The two fair-haired girls, now quite grown, were standing near the gate, they were surrounded by flowers, roses and pinks and geraniums and marigolds, a mass of colour. And behind the house, the compact little trees of the orange groves ran in neat ribs, radiating from the side and the end of the garden, down the slope of the valley. The fruit shone like little round golden lamps in the dark glossy leaves. Edging the orchard were plum and peach trees, purple and pink blossom lay along their slender branches.

'I've dreamed about this all these years,' the old man said.

Bill was looking down at the place too, it was the last time he would be coming to look. He hardly saw the prettiness.

If only his father could die now, at this moment. He was old enough to die. Most old men didn't live this long. Eighty-seven was a good age, too old to be changing your way of life surely. And too old to have to bear such a disappointment. It wasn't that he wished death for the old man. He never had felt like this before in his life, he had never known or even thought before as he was thinking now: it was a deep love for his father he felt and he knew he couldn't bear to tell him the truth about the land.

However could he tell him.

'Shall we go down now?' the old man asked. He was wondering about his daughter-in-law. He had dressed himself neatly in his best clothes for her.

'I hope she takes to me, and them girls too! Let's go down,' he said.

The sight of the old man's new boots irritated Bill and touched him at the same time, he felt an indescribable pain as he looked at his father's boots.

'I've been dreaming too,' he said suddenly in a voice which was quite unlike his own. 'I have to tell you something, Dad,' he began, and his harsh voice trembled and crumbled.

The old man looked at him not understanding what was wrong at first, and then slowly he began to understand. And it was in a moment of deep agony he understood his son for the first time in over forty years. His disappointment was such that he felt he could not bear it, not for himself, what did an old man like him matter, but for his son. He wished for words to offer the love and pity he felt.

They did not look down to the place again, of course it was nothing to them. Without meaning to, in their shame, they crushed little flowers, little clusters of coral and tiny exquisite orchids with their boots as they slowly made their way back through the scrub to the hired car, the prolonged melancholy crow of the rooster following across the deceptive distance.

And Bill Sprockett wondered if he could ask his landlady for a room with linoleum for his father.

A Hedge of Rosemary

No one knew where the old man went every night at dusk. He sat to his tea in his daughter-in-law's kitchen and ate up obediently everything she put before him. She was a sharp woman but quite kind, she called him Dad and stirred his tea for him as she put the cup beside him. She put it a bit towards the middle of the table so he would not knock it over.

'Mind your tea now Dad,' she always said, and without looking up from his plate he answered, 'Thank you kindly, much obliged.' After the meal he would sit for a while with his boots off: he held them in both hands and studied the soles intently, sometimes shaking his head over them, and Sarah would get his dishes done out of the way.

Just about this time, as on other nights, his son John, who had a business in town, came in and he and Sarah had their dinner. When that and the necessary bits of conversation were over they all went into the lounge room and sat in comfortable chairs to watch the television. The house was very quiet with John's three boys all grown up and gone their ways, two to Sydney and one overseas. When the old man had sat a short while with John and Sarah in the lounge he put on his boots slowly and carefully and then getting up carefully from his comfortable chair he went out through the back verandah.

'Mind how you go Dad!' Sarah called after him and he replied, 'That's right, that's right!' and went off into the dusk round the side of the house and through a door in a vine-covered trellis and down into the street. After he had gone Sarah wondered where he was going. On other evenings she had peered out into the dark fragrance to see if he had gone up to the end of the garden. She thought he might have gone up to the shed for something. Sometimes she had looked in there and had even pushed open the door of the whitewashed place next to the shed thinking he might be ill in there. He never would use the one in the bathroom which was so much nicer. But he was never in either place. If she went out of the front door she could never see him: by the time she had picked her way across her neatly laid out suburban garden he was always gone from sight and all she could do was to peer up the street and down the street into the gathering darkness and go back into the house where John was absorbed into the television.

'I wonder where Dad's off to again,' she said, but on this night, as on all other nights, John was not listening to her.

'The Queen's not looking so well,' Sarah remarked as some activities of the Royal Family came on in the news. John grunted some sort of reply and they both sank into the next programme and did not think too much about the old man walking off on his own into the night.

During the day the old man did practically nothing, he tidied the garden a bit and stacked wood slowly and neatly outside the verandah so Sarah had only to reach out an arm for it. Mostly he sat in the barber's shop. He went shopping, too, with his battered attaché case. He laid it on the counter in the Post Office and opened it with his trembling old hands. Glossy magazines lay in neat rows over the counter.

'Mind my magazines now Dad!' the postmistress said, and he replied. 'That's right, that's right!' and when he had drawn his money he said, 'thank you kindly, much obliged,' and back to the barber's shop where the paint was peeling from the ceiling and the shelves were littered with old-fashioned hair nets and curlers and other toilet requisites long out of date and covered in dust. Faded advertisements hung on the walls but no one ever read them.

Towards the end of the afternoon the shop filled with little boys from school and sometimes little girls came in and would take their turn in the chair unnoticed by the barber who did not do girls. The children ignored the old man and brushed past him to reach for old magazines and tattered comics which they read greedily sprawled on the linoleum. The barber greeted every customer in a nasal drawling voice. He spoke to the old man.

'And how are they treating you eh? Pretty good eh?' He said the same thing to everybody, and the old man replied, 'That's right, that's right.' If the children had asked him he could have thought up stories about the Great Red Fox and Brother Wolf, but the children never asked him anything, not even the time.

Some days he wandered by the river watching the weaving pattern of children playing on the shore. They never took any notice of him and he sat half-asleep in the shade of one of the peppermint trees that grew at intervals along the bank. He sat just a bit back from the sandy edges where the kind-hearted water rippled gentle and lazy and shallow. He was always sleepy at noon after his midday meal which Sarah gave him early at half-past eleven so that she could get cleared up in the kitchen. The children never came to him to ask his advice or to show him things. He supposed he was too old. Yet he knew a good many things about the foreshore and about playing in the sand. Back at home he had three things better than plastic spades; he had an iron gravy spoon and an ash scoop and an old iron trowel. These had been for his grandchildren years ago when he had brought them down to the shore to play, minding them for Sarah so she could get on and do the house and the cooking and the washing. He never thought about these three things now, they lay somewhere at home behind the stove, he never thought about the Great Red Fox and Brother Wolf either. But if someone had asked him, he could have thought about them.

There was a little merry-go-round there, a corner of jangling music and laughter, a corner of enchantment. When the children went round and round on the little painted horses the old man forgot everything as he sat on a bench and watched them. They smiled and waved and he would nod and smile and wave and then shake his head because the children were nothing of his and were not waving to him. Once a child was crying on the path and he fished a penny out of his pocket and held it out but she would not take it and hid her face in the uneven hem of her mother's dress.

'You can't get anything for a penny now Gran'pa,' the mother said and laughing quite kindly walked on along the path.

When he went out in the evening he walked straight down the middle of the road, down towards the river. The evening was oriental, with dark verandahs and curving ornamental roof tops, palm fronds and the long weeping hair of peppermint trailing, a mysterious profile sketched temporarily purple on a green and grey sky. Fingers of darkness crept across him and the moon, thinly crescent and frail, hung in the gum-leaf lace. Dampness and fragrance brushed his old face and he made his way to the river where the shores were deserted. The magpies caressed him with their cascade of watery music. This was their time for singing at dusk and all night if they wanted to. Down by the water's edge the old man crouched to rest and his voice sighed into a whisper sliding into the great plate of smooth water before him.

'No one should be alone when they are old.' His thought and his word and his voice were like dry reeds rustling at the edge of the gentle water.

When he had rested a few moments he walked on through the stranded ghosts of the swings and the merry-go-round. The little wooden horses, their heads bent and devout, were dignified in their silence. The old man walked by unnoticed, for why should the little horses notice him, he walked this way so often. A little farther on he turned up the grass bank away from the river. The slope was hardly a slope at all but he had to pause more than once for breath. Soon his hand brushed the roughness and fragrance of rosemary and his nostrils filled with the sharper scent of geranium, and he fumbled the wooden latch of a gate and went in and along the overgrown path of a neglected garden. The hedge of rosemary was nearly three feet thick and sang with bees in the heat of a summer day. Geraniums like pale pink sugar roses climbed and hung and trailed at the gate-posts, and again on either side of the crumbling woodwork of the verandah trellis. Later on the air would be heavy with the sweetness of honeysuckle but the old man was not thinking of this. He fumbled again at the latch of the door and made his way into the darkness inside the familiar place which had been his home and his wife's home and his children's home for more years than he ever thought about now. In the kitchen he felt about with his old hands till he had candle and matches.

Three years back he had been ill with pneumonia and fever and Sarah declared the place unhealthy and smelling of the river and drains, or lack of them; and herself finding it too much to come there every day to see to him and his house as well as her own house which took a deal of doing on her own. So she and John had come one Sunday afternoon in the car and fetched him to their place and had nursed him well and comfortable. And later, had sold his place to the owner of some tea-rooms further along the river, the other side of the swings and the merry-go-round. So far the man who had bought it had done nothing except sell the furniture, and even some of that, the shabby good-for-nothing stuff, was still there. As soon as the old man was better enough from his illness he had started to walk back to his place. At first he had only got as far as the barber's shop on the corner, and then to the postmistress where the road widened before turning down to the sandy wastes by the river. And then one day he managed to get to a bench at the merry-go-round, and after that strength was his to walk right to his place. And he went inside and sat in the kitchen and looked about him thinking and remembering. But he did not think and remember too much, mostly he rested and was pleased to be there. He laid his attaché case on the kitchen table and opened it with his trembling old hands, he unpacked his shopping into the cupboard by the stove. He had little packages of tea, sugar and matches. Then he took out his pipe and tobacco and he sat and smoked his pipe. Sarah objected to the smell of his cheap tobacco in her home, even if he smoked out on the verandah. She complained all the time afterwards, and went from room to room opening windows, shaking curtains and spraying the air with something pine-scented to freshen the place up, as she called it. So every night he walked down home and had his pipe there. He did not say where he was going because Sarah would insist that he stay in her place to smoke and then all that airing and freshing up afterwards.

During the day he sometimes spent an hour tidying up the old tangled garden as much as an old man can. He stacked up some wood and split a few chips for the stove. People passing the rosemary hedge would wish him 'good day' if they saw him in the garden, but mostly people took no notice of him. They were busy with their children or with their thoughts or with each other. The old man came and went in peace and every night he came home to his place and smoked his pipe and sat and rested. He did not think very much because there is no use thinking over things when you can do nothing about them any more. His children were gone their ways, they mostly were like her. She had been a great reader and had sat reading her life away. She read everything the old postmistresss could get for her, novelettes they were called years ago. Bundles of them had come to the house. The children had mostly been like her and she had taken them with her into the kind of world she lived in.

He had come, as a very young man, from the Black Country in England, from the noise and dirt of the chainmaking industrial area where people lived crowded and jostled together in indescribable poverty. The women there had muscles like men and they worked side by side with their men in the chainshops pausing only at intervals to suckle their babies. He had carried his younger sisters daily to his mother and had later cared for them in other intimate ways as he minded them in the blue-brick backyards and alleys which were the only playgrounds. When he had come to Australia he had gone straight to the country, where he had been terrified by the silence and loneliness. He was afraid of the heat and the drought too, but more than that he could not stand the still quiet nights in the bush when he was alone with the silence. And the white trunks of the gum-trees were like ghosts in the white light of the moon. He had longed to hear the chiming of city clocks through the comforting roar of the city and the friendly screech of the trams as they turned out of the High Street into Hill Street. He missed the heave and roar of the blast furnace and the nightly glow on the sky when the furnace was opened. All his life these had been his night light and his cradle song. So he went from the country to the town and found work in one place and then in another and later was employed to look after the foreshore, there was the house there for him too, and though it was quiet, the city and the suburbs were spreading towards him reassuringly.

If anyone had said, 'Tell me about the chainshop,' he could have told them about it and about a place he once visited as a boy where, in the late afternoon sunshine, he had walked with his father down a village street. Standing on the village green were twelve geese. They were so still and clean and white. Beautiful birds, his father had said so. It was the stillness of the geese in his brief memory of the countryside that had made him leave the jostled crowded life among the chainmakers and come to Australia. But no one ever asked him about it so he never really thought about it any more except perhaps for a moment while he sat smoking, but only for a moment.

So on this night as on all the other nights he sat and rested and smoked his pipe in the neglected old house which had once been his place. He was so comfortable there he forgot it had been sold. Though Mr Hickman, the man who had bought it, had called once when the old man was doing the garden. Mr Hickman had said he was having the place demolished in a week or two because he wanted to start building.

'You've got some fine roses there,' Mr Hickman had said after the pause which had followed his previous statement.

'That's right, that's right,' the old man had replied and they had stared at the roses together while the bees hummed and sang in the hedge of rosemary.

But this had been nearly a year ago and the old man did not think about it because there was nothing he could do about it. So just now he sat and rested and enjoyed his pipe and was pleased to be there. When his pipe was finished he remembered he must walk back. He got back to his son's place just after nine and Sarah said, 'How about a nice cup of tea before bed Dad,' and he replied, 'Thank you kindly, much obliged.' And he sat down in the kitchen and took his boots off carefully and stared at the soles of his boots. He shook his head a bit very slowly and set the boots down beside his chair. Sarah stirred his tea and put the cup down towards the middle of the table.

'Mind your tea now Dad,' she said.

'Thank you kindly, much obliged,' he replied.

'Have a good walk Dad?' John asked him.

'That's right, that's right,' the old man said and he drank up his tea.

'Good night Dad,' Sarah said.

'Good night Dad,' John said.

'Good night, good night,' the old man said and he took up his boots and he went off to his bed.

The Jarrah Thieves

High up on the edge of a dilapidated wooden verandah over-looking a shallow ravine of restless eucalyptus and wandoo trees a young man, temporarily expelled from his university, sat opposite his old aunt watching her eat her breakfast with an appetite he was unable to share. She was so thin that when she swallowed he could see the food going down her throat. And all the time she talked in an economical but vivid English which was sometimes only understandable to those who knew her very well. She spoke a great many languages but had never taken the trouble to learn one of them properly.

"Back home in Vienna,' she swallowed, apparently with difficulty, a crust of her own home-made bread, 'back home, you know Manfred, you would spend some time away in the mountains. Here in this country we have no mountains but my place here is a thousand feet over the sea level so breathe while you are here,' she continued. 'More coffee? Drink if eat you cannot, is good, dandelion coffee. I grind myself!' But after his sleepless night in her big empty wooden house he had a bad headache. He had the headache before he came, it was from the noise and the wind and the jokes with his fellow students at the medical school dinner the night before.

'Did you not feel your ears crackle when you came up?' she

asked. 'Mine always! even after all these years. Come along,' she urged, 'another cup, will make you well.'

'No thanks Aunty.' She shrugged her thin shoulders and helped herself.

The wind in the perpetually swaying tree tops was like an endless lullaby in the rocking cradles of branches and leaves. Morning, noon and night, the light and shade and the colours and the outlines of these trees were changing all the time. At all times of the day and at night there was something different about them to notice and enjoy.

He tried to take his aunt's advice: a heron flew alone emerging from time to time between the trees, looking for food. Manfred breathed in the air, it was fragrant with fried eggs and the frail smoke from stumps and tree roots and bits of blackboy burning. And every now and then the heavy scent of fermenting grapes and mulberries came up to them on an extra breath of wind from the neglected, overgrown terraces immediately below the verandah of the house.

From the other side of the valley came a dull rumbling sound and a log-carrying trailer with a blue and white cabin in front went by. The old woman shaded her eyes with one hand, she nodded with approval as the truck passed an open space where a dead tree held up its great antlers into the middle distance between the earth and the sky.

'Quick!' she said to Manfred, 'count the chains, my eyes are not what they used to be, there should be four chains.' The young man looked with obedience, the huge logs were loaded with their glowing cut ends facing outwards, he was not sure where the chains should be.

'One at either end and two in the middle,' screamed his aunt over the noise of the laden vehicle, she was straining across the rail of the verandah trying to see.

'It's all right,' she calmed down, 'I saw them!' The noise gradually became fainter as the truck continued on its headlong journey to the great black smoky scar in the countryside some five miles further on where pig iron was made. The old lady, besides owning the several acres of orchards and vineyards, mostly planted by herself years ago when she had come with her father as a girl to start a new life in another country, also owned some miles of timber, a great jarrah forest acquired with some foresight years ago when the virgin land was being sold, by present day standards, very cheaply. She was selling timber to the foundry.

'Fortunately for me,' she explained to her nephew, 'they are still old-fashioned enough to fire their furnaces with wood. It is a black place, before you go you must see this great black sore we have, but for me, thanking God, it is there!'

There were five log-hauling trucks and before leaving the verandah his aunt remained at the rail till all of them had gone by. The noise of their rumbling and the bright colours of the cabins wherein the drivers sat hidden and his aunt screaming over the heavy traffic. 'Count the chains!' and 'See! Number three is wrongly loaded!' created a diversion, a considerable disturbance in the quiet tranquillity of the little valley.

'Tonight I shall make your dinner myself,' she promised, looking at him fondly. He was her only relative, his father, her younger brother, had died some years ago and as she had never liked her brother's wife, she did not consider her to be a relation. 'Tonight I make a soup for you out of my own head. But first we make little outink to the jarrah forest. I have work for you there. Students are always penniless, is that not so, I give you some work,' she said, 'and then I pay you something!'

They were walking to and fro on the terraces. Every now and then his aunt interrupted her talk with him to scream orders to the two plump girls who kept house for her and who were supposed to do mysterious things to the vines and the fruit trees at the right times.

'They are lazy girls,' she explained to him. 'That is why I have to shout at them all the time.' She has spent most of her life wielding a pick and shovel, digging holes and carting soil and planting trees, and she had spent hours bent in half, weeding or putting potatoes in the earth, muttering prayers and curses to the rain and the wind and the sun and the frost. Everyone who did not do these things all the time was lazy, this was not so much her opinion but rather because of her accustomed way of life.

'Apricots, plomms, nectarines, peaches, almonds, apples,' his aunt showed him the trees. They were all old like she was and their insides were eaten away by white ants, she broke a small branch to show him.

'But we have the fruit all the same,' she said, striding just a few feet ahead of her nephew. She waved her arm to the bottom paddock. 'Down there are pear trees and quince. Do you like quince jelly? I have made! So you shall try!' She poked her stick into some scuffed-up leaves where a goanna, seeking privacy to change his skin, lay unblinking as if dead.

'Strange creatures! We can never know how old they are,' she muttered as if half to herself. Manfred supposed she talked to herself a great deal as she spent all her time alone except when she was ordering the people who worked for her about their business. Her nephew's visit pleased her very much and she did not question why, after all this time, he had come to stay with her when she had not seen him since he was a little boy. He scarcely remembered the place though he had been there years ago with his father. Any uneasiness he felt on the way there (he had been fortunate to get a lift) about his welcome was quickly lost, his aunt had been delighted when he came. They paused beyond the pear orchard by a narrow rotten bridge. The creek, full with its first flow of water after the long hot dry summer, looked stagnant and dirty.

'Is not rain yet,' his aunt explained. 'Is seepage water soaking through, now that it is not so hot, water is not evaporated from the earth, will look clearer later on. Your father,' she continued, 'made this bridge. I bring him up when he was little boy and then he left to go on a life of his own,' she sighed. 'You played here too, you know.'

'Did I?' Manfred tried the bridge with his weight, it sank and water oozed between and over the old railway sleepers from which it was made. The butter-like banks of the creek were slippery and quite steep.

'Careful!' his aunt warned. 'You can repair later,' in her voice was the promise of a treat.

To go to the jarrah forest which was some miles away she drove an old car. She followed the reploughed fire breaks through the bush, as they cut down the distance and, since no one else drove there, she had these tracks to herself and did not have to concern herself at all with the ethics and rules of driving.

'Sometimes I bog myself down,' she said and threw a spade and an old coat and some sacks into the back of her car. 'They make open the old fire breaks,' she complained. 'And this makes the ground too soft for my car.'

It was like turning over a page in a picture book, so quickly did the scrub of blackboys, hakea and sheoaks change into the jarrah forest. First they went through a part from which all the big old trees had been removed. Here a slender forest of secondary growth had grown up, the tall thin trees close together crowded out the sun and the fire break was, as his aunt said, very soft. The car only just went through. They came out at last on to a hard wide gravel track: below them stretching for miles was the forest of big old trees.

'Here my trucks come up,' his aunt said and she drove on down to overlook an area which was being cleared. A kind of devastation of earth and tree moving and cutting and burning lay before them. Huge trees with dark bleeding bark, the colour wrapped round their massive trunks by fires and by the sun, lay about the clearing. All round fires were smouldering, sometimes flames leapt up here and there and men in helmets were going about in this apparent disorder working with machinery, pushing down the trees, heaving them about, cutting them up and loading the trailers.

The air was so clear that the blue smoke hung in patches as if put there for decoration and the great noise of the work came up to them as if from some faraway place. The old lady looked down with approval on the scene.

'Go on down to them,' she said to her nephew. 'The old man in the white hat is the foreman, tell him I have sent you to work, tell him to teach you something. You can get home on the last run to the foundry. Ask for to be put off on the road at the foot of my place. Mind the bridge!' She turned the car and stuck her head out of the window, her shoulder-length grey hair framing her thin face.

'Josst listen to the music of the chain-saws! What an invention!'

The magic of the jarrah forest seemed to be on all sides of him as he walked down towards the place where the men were working. He stepped in and out of the patches of light and shade and the magpies followed him with their song, which was like the sound of water running over clean stones. In this new place it seemed as if the days before this one had never been or as if they had belonged to someone else's life. He longed to go on walking and walking, away from the workmen, as if he might all at once emerge in some hitherto unknown and wonderful world.

'These lady tutors they insist on full-time permanent posts,' his professor complained. He was so absorbed in his problems of administration he hardly looked up from the papers on his desk to glance at Manfred as he diffidently entered the room. 'And then, when they get them,' he went on, 'they aren't satisfied, they weep even, here in my room, see I even have tissues for them, because they say I am unfair, they say they can't get here to give nine o'clock lectures and they can't stay for tutorials and demonstrations after four o'clock in the afternoon because

105

they have domestic duties and baby-sitting problems.' Manfred stood just inside the door while the older man continued his monologue. 'Why can't they themselves stay with their babies and save me from all this worry, I don't understand. Why do they have babies at all?' He looked up suddenly at Manfred as if to say, 'Why are you intruding upon my private worries?' Instead he said, 'So you have refused to register for national service,' knowing immediately, as is the way with an academic mind, how to dispose of the fringes of untidy thought and unnecessary works. 'You refuse yet you know you would be exempt for the present and you are accused of writing an obscene article in our journal. I have seen the article, I am not disposed to discuss it, it has merit. If you offend, you alienate yourself and you do not make contact, you could write what you have written without the use of those certain words. Secondly, if you want to protest for peace then do it in peace. You burnt your cards and resisted arrest. But what is the use, I am not accusing you. All I say is violence will not get rid of violence. Temporarily I gather you are dismissed. I shall do what I can on your behalf. Do not expect too much from me or too little. At all events,' here he gave his smile which he kept for the young men in the middle of their medical studies, 'I shall keep you out of gaol. I want rather to see you in the operating theatre!'

All this now seemed to belong to another time and place, to another person even: as he walked down it seemed as if he had always been with his aunt in her house with her strange mixture of the frugal with a certain luxury of well-being, even her dandelion coffee was not so bad. He had come to her rather than go home to his mother.

'How can you do this to me?' was her phrase always and he felt he couldn't explain that he wasn't doing anything to her, only to himself. If his thoughts and actions could affect the world then he would stick to what he felt were the best thoughts and actions he had to offer even if some part of the world he had to be in found him wrong or obscene. As he walked, it comforted him to think that if the University refused to take him back he could after all perhaps stay on with his aunt. Her meals were a great comfort, or would be when he had thrown off the effects of the students' party, and there was too the great comfort and security in property.

That night his professor was addressing the Thoracic Society at a dinner. How far away that dinner seemed and the professor himself in his half-lensed gold-rimmed glasses. Mahler, his favourite composer, wore spectacles like them. Mahler knew forests and the irresponsible frivolous rustling of leaves and the wonder and praise one could feel about the sight of a tree together with the great sadness and melancholy and the pain of the earth. It was strange that one could know, in a way, more about a man who had written music years ago than about a man one had spoken to and listened to almost daily for the whole of the preclinical course in Medicine.

The smell of the freshly-cut timber and the hot smell of the chain-saws came sharply to him. It was suddenly quiet in the clearing. Manfred, deep in his thoughts walking down through the trees, had not seen the men gather behind one of the little huts they had there. For a moment he thought they had seen him coming and did not want him and had hidden to discuss what was to be done. Then he thought that perhaps there had been an accident. He hoped fervently that no one had had an accident, for though he knew the names of all the bones and systems in the body and had already learned a great many of the things that could go wrong either by accident or by disease or by old age, he was not yet able to fit the frail pages of his books and the words of his teachers to the flesh and blood and the feelings of a human being. He felt quite unequal to seeing the distress and pain of a man trapped under a tree, and was quite sure he would not know what to do in any circumstances if someone should shout, 'Is there a doctor here?' 'A junior nurse in a hospital would know more than I do if someone was hurt,' he thought, and standing alone at the edge of the clearing in the jarrah forest he felt afraid.

'There's nothing in the world like a really good woman,' a voice came out into the stillness from behind the hut.

'True,' another voice helped the story teller. 'Very true.' Manfred stayed at the side of the shed as the first man went on talking.

'At school I sat behind a girl. I never saw her face much, always her shoulders.' The narrator paused to drink tea noisily from a tin cup, he lit a cigarette. 'I used to look over her shoulder and peer at her work, such beautiful neat handwriting, I wanted to copy it and write as well and I tried to see her face but she never turned around.' The men were eating and drinking and smoking, some sitting on the ground, some on cut logs and others standing, they made a pattern of rest and ease as they took both.

'And then later, much later, I saw her again, only the back of her, she was working at a big table in a bakery and I asked her name but it meant nothing to me as you'll never believe how stupid I was. I never knew the name of the girl in front of me at school! I found it was the same girl. She used to get cross with the man who drove the bread cart. He whipped the horse so much and once she came out and saw all the strokes of the whip on the horse and she shouted so much that I, yes men it was me! I, fool that I was! I never went back there. As I didn't go the next day to drive the bread cart,' his voice deepened and broke very slightly in the silence, 'she drove the horse and the bread cart herself. It was only half an hour's drive but she had been so hot in the bakehouse and she went without her jacket and she caught a chill and died quite quickly in terrible pain, you know, what do you call it? pleurisy. Such a lovely girl and only quite young.' A long silence followed the woodman's story and Manfred still waited beside the hut, not liking to intrude.

'I had a dog,' another voice broke in to lighten the weight which had settled on them.

'Yes tell us,' another voice helped the new story teller.

'Well this dog was so intelligent he used to bite the fleas off himself and lay them on the bed.' There was a burst of laughter interrupting the story.

'How could a dog lay a flea?' came from someone.

'But no,' the first voice continued, 'he used to lay them on the bed and count them!' More laughter.

'Ah. Women!' another voice sighed in a foreign accent. 'I have seen the glow of youth and the beauty of being in love and the sweet prettiness of young motherhood changed overnight into weariness and perpetual discontent!'

'Talking about fleas,' said yet another voice, 'I had a dog who had fleas that bad he was quite mad with them. And he went up to a sheep and said beg pardon let me have a bit of your wool. The sheep took no notice, perhaps she was deaf, I don't know, but the dog took a tuft of her wool and holding it between his teeth he jumped in the creek. As you know fleas can't stand cold water, the dog sank in the water so that just the bit of sheep's wool was sticking out and when all the fleas had climbed on to the bit of wool he let it go and came out of that creek without a flea on him,' a burst of laughing followed this.

'That's an old story, I heard that one before or else I read it somewhere.'

'What! *you* read something! That's a story in itself!'

'Anyway I never heard of a dog being able to talk, let alone ask a sheep for anything,' said someone in tones obviously meant to smooth things over. 'Or a deaf sheep, who ever could know if a sheep was deaf or not! Well men! Time for work!'

Manfred came round the hut and the old man in the white helmet set him to sharpening a saw at once, showing him how to wedge the blade in a specially-prepared crack in a log, how to hold the file and then the delicate but firm correct movement of the file. And once more the noise and activity and the dust filled the clearing. The light of the day was coloured with the red glow of the newly-cut wood and the men could not speak to each other because of the noise of the axes and the chain-saws and the earth and tree moving machines. One by one the trailers with the different brightly-coloured cabins came back to be reloaded ready for the headlong rumbling journey to the foundry where the furnaces were hungry for the wood. And back at home Manfred's aunt was busy with her accounts and the profits from the cutting down and selling of the timber which had taken such years to grow and was her good fortune to possess. She was bothered with her accounts, there was a mistake somewhere and never before had she made mistakes and now there was a regular one. She turned back the pages and went through the lists of figures over and over again. Adding up and subtracting, even if it was wrong, gave her pleasure.

All day Manfred worked in the jarrah forest and all day he tried to fit to the different faces the various stories that were told. The stories seemed in themselves to have no significance except that they filled the silence with a kind of philosophical brotherly entertainment when all the machines were quiet.

And yet there was meaning in the stories for they belonged to human beings and the things they thought about, all the things that worried or pleased them. He almost told them.

'I know a young man who punched three policemen and went to hide with his aunt,' but he didn't know the men at all, not like they knew each other. They were kind enough to him, considerate even, the foreman, the old one in the white helmet, sat beside him at noon and offered him bread and olives and a piece of bacon fat from his own hessian bag. But he was too shy to tell his story, he would not have known how to receive their disbelief or their laughter or their boredom or their admiration. They could all take these things from one another. So he worked and looked on.

It was a long day, they worked till dusk, the fires glowed all round them burning the twigs and leaves, they seemed at times to be in a wide circle of fires. He was warm all through his body from the work and from being in the fresh air.

He was to ride home in one of the log-hauling trucks, he noticed it had been loaded with smaller logs, all of them cut and split quite unlike the logs chained on to the other trailers but he was too tired to ask why this was. The trucks set off up the wide gravel track, their engines whining and groaning in low gear. When they reached the top the foreman in the white helmet stood there at the edge of a dark clump of trees and stopped every truck in turn to allow the truck in front plenty of time to start off down the hill on the headlong rumbling journey to the foundry.

When he woke up he was cold and stiff, still in the cabin of the truck: someone had thrown some sacks over him. The driver was nowhere to be seen. The morning was damp and the sun was coming through the trees dispersing the mist in long white fraying ribbons. Cocks were crowing and he looked out and saw he was in a strange place where he had never been before. The truck was parked close up beside the smallest cottage he had ever seen. It was like a nut, brown and uneven, made from old wood and iron and the chimney pipe was rusted and fastened by wires to the edges of the sloping roof. A woman in a blue overall came out and was at once surrounded by hens, and a bit later on seven geese came in a long line from the bottom of the meadow below the little nut of a cottage. All round, in among some old almond trees, were heaps of split jarrah logs, small mountains of logs, once after the other, some of the heaps were as big as the cottage. An axe lay beside a chopping block and a large basket was fixed to a spring balance which hung from the branch of a fig tree in the front part of the yard. There were axe heads and broken handles and discarded toys and two long lines of washing, mostly rags, the things worn by children when they have not enough clothes to wear.

Stiffly Manfred climbed down from the cabin and the woman

asked him, 'Will you stop for some tea and porridge?' The truck driver came slowly from the cottage.

'I'll just unload,' he muttered and climbed back into the cabin after unfastening the chains. The noise of the wood falling brought several sleepy children tumbling from the cottage. The wood roared from the tipped-up trailer into a great heap.

'More wood more wood,' they chanted. The woman tried to send them off but they wanted to hug the driver and Manfred, who was quite bewildered. 'You'll stop for tea?' the woman asked again. But the driver refused in quite a surly tone saying they had not time and must go at once.

The sun came up quickly and lit up the far away tops of the trees in the jarrah forest as they drove towards it.

'She keeps a wood yard,' the truck driver explained reluctantly to Manfred. 'She sells the wood to the people in the township just down the road from where her place is, they come to her for it, it is her living. She lost her husband ten years ago, a tree fell on him, he was deaf, he couldn't hear us shouting at him, he was using the axe, he was the best axe we had.'

'But the children are all little ones,' Manfred began.

'Yes,' the other agreed, 'but so often happens that way to a woman on her own if she has a kind heart,' he shrugged. The truck was coming near to the orchards.

'I should 'ave put you off here last night but you were that sound asleep!'

'Thank you all the same.' Manfred climbed down from the cabin and ran through the sweet fragrance of the summer as it lingered on in the withered grass flattened with the heavy dew which came at night now as the season was changing to autumn.

The pear trees covered in yellow leaves were like little silent watchmen in yellow oilskins. The sun had not reached them yet as they were down on the mud flats near the creek. Manfred trod lightly over the old bridge and almost flew up the rough terraces to tell his aunt how the men were cheating her.

It was quite clear that every night a load of wood went to

112

the lonely little cottage full of children, and all the time his aunt thought she was selling that wood to the foundry. He would be able to tell her the truth and prevent her from losing more money.

'Where are you Aunty?' he called, very much out of breath with running.

His aunt was kneeling on the verandah with her long skirts pinned up, she was oiling the boards with linseed oil and turpentine. The smell reminded him for a moment of the games pavilion at school. He almost felt like a small boy about to tell tales and the sharp smell of the oily mixture brought back vividly the bitter loneliness of the long days and eternal afternoons, of the desolation of homesickness and of hating school and the cloakrooms and the dormitories and the games pavilion where all the other boys always seemed to get on so well with one another. It was better to be with his aunt: the girls laughing about something between themselves were putting the breakfast on the table, the red coffee pot looked splendid, it seemed to be the most beautiful thing he had ever seen.

He thought he would tell his aunt about the stolen wood later on, he felt he must tell her but just now he was so hungry.

Later she was by the verandah rail waiting for the first of the trucks to come by. There was no chance to tell her what he had discovered.

'Always look at a person's hands,' she said to her nephew. 'From their appearance and the way he holds them and what he does with them, in looking at a person's hands,' she said, 'you will learn much about the person. Never take anyone's hands for granted,' she said and then her talk was lost as one of her trailers marked *Martha Dobsova's Jarrah Mills* was rumbling and about to pass the gap where the dead tree implored the pale sky for something with its great antlers which were, this morning, like gaunt arms stretched up.

'Look at the chains!' she screamed above the noise but Manfred was looking at his aunt's hands, they were rough, the knuckles were enlarged with hard work and the skin, though shining with oil just then, was thin like burnt paper and mottled brown with the kind of patches old people have on their hands. Her hands were strong and they were also very kind.

Every day he went to work in the jarrah forest. He even stayed there with the men in one of the little huts and took his turn working at night with them. They remained friendly with a quiet acceptance of him though he was not one of them. Often he went in the specially-loaded truck, the one with the small split logs, to the little nut cottage and listened to the children laughing and shouting over the deafening of the logs being unloaded. He kept thinking he must tell his aunt of the robbery or else tell the men they shouldn't steal the wood but he couldn't bring himself to do either, and often he paused at his work in indecision and despised himself. He had never felt like this before. He was always studying and learning and reading, he enjoyed the company of his fellow students but had no close friend. He took part in the moratorium marches against the war because he really believed all war to be wrong and was overcome with a surprise so deep that it was a pain when he lost his temper and swung his fists at the policemen. It was almost as though he was watching an unknown person do these things and his own voice was unrecognizable to him, the owner of it. It was a kind of shocked state of mind which made him love the jarrah forest and caused him to find the thing he had discovered so difficult and unpleasant just when he was seeking to heal himself.

One day he told his story to the men in the forest '. . . you see I feel that the war is senseless . . .' He felt his voice was not like theirs, his education and the things he hoped to do might not be acceptable to them and again, as at the beginning, he felt afraid. His story was not like theirs except that to him it had the same core of human predicament.

'Ah well!' they say and stood around and made their usual comments, taking their rest as they needed it.

'Who can tell what is best for a man to do.'

'It's easy enough to tell a man what he ought to do but whether it's right or not is another matter.'

'Who can know how a man should be, he can only feel what he feels he is and is the best he can be.'

'True.'

'Too right!' They all shifted their muscular sunburnt bodies a little. Compared with them Manfred seemed to have no body at all, but no one had ever seemed to notice. Some of the men wore thin gold chains around their necks, some had little discs on them and others a golden cross. He felt envious of the wearing of these gold chains, they gave the men an air of distinction as if they had been given a secret blessing; their distinction was the more distinguished as they paid no attention to the chains and took for granted the precious thing they possessed.

'Talking about fleas, have you ever heard of the two fleas who thought they would keep a boarding house . . . ?'

'Who ever heard of fleas thinking, let alone thinking of keeping a boarding house,' the old man stirred himself, he often looked as if he was asleep in the middle of them. 'Time for work! Come on get going!'

And again, as all the other times before, the clearing was busy with work. Fires blazed and smouldered by turns, and the noise of the machinery and the chain-saws made a kind of symphony together with the straining of the heavy chains pulling on the great logs and the whine of the trailers slowly crawling up the slope in low gear.

Of course he couldn't tell them about the article he had written: his first appearance in print had pleased him very much. But now his subject and his choice of words seemed so far away from this life in the jarrah forest, though what he had written concerned them and the woman in the nut of a cottage full of little children. But when he thought of the woman teaching in the university and wanting someone to look after her baby and this other woman in the little hut seeking nothing more than enough food and a few clothes for her children, he began in his mind comparisons of problems. And when he went to the cottage again and saw the woman and the children playing hide and seek among the mountains of stolen wood, he realised he had tried to write about something which was as yet entirely beyond him. How small he felt among these great trees.

On the day he returned to his aunt's house she was surrounded by calico sacks, they looked like little pillows marked with her name *Dobsova*.

'Seed,' she said. 'Blue lupin, Yarloop clover, Wimmera rye grass and strawberry clover.'

It was a poem of seeds: she checked the bags with a list she had in her strong old hand.

'If I can get the hoe going I'm going to sow the bottom paddock,' she explained, 'and on the terraces something too, holds the earth, stops the topsoil from washing away.' She screamed for the girls to bring breakfast.

Manfred after his few days in the forest felt he had to come to tell his aunt about the stealing of the wood. He did not really want to tell her because it would mean the men concerned would be sacked and the woman and the little children would lose the only living they had.

'Always I have troubles with the hoe,' his aunt said. 'Thanking God you are here! You can pull the rope to start it, I am too old!'

Here she was interrupted by the two girls running onto the verandah without the plates and cups they were expected to bring.

'Bassett's place is afire!' they came crying, 'fire at Bassett's!'

'The fools! Blockheads! They always every year do this!' His aunt rose up tall among the little pillows of seeds. 'Always it is the same the day for forbidding fires is passed,' she said. 'But blockheads! they are so stupid, they light to burn off but we have had no rain, it is still not safe to burn just because it is the end of the forbidden time! Every year they do this silly thing!'

She strode across the verandah.

'Get my sacks and wet them,' she told the girls. 'And be quick!' They all went out to her car as quickly as they could.

There was about the morning a strangeness. In the distance the jarrah forest looked quite different as if dusk had come too soon: long curtains of quiet grey smoke were being drawn by ghost hands between the trees. The sky was orange behind a lattice of the same grey smoke. Some trees looked bigger than they really were while others were completely wrapped in smoke.

'Is the forest on fire?' Manfred asked anxiously, he was thinking about the men in the clearing in the heart of it. It was such a short time since he had leapt from the cabin of the truck to run up to his aunt's house.

'Not yet, it is only Bassett's place. Is only ten acres but the tenants are feckless, always no job, always neglect! That place is nothing to me, I go only to save my place, my sheds are that side and my best fruit trees. I won't have my place burned by their stupidity!'

It was some days before he could speak to his aunt, she was restless watching the sky waiting for rain clouds. She kept leaning over the verandah rail, the house behind her quietly waiting too for the rain. She wanted to sow her lower paddock.

'The clouds come,' she complained. 'And always just here they divide and one dark cloud goes over to one side and the other cloud beeg with rain, it goes over to the other side. Always is like this!' And she paced over the rough boards. 'Someone else gets my rain!'

The two girls were sulky and one looked as if she had been weeping. Manfred was on the point of telling his aunt.

'What is wrong with them?' he asked, rather than say what was on his mind. His aunt took her attention from the sky.

'Oh they are sulking a bit,' she said. 'We are a houseful of women. They expected to be seduced while a young man stay

117

in the house. They are disappointed, that is all, they will get over it!'

His aunt was so far from thinking of the men in the jarrah forest, she peered at the trailers as they passed her house and sometimes exclaimed half-heartedly, 'Number three is loaded badly,' but she was busy with the sky. And so a few more days went by.

At last one evening he told her about the small split logs and the little brown cottage and the children.

'So!' she said, 'they are cheating me! And I always try to be a good woman to them!'

She spent the evening thinking, sometimes she shook her head and it seemed to Manfred she was in silent conversation with someone he could not see.

'If you're making the tea,' she called out to the girls, 'I'll have a cup of coffee.'

'If I sack one of them, which one do I sack?' she questioned but went on talking before receiving any answer. 'Or do I sack them all? If I sack no one then they will think to go on cheating. Of course you know,' she said to Manfred, 'the woman was never married and the man who was killed was not working for me. They are all thieves,' she said. 'You go to bed,' she said to her nephew. 'I have to sit and think.'

So he tried to sleep in the spacious empty room which was his and it was as if he kept seeing the men in the clearing working, how clearly he saw them in the jarrah forest.

'There's nothing in the world like a really good woman,' a voice came out into the stillness, and he turned over and turned again trying to sleep.

In the morning they sat facing each other at breakfast. He watched the food going down her thin throat and he found he had no appetite not even for the coffee. He wished he had not told the story to her.

The wind in the perpetually swaying tree tops seemed to sigh with a sadness which was beyond his imagination. Neither of them spoke and then in the stillness of the morning they heard the rumbling of the first trailer. In a few moments it would come along on the other side of the shallow ravine and they would see it pass the open space where the dead tree held up its arms in prayer at all times of the day and night. At once she was at the verandah rail.

'Quick!' she called to her nephew. 'Count the chains! There should be four chains. Regulations you know.' And then she leaned over the rail and screamed at the trailer, 'Thieves! Robbers! You are cheating me! You are all sacked! You won't get away with this!' her voice was lost in the noise of the heavy trailer as it rumbled by in the headlong run to the foundry. Of course the driver, tucked away in the brightly coloured cabin, couldn't hear her, neither could he see her as he had to watch the road and was not able to peer through gaps in the trees.

'There!' she said to Manfred. 'That will teach them not to cheat me!' She sat down again and waved the red enamel coffee pot at him.

'I grind myself,' she said. 'Is good!' After a little time she said, 'You know, it came to me in the night. They wanted me to know about the wood they were giving away. Of course they could not tell me themselves because what could I do then? So what do they do, all night I am thinking it out, they tell you but not exactly, they need not have, they took you there, they could have told you to go on any of the other trucks and never on that one. But, you understand their reason? They wanted to show you so that I would know.'

He hadn't thought of their reason for taking him to the little nut of a cottage, he would never forget that place, left to himself he might never have known why they took him there. His aunt was still talking.

'The woman has to live,' she said. 'In the country one has to help people. There are feckless people who need help all the time, you could give everything to them and they would still need. That is no good. But this woman, this is a different thing.

119

They are good men,' she said. 'And they know I am a good woman.'

Of course his aunt was right, they could have concealed the theft from him, but on purpose they took him to the cottage and let him hear for himself the wood roar from the trailer making those crazy mountains between the almond trees. Now he understood.

He waited till she had screamed her punishment at all the trailers.

'I think I can smell the rain coming,' his aunt turned from the verandah rail.

It was time for him to leave the jarrah forest. He thought he would not be able to bear going away but already it was fading.

'Come again soon,' his aunt said. 'It is healthy here you know.' She thought he had been unwell and for the time being he continued to let her think so. He knew what she meant, there were intangible qualities of light and air and going to bed knowing that close by trees were rocking their branches like green cradles and that under the earth their roots were strong and deep. It was a healthy place, he would have liked to stay but it was time for him to go on to other things.

'Next time you come I cook myself,' his aunt said. He felt he didn't know nearly enough about women. Later he would come back and then certainly he would see that he did not neglect the girls.

The Travelling Entertainer

'You seem to have two answers to everything.'
'I have no answers at all.'

For Leonard Jolley

Da hast du mich erst belehrt,
Hast meinem Blick erschlossen
Des Lebens unendlichen tiefen Wert.

Adelbert von Chamisso

You have first taught me,
You have opened my eyes
To the unending value of life.

The Performance

Early this evening another patient was brought into this ward.

'The packets are everywhere,' he mutters in a low voice. 'Have they picked them up?' he asks anxiously.

'Yes Dear. Everything's all right. Just you have a good sleep,' the nurse says. And Sister comes in then with an injection, which they give him quickly, and then they tuck him in firmly under his sheet and blanket and leave him to sleep.

I've had this room to myself up till now and have been in the habit of spreading all my clothes and things over the other bed. Though I've had to tidy up, I don't resent the newcomer. He isn't the kind of person one could object to; he's big, grey headed and silent. He doesn't sleep after the injection. Instead, he sits up slowly and awkwardly in his bed and, with difficulty, struggles against the weight and tightness of the bedclothes and manages to draw his knees up and sits there as if wondering why he's there. He remains like this for some time.

'Trees in a mass have faces of pain,' he mutters. He doesn't seem to notice me and then suddenly he asks in a shy voice, 'Why did she ask if I'd like a spoon?'

'I don't think she did,' I say. 'I think she said to you to have a good sleep. Perhaps you should lie down.'

After a while he speaks again, restlessly. 'Excuse me, I think there's been a mistake.' He looks embarrassed and turns his head away.

'I'm sure there has,' I say, with my customary good humour. 'They are always making mistakes here. What exactly is troubling you?' I ask him gently. It's clear he can't sleep. He keeps his head turned towards the door.

He clears his throat, it's like a little cough. He says, 'Well I think I'm in the wrong room. I think there's a mistake. Well what I mean is . . .'

'Oh is that all,' I laugh. 'There's no mistake. They're going to cure me so that I'll be what I am, instead of what I want to be. See all those boxes of shirts and the suits of clothes and the golf sweater, I have to wear these, it's part of the cure. Set your mind at rest my dear fellow, it's a men's ward all right. To tell you the truth I'll be glad to get myself sorted out. Sometimes I get so depressed, suicidal really, it's the loneliness, the terrible loneliness. . . .'

He nods his big grey head and I can see he's sympathetic if not quite understanding.

'Well, what's your trouble?' I ask him after the little pause which follows my half explanation. He is quiet for a minute or two. He's thinking, he seems to think slowly.

'It's hard. I don't know where to begin. I suppose I'm here to be cured too but I can't think how they can ever set about it.' He looks at me with his puzzled grey eyes. Even his hair looks puzzled. I wonder what he can have done or be doing. People aren't brought into this hospital for nothing. It isn't just loneliness which has brought me here, it isn't just lying face down on the grass with my head in my arms. It's much more than those endless hours of waiting, something much more, something quite horrible.

'You don't have to tell me,' I say to him and I smile. I'm busy with my hair. The night nurse comes in to take the hot milk cups. She rattles about; she's a real busybody.

'Got a goodnight kiss for me?' she flirts with me, it's part of the plot to cure me. I blow her a kiss and she puts off the light, just leaving the little blue light which is the night light. It's to help us not to be frightened of our own dreams she explains and bustles off down the corridor.

He is so quiet for so long that I think he is going to lie down and go to sleep.

'Goodnight,' I say to him and I lie down quickly.

'It's like this,' he says suddenly in a low voice. He speaks with such urgency that I sit up and lean over on my elbow to hear him better.

'I'm a postman,' he says. 'I've been a postman for years. And now something terrible has happened to me.'

'So?' I ask him. 'What can be so terrible? You killed someone then?'

'Yes, I suppose so.'

'Someone you know?'

'In a manner of speaking. Yes and no.'

'Your wife?'

'Yes and no.'

'You seem to have two answers to everything.'

'I have no answers at all.'

We are both quiet for a while and then I speak.

'So!' I say to him. 'Nothing can be all that bad. . . .'

'It isn't so simple,' he says. 'It's terrible really. It's a postman's duty to see that every letter, every paper, and every package and every card is safely delivered to the correct address. Not much of a job you might think but every work, in my opinion, carries its own measure of responsibility.'

He stops talking as though waiting for me to say something. I haven't anything to say. I don't disagree with him. I agree about responsibility.

After a while I feel he is waiting for me to suggest something. 'Make it a sort of performance for them,' I tell him. 'Tell it to them slowly, bit by bit, a little scene at a time. They're very patient; it's comfortable in here and safe. You can make your material go a long way.'

'I don't quite understand,' he interrupts. I have to explain to him.

'Well put it this way, don't tell them your whole story at once, spin it out slowly. As for myself, I tell them only a very little at a time, some days nothing at all. As I said it's very safe in here and comfortable. There's no need to be in a hurry.'

'I see.' He's so quiet I'm afraid he hasn't been able to understand.

'You can say anything to me,' I tell him quickly. 'You can tell me everything and all at once. I'm not one of them. I'm a patient too. Some time I'll tell you everything all at once, not bit by bit, not the little bits I keep for them.'

He is still sitting up in that awkward way as if he can't, or won't let himself be received back into the clean tight bed.

'It's my wife,' he says. 'For a long time now it's as if she's thought of me as something dilapidated, like the corner delicatessen which is falling to pieces. To her I'm like this derelict place, a man or a place, what's the difference without enough turnover, without money to buy stock, without business, without reason too I daresay. I suppose she's right.

' "How do I look?" she calls out laughing in the evenings from the untidy bedroom which she has taken now quite as hers. The whole warm scented room is all hers, and the double bed. She gets ready in that room for her performance. I want to tell her that she looks lovely but, to tell you the truth, I don't think she listens to anything I say just then. She's radiant, excited and elated just when she's setting off she's so interested and so pleased with what she's going to do.

' "Go on!" she laughs one evening not so long ago. "Tell me if I look nice." She's examining her healthy complexion in her dressing table mirror. It's got gold edges. She likes pretty things.

' "Is there any yoked creature without its private opinions?"

she says. "That's from George Eliot," she says. "It's my title for tonight. They're all supposed to have prepared something, a little personal research." She's laughing and bending down to fasten her sandals. The room is bursting as always with her bright clothes and her vitality. She has so much vitality.

' "Have your own private opinions then, poor yoked creature!" she laughs at me. "But there!" she says, "I expect you're tired. I've left you some dinner in the casserole. Don't burn yourself on the lid, it's very hot." And then, as on all evenings, she grabs up her books and her brief case and she's gone away down the hall.

' "Don't come out," she calls as usual from the verandah. "Don't wait up for me. It's a wonderful class, they're loving every minute of it. I might be late."

'I do wait up for her but she knows when she comes in that I've been asleep all the evening. I can't help it. I eat too much because I'm alone, then I fall asleep as soon as I sit in the armchair afterwards.

' "You're like those sleeping dolls," she says to me often. "You know we used to have dolls, they closed their eyes when you put them down flat. When you lean back your eyes close!"

'I remember the dolls all right. My sister Daisy, she's dead now, had one. I expect, like Daisy, my wife poked the eyes in. I could just see my wife poking at her doll's eyes, till they fell into the pink and white china head, and then it's easy enough to imagine how she would have gone running with her mouth wide open, crying and bawling to her mother, with the eyes rattling round inside the blind doll.'

He sits there, a big shadow in the clean blue light and I try to lie down quietly. Perhaps he'll lie down too. My movement disturbs him. It's these stiff clean sheets; it's impossible to move quietly in a hospital bed.

'I'm on the edge of her performance,' he says as if talking all alone to himself. 'In a sense I'm the rim of her forgetfulness. Sometimes when she's preparing to go I say something, ask her for something, and a quick little frown crosses her face. I hold her up, you see. She forgets so easily what she was thinking and then it's my fault, you see. She's so enthusiastic. Sometimes she tells me things. She has to tell someone so she tells me.

' "Ibsen must have known so much about the frailness of the human being." This is the kind of thing she tells me. "His writing shows us how it is only when we are coming towards the end of life that we can begin to look at life. It's so mysterious," she says. I understand what she means but I don't know how to answer her. "He never stops this relentless search into the self," she goes on and on. "And yet he lived such a lonely life, compelled by his cowardice to conform to those very conventions of society which, he says so plainly in everything he's written, destroy the real self of a person by giving him the limits set by society as an unquestionable standard of values. . . ." '

He waits as if to let his wife's breathless wisdom have its effect on me.

'When I try to read Ibsen I fall asleep,' he says, his voice breaks into the sleep which is beginning to confuse my understanding. I raise myself up again on to my elbow and lean over towards him.

' "You were snoring," she says as soon as she comes home. "I could hear your snores out in the street!" She looks so small and white-faced when she comes home. That's why I wait up for her. Her work exhausts her and there's always the chance that someone might have been rude, you know, she might need comforting. She looks with real dismay at the confusion in the kitchen, all that mess which I'd intended to wash up.

'Quickly she clears up the kitchen, rinsing plates and cups under the hot tap. She loses her temper over the knives and forks and I irritate her by being in the way trying to help her. You see I'm sleepy. I try to anticipate her quick movements but I can't manage, she's too quick for me. Although I get in her way, I always make tea for her. You see I know how to make it just right for her. I know just how she likes her tea.

128

'Later I hear her in the shower. She's already preparing her next class, her next informal lecture. She talks it aloud to herself in the shower and in front of the mirror. I hear her, her voice joyful, eager, laughing, telling, talking to her class, talking to herself.

' "I want you to listen to Beethoven," she says. "It's someone practising on the piano, *Für Elise,* that's what I'll have," she says. "Listen to the piano and it's as if you're walking along the pavement and the music is coming from the open windows of a house, hidden behind oleander and hibiscus; it's the time for the jacarandas to be in flower. I want you to listen to the music and note down your private thoughts, and then suddenly, a woman darts across the road, she stumbles on the pavement and falls and the contents of her handbag spill over the road and over the path. Now write, and while the piano goes on playing Beethoven, write everything as it scatters from the handbag. Write!"

'My wife has her showers quickly and often hurries naked to her room to scribble something down. Sometimes she calls me and asks me to remember a word. Just one remembered word is enough to help her to recall an incident or an idea.

'My wife is no longer young. Of course I'm not young either. I'll be fifty-two on my next birthday. The elation of her performance gives her a kind of youth. She seems young to me and smooth and sometimes I long to give her the kind of love a woman likes and needs to have. Though she looks carefully at her face in the mirror, I'm sure she scarcely ever looks at her own naked body except perhaps to notice that she is soft and bulging more where she was once neat and firm.

'Sometimes I think she has forgotten all the things about her body, that there were sensations, hopeful thoughts of a closeness that matters, that pubic hair is pretty, though rarely looked at, and hardly ever really noticed. But there is something pretty about a woman's pubic hair, it's the way it nestles and curls and is there so secretly. Mostly it seems there just to be shaved off for child-birth, and then later in times of trouble, you know, women's troubles. I suppose it will give my wife a shock when she finds hers has turned grey and she hadn't even noticed it. It must be one of the shocks for a woman when she is getting older and refusing to acknowledge it. Once the little private jokes about pubic hair are forgotten then the whole thing gets forgotten. People forget to love each other, and that's when a woman might have a shock.

'So I always wait up for her even if my clumsy shambling annoys her. You understand, there might be a time one night when she suddenly feels alone.'

In the long silence I can see he is looking towards me. The blue light of the night light is the light in his eyes, they seem to shine blue in the shadow of his big face. He puts his head down on to his drawn-up knees so that he looks like a dark heap. The bed clothes, still tucked in, are pulled and strained because of the way he's trying to sit up.

' "I'll put my giant freesias in the old sink," I told my mother.' His muffled voice comes across.

'I didn't mean to tell her because I wanted to surprise her.

' "It's never a waste of time working to improve property," my mother said, and the branch I was cutting split without warning and fell and killed her. I'd been ill, you see, and I was outside altering the fowl house and yard, making those small improvements a man on his own tries to do when illness has weakened him.

' "Being in the fresh air will make you feel better," my mother had come out to talk to me. . . ."'

'I thought you said you were a postman,' I interrupt him, keeping my voice low.

'Yes, I am,' he replies in a low voice too. 'But let me explain, all my life I was a farmer. Farming means everything to me, the rise and fall and the slope of the land, the changing of the season, the hoped-for weather, the promise of the crop, all these things are my real life. They were my work. I suppose once a farmer, always a farmer in spite of changes. I like to think of myself as a good man on the land. Being a postman too, as I've said, carries the same worth, the same responsibility. . . .' His voice breaks, he coughs and clears his throat. I cough too, and the little night nurse hurrying by our doorway pauses and we are both quiet immediately. We don't want any attention just now.

The silence is so long I think he's asleep at last. It's the injection, it either makes you sleep or you talk.

' "Oh!" my mother was laughing. "I like the smell of this tree. I've forgotten what it's called!" ' His voice creeps across the space between the two beds. 'My mother pulled a handful of the leaves and crushed them and pushed them up towards me. I could smell the bruised leafiness. "It's like Elderberry," she said. "The smell takes me right back to another time and another place," she said, and she looked all down the long paddock, like she was looking down there and seeing into another world altogether.

' "It was in the Black Country when I was a little girl," she said. "It was all coal mines there and chimneys and smoke and the heaving noise of the steel works and then the roar of them, and the red glow in the sky at night when they opened the furnaces and there was this bush on the corner where the slag heaps came down to the back end of our street. These were old heaps and queer tufted grass grew on them and the yellow coltsfoot. Well, this one bush, it was more of a tree really, was growing there all alone in the street full of houses.

' " 'Elderberry! Let's go to the country Elderberry,' we used to shout and all of us would climb into the bush and for hours and hours after I could smell the smell of Elderberry on my hands in my hair and on my clothes. I didn't use to wash so as to keep the smell of Elderberry." '

He stops a minute and then tells.

'It was just then the branch tore away from the stump and my mother, still smiling with the things she'd been telling me, was dead underneath it.

'All at once it was as if a storm had come with heavy steady rains. It was like seeing the house and the sheds and the fence and the paddocks under water. It was like having to grope in a river to gather up her thin body. I took her up in my arms gently like into a cradle. I kept thinking if I could make her comfortable she'd be all right. Because of the way my tears came, I couldn't stop them. It was because of that, I knew inside me I couldn't do anything for her. The branch had killed her. I couldn't bear it. I was weakened with being ill in any case, and there's never a time, is there, when you've enough strength for an accident and death.'

'Tell me about your farm,' I ask him. I'm holding on to everything this strange big man is saying. It's as though he's lifting me up into a kind of cradle, only it's made of steel, not wickerwork, and it's not rocking me to sleep. While he's gathering me up like this, I'm not lying face down with my head buried in my arms. I'm not lying down any longer in the damp grass, outside the public toilets in the park, waiting. While he's talking I'm not lonely.

'I liked the way the road curved.' His voice is louder now and very pleasant, and I can lie back to listen. 'It still does curve, of course,' he says. 'Nothing's changed up there except that it isn't my place any more. I liked the way the road curved so that long before I got home to the farm I could see ahead to the pattern of the buildings. From the road it's all so tranquil. There's the old house built of weatherboard, quite grey now and behind, a bit to one side, is the barn with bright patches on the roof where I've replaced some rusty bits with new iron. And then there's the paddock we called Great Meadow with the neat squares of sheep pens at one end and then at the side of the house the almond trees and behind them the poultry yards all dotted with black and white and red fowls. At one time we had turkeys too and in the long quiet afternoons you could hear them and you could hear the crows and magpies too.

'The farm's high up; from the bend in the road you look up and across to it and water runs down the outcrop. All the year round there's water shining. Water is the last thing to get dark so, if it's late, you can see these streaks of water shining even as the sun goes. I liked the feeling of being high up, especially in the mornings, though the wind is damaging. We had olive trees growing along one side as a screen. They were all bent and their wind-torn tormented appearance gave a wrong impression.

'After my mother's death I worked the farm alone. I noticed things as if she was still there, pointing them out to me and taking pleasure in them. The almond blossom is the first to come. Suddenly the delicate little flowers open all along the almond wands. When the trees are in full blossom the pink and white frilled confusion is full of the noise of bees. As soon as the blossom begins to fade, bright green leaves take the place of the flowers. Every year it's a kind of miracle, the kind of thing you forget about in between times, like the feel of new laid eggs in your hands when you pick them up still warm. It seemed as if my mother was still giving me the knowledge of these things to treasure.'

I don't want him to go to sleep so I ask him, 'Have you sold the farm then?'

'Yes,' he replies slowly. 'Somehow trying to live in two places at once is too difficult. I kept it going for quite a time after my marriage. Somehow the land went sour on me. I couldn't seem to keep up with the seasons, you know, the clearing and the burning off and the ploughing and the sowing. I was always down with the family at home being a postman when it was wet and good for the farm, and when I was at the farm it would be too hot, too hard and too dry for work and too dangerous to burn. Then there was difficulty about stock. In the end all I was able to have there was a few hens, and they went mad. They wouldn't sit and then they were really properly off their heads and began eating their own eggs. That's a terrible thing when hens eat their own eggs. So I sold the place.'

'Why didn't you keep a corner, say five or six acres, for yourself?' I ask him, wishing that he had.

'What can a man do with six acres?' he replies. 'What's six acres when you've been used to a whole hillside with water pouring over granite and paddocks stretching to the fringes of the jarrah forest and the land on both sides of a highway in your name. And then what about the house?' he asks, his voice almost a shout. 'And the barns and the sheds? There's a sort of harmony about farm buildings,' his voice quietens. 'It's all right if it all starts and finishes on the six acres but this didn't.'

He continues in the low voice as before, 'I'm ten years older than Charmian, that's my wife. She came to the farm one day. Her car had broken down and I helped her.

' "I love your place," she told me. She said she meant what she said, "I really do love your place." I could see it was gratitude for being helped.

' "I ought to do it up a bit," I said to her. For some reason I was pleased she was there. I never had visitors. I felt shy with her, but in a nice way. I thought by saying that I ought to do the place up she would feel better about my having spent so much time helping her.

' "Oh no!" she said. "You must keep it as it is, it's lovely!" I could hear the insincerity, very slight, in her voice. It was the embarrassment she felt at being helped and not knowing whether to pay me or not. She didn't know how to leave the place without showing her gratitude.

'After she had gone I went back indoors and looked at the dark wallpaper. It wasn't possible any longer to know what the pattern was. It was lined and parched and smoked. It was a world of deserts and forests and tracks which led nowhere. When my mother died all the pictures went off the wallpaper and now, after the young woman had been through the house, all the mountains and rivers and the gnome figures and faces from my childhood came back, even the torn forest of trees rustled and trembled again above the fireplace. It was just that particular time of the afternoon when the sun went, in those last moments, from one corner of the room across the breast of the chimney to the other corner, lighting up one picture and then another before nightfall.

'The farm being so high and facing west we had the sun a long time, and I began to look again every day for the pictures in the rough cracks and seams in the wallpaper. The young woman, Charmian, had said not to alter anything, so I left everything as it was and went about my work as usual. She said she would come back and she did quite soon. She was a teacher. She was so tired she said and my place was the most restful place she had ever known.

' "It's like a performance every time," she explained. "You put out so much of yourself, you see. You get so terribly tired! You long for peace like this." I listened to her. I loved her tired husky voice. We listened to the magpies together and then the crows were calling across the quiet afternoon and, towards evening, the sheep came up the slope alongside the wire fence below the house, and we couldn't hear each other talking because of their noise.

' "They're hungry," I told her. "I'll have to go." She came with me up to the barn to carry the oats across. No one had been in the barn with me for years. I thought I ought to feel strange but I didn't. She seemed so pleased with everything, especially the fresh air, and she laughed at the animals. She liked the way they trusted me, she said. I'd never thought of it quite like that before.

' "You can come and stay for a rest if you really want to," I said to her, and I was surprised at what I'd said, but it seemed all right if you understand me.

' "Oh could I?" That's all she said. "Oh could I?" It was the

135

way she said it. It was just the time for the almond blossom. She stayed for the weekend.

'The windows of the bedroom were curtained from outside with almond blossom, and we had little flowers of it in our hair and in our clothes. It was the time for the almond blossom.'

His voice is drifting through the edges of my sleep. Almond blossom; he's telling about clouds of flowers.

'It's the terrible loneliness you feel among people.' His voice is harsh now with this very loneliness. 'I never felt it on the farm. But pedalling the post office bicycle along the pavements of the suburb, slowly delivering the letters, I felt so terribly alone. I tried to comfort myself with the quality of the air every morning as the sprinklers made water snakes in the dust. The suburb smells of dogs' dirt and petrol and people burning their food. Every now and then is a freshness of grass and the sweetness of something, Chinese privet perhaps or the datura; scents which lift you into forgetfulness while you're passing.

'People have no real self-respect, sometimes it shows in the kind of letter boxes they have, battered rusty tins, imitations of art, all sorts of stupidities, neglected with tiny slits and lopsided lids, rough and sharp and rusty. And into these things I'm expected to push all kinds of falsehoods and surprises, an envelope which delivered or undelivered might alter a man's whole life. And that's where the trouble starts, once you begin to wonder whether you have any right to put anything at all in these letter boxes. Once you begin to question, that's where the trouble starts.

'I had to poke my hands into these letter boxes sometimes in the dark, sometimes I was so undecided and slow. It was this questioning. It came about because of a certain house I had to pass every day, but I'll come to that later. In the dark when I was trying to deliver the mail, long after it should have been delivered, I could never find the letter boxes, even though I was familiar with them. The bushes and shrubs seemed larger, more enveloping at night and of course people leave their dogs loose and that's not pleasant either.

'The suburb, so littered with people and yet empty of life, became more and more an intolerable place for me to be in, and there seemed no point in pushing packages and letters into the letter boxes.

'It seems that people have no real feeling, either for each other or for their surroundings. It's true the lawns are shaved and clipped and water is drenched over everything. You can see it every day, white spraying mists and jets leaping and dancing across the gardens.

'After a while I stopped trying to deliver in the dark and I began to have to get rid of the mail into all sorts of places. I put some of it into the back of the utility and on Sundays when I drove up to the bend in the road, where I could look across to my old home, I left the bundles in an old quarry near there. I expect it's still there under the sand and lumps of rock. They've been asking me about it.

' "Can you tell us where the letters are?" They ask me ever so gently. "Can you remember what you've done with the letters? They belong to people you know, some of them have money in them. Try and remember."

'I can remember, but how can I tell them. There's such a lot to tell. I don't know where to begin and then there's something else too. Have I any right to tell about that too?

'There's my family. I have to think of them, even though I feel I must get away. I have responsibilities there in my family. You see, it's like this, I had a desperate need to get away from the family situation. I really had this feeling that I must get away, I must get away from them at all costs, to get away from my family.'

'Are things so bad then?'

'On the contrary. Quite the opposite. They're excellent. The house is well built, almost new, comfortable, plenty of space we have all we need. My wife has new clothes whenever she likes; she's perfectly contented, she enjoys her work, she has her performance. We have everything, food, warmth, more than enough. It's like this. Let me try to explain.

'You know the very slight changes in the air? You know the beginning of the change from summer to autumn? In the mornings there's a faint mist in the suburb and the smell of wet nasturtiums and earth and leaves. Instead of the hot restless east wind there's a penetrating calm cold air with a promise of warmth without the fear of the unbearable heat.

'It's on these first autumn mornings that my feelings exceed the boundaries of any possible performance, and I want to leave all their performances and go straight up to my farm. Only, of course, it isn't my place any more.'

'All their performances?'

He stops talking as if my question has interfered with him. 'Yes all their performances,' he says after this pause. 'In the mornings my wife gets up early to get Pamela out on her training. This is her performance.'

'How old is Pamela?'

'What does that matter,' he seems irritated by my question, perhaps it's the injection.

'Whatever age,' he says. 'Whatever age, the child's bed has always been empty. She's been brought up to perform and to compete, her bed's always been empty. Empty early every morning, no sleep-filled child to pull out from the bed clothes.

' "Look at me Mummy! Watch me! Look, over here! Here I am watch! Mummee!", and she'd jump from a park bench and look round for approval. She'd enjoy the approval, not the jumping. Don't you see this seed of competition was sown and cherished in the child even before she jumped from a bench in the park. She's conditioned to compete.

' "I'm better than Samuel aren't I? Aren't I? Better than Samuel? Say I'm better!"

'What does it matter what age she is.

138

'Now it's this fluid movement, she was only a little girl when it was discovered. It's like a gift I suppose, this movement like water from the head to the neck from the neck to the shoulders and then into the arms and down the long thin body and on down the long liquid legs. She seems as if she's made of clear plastic filled with pale apricot pink fluid and with her mother's voice and instruction she flows round the suburb from one little street her light feet moving lightly round into the next flowing round the corners and along the edges of the gardens flowing faster on and on gathering speed but never changing her movements on into more little streets and round endless bends and corners a thin waving flowing flower in her sports tunic which is the same apricot pink as her body.

'Pamela competing for the fast walking; this flexible fast walking which is a restraining from the running and skipping and jumping of childhood.

'She's a fast walker. She's never jumped for joy, only for praise. She recites too, like a water tap. She turns on shamelessly while Charmian makes beef olives and scribbles her notes on Ibsen at the kitchen table.

' "I wandered lonely as a cloud," Pamela's Wordsworth voice from behind the aprons hanging on the back of the kitchen door. She's there pretending to be on a stage and not in the kitchen. I thought she was hiding there because she was shy and might spoil her poem with laughing, but that wasn't it at all, she was making believe it was curtains and footlights and an audience of admiration.'

'Have you any more children?' I think I will turn his attention as his voice is rough with distress.

He doesn't pay any attention to my question but goes on, 'Marks for this and that, her face all distorted with this thing they call speech training. I thought I'd like the poetry and the music at the school, not having had the opportunities myself when I was a boy. But it was all marks in halves and quarters and hot little girls in tears saying the same poem over and over

139

again to be compared, all for comparison, and all the parents not even pretending to listen to each other's children. As if marks matter all that much, but I'm afraid they do matter.'

'Have you any more children?' My question surprised him.

'Yes I've told you haven't I? There's Samuel. He's written a prize-winning essay. Something historical. Charmian typed it all out for him. He cuts out and saves newspaper clippings. Ask him for any item of news. He's got everything in boxes and files. He's neat and well brushed and very clean. He's to be married soon. He's so used to being bossed about, he's become a kind of intellectual masochist. When he doesn't feel constraint of some kind, he seems uneasy so he fits in very well. No troubles of any kind. As I said, my feeling of wanting to escape from the family situation is entirely unreasonable.

'It's when I'm pedalling the bicycle, heavy in front with the hessian bags, and there's the slight change in the air, you know the end of summer, the beginning of autumn, that I feel this restlessness; especially when we have the first rainfall after the long hot dry months.

' "I'll put my giant freesias in the old sink," I told my mother. Sometimes I wonder if I ever saw them flower because it would have been after her death if they had flowered. I suppose I must have done.

'Later I remembered a lot of things. I remembered old refinements. I spread a cloth and cut pieces of cake for Charmian when she came to me. She was always hungry in the country.

'She gets hungry now. It's nice when she's hungry.

'The suburb after the first rain is so refreshed but the take-away food wrappings, the Coca-Cola tins and the dogs' dirt are always there. The sky suddenly seems older and colder, it starts to get dark earlier.'

'But I can't see how all this brings you in here,' I interrupt him. 'Who is it you've killed? If you really have. I can see you've lost some mail, you've said so, but that's nothing so bad, especially as you can tell them where it is.'

'I'm coming to that part,' he replies in a loud whisper. We have to be quiet a moment as the night nurse pauses outside our door with the Night Superintendent. They are making the midnight round. They move on.

'There was something that finished me,' he says. 'Something that made me pack in the whole thing, delivering letters, everything. In a minute I'll come to that. First I must tell you that after the rain I felt I must go up to the farm. I couldn't help it. I had to go. I drove up one evening with a lot of the undelivered mail. Charmian had left for her performance. She was going to be late home. She told me not to wait up for her. "I'm going out for jasmine tea after class," she called out. And she was gone.

'My place is only about forty miles from town. The people who bought it aren't there all the time. It's the weekend farmers who buy these properties now.

'It didn't take me long to get there. I could feel it was being cherished. Everything was very still and quiet and neat in the night. Everything put away till they could get back there. I know it, I've done it myself during the time when I was going to and fro. I just stood there for some minutes in the yard, smelling the land and feeling the cold night air. I like the cold air, you know, especially up there. The farm's high I've already told you, it's cold there at night. I scraped at the sweet earth with my hands; it was only moist on the top.

'It was moonlight. Very clear. I could see the water shining on the outcrop, seeing it again took my breath away. Slowly I moved and touched the weatherboards of the house and ran my hand along the top of the gate. All round was the silence of the deserted farm. They don't have any stock there, so there was no restless movement in the long paddock. I didn't really wonder about them, and of course, I didn't try to go into the house, after all it isn't mine any more. But I did go into the shed and that's where I saw her.'

'Who?'

141

'My tractor.'

'Oh I see.'

'There she was, always a poor sick thing. Whenever I tried to get her going she'd stop in the doorway of the shed like a crippled animal. Oh, I've had some terrible times with her I can tell you.'

'It's not her you've done away with.'

'Oh no! Just wait. I'm coming to that. But first I had this urge, just once more I wanted to plough up the earth. I wanted to feel the earth yielding and turning over and I wanted to smell the freshly turned earth and walk over the crumbling ridges of it and I wanted to look back over the dark new-ploughed part.'

'But it was night time.'

'Yes I know and I wasn't sure I could get the tractor to go, even though I understood her ways, where to encourage her with my boot and so on, you understand. So I took the little rotary hoe instead and, without any trouble, I got her started up and I moved the pin so that the blades would turn deeper into the earth. I thought I'd start at the top end of what used to be the bean field. She rattled over the rocks. I'd forgotten that noise; you can guess what it felt like to hear it again, and being a bit short of oil in the gears there was a terrible noise from there too. But after a bit she settled and I took her right along the field and then back, turning in a great wide half circle of white moonlight. It's very heavy turning a rotary hoe, almost at once the old familiar ache came into my arms. I felt the warmth come at me from the engine. I'd forgotten the smell and the warmth and the reassurance of the strength of machinery. The fragrance of the earth was so sharp I sneezed. I forgot about everything except the earth, the quality of it and the quality of the air. I remembered how I had once shared these qualities with Charmian. The air is sweet and cool up there even in summer at night. It comes through and over miles of trees. The jarrah forest cleans the air and gives it all day long a purity and a kind of golden light which comes from the sun shining on and through all the various shades of green.

'In the suburb, where there are people waiting for me, yes, waiting because they want their letters, I feel real loneliness. You'll never believe this, but one woman says she likes to receive a bill, you know an account, because these days there's an element of surprise. She wants a surprise, life's so boring she says, even paying a bill is better than having nothing to do at all. I hope you don't mind I seem to be talking so much, I've nearly finished.' His voice trembles with his apology. 'I never talk like this. It must be that injection! I'm sorry.'

'Not at all, please go on telling me,' I reply and I'm not even yawning. We are both leaning over towards each other. Gentle snoring comes from the ward across the passage. It's the time of night when even the night nurse, unable to help herself, has unwillingly closed her eyes too.

He clears his throat, it's like a shy little laugh.

'In every village,' he says, 'and I suppose in every suburb is a house which people notice as they pass, a witch's house. And the children say to each other never run by this house, however frightened you might be, always walk by the place slowly, because, if you run to get away quickly your feet will run and run, but you stay stuck in the same place. I suppose you've heard this? It belongs to childhood.' He shrugs as if embarrassed, and his little laugh is partly a cough.

'No never, but go on. I think I can imagine what you mean.'

'Well, in our township, when I was a boy, there was a house like this and when we went for our stores I always passed the house but I never tried it for myself. I always walked steadily with my eyes fixed on the chimney of the next house. I never tried the witch's spell. I never looked and I never tried to run.

'Where I deliver letters is just such a house. It's so neglected, long grass and wild oats and the castor oil plant have taken over completely, right up to and over the window sills. The

143

verandahs have been covered in with asbestos and that's all cracked and broken. Some sort of bedspreads are nailed on the insides of the windows, no curtains, just these faded cloths sagging across. The house belongs to an old woman. Most days she comes out on the pavement looking incredibly old and withered, her stockings all in wrinkles round her old woman legs and, instead of a proper dress, she'd have some rags hanging over her shoulders.

' "You got a letter for me today?" she used to ask me every day and she'd reach out her dirty thin hand. "I've got a boy married in England. He's got a lovely wife and four children. I've four grand-children, all lovely girls," she'd say proudly.

' "No, I'm sorry nothing for you today."

' "Ah well, they're writing tomorrow, I daresay."

'And I'd pedal the heavy bike on steadily to the next house not really looking at her. I couldn't bear to see her hope die away at my reply.

'There wasn't ever a letter for her and she was always asking. All this, of course, was before I began to lose heart about delivering the letters. In a minute I'm going to explain.

'It was like this, you see, around Christmas time it was hot and there was all the extra delivery to do and one morning there was a letter for her. It had come from England. It was a thick envelope with the name and address clearly typed. I tried to hurry to her place but there were so many envelopes and packages I thought I'd never get there.

'I really hurried, stuffing things into letter boxes, kicking dogs and tricycles out of my way, and when at last I got to the old witch's house there was no sign of her. I thought what if she'd died in there, and no one would know, and she'd never know she'd got the letter. I wondered what to do. In the end I propped up my bike against the side of the house and I went round the back with the letter and I kept calling out, "Anyone at home," and as there was no answer, I pushed the fly wire door and went inside.

'You'll never believe this, the whole house was piled up with rags, heaps of them. They were all over the few bits of furniture, in the corners stuffed into cupboards and falling out, all sorts of rags, men's coats and women's dresses, all old and out of date I suppose. And there were indescribable rags, not clothes or anything, just tattered cloth, all colours and all filthy dirty, that's how they looked to me. It was dark in the house, I didn't see the old woman at once. And then I did see her. She seemed like part of the rag heap, only she was moving about fidgetting from one side of the heap to the other, pulling first at one rag and then at another. I thought she was singing and then I realised it wasn't singing. She was talking. She was talking to the rags. She was telling them off! One after the other she pulled the rags and shook them angrily. She even slapped some of them. I couldn't hear the exact words of her muttering but she seemed to be accusing them. And then suddenly, "You fool!" she screamed at one of the unfortunate creatures, I mean rags. And the whole heap seemed to be moving as if uneasy and afraid of her rage. I couldn't believe it, this mass of trembling rags trying to edge away from the angry old woman. I noticed she was more dressed up than usual. Well, perhaps rigged out is more appropriate, you couldn't call her rags dresses.

' "Hurry up!" she screeched. "And get ready! It's time to start." She pulled another rag forward, her voice changing a bit. "I'll really have to slap you hard you know." Her voice softened and gently she drew the rag nearer so that it seemed to stand ashamed before her, out there in front of the shifting whispering heap, as if in disgrace. "Hold up your head," she said. "You remember your lines don't you, well don't be shy," giving it a gentle shake. "Come on, you're my best girl. . . ."

' "Missis!" I said. "Missis, there's a letter for you," I said, holding out the envelope towards her.

'Immediately she stopped talking and the rag withdrew politely to one side. She turned to me and looked at me and waved her hand towards the door in an imperious gesture. "Not now,"

145

she said. "Can't you see we're in rehearsal? Come back later. Say, in about an hour. We should be through in an hour." And with a sharp flap of her hand she dismissed me, and turned and nodded to the rag as if to say "Begin."

'I didn't wait, I can tell you. As I left I could hear her voice soothing and comforting.

' "There, there I didn't mean to be sharp. Don't cry! There's my good girl! How can you say those lines if you're crying? They're poetry you know, you can't speak poetry and cry at the same time. Dry your eyes, do! There, that's better." She was somehow singing. As I closed the fly screen, I saw her sink down, take the rag in her arms close to her withered old breast and gently rock backwards and forwards, as if to console forever the upset, hysterical rag.

'Well, I kept the letter. I kept thinking she'd come out as usual and ask if there was a letter for her from her son in England. This letter had an English stamp and post mark. It was dated the previous October and by this time it was already April.

'She didn't come out and I didn't go into the house again. What was the use of giving her the letter if her mind was gone, I thought. She'd only lose it or destroy it while she was off her head like this. Better keep the letter, I thought, till she was recovered and then she'd be so pleased. I began to look forward to seeing her pleasure at receiving the letter. I kept it in my pocket which is against the rules, but never mind; it was something to think about, seeing her hold out her dirty thin hand for the letter and seeing her smile when she'd got it.

'But the weeks went by and she didn't come out. And then I had this idea. I thought if I went in the house and interrupted her while she was busy with the rags, and if I opened the letter and began to read it to her it would make her remember; she'd be forced to realise it was her son talking to her in the letter.

'So, in the evening when Charmian had left for the performance and I had the sitting room to myself, I broke all the rest
of the post office rules and opened the letter. You see, I wanted
to make sure it was from her son.'

He's so quiet for a time I want to ask him, 'Well, who was
the letter from?' I do ask him. He seems to have forgotten
everything he was saying and in the blue light he peers at me.
It's beginning to get light outside, not the dawn but that paleness
of the sky before the dawn. Only people who work at night,
or who can't sleep, ever see this watery pale sky just before the
dawn.

'Well, who was the letter from?'

'Eh? Oh yes the letter.' He lies back, as if tired, and his voice
rasps. 'The letter. Yes the letter. It was from her son all right,
and from her daughter-in-law and from the four grand-daughters
who must be quite grown girls. Though that growing process is
a slow thing I can tell you.

'The letter. Yes, the letter. Yes. It was one of those duplicated things. Her daughter-in-law must have sent off a whole
lot of them, you see, about the beginning of October last year.
Someone had written Grandma, in ink, next to the duplicated
Dear and then came the letter and their names were all at the
end, duplicated too. I read it. I read it to the end. I can remember every word of it. I'll tell it to you. It'll help you to
understand why I've done what I've done.'

'With the mail?'

'Yes, with the mail and everything else.' And then he begins
to recite in a flat dead voice.

' "Dear Grandma, once again it's time to catch the Christmas
mail. We send you our warmest greetings and our best wishes
for a happy Christmas and a good new year. The year has been
a busy and eventful one for all of us. The twins recovered from
measles and had their tonsils out and joyfully entered secondary
school. It has been a successful year for them, both gaining the

highest marks in every subject in their class. Their taste in music is classical rather than pop and they read non-fiction for pleasure.

' "Half way through the year our new house was finally completed and we moved and settled in, all of us coping with the necessary changes in our routine. As we are only six houses away from the arcade, Mavis can shop daily and Peter can have the car without argument. The suburb is very attractive with Tudor houses and a large fifteenth-century church." ' He stops and draws breath.

' "Shortly before we moved . . ." ' His voice has taken on the singsong quality of a school recitation, up and down now his voice goes on.

' "Shortly before we moved, Edwina announced her engagement and after graduating, with honours, she was quietly married and the buffet reception was held at a nearby hotel. . . ." ' His voice crumbles and fades; he clears his throat. The sound is something between a little cough and a little laugh and the beginning of a sigh. And then he says, 'I had to read the rest of this, it went on for two long pages. There was nothing in it for her. Nothing of her son for her, you understand. The letter, I can remember it all, was all examination marks, interior decoration, you know, bathroom colours and matching towels, food prices, holidays in the Swiss Alps telling which hotels included mushrooms in their breakfasts, art galleries and picture galleries, museums, plays and concerts. It's true their names are all there at the end but they're machine copies. Just at the end, too, is a part about politics in England. I'll remember it for ever. I'll never forget it. It's how a letter dies, it's the death of a letter. How can a man deliver a letter that's died. This is how in the end it had died from being strangled, strangled to death. Listen. "At the moment we're facing another election with no party really knowing how to solve the serious economic problems arising from increased oil prices particularly in view of increasing militancy and the tendency still to demand more despite a reduced national income." '

'So you did away with the letter.' My voice fills the quiet.

'No, there was no need, it was already gone, as you might say.'

'You never took it to her?'

'No, how could I?'

'Did she come out and ask? I mean, did she get over the rag bit and come out and ask? For a letter?'

'No. Not again because something happened.' He's still lying back and I can just make out the outlines of his troubled face.

'I'll tell you something about trees,' he says suddenly, and I remember he had muttered to the nurse about trees. He raises himself on one elbow. 'There's something about trees, there's all kinds of expressions in their restless foliage,' he says. 'Have you ever noticed that trees on the other side of a valley, trees massed on the other side of a narrow valley and along a bit, trees piled together, seem to have troubled faces and these faces are sometimes faces of pain? It's the same with clouds. It's as though all the perplexities of our lives are reflected in these faces they look back at us in the same pain.'

'Do you want to tell me about the old lady?' I ask him softly.

'Yes,' he replies. 'It won't take a minute. The very next morning I'm pedalling up the street where her house is and there she is out on the pavement with her old rags dangling all over her and as usual her stockings are down in wrinkles. She's got her arms full of packages of some sort.

'I pedal steadily along the pavement. It's a bit uphill but I've a great strength still from the kind of life I've had, even if I am heavier now than I really should be. I keep going. I think to myself how I'll go straight on by. I'll really hurry by her place without seeing her without stopping to hear her asking me for a letter from her son. I keep thinking how I'll go straight on as fast as I can just looking steadily ahead to the chimney of the next house and she'll be obliged to step back into her yard out of my way.

'I don't look at her at all. I keep right on pedalling as hard and fast as I can, not looking. All I see is the next chimney.

'It's the squeal of brakes that makes me stop and get off my bicycle, and when I look back, there she is in the roadway knocked over, run over and crushed by a car. All at once quite a few people have gathered in a little crowd there.'

'She must have stepped the wrong way,' I say.

'Yes, she must have,' he replies.

'It's not really your responsibility,' I say to him. 'It's not your fault if a woman steps in one direction instead of another.'

'It is and it isn't,' he says.

'There you go with your two answers to everything.'

'Yes, it's terrible when there's two answers,' he says. 'I haven't any answers at all really, only questions. Only questions.'

'I don't see,' I say to him after a while. 'I don't see where your wife comes into all this. You haven't done anything to her. She seems to be very much alive and enjoying her life and her work.'

He sits up in bed trying to untuck the bed clothes even more. He shakes his head slowly as if he's got a headache and hopes the movement will ease him.

'Charmian?' he asks, he's grey this morning and puzzled. 'Charmian? Oh yes. Charmian. She was upset to read a description of the accident in the paper the next day. She read it aloud while we were at breakfast, "the victim's face was all crushed like a spoon?"

'I looked at Charmian, I remember looking. I thought then a face could be crushed and hollowed out like a spoon.

' "Like a spoon?" she asked me, repeating a question I didn't understand.

' "Do you want a spoon?" she asked again.

' "What for?"

' "To eat your cornflakes with." '

' "Oh yes, of course." '

The small ward is quite light and raw in the grey morning. There are noises reminding us that the work of the hospital is going on in spite of everything.

'I'm afraid I've kept you awake all night,' he apologizes.

'Think nothing of it,' I say with my customary good humour. 'We can sleep all day if we want to.' After a moment I say again,

'I still don't see, unless you've done something else, what you have done to your wife?'

'No, I haven't done anything else. I've told you everything.'

'I think you're blaming yourself too much.'

'No, I can never be given enough blame, enough punishment. Don't you understand. I used to wait up for her. She comes in you see all white-faced and small; tired out! This performance of hers every night takes a great deal out of her. She puts a lot into the performance. I always made tea for her and I sat there while she told me all about the class, what the students said, what they laughed about together and all the things they'd discussed.

'She puts tremendous energy into everything she does. You know I told you about the almond blossom, she came up into the barn with me that evening and I said, "You can come and stay for a rest if you really want to."

' "Oh could I?" That's all she said. It was the way she said it and it was there in the barn she said something else.

' "Kiss me!" she said. I'd never known anything like it before; the kiss I mean. I kissed her more than once. She stayed with me, I told you. She wanted me. I wanted her. We could hardly wait for the night. I'll never forget the almond blossom.

'Well, as I was saying she'd drink her tea and tell me things. You know, it restores her to do this. She restores herself, regains her energy while she's talking to me. She needs to talk, and now if I'm not there because I have to be in here, because

151

of this, it's the same thing as I've done to the old woman by not looking at her. Don't you see I kept going on the bicycle and I didn't look on purpose. I looked at the chimney of the next house.

'Oh!' he says in a deep sigh and after a while he repeats in a lower tone, 'Oh! Oh! . . . Oh don't you see,' he says. 'The scattered groceries all over the pavement showed so plainly that she had intended to go on living.'

Winter Nelis

Leonora Brown, lying in a hot bath in the middle of the day for gynaecological reasons, relaxed into the drifting thoughts which accompany hot water and steam at an unaccustomed time.

All night old Smith's rooster had crowed with a mechanical regularity, as though the old man had wound up the bird before going to bed himself. Two cars crashed somewhere quite near and through the noise of the car, bodies indescribably wounded, dragging their tormented wreckage, she heard someone crying and crying.

'I think there's been a crash,' she said to her husband, but he said he'd been awake all night and had heard nothing.

'It's only your imagination,' he said. And she lay beside him, separated by a knowledge, which he did not share, of something sinister; of wounding, of unhappiness and of pain.

At breakfast she asked him, 'How much water does the bath hold?'

He was hidden behind the newspaper.

'Water? The bath? Absolutely no idea, but there's no shortage just now is there?'

So Leonora guessed the quantities of vinegar and bicarbonate of soda for her remedial bath. A person couldn't dissolve in a mixture of this sort. In any case, the vinegar in the hot steam was sharp and medicinal, very reassuring.

She sang. The bathroom encouraged her.

'I had not,' she said to herself in a rich deep contralto. 'I had not known Ludwig many months before he decided to make me the heroine of his opera. . . .' She laughed and then stopped laughing. There was nothing, nothing in that, especially her singing, nothing at all that was laughable.

'I've had some bad times. Oh but these bad times!'

'That's no way to speak to a guest!' Leonora remembered it clearly, her own voice sharp and unpleasant in the foyer of the unfashionable hotel she had misguidedly chosen.

'That's no way to speak to a guest!' And the young receptionist looked up from the counter and at once she saw her mistake. An unbearable mistake. She remembered his pale eyes bulging as he looked in disbelief, and the little veins and capillaries misplaced on his crooked boyish face slowly reddened. The painful blush was to her a greater pain, she had not imagined she could, and had, stripped him of covering and dignity. It was as if she peeled off his unhealthy skin leaving him raw. Later that evening the memory of it was so close she couldn't bear it. Miss Butterick, sitting with her third brandy, couldn't possibly have understood so why try and tell her. But she did tell, concluding with, 'I can't imagine why I was so rude and impatient.'

Miss Butterick's speech was somewhat slurred, and her voice deepened with alcoholic compassion,

'It's awful when you know you've hurt someone.' She didn't care really, Leonora knew, she just said the safe thing. For the moment Butterick was warm, and she'd had her brandy, and she might even have something else later on if Leonora felt sorry enough for the whole world to feel she should satisfy Miss Butterick's repetitious physical need.

All too vividly Leonora recalled the bandy goblin legs clambering up into the Paris Express, and the stuffy warmth which came from that region under the tweed skirt where those concave thighs met with so little magic. She followed Miss Butterick with misgivings which told all too plainly at the outset that she had made a mistake. . . .

The bath water was cooling off. Leonora turned on the hot tap with one foot and the warmth surrounded her reluctantly.

'I hardly knew Ludwig when he insisted on making me the heroine. . . .'

What did Miss Butterick know of Beethoven, so how could one make that sort of joke? At dinner, she remembered, the Butterick pretended a preference of wines. For sophistication, she scooped a tiny fragment of melting camembert and ate it hastily, without relish, as if it was a medicine. She ate furtively, wiping suspected crumbs from the corners of her boring mouth.

Leonora remembering, shuddered. The rhythm of the railway wheels seemed to send the knowledge of the mistake straight into her, just as the rhythm sent another experience into Miss Butterick sitting opposite. Leonora couldn't fail to notice the furtive moment of feeling so quickly achieved and so quickly brushed aside like a mistake in a typed letter, as it was followed by the all too familiar, "Oh! Naughty me!"

The bitter drops of the after dinner coffee had to come to an end and there was nothing to do but shepherd Miss Butterick, pathetically proud of having had more than enough to drink, upstairs to the cold dingy room.

'But Butters, you can't possibly sleep with me without washing!' Leonora came from the unexpectedly pleasant comfort of a hot bath to where Miss Butterick sat like an imp in the bed.

'Try me!' She twisted her mouth in a smile and Leonora opened the tall window. She wanted to call out her unhappiness to someone, she wanted to call it across the clean moonlit roofs and chimneys of a strange city.

'If Ludwig had only known me a few months he would have made me the heroine. . . .' There are times when the imagination is not enough. . . .

Tears trembled on Miss Butterick's eye lashes and her hands were cold and Leonora knew, and went on knowing, how wrong it was to explore, to unmask, to get complete revelation and then to leave off, to discard; no, it was not discarding, it was more a moving away because of being too frail to continue. She never meant to be guilty of discarding. Never.

Leonora added more hot water, it brought poetry. Horace? Campion T.? *The man of life upright/whose guiltless heart is free/from all dishonest thoughts/and deeds of vanity: that man needs neither towers/to shield him from the sky/nor armoured vaults to fly/from thunders tyranny.*

The water slapped the bath in lukewarm idleness.

'Whose are these?' With a terrible voice the Night Superintendent held up the scattered shabby underclothes indecently inadequate, ragged with black lace and, with them, more than a hint of leather and feathers. Peacocks are supposed to be unlucky but Haddon said that was rubbish. With her had come things which had never existed for Leonora before, the Beethoven and the poetry. The feathers were crushed and broken as if from some kind of indescribable wounding.

Leonora never owned up to the clothes but kept her eyes turned away and let Sister Haddon in her well-bred voice say in front of the assembled staff,

'I'd like to explain in private please, if I may, to Matron.' Haddon, who off duty was well tailored and wore shirts with collars and ties, left that night and Leonora stayed.

In the school of nursing she was not allowed to have curled hair showing, or to wear lipstick, bracelets or rings, and she had to have the gold studs removed from her shoes. There was something indefinable about her. The Home Sister and the Tutor Sister felt this intangible quality which they did not quite understand or like. She seemed in some way shop soiled, but they were never able to openly accuse her of anything to do with that odd collection of clothing and accessories. Only in their secret imagination could they reconstruct what might have been confessed in Sister Haddon's explanation. It was agreed that Leonora was a conscript, and that she would probably fail her examinations. So many only chose nursing to avoid the forces or the munition factory.

The Buyer for Fancy's Fashions straight away liked Leonora's way with the customers, only fresh from school and she could do it! Fancy herself approved.

'Take Lady Moneybags to the fitting room,' Fancy whispered from the side of her soft red mouth. 'Take the sequins, the gold leaf and the ermine, take the lot in with you.' The hoarse whisper intended for Leonora alone came through the racks of dresses and furs. Even in her youthfulness she was able to match customers and clothing and the expensive vulgarity of certain kinds of jewellery.

Big Fancy, trying on in advance the summer beach wear, stood partly naked, surveying her creamy folds pressing her pale flesh with her palms. There was a smell of fresh new cotton.

'Leonora! Zip me up!' she whispered. 'Try harder! Do it harder!'

If Leonora at times seemed to stay too long in the fitting room, Big Fancy, with a flurry of the beaded curtain, would pull out the bent-wood chair from under her, violently, and a few minutes later, with equal violence, would send the chair screeching over the inlaid linoleum back through the frantic leaping beads.

'Thanks Fancy,' calmly Leonora reseating herself would continue her contemplation which often became a kind of simultaneous act of praise and betrayal.

. . .

157

Leonora, lying in the indifferent water, walked with her mother who said, 'No one can earn a living singing. When I was your age I already had four children.'

She remembered the smell of the promise of summer between deep hedges, darker at the tops where they had not been cut. There were delphiniums in her mother's garden, blue and white, thrusting right up into the apple tree as if feeling for the little hard nipples of the ungrown fruit hidden in the safety of the leaves.

Telling a lie about her age, she married Desmond. He was ten years younger and this showed quite quickly. Horribly. It really was unimportant, but she did worry. There was the constant watchfulness over the persisting truth in the parting of her hair, and that exhausting search for dresses with high necks. She had pills to take but they made her sleepy and, even worse, she was sure they made her fat.

In the mid-day silence, the next-door car came home. The car door opened and slammed shut and the new little next-door woman ran quickly, gack gook gack gook, up the concrete path.

Leonora heard the neighbour woman give a moan, a subdued cry suggesting a burst of tears and the front door opened and slammed shut and across the silence came the muffled sound of crying.

Leonora wondered whatever could have happened to make her come rushing home like that, hardly able to wait till she could reach the seclusion of the house before crying, and then to go on crying as if there was something unbearable for her, as if something terrible had happened, or was going to happen. Whatever could there be in the lives of the newly married young people to wound and torment, to make her weep in such a broken hearted way.

The Browns did not know the Banks at all yet. They had only moved in a few days before. Mr Banks looked fresh faced and quiet, he went to the bus in the mornings with a brief case. So many people had a brief case now it was impossible to draw

158

any kind of conclusion. Mrs Banks was small and neat, and pink like a hygienic doll. She usually had the car.

Leonora had not liked to intrude, she and Desmond were so much older. Leonora lately resented people, even disliked them. Often the only conversation she and Desmond had was to talk about people they knew, and find fault.

The noise of the sobbing went on and on. Leonora dressed herself quickly and went round to the other house. She wished she had a little jar of something home-made to take, but she had given up long ago shredding orange peel and removing plum stones. It was so much easier just to buy a tin of marmalade somewhere, it was too sweet, but she did not bother about flavours enough now to mind.

When she thought about it, what did any of it really matter. There was always this feeling of being only temporary. Thinking back about Miss Butterick, of Haddon, of Big Fancy and of her mother, life seemed endless and yet one's turn of being was so limited, so brief, it really was a waste to care. Sometimes Leonora cried, not out loud like young Mrs Banks, but quietly inside herself. On these days she did not dress and she did not even comb her hair. It seemed to Desmond then that women in their wanting wanted something indefinable and, when he could, he persuaded Leonora to go into a nursing home for a rest.

The little hospital was high up overlooking a place where some old houses were being pulled down to make way for a new shopping centre.

'Why don't you go for a little walk,' the Sister said. 'It'll do you good.' So Leonora went out.

The road went below the escarpment; two men were working, as if chained to the steep dusty slope, with their hand drills and shovels, trying to build up the crumbling side. It seemed so hopeless, and a sunburnt young man went to and fro on a bulldozer, like a clockwork toy wound up and rewound, destined to go on in the noise and the dust for ever.

'Take me home!' Leonora sobbed when Desmond came to see her. 'I can't stand being here.' So she went home somewhat worse than before.

Mrs Banks had dropped some of her shopping. Little russet pears lay scattered all over the red path and on the grass and on the doorstep and on the new door mat.

Leonora knocked on the door too softly. The sobbing could be heard quite plainly. She knocked again. She waited but no one came to the door. The garden was untidy with the little pears. They had a look of autumn about them. They were shining and healthy and nut brown. Leonora wondered what they were like, so often appearances were deceptive.

She tried again knocking at the door, but no one came. She felt a curiosity mixed with concern and she was irritated too because Mrs Banks did not come.

In the end she went home.

The afternoon was peaceful with the soft voices of the doves. Leonora sat on the edge of her verandah. She seemed to notice, as if for the first time, the warm fragrance of the earth. Leaves, like approaching footsteps, rustled and fell from the flame trees, a few scarlet flowers were already splashed on the blue sky and the monotonous climbing notes of the rain bird sounded from somewhere quite near. It really was the autumn.

Across the road, two women were talking together. Expensively dressed and well groomed they were sitting on a lawn. Their high-pitched voices pierced the tranquillity, they sounded conceited and false and then serious in their own self importance as they asked questions and did not listen to answers. Every now and then one sighed but the other paid no attention and, occasionally, one of them or both of them together burst out with little cries of insincere mirth.

Leonora never went to her hairdresser these days. Most of the time she just sat doing nothing. And if she did force herself to do things, perhaps to weed the flower beds, it always seemed afterwards that the tall feathery grasses and the wilderness of nasturtiums really looked better than the bare fences and the edges of the garden where her restless hands had torn up everything in order to neaten. The sight, on these occasions, of the ragged and bruised flowers was so appalling that she often did not go out of the house until the memory of them had faded a little.

The women across the road went indoors. Leonora, on this day, did not mind them. She was listening to the house next door, but all was quiet there. She did not pause to be surprised at herself as she went into her kitchen where she cut bread and butter on a clean white cloth. While she worked she sang in her deep rich voice, she had forgotten how much she enjoyed singing. She said to a saucepan,

'I had not known Ludwig many months when he decided to make me the heroine of his opera . . . ,' she was laughing at herself when Desmond came home. Quickly she told him about Mrs Banks and they both wondered what dreadful thing could have happened.

'I'll go out and have a yarn with young Banks,' Desmond said. 'He's just out there in his yard now.'

'Hullo there! How're you making out?' he called across the low fence to Mr Banks.

'Good, thanks!' Mr Banks called back as he went into his own house.

The Browns were disappointed and after their meal Leonora said, 'Go round and ask them in for the evening.' She seemed quite eager. Desmond was surprised and pleased. This was an improvement in Leonora beyond any hopes he might have dared to have. He noticed the golden sponge fingers on the table. Leonora hadn't baked anything for a long time.

'They were pleased to be asked,' he said when he came back. 'But they want us to go round there to sort of warm the house, you know, their first real visitors,' he added. He was afraid Leonora would lack courage at the last moment. But he need not have been afraid.

'I'll change my dress then,' she said. 'I'll not be long.'

Perhaps the Banks needed to talk to someone about what had happened. She and Desmond were older and would be able to help in some way. Leonora had never heard a woman weep like that.

When Miss Butterick cried all those years ago, her tears, in an attempted silent restraint, hung as if held back shining on the lashes above the bluish puffed cheeks. With those furtive tears it had come to Leonora that it was wrong to give the appearance of loving when there was no love. How bitter is understanding when it comes through someone else's pain. It was something she would never be able to forget.

But this weeping was different. Leonora could not think of anything sinister, painful, frightening or sad ever happening to little Mrs Banks. She always looked so well and so happy, and so competent too.

She changed hurriedly and combed her neglected hair. Somehow, for the first time, it did not worry her that she no longer looked young. Soon they would know what had upset Mrs Banks so much.

And the Browns went quietly together to visit the Banks.

'Come in! Come in, please.' Young Mr Banks led them into the sitting room which gave the impression of being lovingly arranged. They sat in matching chairs drawn up to the hearth, lively with a small fire which had just been lit. The new warm flames ran laughing all round the dry crackling sticks. The russet pears were arranged with other fruits in a pyramid on a polished silver tray.

'What nice little pears!' Leonora said as Mrs Banks came in. Perhaps the pears would lead them straight to the necessary conversation. She smiled as kindly as she knew how at Mrs

Banks whose serene face and dress were as if embroidered with matching pink and white silk.

'Yes,' Mrs Banks said, and her voice suited her; it was clear and full of confidence. 'Aren't they exquisite! They're called Winter Nelis. You must try one,' she said. And then she said, laughing, 'D'you know, I think I've forgotten the pepper!' With a pink finger-tip she lifted the corners of one or two of her tiny sandwiches.

'Fetch the pepper please Honey,' she smiled prettily at Mr Banks.

Leonora chose a little pear, one of the Winter Nelis. She wondered if it had any flavour. So often things which looked attractive were not.

And she took a polite little bite nervously.

The Outworks
of the Kingdom

'How can a man be angry with his land,' Uncle Bernard said, when his nephew Walter asked him, 'Oncle do you feel angry with the land?'

They stood together at the edge of the great clay pit.

'No, I don't feel angry with the land,' Uncle Bernard continued. He picked his teeth with a sharpened match. 'How could I live if I feel angry with my land? Is josst like a woman. She becomes what the man who loves her makes her to himself. Same with the land.'

The forsaken pit was full of milky water and the cold air smelled of wet clay. As they walked back up the slope their boots sank in the mud. Big drops of water trembled on Uncle Bernard's woolen cardigan. The drops clung to him and were shed in small showers of tears whenever he moved.

Every time Claus and Walter visited their uncle, it seemed they had to go down more steps into his kitchen. His whole house, once quite visible from the bend in the road, no longer showed its iron roof and crooked chimney pipe above the side of the hill. A trace of smoke through the trees was the only evidence that there was a dwelling there at all.

When Walter asked him, 'Oncle, is your house sinking?' he

simply laid one finger along the side of his nose and replied, 'Perhaps the earth moves.'

'Oh earth can't move Oncle!'

'In the outworks of the kingdom,' Uncle Bernard said, 'earth moves in slides and quakes, earth goes to and fro.' He paused in the middle of his wisdom. 'What is a man?' he continued. 'Josst some meat on some bones and who can tell how long he will walk on his land. Sometimes is very good for a man to move his earth before some bodies else do it for him.'

Slowly they walked back to the house and, as they went indoors, Walter counted the steps. There were five and he clearly remembered counting four last time. He nudged Claus as they went down into the kitchen, and the brothers, nodding their heads behind their uncle's narrow back, each held up a hand to show five fingers to the other.

The kitchen smelled of baking apples. Aunt Mitzi and the two girls sat smiling in their Sunday dresses among the plates and cups. Uncle Bernard placed two chairs for his nephews.

'Back home in Holland, a long time ago, I bake bread,' he said. 'Now I bake clay bricks and today I am denking that Claus and Walter are coming so I am baking epples.'

With a small movement of reverence, he put Mitzi and the two girls behind the clock on the high mantle piece.

'First we eat,' he said to his nephews. 'And then I tell you why I ask you to come.'

'Smells good Oncle!' The two young men seemed to fill the small kitchen with their strength. Clove-scented steam from the hot apples made their ears red while they ate. The three men sat for a time completely happy to be together.

Later they walked outside. Uncle Bernard led the way, his unconcerned boots crushing fragrance from fallen eucalyptus leaves. The brothers couldn't help noticing at once that the land looked different. There were holes and hollows everywhere as if some strange animals, grazing with an industry beyond instinct and common sense, had eaten right down into the earth itself. The nephews were puzzled but followed their uncle quietly. They had not forgotten his tremendous disappointment years ago.

'You'll not do much up there,' the shopkeeper woman had said to them the day after they had taken possession of the land. 'Your creek floods in winter and it dries up in summer and the water's salt. Your soil's all salt and clay and up the hill it's gravel and outcrops of granite, nothing'll grow there. You've got poison weed too, so if you put stock you'll lose the lot.'

After years of selling macaroni, carried in two suitcases from one house to the next, Uncle Bernard had been so pleased to buy his own small property. 'All land is someone's land,' he had said to Claus and Walter then. 'And this land is ours!'

He had wanted to grow grapes. He longed for a vineyard of his own and, on that first day, it was as if he saw the vines already growing, their neat rows stretching towards the setting sun.

The woman in the shop warned them of frost and failure. And one by one all her predictions came true.

Claus and Walter, preferring not to think back to those failures, stared at the irregular excavations, both wondered what Uncle Bernard was doing. Surely, after all these years of bearing his disappointment so well, he couldn't have gone out of his mind now. Making clay bricks was not the same as a vineyard, but the bricks had brought success and a good business had been built up. The holes in the earth suggested a terrible truth.

'I wonder if he's trying to . . .' Walter started to speak.

'Let's hope not . . .' Claus said quickly. With dismay in their hearts they hurried through the scrub after their uncle. They knew how dedicated he could become to an idea.

Every night in those other days he sat studying from some old text books. 'Josst listen to the vines. . . .' Sometimes during those long evenings he read aloud to Claus and Walter. 'Tokay, Shiraz, Muscat, Grenache, Pedro and Frontignac. Is the poem of the grapes,' he said. 'Later I read you the poem of the soil!' He spent a lot of time with plump ladies, smudged naked in red and blue ink on the pages of an old exercise book. He was designing his own wine labels. The names of his wines were familiar, Claret Bernard, Bernard Burgundy, Bernard Rosé Sec and all had impossible dates and descriptions of soil and climate which bore no resemblance to reality.

The three men began to cross the neighbour's land. Similar hollows and pits disfigured this place too. The brick kilns and the sheds straggling at the bottom of this slope had, like the pits of milky water, the stillness of being forgotten for the time being. Uncle Bernard had something more urgent on his mind. The neighbour and partner in the clay brick company was a widow, long retired from a rice farm in New South Wales. She was outside her cottage contemplating her chimney which hovered between the intention and the accomplishment of a fall.

'Gut mornink Madam. How is your health?' Uncle Bernard enquired.

'A ball o' dash,' the old woman replied. 'How's yerself.' She looked with approval at Claus and Walter.

'Pheebe ain't too good,' the old woman continued. 'She's very uneasy. I think she's eaten something disagreeable . . . I think she's going to throw up any minute.'

'Dogs never do anything inside a house Madam,' Uncle Bernard said politely.

'No that's just what I mean, she'll suffer in her mind. I can't get her out of the kitchen see, she's too old. It's as if she's down a well in there. She's too old and too fat to climb out. Just take a look down there.'

Claus and Walter looked down into the kitchen. Not so long ago there had been steps up to this house. They looked at each other with eyebrows raised like question marks.

'I tell you!' Uncle Bernard interrupted. 'I and my nephews here will lift your house up from the dog and then she, too, will be outside the house.'

The widow thought for a moment, chewing on her gums. 'Fair enough!' she said. 'How soon can you start?'

'Right away!' Uncle Bernard was excited.

'But Oncle!'

'Never mind Walter! We pick up house bit by piece and shovel the earth into your truck and make nice flat place and put house back. . . .'

'But Oncle!'

'Never mind Walter! We do same with chicken house und shed. We make whole land neat. You will see. This is why I send for you to come and help me.'

'But Oncle!'

'Work now! We must hurry. We have to move my house too. You see,' he gave a small shrug of apology, 'one man can only dig out a little land by himself, and little digging makes troubles as you see.' He indicated the chimney which trembled above them. Uncle Bernard lowered his voice.

'There is very good price for earth and rocks, but is easier if we move whole house. Very hard digging inside a house!' he said. 'Very good price for land fill.'

For some weeks they toiled together, straining to move weatherboards and timbers, and then there was the moving of the earth itself. Every day they filled the truck and Claus drove the heavy load, the engine whining and groaning, along the winding roads to deliver the rocks and earth and to receive the payment for it.

At the bottom of the slope the water was smooth and secretive, milky, in the deserted pits. Every now and then the odour of wet clay came up to them as they worked. When they had finished on the old woman's land, they set to work on Uncle Bernard's place. His furniture looked small and out of place on the disturbed earth. Though Claus and Walter no longer lived with him they would always leave their own work to help him for it was he who had made the new life for them in the new country. Aunt Mitzi was to have followed with the two girls, but first it was school which prevented them, then sweethearts, then marriage and then grandchildren. Mitzi simply never had a chance to join Uncle Bernard and she remained fresh and youthful for ever on an old photograph.

At last the work was finished. Both properties were some six feet lower over all, perhaps a little more in places. The houses and sheds had been neatly replaced and Uncle Bernard divided out the money, giving the rice farm widow her share too.

'Tonight I go back to Holland,' he suddenly said when they were having their meal.

'But Oncle!'

'Is all arranged.' Uncle Bernard waved a pale blue letter. 'I have written to Mitzi.'

On the way to the airport Uncle Bernard asked Claus to stop at the cross-roads before the bridge. From the corner, the vineyards sloped in two directions towards the curving river. They stood in the long grass by the fence, which was covered in "For Sale" notices. The air was sweet with the scent of the bean flowers.

'When the beans are picked,' Uncle Bernard told them, 'the stalks are ploughed in between the vines to nourish the earth.' He sighed softly to himself.

In the moonlight Uncle Bernard's white hair showed like a bandage beneath the brim of his hat. The gnarled vines were kneeling on the earth, as if praying alone in the night.

'Perhaps they ask for kind owner,' Uncle Bernard sighed again. 'Even though I sell my land twice over and have enough money at last to buy this place, I haven't time any more.' He said nothing about strength, only steadied himself against the fence post. 'I haven't time any more,' he said again.

'Oncle,' Walter said shyly. 'At first we thought you were looking for gold.' Uncle Bernard laughed.

'How do you mean you sell your land twice?' Walter asked.

Their voices went to and fro softly in the sweet-scented night.

'Is like this,' Uncle Bernard said. 'If some bodies want to remove your land, is best to move it yourself first.'

'You mean,' said Claus. 'The government?'

Uncle Bernard laughed a small laugh. 'Yes. Tomorrow the outworks of the kingdom resumes clay bricks, pits, sheds and gravel. Is still some left!' He winked one eye. 'They want to build a six-lane highway through my place, and in exchange is fair words and money.' After a little silence he said, 'And I, I shall get home before my letter. Only denk! I shall telephone Mitzi from the corner of her street. "How is everyding over there?" I shall ask her. "How is everyding over there!" His voice seemed to ring across the vineyards. "How is everyding over there! Mitzi how are you!" I shall ask her. Then I wish her, "Happy Birthday." "Happy Birthday over there!" I shall say to her, and she will denk I spik from twelve thousand miles away. "Happy Birthday!" I shall say again, and then in five minutes I shall walk in her kitchen!'

'But Oncle!' Walter said. 'That air letter is an old one, it's out of date, it's got a Christmas angel on it.'

'Yes, you'll need more stamps,' Claus said. 'Postage has gone up several times since you wrote that letter.'

'Yes, yes,' Uncle Bernard agreed. 'I can get stamps. No troubles!' He smiled fondly at his nephews. 'And as for the angel. There's no harm in an angel all the year round, is there?'

The Agent in Travelling

'How can a man reproach himself?' Uncle Bernard said when his daughter, who was pretending to be his niece, asked him, 'Uncle, don't you reproach yourself?'

'No, I don't feel any reproach to myself,' Uncle Bernard replied. 'How can a man live if he reproaches himself?' he said. 'Spik Enklisch please or else spik more slowly. After so many years, you know, I forget everyding of mine own country and of mine own language.' Uncle Bernard sat propped against white, plastic-covered pillows; his white hair was like a ragged bandage fringed round his head. He seemed small and shrivelled and clean, tucked inside the stiff sheets of the hospital bed.

Stephanie was so like Mitzi; it was confusing. She was the same heavy shape. Her pale hair was drawn tightly back from her big face. And her clothes too were big, as if sewn on as neatly as possible round her well-fed body. Like Mitzi, she chose skirts and jackets and hand-made blouses made of spotted silk. Stephanie sat beside the bed. The visiting time was nearly over.

'You frightened the children dreadfully,' Stephanie persisted. Her English was good for she had been well educated. 'How could you!' she accused him. 'How could you do such a thing! Being ill like that in front of them and in a restaurant too and

171

so many people there to look and see you!' She made a quick impatient movement backwards with her chair. Uncle Bernard sank lower in the pillows and looked at his daughter.

'Oh yes. For that I do reproach myself. Yes,' he sighed. 'For that I can never be blamed enough! My two dear little angels, how could I frighten them! Oh my little angels.' He moved his head from side to side on the pillow. His blue eyes were deep and misty but the eyes of old people often look as if they are full of tears.

After Stephanie had gone he lay very still in his bed. He wished for his nephews, Claus and Walter, but they were far away, busy with the new life he had helped them to make. He tried to forget the hospital and to think about the letter they had sent him; the earth moving was going well.

Trying to keep his mind on that far-off place, he thought he could smell the stagnant water of the clay pits. He seemed to hear, somewhere in his head, the groaning engine of the big truck as they drove the heavy load of earth and rocks to sell for land fill.

'In the outworks of the kingdom,' Uncle Bernard said softly to himself. 'In the outworks of the kingdom, earth moves in slides and quakes, earth goes to and fro. If some bodies want to remove your land, is best to move it yourself first.' He laughed, he had been pleased to have the letter.

Claus had written, 'Oncle, all the time we are some miles ahead of the new highway. Most farmers of the resumed land are pleased to sell their top soil and business is very good. In some places you may be sure the six lanes of the new highway will be going through a deep valley.'

Uncle Bernard tried to dwell on the pleasure of selling land twice over. The government had been fair in their dealing over the resumption of the clay pits. The whole clay brick business had to be given up, but then there was the sale of the soil and the rocks before the land was actually resumed. Of course the earth-moving business would be good. What man could refuse two payments for his land.

'The children couldn't sleep.' Stephanie's persistent voice came to him again. 'Your illness frightened them so much, and in public too. Aren't you ashamed?'

'Oh!' he sighed. Yes, he was ashamed and he did reproach himself and a man cannot live reproaching himself. He sighed again and his thoughts went back over the last few weeks since his return.

'A man does not, in his life, always do what he hopes to do,' he told a new acquaintance, a man he didn't know, but someone who, like himself, sat every evening in the Café Maximillian. This café was on the corner of the street where Mitzi had found a small, but clean, room for him. There were thick green cloths on the tables and the two men sat in a kind of tainted respectability, slowly drinking their coffee. He explained to this stranger all about his years abroad and how he had wanted to have a vineyard and grow grapes. 'I buy the wrong land,' he confessed. 'But clay brick business very good.' He didn't want to show off about the clay bricks, but he would have liked to describe the vineyards spreading round the curve of the river, and the neat rows of vines and the narrow orchards of fruit trees, which seemed to run in ribbed patterns up and along the low hills. The varying greens and browns deepened at sunset, and the plum blossom looked like a trimming of white embroidery. Though these orchards were not his, he would have liked to talk about them. And this had given him an idea. Carefully he wrote out a little advertisement, *Agent in travelling. Enquiring welcome,* and paid to have it displayed in the window of the little shop, which was the Café Maximillian.

Of course the travel agencies in this city were in modern offices of glass, and had an appearance of wealth with coloured posters, deep arm chairs and pretty girls to tell intending travellers where to go and how to go. He couldn't offer all that, but he could describe the soil conditions in far-off places and the rough, sun-streaked bark of foreign trees. And he could tell of the smell of the rain in the wind and on the eucalyptus-laden earth. Though he sat patiently at the green-covered tables no one, in these first few weeks, had come to consult the agent in travelling. He pondered on the possibilities and wondered whether he could describe the pleasure of rain when it was raining all the time and people complained about it. He supposed too there might be difficulties in talking about the poetry of the soil in this place, where it was impossible to put a soup spoon in the earth, let alone a spade.

'Listen to the poem of the grapes,' he would have liked to tell them as he used to tell his nephews, Claus and Walter, in the days when they were working together and saving to buy some land.

'Tokay, Shiraz, Muscat, Grenache, Pedro and Frontignac is the poem of the grape,' he said it often to himself, and once he had even designed a new wine label on the table napkin. It was just a small sketch of a label with a plump naked lady, not quite resembling Mitzi, smudged in blue biro and provokingly decorated with smudged blue biro vine leaves. The proprietress of the Café Maximillian resorted to her knowledge of English for Uncle Bernard's benefit.

'You pay me Mr Oons!' she cried. 'One spoiled napkin cost. . . .' and she made a wide gesture with both arms out-stretched, filling the small room. 'One spoiled costs whole set because one spoiled, spoils whole set. Whole set ruined! When you pay me?'

The street where he lived now was the one where all the shameful things went on. The ladies sat in their partly unlaced corsets with their round knees bare above gaily striped woolen socks. They sat comfortably in pink-lighted windows, smiling with that benevolence which largely provided the inspiration for the sudden unexpected creation of the new wine label.

Every day he hoped for an intending traveller to come for

advice. The café seemed less lonely than the room he rented. It was a narrow room where nothing could happen and where thoughts never came. From this room he had a glimpse of the canal and sometimes it seemed as if the narrow strip of water could lead directly to some distant place, where he would be able to breathe freely in the fresh air again. He was used to such rooms but had not expected his homecoming to yield this repetition.

All through the years, every time he lifted Stephanie and put her with her mother and sisters behind the clock, he had looked upon her and upon the others with reverence and with love. Mitzi and the girls were to have followed Uncle Bernard to the new country. But first it was his own hard times which prevented this, and then the education of the girls, and then came sweethearts and then marriages and then the grandchildren. Always something to prevent them from travelling. Mitzi was a grandmother now, in spite of her rosy youthfulness preserved forever on the tinted photograph.

'How is everyding over there?' He telephoned Mitzi on the night of his arrival. 'Happy Birthday Mitzi! How is everyding over there?' he called into the telephone. To surprise her, he telephoned from the corner of the street and five minutes later walked into her kitchen after being away for more than thirty years.

'But where is Mitzi?' At first he didn't recognize the ageing, but well-preserved, woman.

'Ach!' Mitzi cried out.

'Spik Enklisch please!' Uncle Bernard said as if for a joke.

'Spik Enklisch or spik more slowly please! I have lost my practice!' His smile spread over his face and he did not see dismay advancing in an avalanche of tailored jacket and skirt, rounded off with extensions of spotted silk.

'Ach mein Gutness! I thought you was dead years ago!'

'But, Mitzi, I telephoned.'

'Ach yes! But how I am to know if it is really you? And

something else, if you telephone from over there, how you get here josst now?'

There was a short uneasy pause.

'But Mitzi! It is I, Bernard, your husband. Can you josst remember what I was like when I was young? I have come home!'

Mitzi's dismay turned to anger. With a quick movement and unexpected strength, she hustled him through the back door.

'I am married again since nearly twenty years.' She failed to keep her voice to the whisper she intended. They faced each other in the dusk, but only for a moment, as Mitzi hurried him out through the gate.

'How do I know vot you doink with other vimmin?' Wrath came down on his white head. 'That Schultz! Who is she?' Uncle Bernard couldn't remember. It flustered him to be hustled down back streets away from the place he thought was his home. And then he remembered.

'Ah! Yes! Ya! Schultz!' he said. 'Frau Schultz.' A smile spread over his kind face. 'A splendid lady. Mine first landlady in Australia. You know Mitzi,' he said, 'when I leave her, she give me two hens to take to my place. One hen was sick but she said to make soup from the good chicken to cure the sick one. . . .'

'Landlady! Vot land und vot lady!' Mitzi pounded him through another gate. She was panting. Years behind a cash register had improved her purse but not her health.

'I loose my breath,' she gasped. 'But I do not loose my head! I am married!' she warned in another loud whisper. 'You have to be my brozzer who is returned. There is no ozzer way. I get you nice upstairs room here in this house with my friend. Always use back entrance! The front rooms is for other cominks, you know, the rooms facing the street is for her livink,' she lowered her voice. 'My friend also has to earn livink. Her husband go

176

away like you. Now we mosst be quick, mine husband is comink soon for his meal. A woman cannot have two husband in one bushes, as the sayink goes.'

'But I am your husband, your first. . . .'

'Yes, yes I know you are the first, but the second has very good, failed business which I build up. Is really mine now,' she said. 'I do not intend to loose it for any husband. You will be very comfortable here. And to everyone who will not remember you . . .' She looked at him with a critical eye, 'You have grown so old,' she said. 'You can be mine older brozzer back from Africa.'

'Australia, Mitzi!'

'Oh Ja! India. Who here will know the difference?'

Uncle Bernard during his long absence had become a grand-father several times. Grand Oncle they all called him, all those children. For the first time in his life he was not short of money, and it would have pleased him to take the grandchildren to films and concerts and to museums and on little journeys to places he remembered. The grandchildren were all too busy with their own lives, but there were still two little ones, Stephanie's young-est daughters. Grudgingly she allowed him to take them to a restaurant. It was high up, on the top floor of a tall building, the whole floor turned round slowly so that there was an ever-changing view. Together they looked out and saw the trams going from the crowded squares, where fashionable hotels faced each other, to the places where there were lawns made of water. These lawns were smooth and quiet and enclosed in low walls. What long journeys the trams made from the old part of the city to the broad wide streets full of new clean houses. It was there in the middle of their delight with first, the shining canal below them, and then the wild colours of the fairground, and then the mysterious railway station and, beyond all this, all the various lights and shadows of the city turning round like a great wheel, that he was ill.

He had no memory of the illness overtaking him, only the memory of Stephanie's persistent voice.

'The doctors said it was a stroke,' Stephanie said. 'People of your age should not go to restaurants.' Uncle Bernard tried to forget the things Stephanie said. He never wanted to upset the children. Never. They were his little angels. He wanted only to please them.

He thought he could hear a small confusion of whispering near the door. The Sister came across to his bed.

'The doctor says these two children can come in for a few moments,' she said. He saw with pleasure the two youngest grandchildren. They came quickly towards him climbing on his bed and kissing him with their soft little kisses. Their hands were full of tiny flowers and small toys and sweets in coloured papers.

'Oh Grand Oncle!' Paula said. 'You must get better quickly.'

'Yes,' Toni, the smaller one, said. 'At school everyone wants us to tell about the world turning round like you showed us. We have promised all the girls and boys that you'll take them too . . . the next time when you take us. . . .'

'When you're better of course,' Paula interrupted. And then both the little girls were laughing and laughing.

'Look!' Toni cried. 'That's why we've been given all these presents to bring to you. Everyone in school sends you something. . . .' He felt the warmth of their eager little bodies.

When they left, his bed was strewn with delicate leaves and petals and those sticky treasures which are cherished and repeatedly examined in the long leisured, never passing, hours of childhood.

The Sister came to tidy his bed. She turned off the light.

'Sit down will you please,' he asked her, but because of the hospital regulations she remained standing at his bedside. She was not pretty but her scrubbed round face, enclosed in the

178

wide flaps of her head dress, looked kind. He felt sure he could discuss with her his intention to travel.

The headlamps from a car turning in the street outside shone for a moment on Uncle Bernard's quiet face. The Sister was not sure, but it seemed to her that the Virgin, caught briefly as the turning lights passed across the alcove, without in any way changing her tender expression, slowly winked one eye.

The Long Distant Lecture

I'm on my way to give a lecture in a country town; an informal lecture, a mixture of fact and imagination from chosen writers and the ways in which they approach death.

That death is a part of living I find unquestionable, and keeping one hand on the skull, like St Jerome, has become a part of my life. There is to me a strange fascination about the ways in which the writer presents the long illness and subsequent death. My lecture is called *The Deathbed and the Chaise Longue*.

The journey is long. I have the directions written on a piece of paper. I made a detour to leave the china painting tutor at the place where she was expected.

I'm enjoying the journey. The road is well made and the wheat is standing in that golden stillness just before the harvest. Two girls are on horseback at the side of the road. They look just old enough to be admired. They are part of the landscape with their sun-brown skin and honey-coloured hair. Their horses are this same colour, palomino, cream and gold, well bred. It's a pity their youth can't be part of this afternoon for ever.

Just now, the unknown people who will attend my lecture are driving from the outlying farms. They will see this same sunlit and shadowed landscape. They will see the same far-off patches of gold where the sun shining from between distant clouds catches, with its last brightness, the curve of the land as it falls towards the horizon.

All the time during my lecture there will be doves overhead, to and fro on the roof, their voices softly persistent like the contented voices of a middle-aged couple in bed. I remember this from last year. Coming back to this far-away place is like stepping back into another life.

Often as a boy, lying in bed at night, I could hear my mother's voice, like a stream running as she talked up and down to my father. And, every now and then my father's voice was like a boulder in the way of the stream, and for a moment, the water swirled and paused and waited and then rushed on round the boulder and I heard my mother talking on, up and down.

The place where I will have my room has all the qualities which belong to concrete, cyclone-wired enclosures and store-houses on concrete stairways stained blamelessly as if from other innocent imprisonments. It has the cracking associated with concrete and water unable to soak through sluggish drains. Wherever you go in the world, Singapore, Bangkok, London, Paris, Berlin, Rome, New York, and even here in the wheat, all motor hotels are the same. It's hard to remember where you are when you wake up inside this concrete.

I remember, last year the township at dusk seemed to be a desolate scattered poverty; a shabbiness of blistered little houses, stacks of poles and empty drums gathered near a closed petrol station, and a wheat silo alongside a deserted overgrown railway line. The place reverberated with generators in a tin shed up against the hotel.

Tonight, when I arrive, I'll have to go into the bar with my books and my brief case. Building was in progress last year, and building is always being held up by some sort of anger.

I'm too tired to think about the anger of men. The dinner party seemed to go on forever last night with people trying to outwit one another through literature and music, nodding heads and waving hands.

'A la recherche du temps perdu! Aren't we all recherchering our perdood temps?' said the man opposite.

'What is it about Proust?' said the man next to me.

'With love from the lettuce.' I passed him the salad. 'Vitamin E prevents sterility in rats.' But he was nodding off to sleep.

'What about Proust,' he managed to murmur.

'Ah yes! Well,' I told him. 'I'd cut out the first volume, all that enchantment. . . . Cut that out, and start in at volume three with Monsieur de Norpois at the dinner table. Now that's superb conversation my dear fellow . . . it's the same with Beethoven. . . .'

There's no reception office at the place where I'll be staying for two nights. The building still won't be finished. When I see the men ranged along the bar there, I won't be able to imagine anyone being interested in what I have to tell them. How can I tell them, 'We sail with a corpse in the cargo.' That this is the poet's direct reference to death being a part of life. We all shrink from death but the writer shows there is no need. Can I explain this to them?

'In place of death there was light,' Tolstoy wrote. 'So that's what it is. What joy!' The writer approaches death with a certain knowledge, yet with no knowledge because, like birth, death remains a mystery. Tolstoy, at the moment of death, takes his character, in a supreme moment over the pain and the dishonesty and the destruction of illness, to something joyful beyond. . . .

This is where I turn off. What a great wide place this is. All those miles of wheat in all directions, folded and mended in places, pulled together as if seamed by little dark lines of trees. Sometimes in these seams there is the darker green of something cherished, growing beside a house. Just now, the wind comes with restraint across this harvest, a gentle sound like the faint playing of a flute being carried on the wind. There is peace here in the ripened corn and the light and warmth of the sun.

In the rain-misted fiord a dying man calls to his mother for the sun. 'The sun, the sun!' Another man lost in snow-bound country, trying to follow a dark hairline trail, making his journey through life, bargaining for more time, tries to build a fire. The approaching death is heralded by the lack of the sun and by the pall over the countryside. The man's spit freezes and his mouth is clenched firmly shut in his beard, lengthening, amber-coloured with frozen tobacco juice. How will people listening to my lecture be able to imagine, in this sunfilled place, the deep snow and a man contemplating the killing of his dog so that he can thaw his frozen hands inside the carcass of that dog? Will they understand a man's desperation as he tries to make his little fire, twig upon twig, trying to hold the matches in his stiff frozen hands? When a match struck and dropped here would send a fire raging to the horizon, causing the work of a lifetime to disappear in a few hours. I remember a farmer telling how he lost everything in a fire, his home, his sheds, his stock. 'And I lost my grass,' he said, and he wept for his grass.

There's no one here at all, no one in these paddocks and no one on this road. What kind of people will come to my lecture? Will there be anyone there?

The poet writes of ghostly forests and rocks and of frail bridges crossing the emptiness of immense grey unreflecting pools hanging like the grey rain-filled sky above the landscape. He writes of meadows, soft and full of patience, with pale strips of pathways crossing and recrossing endlessly.

I am travelling alone on this single pale pathway.

'I can't endure all this agony of mind alone,' the dying man cries out. 'But there's your mother to share it with you,' his mother replies. The 'corpse in the cargo' means of course the old ideas, old infections, diseases and opinions, tainted and inherited. Previous actions always returning to haunt and spoil and destroy; secret symptoms which imprison a man and his soul. Every pregnant woman carries death as well as birth inside her. As soon as the human being is born, the slow process of death begins.

183

'For that which befalleth the sons of man befalleth beasts. Even one thing befalleth them; as the one dieth so dieth the other. . . . All go unto one place, all one of the dust and all turn to dust again. . . .'

In my lecture I want to describe the strong arms of fantasy, the imaginary sleigh ride over frozen fiords to the fairy castles of childhood. The young man, an outcast, comes home to his dying mother in time to harness the bed posts. . . . But wait a moment! Am I going in the right direction? Perhaps I should have turned off again, but I haven't noticed a turning. . . .

So much land and so much sky and a smell of something dead, there at the edge of the paddock. Someone must have hit a heifer. It's tremendous, dead and swelling at the side of the track with its legs pointing towards the sky. If you hit such a big animal you'd be killed immediately.

How could this enormous creature come to be here. Perhaps cattle feed in this salt scrub at the edge of the wheat. Perhaps they get lost out here.

'Man also knoweth not his time!'

Writing and studying has become my habit. A writer who wants to achieve something must isolate himself and live alone in his thoughts. I long for solitude. I want to sit alone at my table and lose myself in the green leaves of the table cloth.

Here in the wheat is solitude and already I am feeling, not afraid exactly, but I feel the silence all around me.

Last year the china painting tutor accompanied me, purely a matter of convenience. She quoted the whole time from Tolkien and Winnie the Pooh. She stole the solitude I long for. She stole my time and my thoughts and, in her company, I felt I would weep with all the forgotten bitterness of homesickness. In the chill wildness of a supermarket while she hunted for cheaper cheese, I fought with that alienation and that sorrow which wells up in school cloakrooms, and dancing classes and in boarding schools during the desolate hour between afternoon school and tea. This same loneliness is there, too, in the smell of linseed oil in far-away cricket pavillions. It belongs to un-marked railway stations during the war. It's in railway com-partments, in trains without corridors, in out-patients' waiting halls and afterwards in hospital beds. . . .

The soft, little click of a case closing in the night reminded me so much once of my mother's hands, hovering above an earache, that I sobbed with the sadness of a future lifetime condensed into a few years, hiding this grief in the single pillow.

Men and women believe it is given to them to know what they need in life. They believe they need money.

So the china painting tutor is in demand. 'Can you take Miss Burton with you in your car?' This request is repeated to gain more time as papers are shuffled to and fro on that distant desk below the telephone.

I have taken Miss Burton to an isolated craft centre. It was a disadvantage to have to drive so far out of my way. It is several hours since I left her there. By now bowls and dishes will be covered with gentle piglets and red and blue Hobbits. And, on the greater spaces available in soup plates, will be the four false Farthings, North, South, East and West, of Tolkien's Shire of Make Believe.

For some reason I feel alone.

The gravel's like sand. I'll have to change down and keep the car steady. I don't want to get stuck here.

Now about my lecture. 'Black flowers are dead flowers and who would send dead flowers to a funeral?' That's a quotation of course, better spoken with an American accent. When I think of the sacrificial heifer I'm appalled at the sheer waste! We simply have no on-the-spot industry for blood and bone. Blood and bone. What is a man? Just some blood and some bones and who can say how long he will stay on the earth. How can a man make any arrangements even for a few days ahead? He can be measured for an expensive suit in the morning and by night-fall require only a cotton shroud. Even in the short time allowed, a man can lose his way in his life. He can lose sight of living. The successful man forgets the promises he made when he was struggling, and he forgets the humble act of giving thanks.

I can't have lost my way, can I? I must be on the right track as no other track has turned off this one. The instructions say quite clearly, 'Keep the barn on your left and take the right-hand fork by the home-made bus shelter.' Bus shelter! So a bus actually comes along this hairline trail!

What is this? The whole countryside suddenly seems subdued and the road ends in a wide valley. I could have gone straight over the dizzy edge here. How can there be a valley? I thought the land was flat and that the road was straight. Where is the barn I'm supposed to see? It's as if the land has fallen away into a depths, unbelievably deep. I could have fallen to my death.

It's only a sudden mist of rain cloud, coming purple across the wide land. Almost at once, it's gone; it's stopped raining. I'll stop and smell the sharp smell of rain on the dry earth and on the dusty crop.

It's as if the cloud had never been. This cloud was part of some immense pattern of cloud, the result of a great storm thousands of miles away. In the sunlight now there is no sudden valley and the road is there, going on and on. There's nothing here. No house in sight and no harmony of sheds and farm machinery. All life is withdrawn from this place. I want to see the barn.

The track, now orange gravel, now white sand, goes on and on very slightly uphill, now to the left and now to the right. The track moves like a snake; soft, soft, disappearing, merging with the scrub and appearing beyond the scrub. The scrappy salt bushes invade and fill the narrow path, hitting and scraping my car. And all around is an indifference of wheat. In this deserted place the sky seems nearer and the land wider.

'There is a path which no fowl knoweth, and which the vulture's eye hath not seen. . . .'

Who said that? What voice was that? Is anyone there? I can't be afraid of my own voice! I'll get out of the car and run. I must find the bus shelter. It must be along here somewhere, yet I can see so far ahead and there's nothing. Have I missed a faint turnoff? I must find this crazy bus shelter. It's sure to be crazy, two bits of tin leaned up together with names splashed on in white paint. People paint their names everywhere.

There's no one here at all. I can run, but where to? Oh, this soft wind, like a flute, brings all the loneliness of the world to this one place.

Where are you? Was that me calling out? There's no one here to call. It's all around me this quietness and loneliness.

Whose voice was that screaming so terribly? I've never heard such a scream in my life.

There's no one here to scream except me. I'll whisper. Those people shuffling papers on their distant desks, what do they know back there, in that gossiping rat's nest of paper admin-istration, about all this.

If I'm lost I can go back the way I've come. When I look back there is the track going back and when I look forward there is the track going forward. I can do one of two things, but I must get my breath. I can feel the scream coming in my chest. It's quite without reason. I know there's no reason to scream. I can't go on!

I can't go on screaming out here alone. How strange and uncontrollable this is, this fear of being afraid. I'm not even lost. If this track is not the right one I can go back and try one of the others. There they all are, winding across this empty world.

How many ways can I try before nightfall? I'll follow the track and I'll turn off at the first homestead I see and I'll ask the way. There's sure to be a house and some sheds, or that barn, or even a home-made bus shelter. I'll simply drive on calmly, up the slow rise of the land, follow the track, slowly, look for a turnoff, look along the turnoff . . . slowly up the track. This is a long rise, very gradual like something in a dream.

Perhaps over the next rise I'll see the barn. . . . The car's going very well. It's a quarter past three, plenty of time. I'm coming to the top of the rise. The track's very narrow, it's the hairline trail of a man's life. I'll just keep going. I know it's not a firebreak. I know I'm not going in a circle round one wide paddock of wheat.

I see now that the way ahead of me is the same as the way I have come. Wide stretches of wheat, golden in the sunshine, and the track narrowed with dark saltscrub going on and on as far as I can see.

I'll drive on to the next horizon and see what lies beyond. I want to come to that place where the wheat drops suddenly into the sea. The place where I am to give my lecture crouches between shorn headlands, half hidden in rain mists and surrounded by that bewilderment of movement where land and water meet. The wheat runs in golden rivers all down that valley and there are sheep on the headlands. Last year I walked alone early in the morning by that rolling, green sea.

There is a turnoff here, to the left, and over on the left is a narrow seam of trees, in the fold there may be the barn. I'll go to those trees. I don't know if I can face the desolation if there is nothing there.

Last year it was uncomfortable at the hotel. I expect it will be the same this year.

In the dining room the hungry builders sit at crowded tables. The ancient carpenter sits alone. There is always some sort of anger. Perhaps men, having lost their way in living, lose their dignity too. They say it is the carpenter who brings all the trouble.

Some of the builders are fleshy, filled with food, dimpled, curly and big, and others are slender, with naked waists and long fair hair. Some, in little coloured caps, smile at each other and eat quickly. Others eat their food slowly and never raise their eyes. I think of Beethoven's death in my brief case and begin again to question if my world can ever meet this world. These notes of mine so carefully prepared from years of studying, whatever can they mean here?

'What are you here for anyhow?' The hotel manager asked me last year, and I couldn't explain. He didn't know lectures were given in the country towns. He didn't know about the china painting and the other crafts which are offered. And of course, the builders, concerned with their rightful shares of food and work, were not interested either. Neither could the waitress be interested. She had squeezed her childish body into tight white clothes and was slowly gathering and replacing plates.

The concrete passage to my room contained, within its blemishes, all the fear people have of each other. Coiled in the dusty bedspreads were the nightmares men have when they no longer trust other men.

I'll leave the car and walk down through these trees. Suddenly there are blue bricks, the pale strip of a single pathway as in a poem. Blue bricks, brought here long ago from the far-off place where they were made, and laid in a path through the sweet-smelling, long grass. There is a house and there's a white doorstep. A donkey-stoned doorstep! The doors of my childhood had whitened steps and opened straight on to the pavements. Tram lines shone in the rounded cobbles of lamplight and sparks flew from the heavy iron-shod dray horses.

I'll run to get to that house. I can't run like this. It's too much at my age. These bricks are uneven, that's why I've fallen. I've torn my clothes. My knee's bleeding. What a mess. It's painful too. How white and stupid my skin is, like something shut away from the light and the sun. What a long way it is to that house though I can see it so clearly. They say, never panic, never run from a car. They say, people lost in the heat throw off all their clothes; my knee only shows because I fell. I can see the old house like a nut, brown and crooked. It's derelict! It can't be! Someone must be there. I'll shout.

'Hey you, old man! I'm on my way to give a lecture. I'm lost. I've missed my turning. Can you please direct me? My car's back there.'

There are two old people here. The old woman welcomes me, draws me into the cool dark room. She's laughing, telling me, 'Grandpa's deaf.' Telling me to sit down. I can hear her splashing water into a pail. 'Grandpa's deaf,' she says.

'Here,' she says. 'Have this cup of water, it's nice and cold. Water's good. I'll fix your clothes and bathe your knee.'

'He's lost,' she shouts at the old man who watches from the doorway. 'He's lost his way. He's lost. He's lost.'

'I hear you,' the old man replies with a thin reedy voice. 'He's lost, is he.' He laughs his reedy laugh. 'Everyone gets lost sometime. But let me tell you this,' he cackles. 'No one can ever be lost in the middle of the harvest.'

'Just hearken at him!' the old woman says. 'Sit you down and let the water soothe away the pain. I'll make your tea directly. I expect you could eat some bread and butter. What about a boiled egg? And look you, there's biscuits in that biscuit barrel on the sideboard there. It's dark in here, you can just see the pattern of the roses. Them's faded roses and the handle's all tarnished.' She laughs softly to me. 'I haven't given biscuits to comfort a hurt knee for years!'

And I find I'm smiling up at her.

'It's nice to have you come,' she says, and her old hands are quick with the bandage and with the needle and cotton. 'Even if you nearly broke your leg on the way. You can forget all your troubles in a bit of company. I think you'll have a bruise,' she says. 'But better a bruise than a break.'

'Here, looky here.' The old man is cackling. 'Looky here, looky here.' He's got four little bright coins on his outstretched trembling hand.

'Thank you,' I tell him, and I take one.

The old woman, busy at the white cloth on the table, is laughing. 'He doesn't hear you,' she says. 'He's just showing you the farthings. If you'd give it back to him. Gran'pa's only *showing* the farthings. You see, he used to show them farthings when they fell and hurt themselves. You know, to take their minds off while I washed their poor scraped knees. Gran'pa's only *showing* you the farthings, I'd explain to them. And they'd give them back to Gran'pa.'

I give the old man his farthing back.

'You'll stay for tea?' the old woman asks. 'I'll show you the garden while the kettle boils.'

'I should be on my way,' I tell her. 'You've done such a lot for me, thank you,' I tell her. 'If you'll just direct me. . . .'

'Oh the water's on the boil, you've time enough,' she says and leads the way down some steps through the cool stone-flagged passage into a long narrow garden, watered green, fenced in between the paddocks. Sheds and fruit trees are in this cherished strip and the windmill is clicking and turning.

'It's nice to hear the mill,' she says. 'We've got a well. It's never dry. There's sunflowers. Did you ever see them?'

' "Ah, Sunflower! weary of time/Who countest the steps of the sun. . . ." ' I start to say the poem softly as I follow her to the hens. She tells me about her hens.

'Sunflowers and carrots,' I say. 'They grew in the garden when I was a child, far away from here.' Suddenly I'm telling her things I'd forgotten about. I'm telling her that her voice and his voice remind me of other voices from another time and another place, long ago.

'Yes, I daresay.' She gives her little laugh and turns back towards the house. 'When you think about it we all come from the same place.'

More than anything I want to hear his voice again. I feel I must get back into the house to hear his voice once more. I want to catch what I almost caught in the sound of his voice. There's a half remembered kindness and comfort in his voice, and there's a forgiveness. I want to hear him speak again.

The rooms of the house are built one onto the next, so it is

191

a slow journey through the small jostled rooms piled with unused furniture, smoothed-over beds, cupboards with faded photographs and ornaments.

The old man is asleep in his chair, small like a child in the sleep of an old man. She'll rouse him, she says, but I tell her, 'No, I must be going.'

The place is like a place I used to know. I want to tell her, a place of peace and love to come back to. I want to thank her; I tell her. She tells me the way. 'Keep on going the way you were going,' she says. 'You were on the right road. You'll come to a big barn on your left and then you'll come to a home-made bus shelter.' She gives her little laugh which matches mine.

'Yes, I remember all that,' I tell her, and again I thank her and she, smiling, stands at her door as I run back along the blue brick path. It hardly shows, hidden as it is under the long grass, flattened in the withering of summer.

All the time during my lecture tonight there will be the doves overhead, to and fro, their voices softly persistent, to and fro in the roof.

The sun is lying low along the wheat. I should reach the place just before nightfall. There is an excitement where land and sea meet. It was where land and sea met that life first came into being. What was it the old man said? 'No one can be lost in the middle of the harvest.' The girls on horseback, just old enough to be admired, can't stay for ever on the edge of their ripening. Someone is sure to come along and gather every harvest.

The sun is lower now over the wheat. How still the harvest stands, waiting. I'll come again and find that little farm. I'll see the sunflowers. I'll step into that other life again.

'Ah, Sunflower! weary of time
Who countest the steps of the sun,
Seeking after that sweet golden clime

Where the traveller's journey is done.'
The sun sinks lower now and lower.

Early in the morning I'll walk alone at the edge of that rolling green sea and the little hills will rejoice on every side. The pasture will be clothed with flocks and the valleys covered with corn.

'Ah sunflower weary of time!' Like the poet, I want to transcend time so that mortal time doesn't matter any more.

I'll count the steps of the sun.

The setting sun, just now, lights the gilded face of the town hall clock down there. In a few moments I can reach the main road and then it will be dark.

Memories piling on memories, the desolate scattered poverty of the township is deceptive at dusk, for when the morning comes it is filled with the sunrise and the rosy breasts of birds screaming low across the waves.

I'll take out the treasures from the enclosures in my mind and unfold the layers of mountains and rocks and forests and streams. Stored away are sunsets upon sunsets. There are other things too; there's freedom and fantasy and there's tenderness. Above all, there's the tenderness. . . .

The Fellow Passenger

Dr Abrahams stood watching, for his health, the flying fish. They flew in great numbers like little silver darts, leaping together in curves, away from the ship, as though disturbed by her movement through their mysterious world. Nearby sat his wife with her new friend, a rich widow returning to her rice farms in New South Wales. The two women in comfortable chairs, adjoining, spoke to each other softly and confidingly, helping each other with the burden of family life and the boredom of the voyage.

'Who is that person your daughter is talking to?' said the widow, momentarily looking up from her needlework.

'Oh I've no idea,' Mrs Abrahams said comfortably. And then, a little less comfortably, she said, 'Oh I see what you mean. There are some odd people on board.' She raised herself slightly and, raising her voice, called, 'Rachel! Rachel dear . . . mother's over here, we're sitting over here.'

As the girl reluctantly came towards them, Mrs Abrahams said in a low voice to her new friend, 'I'm so glad you noticed. He does seem to be an unsuitable type, perhaps he's a foreigner of some sort.' She lowered her voice even more. 'And they do have such ugly heads you know.'

Their voices were swallowed up in the wind, which was racing, whipping the spray and pitting the waves as they curled back from the sides of the ship.

Dr Abrahams walked by himself all over the ship. The sharp fragrance from the barber's shop excited him, and he rested gratefully by the notice boards where there was a smell of boiled potatoes. The repeated Dettol scrubbing of the stairs reminded him of post-natal douchings and the clean enamel bowls in his operating theatre.

Whenever he stood looking at the front of the ship, or at the back, he admired the strength of the structure, the massive construction and the complication of ropes and pulleys being transported, and in themselves necessary for the transporting of the ship across these oceans. It seemed always that the ship was steady in the great ring of blue water and did not rise to answer the sea, and the monsoon had not broken the barrenness. Most of the passengers were huddled out of the wind.

When he returned to his wife he saw the man approaching. For a time he had managed to forget about him and now here he was again, coming round the end of the deck, limping towards them in that remarkably calm manner which Abrahams knew only too well was hiding a desperate persistence.

Knowing the peace of contemplation was about to be broken, Abrahams turned abruptly and tried to leave the deck quickly through the heavy swing doors before the man, with his distasteful and sinister errand, could reach him. There was this dreadful element of surprise and of obligation too. For apart from anything else, the man had an injury with a wound which, having been neglected, must have been appallingly painful. It was something, if seen by a doctor, could not afterwards be ignored.

'All you have to do is to treat me like a fellow passenger,' the man had said the first night on board. He entreated rather, with some other quality in his voice and in his bearing which had caused Abrahams to buy him a drink straight away. Perhaps some of the disturbance had come from the unexpected shapeliness of the man's hands.

The Bay of Biscay, unusually calm, had not offered the usual reasons for a day of retreat in the cabin. Abrahams, excusing himself from the company of his wife and daughter, had again invited the man for a drink.

'What about a coupla sangwidges,' the fellow said, and he had gobbled rather than eaten them. A little plate of nuts and olives disappeared in the same way.

The two stupid old ladies, they were called Ethel and Ivy and they shared the Abrahams' table, were there in the Tavern Bar. They nodded and smiled and they rustled when they moved, for both were sewn up in brown paper under their clothes.

'To prevent sea sickness,' Ethel explained to people whenever she had the chance.

A second little plate of nuts and olives disappeared.

'That'll be good for a growing boy!' Ethel called out. Like Ivy, she was having tomato juice with Worcester sauce. Already they had been nicknamed 'The Worcester Sauce Queens' by the Abrahams family.

Abrahams, with the courtesy of long habit, for among his patients were many such elderly ladies, smiled at her. His smile was handsome and kind. The very quality of kindness it contained caused both men and women to confide. It was the nature of this smile, and the years of patient, hard work it had brought upon him, that had necessitated a remedial voyage. For Abrahams was a sick man and was keeping the sickness in his own hands, prescribing for himself at last a long rest. He had been looking forward to the period of suspended peace, which has such tremendous healing power and is the delight of a sea voyage.

At the very beginning the peace was interrupted before it was begun, and Abrahams regretted bitterly the sensitive sympathy his personality seemed to give out. It was all part of his illness. It was as if he were ill because of his sympathetic nature. The burdens he carried sprang from it. That was what he allowed himself to believe but it was not all quite so simple. There were conflicting reasons and feelings which were all perhaps a part of being unwell, perhaps even a part of the cause. He tried to make some sort of acknowledgement, to reach some sort of inner conclusion in the all too infrequent solitary moments.

At the first meeting, Abrahams' feeling was, apart from a sense of obligation on the good manners of not liking to refuse to buy a drink for the stranger, a feeling of gladness, almost happiness, perhaps even a tiny heart bursting gladness which could have made him want to sing. He did not sing, he was not that kind of man. His work did not include singing of any kind. There was not much talking. Mostly he listened. His work kept him quiet and thoughtful. He often bent forward to listen and to examine and to operate. He had good hands. His fingers, accustomed to probing and rearranging, to extracting and replacing, were sensitive and capable. If he frowned it was the frown of attention and concentration. It was his look of kindness and the way in which he approached an examination, almost as if it was some kind of caress, which made his patients like him.

In the bar that first night, he reflected, he had come near singing. A songless song of course because men like Abrahams simply would never burst into song.

Once he did sing and the memory of it had suddenly come back to him clearly even though it had been many years ago. Once his voice, surprisingly powerful, it could have been described as an untrained but ardent tenor, carried a song of love across and down a valley of motionless trees. Throughout his song the landscape had remained undisturbed. He had not realised how, in the stillness, a voice could carry.

'Heard yer singin' this half hour,' the woman had said, holding her side, her face old with pain.

'Oh? Was I singing?'

'Yerse, long before you crorsst the bridge, I heard yer comin' thanks to God I sez to meself the doctor's on his way, he's on his way.'

It was during a six-month locum in a country town. That day he sang and whistled and sang careering on horseback to a patient in a lonely farm house. He remembered the undisturbed fields and meadows, serene that day because he went through them singing.

The stranger's voice in the bar, and his finely made hands taking the glass from Abrahams, brought back so suddenly the song in the shallow valley.

On the track that day he thought he'd lost his way and he was frightened of his surroundings. The landmarks he'd been told to watch for simply had not appeared. There was no house in sight and no barn and there were no people. He'd been travelling some time. Joyfully he approached some farm machinery but no one was beside it. He almost turned back but thought of his patient and the injection he could give her. In all directions the land sloped gently to the sky, the track seemed to be leading nowhere and he was the only person there.

He came upon the man quite suddenly. He was there as if for no reason except to direct Abrahams, though he had a cart and some tools, but Abrahams in his relief did not really notice. The man's eyes shone as he patted the horse and Abrahams felt as if the intimate caress, because of the way the man looked, was meant for him. He continued his journey feeling this tiny heart-bursting change into gladness, which is really all the greatest change there is, and so he sang.

As he walked or stood on the deck he thought about loneliness. The crowded confined life of the ship was lonely too.

'Give me some money,' the man said. 'It'll look better if I shout you.' So in the temporary duskiness between the double swing doors Abrahams gave him some notes and small change and followed him as he limped into the bar.

'What'll you have?' the man asked the old ladies. They were

there as usual, before lunch, their large straw hats were bandaged on with violently coloured scarves. They sat nodding those crazy head-pieces, talking to anyone who would listen to them.

They were pleased to be offered drinks. Abrahams had a drink too, but it was accompanied by disturbing feelings. The thought of his illness crossed his mind. The man's hands had an extraordinary youthful beauty about them, out of keeping with his general appearance. As on the other occasions when glasses had passed between them, their fingers brushed lightly, but it was not so much the caress of fingers as a suggestion of caress in the man's eyes.

Abrahams, with a second drink, found himself wondering had he been on horseback that time in the country or in a car. Had that other man touched the horse or merely put a friendly hand on the door of the car? With his hand he had not touched, only the expression was there in his eyes. This time, all these years later, it was a touching of exceptional hands together with an expression in the eyes.

In the afternoon there was a fancy dress party for the children. Mrs Abrahams had been making something elaborate with crepe paper. Already the cabin blossomed with paper flowers. Abrahams discovered his daughter sulking.

'Look Rachel darling,' Mrs Abrahams persuaded. 'You will be a bouquet, we shall call you "the language of flowers," ' she said holding up her work. 'White roses—they mean "I cannot," and this lovely little white and green flower is lily of the valley, it says, "already I have loved you so long" and here's a little bunch of violets for your hair, Rachel, the violets say "why so downhearted? Take courage!" and these pretty daisies say . . .'

'Oh no, no!' Rachel interrupted. 'I don't want to be flowers, I want to go as a stowaway,' and she limped round and round the cabin. 'Daddy! Daddy!' she cried with sudden inspiration. 'Can I borrow one of your coloured shirts, please. Oh do say I can. Do let me be a stowaway, please!'

Abrahams took refuge among the mothers and photographers at the party. He joined in the clapping for the prize winners, "Little Miss Muffet" and "Alice in Wonderland." 'All so prettily dressed!' Mrs Abrahams whispered sadly. A girl covered in green balloons calling herself "A Bunch of Grapes" won a special prize. The applause was tremendous.

'They must have made a fortune in green umbrellas,' the rice farm friend said with delight.

'Spent a fortune on green balloons,' Abrahams muttered to himself, almost correcting her aloud. He was unable to forget, for the time being, his sinister companion who was somewhere on the decks waiting with some further demand. Silently he watched his little daughter's mounting disappointment as she limped round unnoticed in one of his shirts, left unbuttoned to look ragged.

He thought he would like to buy her a grown-up-looking drink before dinner, something sparkling with a piece of lemon and a cherry on it, to please her, to comfort her really. If only she could know how much he cherished her. He longed to be free to play with her, she was old enough, he thought, to learn to play chess. But there was the fear that he would be interrupted, and she was old enough too to be indignant and to enquire.

'I am not quite well,' he explained to his wife after the first encounter with the man. 'It is nothing serious but I am not sleeping well.' He did not want her disturbed by something mysterious which he was unable to explain. So he had a cabin to himself and arranged for his wife and daughter to be together. Their new cabin had a window with muslin curtains and a writing table. Mrs Abrahams took pleasure in comparing it with the cabins of other ladies on board. Dr Abrahams called for her and Rachel every morning on the way to breakfast.

The children's fancy dress party was depressing. The atmosphere of suburban wealth and competition seemed shallow and useless. The smell of hot children and perfume nauseated him. But it was safer to stay there.

The ship remained steady on her course and the rail of the ship moved slowly above the horizon and slowly below the horizon. There were times when Abrahams felt he was being watched by the stewards and the officers, and even the deck hands seemed to give each other knowing looks. These feelings, he knew, were merely symptoms of his illness which was, after all, nothing serious, only a question of being overtired. All the same, he was worn out with this feeling of being watched. He avoided the sun deck for it was clear from the man's new sun-burn that he lay up there, anonymous on a towel, for part of each day.

'You'd better let me have a shirt,' the man said. 'I'll be noticed by my dirt,' he said. He took a set of three, their patterns being too similar for Abrahams to appear in any one of them. He needed socks and underpants and a bag to keep them in. The nondescript one Abrahams had would do very well. It was all settled one evening in the cabin which Abrahams had said he must have to himself. The fellow passenger slept there, coming in late at night and leaving early in the morning. It was there in the cramped space Abrahams dressed the wound on the man's thigh with the limited medical supplies he had with him.

'Easy! Easy!' the fellow passenger said in a low voice.

'It's hot in here,' Abrahams complained. He disliked being clumsy. 'It's the awkwardness of not having somewhere to put my things.'

'It's all right,' the fellow passenger said. 'You're not really hurting me.' He seemed much younger undressed, his long naked body so delicately patched with white between the sun-burn, angry only where the wound was, invited Abrahams.

'I'm not wounded all over,' he said and laughed, and Abra-hams found himself laughing with him.

'Easy! Easy! don't rush!' the younger man said.

That laughter, the tiny heart burst of gladness was a fact, like the fact that the wound was only in one place. They could be careful. It was a question of being careful in every kind of way.

Abrahams knew his treatment to be unsatisfactory but there seemed nothing else to do in the extraordinary circumstances. If only he had not answered the smile in the man's eyes on that first evening; he should have turned away as other people do. Knowing the change and feeling the change, in whatever way it brought gladness, was the beginning and the continuation of more loneliness.

Incredibly the ship made progress, her rail moving gently up and persistently down.

Like many handsome clever men Dr Abrahams had married a stupid woman. She was quite good at housekeeping and she talked consolingly through kisses. Her body had always been clean and plump, and relaxed, and she was very quiet during those times of love-making, as though she felt that was how a lady, married to a doctor, should behave. Abrahams never sang with her as he sang in the cabin.

'Easy! Easy!' the fellow passenger said, he laughed and Abrahams put the pillow over his head.

'They'll hear you.' He buried his own face in the top of the pillow. He could not stop laughing either.

'And they'll hear you too!' Abrahams heard the words piercing through the smothered laughter.

Always unable to discuss things with his wife, Dr Abrahams did not want to frighten her now and spoil her holiday.

'Your husband is a very quiet man,' the rice farm widow said to Mrs Abrahams. 'Still waters run deep, so they say,' she said. That was very early in the voyage after a morning in Gibraltar, spent burrowing into little shops choosing antimacassars and table runners of cream coloured lace.

'Did you go to see the apes?' Ethel enquired at lunch.

'Plenty of apes here,' Abrahams, burdened and elated by

202

discovery and already bad tempered, would have replied, but instead, he smiled pleasantly and, with a little bow, regretted the family had not had time.

'You see Ethel and I have this plastic pizza,' Ivy was explaining to Mrs Abrahams and Rachel. 'At Christmas I wrap it up and go down to Ethel's flat, "Happy Christmas Ethel," I say, and she unwraps it and she says, "Ooh Ivy you are a dear it's just what I wanted," and then next year she wraps it up and gives it to me, it saves all that trouble of buying presents nobody really wants. Thank you,' she said to the steward. 'I'll have the curried chicken.'

Rachel, accustomed to good meals, ordered a steak. Abrahams could not help reflecting that Ethel and Ivy had both the remedy and the method which simplified their existence. They appeared to be able to live so easily, without emergency, and without burdening other people with their needs. They could, of course, require surgery at any time, though he doubted that this ever occurred to either of them. Perhaps he too, outwardly, gave the same impression.

The fellow passenger's demand was both a pleading and a promise. At the beginning Abrahams had risen to the entreaty, but, as he understood all too quickly, his response was complicated by an unthought-of need in himself. Walking alone on the ship he was afraid.

The begging for help had, from the first, been a command. Abrahams knew his fellow passenger to be both sinister and evil. In his own intelligent way he tried to reason with himself what, in fact, he was himself. At the start, but on different terms, it was a matching desperation of hunger and thirst and an exhaustion of wits. The fellow passenger had certain outward signs: for one thing, he had a ragged growth of beard which in itself was dangerously revealing. He was dirty too. He needed help, he told Abrahams, to hold out till the first servings of afternoon tea in the lounge, and until such time when the weather would improve and cold buffet lunches would be spread daily in the Tavern Bar and on little tables on the canopied deck by the swimming pool. To be in these delightful places, in order to fill his stomach, he needed to mingle in the company.

'It's dangerous,' he said. 'Being alone. Being on my own makes me conspicuous and that's what I don't want to be.' A companion who was both rich and distinguished was a necessity and it had not taken him long to find the kind of fellow passenger he needed.

'I better have a bit more cash,' he said to Abrahams. 'I'll shout you and them old Queens. They know a thing or two about life, those two. I'll take care of them.' His words sounded like a threat.

They had, without laughter, been sorting out what was to happen next. The cabin had never seemed quite so tall, quite so awkward. He had plans to alter a passport, he knew exactly what had to be done, he needed a passport and it only needed the doctor to produce one.

Like many clever men Dr Abrahams was easily tired. He had come on the ship, as had the fellow passenger, exhausted, already an easy victim. Now, more tired than ever he hated the man and saw him as someone entirely ruthless. It seemed impossible to consider what might have been the cause. It was clear that there would be no end to the requests. Abrahams realised that soon he would be unable to protect his family and quite unable to protect himself. The voyage no longer had any meaning for him. Together, the two of them went to the bar.

Ethel and Ivy were there as usual.

'It's on me today,' Ethel cried and made them sit down. 'You must try my tomato juice,' she cried. 'It's with a difference you know,' and she winked so saucily everyone in the bar laughed.

The fellow passenger drank quickly.

'Now it's my turn,' Ivy insisted. 'It's my turn to shout.' She watched with approval as the fellow passenger drank again.

'So good for a growing boy,' she declared and she ordered another round.

Dr Abrahams held his glass too tightly with nervous fingers. After the conversation about the passport he felt more helpless than ever. He could scarcely swallow. He should never have lost his way like this. Quickly he glanced at all the people laughing and talking together and he was frightened of them.

'More tomato juice for my young man,' Ethel shrieked. Her straw hat had come loose.

'Ethel dear, watch yourself!' Ivy shrilled. 'We're in very mixed company you know dear.' Their behaviour drew the attention of the other passengers.

'Steward! Steward!' Ethel called. 'Don't forget the you-know-what-oops la Volga! Volga! It makes all the difference. There dear boy, let's toss this off.' She raised her fiery little glass to his. 'Oops a daisy!' Her hat fell over one eye.

While the fellow passenger drank, Ivy retied Ethel's scarf lovingly. She rocked gently to and fro.

'Yoho heave ho! Volga-Volga,' she crooned. 'Volga Vodka,' she sang, and Ethel joined in.

'Yo ho heave ho! Volga-Worcester-saucy-vodka-tommy-ommy-artah—All together now—Yo ho heave ho-Volga-Vodka,' they sang together and some of the other passengers joined in. Above the noise of the singing and the laughing Abrahams heard a familiar voice, but it was much louder than usual.

'Go on dear boy! Go on! Go on! Don't stop now!' Ethel and Ivy cried together, their absurd hats bobbing. 'Tell us more,' they screamed.

It seemed to Abrahams that the fellow passenger was telling stories to Ethel and Ivy and to anyone else who cared to listen. Hearing the voice he thought how ugly it was. The ugliness filled him with an unbearable sadness.

'So you're wanted in five countries!' Ethel said. 'Why that's wonderful!' she encouraged. She bent forward to listen. Ivy examined the young man's shirt. She patted his shoulder.

'This is such good quality,' she breathed. 'Look at this lovely

205

material Ethel dear.' But Ethel would not have the subject changed.

'Rape!' she shrieked with delight. 'And murder too, how splendid! What else dear boy. Being a thief is so exciting, do tell us about the watches and the jewels and the diamonds. You must be very clever. Ivy and I have never managed anything more expensive than a pizza and then it turned out to be quite uneatable.'

The fellow passenger did not join in the laughter. He began to despise his audience.

'Look at you!' he sneered. 'You two old bags and you lot— you've all paid through the nose to be on this ship. But not me, I'm getting across the world on my wits. That's how I do things. I've got brains up here,' he tapped his head with a surprisingly delicate finger. 'It isn't money as has got me here,' he said and he tapped his head again.

For the first time Abrahams noticed the ugliness of the head. He thought he ought to find the Purser and speak to him.

'It's all my fault about the head,' he would confide, and explain to the officer about the arching of soft white thighs and the exertion. 'It's like this,' he would say. 'When you see the baby's head appear on the perineum it's like a first glimpse of all the wonder and all the magic, a preview if you like to call it that, of all the possibilities.' The Purser would understand about the shy hope and the tenderness when it was explained to him. Abrahams thought the Purser might be in his cabin changing for lunch. He could find the cabin.

'What has happened?' he wanted to ask the Purser. 'What has happened?' he wanted to shout. 'What is it that happens to the tiny eager head to bring about this change from the original perfection?'

He walked unsteadily towards the open end of the bar. Really he should speak and protect his fellow passenger. He felt ashamed as well as afraid, knowing that he needed to protect himself.

Of course he could not speak to anyone, his own reputation mattered too much.

He was appalled at the sound of the boasting voice and, at the same time, had a curious sense that he was being rescued. The fellow passenger was giving himself to these people.

Abrahams did not turn round to watch the man being led away by two stewards in dark uniforms.

'Mind my leg!' He heard the pathetic squeal as the three of them squeezed through a narrow door at the back of the bar. It was a relief that the wound, which he was convinced needed surgery, would receive proper attention straight away.

There were still a few minutes left before lunch. For the first time he went up on the sun deck. Far below, the sea, shining like metal, scarcely moving, invited him. For a moment he contemplated that peace.

'Yoo hoo Doctor! Wear my colours!' Ethel shrieked. Turning from the rail he saw the Worcester Sauce Queens playing a rather hurried game of deck tennis. Ethel unpinned a ragged cluster of paper violets from her scarf and flung them at his feet. Politely he bent forward to pick them up.

'You must watch Rachel beat us after lunch,' Ivy shrilled.

The pulse of the ship, like a soft drum throbbing, was more noticeable at the top of the ship. To Abrahams it was like an awakening not just in his body but in his whole being. He stood relaxed letting life return as he watched the grotesque game and, with some reservations belonging to his own experience, he found the sight of the Worcester Sauce Queens charming.

Mr Parker's Valentine

After only a few weeks Pearson and Eleanor Page were tired of living in the rented house. The rooms were small and stuffy, and the repetitive floral carpet depressed them every time they stepped into the dark hall. Pearson felt his wife would be less homesick if they had a house and garden of their own.

'House hunting will do you the world of good,' he said to her. Friends of theirs, just as recently arrived from England, were happily settled already, busy with paving stones, garden catalogues and plans for attractive additions to their new home.

So Eleanor looked at houses and quite soon she found exactly what she had always wanted. In the evening they went together to see it. It was old and had an iron roof. Wide wooden verandahs went all round the house, and faced the sun, or were shaded at just the right times.

On either side of the street were old peppermint trees, and there was an atmosphere of quiet dignity in the decaying remains of a once well-to-do residential area.

There was, however, a difficulty about the house. They stood together with the land agent out in the back garden, surrounded by a wilderness of full-skirted red-splashed hibiscus and flower-laden oleanders. All round them tall trees in a ring, sighing now and protesting, tossed their branches in the afternoon sea breeze. Cape lilacs, jacarandas, flame trees and Norfolk pines, green, light green upon dark. And, nearly as big as the house itself, a gnarled and thickly-leaved mulberry tree, with early ripened fruit dropping, replenished the earth.

They stood in the noise of the wind, as if at the edge of waves, and were submerged in the swaying green, as if in water of unknown depths, to ponder over their problem.

At the end of the garden was a tall shed, stone-built with a patched corrugated iron roof. The door of the shed opened to the western sun and, in a little plot edged with stones and shells, herbs were growing and wild tobacco flowers. A short clothes line stretched between the door post and the fence. An old man lived in the shed.

'The trouble is,' the land agent said, 'he's lived here for years. The owners hope that whoever buys the house will let him stay on. He has no other home.'

'I'm afraid it's out of the question if we buy the house,' Pearson Page said, shouting a little to increase his authority and determination. He was a short man, fresh faced, looking younger than he was.

'Oh! I do so want the house,' Eleanor said. They stood re-membering the recent pleasure of large fireplaces and polished jarrah floor boards, of high ceilings still with their graceful mouldings and, of course, the windows. Tall windows, each one framed and filled from outside with green leaves and woven patterns of stems and roses, jasmine and honeysuckle. And all the rooms so fragrant just now with the scent of Chinese privet.

'I never had a house with such a spacious kitchen,' Eleanor said, adding to their thoughts. She wanted the house very much and felt the old man being there could make so little difference.

They all moved down to peer into the shed.

A great deal was crammed inside the shed, an old man's life-time of experience and possessions. Boxes were stacked and his lumpy bed was smoothed and tucked up in a black and grey plaid. Some matting covered the floor and there was a plain wood table and three scrubbed chairs. Over the wood stove were shelves piled with pans and crockery, and a toasting fork hung on a nail. Ivy, growing in under the roof at the far end, hung down in a dark curtain catching and concealing the full sun as it flooded in through the open double doors.

'Place would make a good biscuit factory,' Pearson tried a joke, as he saw disaster in the corrugated iron and an old man's clothes hung out to dry in the sun.

The character and possibilities of the house were overwhelming; Beethoven in the evenings and perhaps the writing of poetry. Eleanor longed for such evenings on the verandah. She stepped into the shed.

'Pity to turn the old man out,' she said. 'But it would make a marvellous rumpus room for the boys.' She used the word 'rumpus' with the self-conscious effort of fitting in to the phrases of a new country.

'Ah, you have sons?' the house agent asked gently.

'Yes, two,' Eleanor explained. 'They are just finishing off the year at boarding school in England and will be joining us later.'

'Mr Parker's out shopping just now,' the house agent continued in his soft voice, his knowledge suggesting years of experience of Mr Parker's habits. 'He does not trouble the house at all,' he said.

The wind tossed the tumult of branches to and fro. 'Think it over,' the house agent said.

The Pages had always enjoyed a single-minded, smooth partnership in their marriage and now, for the first time, they were unable to come to some kind of agreement about the old man and whether he should be allowed to stay.

'I can't think why all this fuss,' Pearson said, his face very red because of the sun; he scooped out the fragrant flesh of a rock melon. Juice stayed on his lips. 'We can buy the house if we want it. There's nothing about the old man to stop us buying the house. It can be ours tomorrow. All we have to do is to say we don't want him there. And he'll have to go. It's as simple as that. I can't think why you're so worried.'

'But Pearson, where would he go? We can't just turn him out. I couldn't live there if we did that.'

Neither of them slept.

In the end Pearson agreed to the old man remaining. 'Any trouble,' he shouted, 'and out he goes!' He did not want to disappoint Eleanor and, in any case, he wanted the house too.

On the day they moved in they were too pleased and excited at being able to unpack their own things at last to think of the old man.

Pearson strutted in and out of the empty rooms giving instructions. He was a sandy man and his face was fresh and rosy coloured, contrasting with the tired grey cheeks of the two men who were carrying in the furniture and the countless boxes; for Pearson and Eleanor had many books and pictures and other treasures.

In the evening the old man came up to the back door and introduced himself. He was small and clean and had the faraway voice of a deaf person.

'I've roasted a half leg of lamb, the shank end, I thought you'd like a bit of dinner. Six-thirty sharp, down at my place,' he said. 'Plenty of gravy.'

Eleanor in her dirty removal dress was embarrassed. 'Oh, no thank you. We couldn't possibly spare the time . . .' she began, smiling kindly at his best clothes. But he could not hear her.

'Don't be late! Six-thirty sharp; hotting up a roast spoils it,' he said, and went off down the garden.

So there was nothing to do but leave their unpacking and arranging, tidy themselves up and go in an awkward little procession of two down to the shed.

Inside the shed it was surprisingly bright and cosy; it was the wood stove and the smell of the hot meat. The old man told them about his life when he travelled round Australia at the turn of the century. He was just explaining about the quarantine camps of those far-off days, when he suddenly stopped, and said. 'Yo' know what day it is?' Eleanor, smiling, shook her head.

'Valentine's Day!' he said, and he climbed up on the boxes and fetched down a grimy envelope from behind a rafter.

'Fifty years ago that was sent to me,' he said proudly. And he showed them the dusty paper pillowed heart, stuck all over with faded daisies.

'Who sent it?' Eleanor asked. She had to shout the question three times, self-consciously, trying to hide Pearson's boredom.

'Ah! You're not supposed to know who sends a Valentine,' the old man creaked with the far-away reedy laughter of the deaf.

Late in the night, they made their way up the dark garden. The house, neglected, was hostile with nothing done. Confusion in every room.

'Not even the bed made,' Pearson's voice was disagreeable with the wasted evening. He had wanted to put up pictures and arrange their Venetian glass.

'Oh Mr Parker's delightful.' Eleanor hurriedly found the sheets. Really Pearson's sulky ways made her very uncomfortable, especially as the old man was so friendly.

In the next few weeks there were some things to trouble them. Old Mr Parker, early one morning, painted all the verandah posts blue, spoiling the appearance of the house.

'Protection against the weather,' he explained. He chopped down the passion vine, his thin stumpy arms whirling the axe as if he had unlimited strength.

'Too old,' he pointed at the gnarled twisted growth of the vine.

Every time Pearson started to do some gardening, Mr Parker was at his elbow.

'Wrong time of the year to prune them lemon trees,' he said.

And 'Yo'll not pull up all them bricks in that path, I hope.'
The reedy voice irritated Pearson; he longed to work without
interference. He sought for something to heal himself in the
garden. He had come to a new post, his first university ap-
pointment, thinking to pour the culture and refinement of his
mind over his new colleagues. It had been a surprise to him to
find thoughts wider and greater than his own, and a wider
establishment of learning than he had thought possible in the
far-away place he had come to. Every day he had to adjust to
some new discovery of his own ignorance. The garden could
have been a place for a quiet renewal of his spirit and energy,
but it was not so with the presence of the old man.

Eleanor too was strange, she seemed to like Mr Parker so
much. Pearson wasted hours waiting for Eleanor, who had slipped
down to the shed for two minutes. Sometimes she was there in
that biscuit factory, with the stupid old goat, for a whole evening. Really, the old man would have to go. Pearson felt he
could not wait to get him away, together with all the rubbish
there was down there.

Eleanor said the old man meant well, but Pearson was not
so sure of this. He could not understand her attitude, and she
was unable to accept what she suddenly saw as a cruel side in
his nature.

In the night Eleanor thought she heard a tiny shout. She sat
up. Again, a tiny far-away shout in the night.

'It's the old man! Mr Parker's calling us.' She roused Pearson.

'Oh don't fuss,' yawned her husband. 'He's used to being
alone. He can look after himself!' He turned over and went on
sleeping.

Eleanor went down, in the dark, to the shed. The night was
fragrant with the sweet scent of the datura, the long white bells
trembled, swinging without noise, and the east wind snored in
the restless tree tops. Fantastic fire-light danced in the shed and
the old man called to her from his dishevelled bed.

'I've got the shivers,' he said. 'There's a good girl! Make up the stove for me and squeeze me some lemons and boil up the kettle.' He gave his orders and his teeth chattered.

'Just a chill,' he comforted Eleanor. 'Get me warm,' he said, 'an' tomorrer I'll be right you'll see.'

Eleanor did as she was told.

The old man slept a little and Eleanor sat there beside him. In the small light he looked ill and frail. She thought he might die. She thought it would be much easier if he did die. It was not that she wanted him to die, only that if this was the end of his life, and he had lived a long time, it would solve all their difficulties. Lately she had been so unhappy.

'Shall I get the doctor?' she shouted to him when he opened his eyes. But he laughed at her.

'Put some more wood on the stove, my dear. I got the shivers that's all, it's nothing.'

A bit later he opened his eyes.

'Yor husband's a quiet man,' he said. 'Still waters run deep they say.' He gave a little far-away laugh, and then he said, 'Thank you, my dear. I'm much obliged to you,' and he slept.

Eleanor went back up the dark garden, the moon rode on the restless fragrance and she felt grateful for the old man's call.

'I think I should sit with him.' She woke Pearson.

'Whatever for, if we weren't here he would be alone.'

'But we are here.' Eleanor stood uneasily by their bed.

'I don't see that that comes into it. We bought the house it's true, and we live in it, but that does not mean we are responsible for the old fool, and his so-called illness.'

'But Pearson, he's really ill.'

'That's his lookout. We can't look after all the old men who are ill. If he doesn't want to be alone, he shouldn't live there. You'll only wear yourself out.' Pearson added his warning.

They seemed to face a wall in their marriage, and they tried to sleep and could not.

By the next weekend Mr Parker was quite recovered.

Pearson was disappointed and angry to see him emerge from the shed as if nothing had been wrong with him. Ignoring advice, 'It's not the best time for it,' Pearson cut dead wood out of the hibiscus. 'Yo'll not touch them roses I hope,' the reedy voice followed Pearson, so he turned his attention to the flame tree. One great bough, he could see, was a danger to the house.

Collecting necessary materials, he set to work. He sat in among the thicket of leaves, straddling a branch near the trunk, and began with his well-cared-for saw to cut the offending limb. Slowly and methodically the saw went to and fro. Pearson was surprised the wood was so soft. He was surprised too at the sharp thorns the tree had all over the branches; from the ground the bark looked quite smooth.

Mr Parker stood under the tree.

'Yo' want to take that branch bit by bit,' he shouted, cupping his mouth with one hand, though Pearson was only a few feet above his head.

'If yo' cut it there it'll tear,' the old man warned. 'Them trees is best cut when the leaves is off.'

'Too heavy,' he explained to Eleanor. 'Too heavy!' he shouted up to Pearson.

'Oh mind your own business you old fool,' Pearson said, but of course Mr Parker was so deaf it didn't matter what anyone said.

Eleanor, standing by, wished Pearson would not look so irritable. There was no pleasure in anything they did now. She smiled at the old man.

'Mr Parker says the branch will tear,' she called up timidly.

'I heard,' Pearson replied grimly, the saw was stuck and he could see he needed something to pull on the branch.

'Throw me the rope,' he called down. Eleanor could pull at the branch from below.

'Yo'll rip right down the trunk,' Mr Parker called. 'He's new to our trees,' he explained to Eleanor.

215

'Yes, yes, of course,' and she smiled at him.

'Pull! Haul!' Pearson called to Eleanor when the rope was secure.

'What if the branch falls on me?' she cried.

'I'll shout and you run for it,' Pearson called back.

'Pull! Haul!' He saw her straining, but nothing happened. The white smile of wood remained tightly clenched on the saw.

'Yo' need to work at it bit by bit,' Mr Parker said to Eleanor. 'I'm a comin' up!' he called to Pearson. And the next moment he was up the ladder with Pearson's new pruning saw, and off onto the swaying branch along to the end of it, cutting twigs and little branches. Leaf-laden tufts fell to the ground below as he cut this side and that.

'Yo' want to lighten the branch and cut further out to start with,' he explained to Pearson who, red-faced with anger, still sat straddling his branch.

Pearson, before becoming a university professor, had a short but brilliant army career behind him, and he was not going to be ordered about by old men.

'Go down this instant!' he shouted at the old man. His voice was so loud Mr Parker heard it. He stopped his prancing on the branch and stared at Pearson as if unable to understand the reason for the anger.

In that moment Pearson seemed to see the old man as something more than a nuisance; he saw in him something tenacious and evil. And the thought came to him that perhaps many people had taken the house and been forced by reasons, unknown to the land agent, to leave.

'I must be ill,' Pearson thought to himself, 'to have such stupid ideas.' But as he saw Mr Parker coming slowly along the swaying branch he felt he would fight this thing, whatever it was, and he would keep the house; he would fight with all his strength. Mr Parker advanced slowly, in his hand he held the pruning saw and on his face was a strange expression.

From the ground, Eleanor thought he was going to cry, but

the awkwardly pointing little saw, with its curve of sharp teeth, frightened her.

'Pearson!' she cried out.

'Go down this instant!' Pearson's voice was deep and loud. And still seated astride the branch, his back against the trunk, he pointed down towards the ground with authority.

'Yo' go down then,' Mr Parker said. In his reedy little voice there was no anger. 'You've more weight nor me. Yo' pull on the rope, an' I'll get her out.' He indicated the saw.

Pearson recognized this as commonsense, but he was not going to be told what to do by this old fool.

'Go down. This instant!' he shouted, still pointing down.

'Well, orl right. I'll have a go on the rope with 'er then.' Mr Parker scrambled down the ladder.

'Come on Missus,' he said to Eleanor, and together they took the rope.

Pearson watched the pantomime below. Eleanor, in her un-fashionably long skirt, pulling on the rope with the little old man dangling behind her. The morning had become ridiculous.

'Pull! Haul! Heave! Haul!' he bellowed.

And then, to his amazement, the cut in the branch suddenly widened and, with a roar, the great leaf-laden bough fell away, grazing his thigh as it tore down the side of the trunk. He caught the saw before it fell.

'Timbah!' he yelled. 'Run for it!'

Of course Mr Parker heard nothing of the warning. And Eleanor, leaping clear of the heavy falling foliage, tried to grab his shoulder to pull him away, but a forked branch came sharply and painfully between them, and Mr Parker was left there under the heavy fallen mass.

'Oh my God!' Pearson sprang from the tree and pushed through the leaves and branches.

It was an action accompanied by feelings he was never able to forget afterwards.

Eleanor could only stand and watch. She saw her husband's

bare feet, competent and clean in rubber thongs. She thought his feet looked cruel, and she realised they must have always been like that.

Pearson toiled like a sick man to clear out the shed. He cleared and destroyed as if cleaning himself of an infection. The whole place would be different by the time his boys arrived from England.

As he worked he found himself thinking all the time of the old man. He kept expecting to see the washed-out shirt between leaves and bushes, and he missed the persistent reedy voice at his elbow. The garden, so much the old man's place, seemed deserted.

He tried to discipline his mind. He thought about his boys and longed for the time when they would come. He longed for their voices and the noise of their healthy bodies about the house. He wanted to be concerned again with examination results, sports training and dogs and bicycles and the choosing of birthday presents.

The envelope, treasured up all the years, fluttered and fell with the dust being brushed from the beams and rafters. The old man again.

'Who wins a fight anyway,' Pearson muttered to himself. He had to put aside too, the thought that his boys were hardly boys now and would not want the same things from him.

'It's Mr Parker's Valentine.' Eleanor picked it up. 'And he never knew who sent it to him.' She experienced curiosity sadly. Beyond the double doors of the shed, doves laughed softly in the silky morning.

'Put it on the fire,' Pearson ordered.

He thought, as he dragged boxes and tore down ivy, that everything would have been different if the old man had found out all those years ago who had sent him the Valentine.

Eleanor, carrying the dirty envelope up to the house, was thinking the same thing. She had been fondly patient with Mr

Parker and knew she was without blame, yet she felt the burden of Pearson's anger and resentment. He had shown how he felt, while she hid her feelings, so giving him full responsibility. She knew they would never speak of any of this now, and she could not reach Pearson in his grim remorse. All day they worked, separately.

'Pearson.' Eleanor called from the house.

'Coming.' He went slowly up the garden.

Some time earlier they had arranged to have a party, a kind of house warming. Neither of them had suggested putting it off. It was time to start preparing for the evening and they tried to smile in readiness for their visitors.

A New World

'Now that I am old I get up very early and
feel like God creating a New World.'
From a Chinese poem, translated by Arthur Waley

Every morning the old man in bed twelve was shaved by the ward orderly.

'When can I get a shave?' he kept calling across the ward and the orderly, who had to polish the ward table, called back, 'Soon as I'm ready and not before,' and the old man muttered, 'Very well, very well,' and sat there in his bed.

And after a while, forgetting he had called once, called again.

'When can I get a shave?'

And the ward orderly, sliding his dusters up and down over the smooth shining table top, replied, 'Soon as I'm ready and not before.'

Mostly the old men were dozing; they had all been washed and tidied and the nurse had rushed round with the breakfasts and everything was cleared away early. At last the orderly was free to come with a little shaving mug of hot water and the shaving brush and soap. He wrapped the old man in a towel and lathered his face, rubbing in the soap round and round with the brush; the old man turned his face a little from one side to the other to help. Then the orderly set about the shave and the old man blew out first one cheek and then the other and tried to stretch the skin between his nose and mouth and against his soft old chin by twisting and turning his mouth in all ways. His face was old and sunken and because of this it was not easy to shave, but because he had always blown out his cheeks, first one and then the other, and twisted up his mouth, he did so now; it was from habit. The orderly was quickly finished with his task and the old man ran his fingers over the rough stubble of his cheeks and chin and nodded and muttered, 'Quite good, quite good. Thank you, much obliged.'

And then the orderly fetched mouth wash for him and he gargled and spat twice. Because he had always done this he did it now. He tried to comb his hair too and with the other hand, in between the combing, he smoothed the few hairs back in strands.

Later on the old man, Twelve, asked the man in the bed next to him if he would like a smoke, and the old man, Fourteen, said he would very much. And as he was allowed up, he slowly got out from his bed and groped for his slippers.

'They're in my locker, Fred,' Twelve said. 'Down at the bottom they should be.' And Fred shuffled round to get them.

'Fetch 'em out then,' Twelve said. But there did not seem to be any cigarettes in the locker. There was nothing there except a dish with a square of lint for a face flannel and a bit of red soap. There was nothing in the locker except this and the cleaned-out emptiness. So he went over and asked the ward orderly about it.

'Oh, Twelve's a bit confused these days, Dad,' he said and went on with his polishing.

So Fred Nash went back and sat on a chair by the old man's bed and the old man sat there in his bed and after a while they both slept a bit and quite soon it was dinner time.

When he became old he, Fred Nash, got up very early and felt like God creating a New World. It was as if the world opened out on all sides fresh and clear spilled all over with hibiscus and oleander, fragrant with roses and lavender and pinks, and sounding softly resounding with the running of the voices of the magpies and the gentle laughter of the doves. He liked to be up first. And with his hand-knitted socks and cardigan he was nice and warm, and he went out into this first freshness of the day with his dog into his little garden. He put more wood on his verandah near the back door so that Edie, his wife, need only stretch an arm out to get nice small bits ready for kindling and then plenty of suitable bits for keeping the wood stove just as she liked it all day. He swept up the little paths and tidied the beds and rearranged flower pots and hung things in the shed he had built years ago. Sometimes he painted things. He painted the window sills and the door and the white trellis along the verandah. He liked to keep things nice and neat. And all the time the doves caressed the morning as the sun warmed the leaves and the branches and the grass and the flowers and he felt the warmth of the sun on his back. And he thought and planned in his new world where he would grow sunflowers, and how he would rebuild part of the shed; it was held up, he guessed, only by the vines. All these things he had liked to think about and plan to do in the peacefulness of his life as it was first thing in the morning.

On Easter Sunday the nurses coloured all the boiled eggs with acriflavin and gentian violet and took them round with the breakfasts, saying, 'Happy Easter, Dad,' and 'Happy Easter, Grandad,' all round the ward. But the old men looked with suspicion at the purple and yellow eggs in front of them.

'I'm not eating that thing,' one said and then another said, 'I'm not eating that!' And in the end, none of the old men ate their eggs and the nurse had to rush off to the kitchens to ask for a can of porridge for them. And the orderly put the eggs, with their despicable colours, in with the dirty laundry and so had them safely removed before the charge nurse came on.

Every day the old man, Twelve, had a visit from his daughter. She lived near the hospital and worked in the kitchens and so was allowed up to the ward for just a few minutes before she went home. And every night in the night, Fred Nash, in the next bed, bed fourteen, could hear a munching and crunching and a smacking of lips and a licking up of crumbs. It made him feel hungry to hear those noises. The rustling of the paper, quietly as it was done, carried the suggestion of a piece of home-baked cake or a slice of apple pie, and the old man, Fred, sighed and turned over, his mouth watering at the thought of whatever it was the old man, Twelve, had to eat in the night.

It was best then to think back and dream of those other times. Sometimes during the day when Edie had gone somewhere on the bus he sat in the back porch listening to the bees in the branches pressed against the trellis, and watching the small birds, Silver Eyes, darting in and out of a lantana bush and he would remember. Remembering at dusk the dirty streets where there were derelict back-to-back houses, remembering this cramped street where he had lived as a boy. Once he had seen a man, terrified and weeping, crouching with his heels pressed into the greasy bricks, trying to hold back from being dragged off by two policemen. He had seen women weeping and ill and children cold and hungry and people pausing on their way home from work to see things, dreadful things. Like himself, not knowing why it was.

As soon as he could he left these streets and went to work on the ships. His mother was pleased. She told everyone, 'He's on the ships.' And every time he went home he took money and presents for her and for his sisters. From far-away ports and cities he took home smooth yellow and green and orange beads and bracelets and necklaces of something volcanic, sparkling and shot with intangible delicate colours. He took bright little bags of red leather embossed with gold, woven glittering slippers and little boxes of inlaid wood. Some of them played

223

tunes when you lifted the lid, *Come Back to Sorrento* and *O Sole Mio*. And one revealed a tiny couple revolving, embraced in the waltz, exquisitely dressed in silk and entombed forever in quilted crimson plush.

But it was chiefly the money, for he spent sparingly even on the presents, and he saved. He worked first at scrubbing the baths and lavatories and later in the cabins. The ship and his cabins and his passengers became his world. Back and forth, his ship moved on her course night and day.

His ship had everything—space and cleanliness, comfort, chairs, swimming pools, ballrooms, lounges, films, games, toys, even a peal of bells for the Sunday morning service.

He worked on the ships for eighteen years, till his mother was comfortable in a house of her own and his sisters all through school. And then he married his girl, Edie, and they took a final trip on the ship and settled in Western Australia. He bought himself some land on the coast down the south west and he built a small house there and half a dozen holiday cottages, mostly of weatherboard and iron. And he began again his service to people who came there throughout the years to have a holiday. It was very hard at first. The cottages were simple but all were fitted out in detail as a ship is. He collected old stoves and fitted them in his kitchens and made wood boxes which he kept filled with kindling. He laid coloured linoleum over the boards and Edie sewed at curtains and covered the mattresses with calico so they would keep nice. He used up all his money and his work was never done; it was a round of repairs and improvements. One winter he got himself a load of used bricks and chipped them even and built a wash-house and fitted in an old copper and next to that he put in a chip heater and a tank and the next summer his visitors could have showers and do their washing.

Always he could hear the sea. It roared far out over a fringe of rocks, surf waves out there throwing up forty feet of spray.

He could hear that at night and the croaking of the frogs in the swamp near his place. Before very long he had to make his front room into a shop and all the time his people came to buy groceries. And there were some kangaroos; they came down there of an evening and his two children and the holiday children fed them slices of bread.

He did not think of all these things at once; he remembered only in snatches when Twelve had done mumbling. It was a comfort to be at the edge of the dream at those times, as if he were able to step back into any part of it. He liked to think of Edie's kind smile that came from her kind grey eyes and lit up her whole face.

Of course the nurse would be round soon. He always woke early, it had always been his time of day, the early morning, especially when he was old and in his own place which he made into a new world of his own. Things were different now; to wake early was not the same.

Of course his boys had helped him but the time had come and school finished when they had gone off to other places, towns where there were garages and radio shops.

He liked to see the pleased look come into the people's faces when they arrived the first time and stepped into one of the little cottages. They exclaimed at the neatness and the cleanliness and at all the things ready for them to use. They were pleased to look through the window the whole wild way down to where the waves were breaking over the rocks. The rocks were wonderful there, steps and slabs and tables, pinnacles, piers and palaces of rock, strewn like gigantic playthings abandoned. The children always ran down there straight away.

When he had been to the township for supplies and letters and come back to the road fork and the signpost, the same all the years, he felt a deep excitement. There was the road going off to the right, a narrow white strip between the fringes of red dust gravel. On either side the bush spread very quiet and mysterious, untouched and unchanged for miles. There was something about the bush that was like the sea. He felt the same as he had years ago on the ship.

The road went down steeply through a place overgrown with trees and creeper, over a creek with a narrow wooden bridge and then steeply up and round to emerge suddenly higher than before, splendidly overlooking the wide wild bay. The uneven edges of the land ran down, with the river between to the sea. The smooth sea and the rippled sky met on a horizon so wide and light and open, it was the very joining of heaven and earth.

Always he felt as if he had come there for the first time. It was a place where he could feel at once restored and remade.

At the time it seemed a long life of working and improving and caring for so many people. And then it suddenly seemed a short time, his being there. One day the local authority came. They built a public toilet with showers and changing rooms. Not on his piece of land, of course, but right up against his cottages. And in front of his place they levelled the ground and filled in the frog-haunted swamp and made a lovely big car park.

Edie made tea and sold pies to the men working there and they were pleased to sit on the little verandah.

'It's progress, Dad,' they said to the old man. They cleared the bush beyond the toilets and put up a sign saying:

Happy Days. Campers Only.

The men said they were bringing out water and electricity.

'It's a new world, Dad,' they said. The road was up everywhere and it was noisy and dirty with tractors and lorries and building materials. For the next thing was that the land was sold off in small blocks and people began building their own holiday houses, elaborate with concrete and glass and lights and flushing lavatories. The view from the little windows of the cottages was quite changed and it was impossible now to see the sea. And with these modern houses who would want to bother with kerosene lamps and earth closets and a chip heater in a shabby place, up the back, filled with leaves and twigs, visited nightly by possums, and open to the sky. The water tanks put there by himself seemed suddenly decrepit and he could see quite plainly when Mr Barker, quite a kindly man from the Public Health, showed him that his home-made, soak-away drains were quite inadequate, perhaps even dangerous to the people.

Edie said it was all for the best really, as they were both of them getting on and it would be really nice to get the garden done how she had always wanted it. So when a road was put through where their cottages had been they hardly noticed it as their trellis was covered with vines and they were hidden in honeysuckle and hibiscus and lantana; there was oleander too, pink and white, and all threaded in and out with blue cupped bindweed.

Later when he was on his own, the ladies brought him a hot dinner every day. It seemed every convenience had come to this place where there had once been nothing. They told him to spread a nice clean newspaper on the table and have his fork and spoon ready, at noon, and his plate put to warm. They chatted to him while they served him, but when they had gone, he forgot about the beef and vegetables and the custard pudding. He forgot so often that it was decided it would be better if he were looked after properly.

For a few days the old man, Twelve, had not had his usual visit from his daughter. He sat there in bed waiting and waiting and hoping for her to come. And then the charge nurse came just before teatime to tell him that his daughter would not be coming again. Afterwards he just sat there shaking his head. He couldn't get up and walk to the window to look out or anything, there was nothing he could do. So the old man, Fourteen, got up

227

slowly and groped for his slippers and sat on the chair beside Twelve.

'What'll you have,' the nurse asked them. 'Soup or cheese or hot Bonox?' They chose the Bonox and she gave them each a little tray and helped them each to bread and butter, forking it skilfully from her piled-up plate.

They liked to blow into the hot Bonox and sip slowly and dip their bread and butter in it.

The old man, Twelve, had been restless the last few nights; Fourteen had heard him turning and muttering and he was sorry for him. He thought and thought what he could do about it. While he blew into the fragrant steam of the Bonox he watched Twelve stirring his and sucking at the spoon and he watched him enjoying his bread and butter, and an idea came to him. He took up one of his own slices and was about to dip it in his mug and he hesitated and put the slice down. And he sipped a bit and blew and picked up his bread again from forgetful habit and, as if remembering something, he laid it down again. After the Bonox was all gone he took the piece of clean paper, which was the tray cloth, and carefully wrapping up the bread and butter he placed it in Twelve's locker. He patted it lovingly with his old hands. Twelve looked at him and at the crumpled little package; both the old men seemed a bit perplexed. Fourteen patted the package again and looked at it, and after a little while he went to bed to wait for the night.

In the night towards morning he heard the rustling of paper and the munching and scrunching and the licking up of crumbs. The noises made him feel hungry and he turned over and sighed and his mouth watered but he stepped quietly back into the edge of his dream.

The Travelling Entertainer

Everything was so wet after the rain. Drops of water quivered like spangles on the wire fences and hung from leaves and flowers, tremulous, ready to fall in a glittering shower at the slightest movement.

Morris Bernard, as usual, drove his wife to the university. The road, fringed with shivering nodding grasses, followed the curve of the river; and across the wide water the city lay in repose as if painted on a pale curtain. It had a quality of unreality as if no life could unfold there behind the shreds of blue mist.

Morris Bernard stopped the car and eased himself out. He walked round crushing eucalyptus leaves into the damp earth and, in the hovering fragrance, he opened the car door for his wife. The rain bird called, little phrases of bird notes climbing up in among flame tree flowers, brilliant against the dark clouds, and the thin narrow leaves of the eucalypts trembled.

Morris looked at the river as he waited by the car door. The water was purple-brown with top soil washed from the vineyards further up the valley. It was the time for black cockatoos. They flew now in formation low across the choppy tumult of the river in flood.

'More rain coming,' he said. But already Natasha, his wife, was thinking about her work.

'Goodbye, my Precious.' But Natasha had gone.

On the way back across the campus he saw people whose lives were connected with his wife's, the Professor of Divinity, the German tutor, the senior lecturer in Physics and the man in the white coat who came every day with sweet yellow cakes and jam tarts for the students' coffee shop. He nodded and smiled and waved to these people as he passed, for though they were not acquainted with him, they were, after all, Natasha's colleagues. Mostly they ignored him.

He supposed they could have been customers, except that Natasha forbade it.

'No selling on the campus.' She said this years ago, and he respected her wish. The cake man was leaving. Mr Bernard waved to him.

Yesterday the cake man's wife, longing for the white-washed walls of her home, a village in the Ukraine, wept when Mr Bernard was in her kitchen.

He juggled with a powder compact and a toothbrush. 'I'll take a deodorant powder,' she said, drying her eyes and laughing shyly. 'You made me feel better already, Mr Bernard,' she said.

'I must fly!' Morris Bernard said, trying to flap his arms but only awkwardly because of his case and display basket. He began dropping things, his docket book, the wrapped toilet soap and his pencil.

'We have just this saying.' She gathered up his things with delight.

'Your English is very good. Very good!' He always shouted at foreigners. And he continued his ungainly flight, to make her happy and laughing, down her verandah steps, ignoring the pain in his groin and the knowledge that in all the time he had spent there, he had only sold one small item. Yesterday was a very bad day.

Already this morning he felt old.

'I must improve the business in some way.' He was used to the sound of his own voice in the car. He wanted, more than anything, to buy for Natasha a present, something very special. For a long time he had had this wish.

Every day he felt the age of himself and the tiredness coming upon him, often before he had even started out. It was time really to take orders for fly spray and to push the shampoo specials. Instead of yawning all evening in front of the television, he should have been gift wrapping Christmas packs in cellophane for advance display.

Every day, after driving Natasha to the university, he did the household shopping and then he wished he could go home. His area stretched in unwieldy distances; the streets of closed doors, blank venetians and drawn curtains burdened him. It would be easier to go home and rest but, of course, it was unthinkable. Natasha often cleaned the whole house before they left in the morning and, even then, was fresh and trim to face her day at the university, where she lectured and demonstrated in physiology.

'How will I ever be able to buy for Natasha what she wants if I give up now?' He recognized his own moan as it burst from him. 'In any case, how can a man allow his wife to keep him? I can't allow Natasha to keep me!'

And really he loved his work. He liked to be out in the familiar streets in the fresh air and the sunshine. His area was between the railway line and the sea. There were certain places, a bend or a gentle rising of the road from where he could see the sea. Serene blue surprises in glimpses between the trees and houses. The smooth blue sea, beyond his reach in a silent place, seemed to meet the sky in a rippled quietness and a gentleness only possible in dreams.

The street lawns, neglected, were spotted all over with yellow daisies and there was a freedom about being in these clear sun-washed streets; the freshness of the air so often sweetened with

231

the smell of cut grass. Often he wanted to tell his wife about the air and the sea.

'Oh you have a mind like a slot machine,' she said, and he realised again that he had spoken of the commonplace with the unforgiveable cliché.

As well as feeling old, his shoulders ached. It was from standing in the cold porch of a house yesterday. He knew the ache well, it was his losing score in the game played by the customer.

'What's the lipstick like?'

He held them out to her from the case.

'Honey, Peach, Parasol and Miami.'

She undid them all, tried them on her forearm and handed them back, cascading little gold bullets in among the coloured packets and bottles and jars.

'I don't really use lipstick. What's this? And what's this?' Her fingers delved and picked, and she unwrapped, unscrewed and unstoppered; she sniffed and tasted and handed back.

'I can get all these at the shop round the corner. What's this?'

'Allspice.'

'Never use it. I don't use this or this . . . No, nor that . . . Nor this. . . .'

So he surprised her big teeth in the middle of a mouthful of words. Gently he said, 'Perhaps I will have my catalogue back,' and waited confused and ashamed, remembering the moment of hurt in her eyes, while she pretended to look for it somewhere in the house.

Later he sang softly in the car, 'I'll not go back to that house,' over and over again and his singing comforted him.

The day was so bad that he thought he would call on Helga. They met at the corner where Helga's path came down to her neat white-painted gate.

'I had a death this morning,' she said with an affectation of a shudder. She was just coming home from the nursing home where she was temporary matron, six weeks relieving. Helga had no need to work, no need at all. Morris was about to say something about her not needing to work, but she spoke, 'So if you'll excuse me,' she said. 'I just can't wait to get inside and get washed and changed. See you!' She brushed by him and hurried up her path of coloured flagstones, laid by herself, and into the white front door which she closed smartly behind her. Morris went on, trying not to feel the loneliness left by the encounter.

So that was yesterday. Already today he felt he could not face Marlimont and the searching for customers. He was walking the long quiet morning knocking at this door and then at the next one. He thought he heard someone coming to the door and quickly he combed his already tidy strands of hair and turned the frayed edge of his coatsleeve away from the searching sun. He thought he could hear someone coming quietly pad pad along the carpeted hall on the other side of the door, but it was only the beating of his own heart he could hear. Again no one in.

'It's climbing all these steps makes me so out of breath these days.' His crackling lonely voice filled the stillness and he paused a moment on the deserted verandah, resting in the sweet forgetfulness, the fragrance of frangipani.

Sometimes he thought he ought to do exercises in the garden at home but he was afraid Natasha would peer from behind the white curtains of the bedroom and be scornful. So he remained flabby and out of condition.

Years ago, on his first day as a travelling salesman, he wished no one would be at home. He said to his supervisor, 'Sometimes I hope there will be no one in.'

And he had replied, 'How can you make a sale then? You can't sell to an empty house.' The supervisor had then said he enjoyed the excitement of waiting for the door to open.

Housewives were always at home in those days and, of course, there was no modern shopping centre to take away the trade.

Morris, whenever he looked at the car park and the arcades of shops with their mosaic tiles and coloured advertisements in

American spelling, remembered the road going through the bush and the rough tracks going off to the homesteads. There was a swamp there then, and in the mornings the still water shone on both sides of him as he drove, jolting, over the narrow causeway of packed earth, to the farm. They were all stout, the women and girls on the farm, and they stood waiting in their aprons and boots to choose their purchases from his cases with their rough hands.

And the melancholy crowing of the roosters followed him across the causeway as he slowly drove back; the shining water, invaded by thickets of rushes stretching on either side, echoing and echoing with the croaking of the thousands of hidden frogs. And afterwards, in a sunny peaceful place on the other side, he stopped and added up his sales.

There was a car outside Helga's neat brick house.

'Yoo hoo!' Morris called from the path. 'Playing ladies I see! I heard about the chocolate cake so I thought I'd come along.'

'Heard the story of the year,' Helga sighed and turned her eyes towards the ceiling. 'Look who's here!' She went for another cup.

'Pardon my slacks!' Morris said and minced into a chair. 'I didn't have time to change.' The coffee had gone cold but he drank it off quickly, grateful.

He entertained them then with his products. He demonstrated the carpet cleaner, clowning with the squeeze bottle. He laughed and laughed and told them funny stories.

'See, I leave this woman sample, free sample, of hand lotion and sample of shampoo. Next day she rings me. *Oh,* she says, *I like the furniture cream very much. Will you bring me a bottle please?*' He roared, laughing, slapping his thighs and carefully explained it to them once more. 'So what she used on her furniture I'll never know,' he said. But Helga didn't get it, neither did her friend, so he let it go. The friend had to go to the bathroom then and while she was gone Morris said to Helga.

'When can I come?'

'Oh, some time.'

'Soon?'

'Oh, some time.' She yawned and stretched and showed all up her legs because of the way she was sitting.

'I can see all up your stockings,' Morris reprimanded.

'It doesn't matter,' Helga said. 'They're tights,' she explained.

'Colour of pig,' she said laughing. 'Pig-coloured panty hose,' and she stretched out her short thick-set legs, and laughed some more.

And when her friend came back, Helga poured drinks.

'This sherry tastes like urine.' She held her glass to the light. Really Helga did think of some dreadful things.

'Of course it isn't urine, Helga.'

'Well, of course, *if* it is, it can only be Robert's and one couldn't mind drinking his.'

Robert was Helga's son, her younger child. His habit of stealing alcohol had always annoyed Morris and the idea of his replacing it in this way, and Helga's pride, she was always proud, in him, was altogether too much.

Morris gave the two women a nutmeg sprinkler each. These were not free samples, they were two of the more expensive things in his case.

'Well I must fly! Idle bodies only busybodies.' Morris pretended to fly down the steps.

'Oh you, you make my heart go ticketty boo,' sang Helga, out of date, from the porch, shaking the nutmeg playfully over his bald head. The afternoon was suddenly screaming with laughter and sprinkled nutmeg.

'Time is money!' Morris called, laughing, trying to wave the ugly heavy case, his knotted groin catching painfully in the awkward movement.

And their laughter followed him down to the car.

235

'Who says I feel lonely. Of course I'm not lonely,' he spoke softly in the car, reassuring himself. 'Tarrara bumde ay,' he sang.

And he consoled himself with a vision of nude buttocks and bosoms; pale melons, alternately swaying. Someone, years ago, had told him a joke which had left behind this picture in his mind.

'Bum-titty, bum-titty, bum-titty,' he sang. 'Bum, bum, bum titty, Bum. . . .'

'Knock, knock, anyone at home?'

'Hullo there! Anyone at home?'

'You there, little dog, is your mistress in? You don't have a mistress? Ha ha. No one in!'

'Knock, knock, here is your friendly travelling salesman. Here's your travelling entertainer.' No one was in. House after house, everyone out, or watching television and not wanting to get up to open the door.

Years ago Helga was a good customer. She lived then in an old weatherboard and iron house. It was later she built the neat little brick home on the tennis court of the old house and moved in, selling the rest of the property. She had had a large household. She bought everything years ago; she wanted it all. One day she said to Morris, 'I've been given a coffee percolator Mr Bernard. I've always wanted one and now I have it will you stop, please, and have a cup of coffee with me? I'm dying to use it.' So Morris stopped that morning, and other mornings, and sat among the boarders and the children and the dogs and toys and fowls, and Helga played with her percolator and told Morris things about herself.

'How can I manage if I give away the nutmegs?' Morris Bernard spoke softly to the hibiscus hedge of yet another empty house. Last week he gave Helga bath crystals.

'Give me for my friend also,' she said.

'But I am your friend,' Morris said.

'Oh, I mean my girl friend,' she said and chose a pink urn

of bath crystals for this girl friend, who was, of course, not a girl at all but a middle-aged, unattractive greedy woman.

'Oh you girls!' Morris said playfully slapping Helga's bottom.

'The church has one foundation,' she sang, 'and that's so firm . . . I never felt a thing!'

He felt invited to repeat the slap a bit harder.

'Oh you mind,' she warned. 'It's superannuated!' And she went off to put her own bath salts, blue, into her own blue bathroom.

'Now,' Morris said, when she came back. 'What do you want to "buy"? Give me your order.'

'Oh you know I've no one at home now. What do I want with any of these things? I get all these lotions and creams and perfumes on my birthday. The house is full of them, not touched. And I never bake anything these days so it's no use me buying spices. Years ago, yes. . . .' she said. 'But not now.'

'Oh no Helga,' Morris Bernard's voice moaned aloud alongside the hibiscus. 'Not you too!'

And he had then taken out the new product, the new sun tan cream; the bottle had a pinched-in waist.

'How do you like this? More expensive of course, but modern!'

'Oh Morris! Another present! Oh Danke! Danke!' And she kissed the top of his head where the strands of hair lay carefully combed.

'Oh Baldpate!' she laughed and laughed. 'Baldy Baldpate!'

So that was two things he had given her last week.

'It can't go on like this.' His voice slid along the footpath.

'I must somehow improve the business. I can't allow my wife to keep me.'

Sometimes, now, when he walked from one house to the next he thought about Natasha. There was something clinical about Natasha. It was this quality which attracted Morris, a kind of hygienic prettiness. And the fact that she knew so much about the body and the privateness of the body, and yet was so innocent, made her irresistible to him. He thought he would be Lord of all this secret knowledge, but she soon turned him out of the bed. She said he snored dreadfully.

'I love my wife. I love Natasha as I did all those years ago.' He muttered into his case as he sorted it by the side of the road.

He remembered details of their love making. He could only think about them now, if he spoke of his love, she would, he felt, turn aside her neat head and refuse to listen or believe. But he could remember her body twisting and quivering with passion, and her teeth shining in the half light as she called his name.

'Morris,' calling in love, her voice strangely hoarse, calling his name in love, 'Morris!'

Recently he had been thinking too much about those times. Sometimes he stopped the car and slipped into a dream about Natasha, and then he would remember all too soon how he had aged so quickly. The difference in their ages, which had scarcely seemed to matter at the beginning, became suddenly so very apparent. His wife had stepped immediately on to her plateau of clinical beauty; she was youthful and intelligent too, and she had not come down from this table top of vitality. And he could only admire her from the flabby disadvantage of old age.

Of course then, he began to think of Oriana. She was their daughter. Oriana was nearly twenty-seven. He couldn't think why Oriana was so fat and lazy. She sat on the sofa in the evenings and slept. Morris tried telling her funny stories.

'Laugh, Oriana, laugh like me!' he shouted at her. Lazily she opened her eyes and made as if to knit but, almost at once, dozed off again. He supposed she was tired after the kitchen work. 'If only someone would come along and want to marry Oriana, someone kind, to give her a comfortable home and look after her when I'm gone.' He continued to rearrange his display case on the roadside, putting the little bottles of food flavourings, peppermint, banana, raspberry, strawberry, vanilla and almond neatly side by side.

238

And then he began to think of something else. For some time an idea had been in his mind and, repeatedly, his thoughts turned in the end to this idea.

Helga in her neat brick house boasted so much about her own daughter, when she wasn't boasting about Robert. Last week twice she boasted.

'Of course Morris, when Jan's baby comes I'll be up there on the property.' Her bulgy eyes gleamed with the successes of her son-in-law and his farm and her daughter's happiness. The third grandchild was expected, and Helga would be only a stone's throw across the paddock in the little house they had had put up there for her. She told Morris, 'Everything is in the house for me.' She could be entirely self contained, she explained, and yet be on hand whenever her daughter needed her. And of course she would be needed. A girl always needs her mother.

'So you see Morris, I'll be going up there. I'll be away for some weeks, this place'll be closed up and I'll . . ."

Morris closed his eyes in the weariness of listening to the successes of Helga's children and his heart ached for Oriana who, as the years went by, seemed to become more dull and lifeless, spending more and more time in the kitchen. For though Natasha did a lot of housework, she left the kitchen and everything to do with kitchen work to Oriana. Helga went on talking and Morris, still with his eyes shut, resolved to burn down her house. Frequently his thoughts turned in this direction. He thought he would rob Helga and buy a car for Natasha to have of her own, in the hope that it would soften her towards Oriana. Of course a daughter needed her mother. Helga was right, Oriana was lonely and needed her mother to help her. There was so much Natasha could do.

'Here is a new car for you Natasha. Take Oriana to town and buy new clothes for yourself and for her. Go on, pretty yourselves up! Have a good time!'

He hovered over his case of cosmetics and flavourings, dreaming in a kind of forgetfulness, and the sun warmed his back.

Already it was mid-day and no sales yet. No one at home except Helga and she didn't want anything.

'Oh whatever about Oriana!'

Often he worried about Oriana. Who would feed and clothe her for the rest of her life? She liked food so much and seemed to need a lot. In his heart he felt the burden of her.

When Oriana was a little girl she used to run out to meet him. She loved all the things he had in his case and she used to dust the little jars and bottles with a piece of clean rag. The rag he still had; it was the opera top of an old underslip of Helga's. All the years he had used it, washing it from time to time, hanging it up carefully in such a way that no one could tell what it was.

Sometimes he drove slowly past the playground of Oriana's school when the children were all out so that he could wave to her.

'That's my Daddy.'

'There's Oriana's Daddy.'

And the little girls would be all linked together, arm in arm across the yard, round and round they went chanting.

'Who'll join on. . . .'

'Who'll join on . . . Who'll join on. . . .'

Sometimes at school coming-out time he was there at the gates and threw jelly-babies onto the green for the children to find; they ran scrambling and laughing.

'I got one!'

'I got one!'

And Oriana left her playfellows and ran to him.

Now when he was out he was always alone. It was lunch time and the children were spilling across the street to the little corner shop. It was an old shop, standing alone in a group of tamarisks and eucalyptus trees, and the children went there for pies and ice-cream. Morris Bernard felt he was in the way. He felt, if he started to throw sweets now the children would only look at him with their school eyes and they would be afraid to take sweets from a strange old man. He waited his turn at the counter to buy a green cool drink.

He supposed they would think he was an old man. How could they think anything else. His wife thought he was old. He was ill at the beginning of winter. It was a bladder complaint, an inflammation and very painful, and it took his strength out of him.

'Why don't you give up the products,' Natasha said. He was sitting on the verandah, dead tired after the illness and the bad nights, thinking he should try to be off out into the streets, out in his area. And he knew she was thinking, 'He's too old.' But he was not so old.

'I am not at retiring age yet, my love,' he said, but she had already gone back inside the house. He felt that she found the house pokey and commonplace. It was small and had small flat windows squatting in red brick. It was a stuffy house filled with relics from Morris's mother; ugly things brought with her from the small central European town which had been her home long ago.

'I'll buy some land,' he had promised Natasha. 'You can design and build your own house just as you really want it.' But as the years went by he was never able to keep his promise.

Natasha had, in the small of her back, a very fine soft down. Of course he could not speak about this to her now. She never knew she had it. It could hardly be seen; it was a kind of delicate, primeval inheritance and it was Morris who, years ago, made the discovery in a moment of tenderness.

In the fragrant doubtful shade of the eucalyptus trees beyond the faded verandah board of the little shop he ate his sandwich. Quickly he got up, his pain rising in his chest, it was only indigestion, to start off again.

'Father Christmas,' he said, bowing low to the first open door. 'Today I have something free for you,' and he handed a quilted coat hanger to the woman who stood in her dressing gown before him.

'I was just in the bath,' she said. And for the first time in his life one of his own products made him nearly sick; the odour of pine antiseptic, the house behind the woman was all steaming with it. Quickly he turned for the gate.

'I must be ill,' Morris said to himself on the kerb. He edged himself and his case and basket into the squalid comfort of his old shabby car.

'Really ill,' he murmured. 'It has never happened before.' He sat in the car for a while. He thought he would feel better after a little rest.

'Perhaps it was something I've eaten,' he muttered.

This was the street where, years ago, he first took Natasha in the car. He remembered every detail of this street as it was then. The broom had been in flower, splashes of yellow every-where and the scent of it sweetly in the air. The hibiscus hedges with yellowing leaves were mostly unchanged and some street lawns were still covered with prickly weed. One or two old houses had been pulled down and replaced by flats. Otherwise nothing had changed, except his life and his business prospects and Natasha.

On that day he drove a little way down the street and when he stopped the car Natasha suddenly sat very close to him and sighed and put her head on his shoulder. This movement of hers said something to him which he had never forgotten; he still felt the same tenderness over her whenever he was in this street year after year.

In those days Natasha was living in Helga's house. It was a house full of children and animals and the smell of cheap meat stewing. When Helga was choosing and buying, Natasha some-times wandered into the room, and in her quiet way, looked over the things in his case. She hardly spoke and quietly she wandered off again to the louvred sleep-out which was her room in the house. But this day she asked Morris, 'Can I come in your car to the bus stop?'

'Dear young lady I shall be delighted,' Morris said. 'We'll hire Helga to push,' he joked, laughing and laughing.

Natasha piled her books in the car and sat by Morris.

'All set like a jelly!' he said and drove off.

But Natasha did not want to get out of the car. 'Mr Bernard,' she said. 'Let me stay with you.'

'But you must go on the bus,' Morris said gently. 'And study. What about your exam?'

'Let me stay with you. I hate school and I hate it at Helga's. Let me stay, just today.'

So she stayed with Morris, waiting in the car, reading a bit, waiting while he went up and down to the houses selling.

'Leave off now,' she said when Morris came to replenish his case. So Morris sat in the car.

'Funny thing you having two Christian names, Morris and Bernard, Mr Bernard,' she said. He drove a little way down the street and it was when he stopped the car Natasha put her head on his shoulder.

'Morris,' she said.

'What is it Natasha?'

And after a little while they went on down to the sea together.

'She's so young,' Helga said. 'Really only a schoolgirl. And you know she has no one, no one at all.' Her voice went on reproaching.

'She's not at school,' Morris protested, awkward, his case unopened on the kitchen floor. 'She's at the university now.'

'Yes, yes,' Helga agreed. 'But for how long, a few weeks only. How could you!' The reproach scalded. Morris wished to sit down but Helga remained standing; so he stood.

'We tried everything, but nothing has happened. How could you!'

'She, she wanted me,' he said in a low voice. 'How can a man refuse?'

Helga made an impatient movement.

'Would she marry me?' Morris asked after an uneasy pause.

'Why don't you ask her?' Helga put her head round the door and screeched into the hollow echoing passage, 'Nat-ash-a!'

After a few moments Natasha came. Morris was shocked at her appearance. She was very pale and looked as if she had been crying a great deal. She came in slowly with her head bent. She did not look at Morris.

'My Precious,' Morris said gently. 'Why didn't you tell me at once?' He put his arm behind her and drew her out through the back verandah to the garden. 'Pom pom pa pom.' He sang the Wedding March.

'I don't want a baby.' Natasha sobbed and then she was sick in the long grass of the neglected tennis court.

Morris tried to soothe and comfort her.

'But I want our baby, my Precious,' he said.

Natasha continued to go to the university after the marriage. Morris drove her every morning. She seemed withdrawn in her pregnancy and suffered from morning sickness, and she sat quietly in the car, upright and very close to Morris. Tenderly, every day, he helped her from the car. Some days she worried about her work and he tried to comfort her.

'Goodbye, my Precious. Everything will be all right. You'll see.'

'Goodbye, my Gingerbread Daddy.'

And he was always waiting for her in the students' car park at the end of the afternoon and they drove home together. There, in the stuffy privacy, Morris cherished Natasha, making her scrambled eggs and tea which he brought to her on a tray. And all the time he looked forward with joy and hope to the birth of their child.

Helga always kept a great deal of money in the house, together with a box of valuables and old jewellery and silver. A one-time refugee, she trusted no one but herself, and had escaped, crossing hostile frontiers, with her possessions on her person and thereafter kept them as near to herself as possible.

Morris knew a great deal about Helga from the percolator mornings when she, in varying moods of self pity or self importance or sheer boastfulness, related incidents from her life. She loved talking about herself.

Once she had even shown him the box.

'I must burn down her house,' he muttered in the car, retching still from the penetrating odour of pine antiseptic.

'Funny thing, the antiseptic's never upset me before. Might have been the sandwich.'

But he always made his own sandwich and knew what he put in it.

'Home cooking's best,' he said to Oriana every morning. 'You know what's in it when you've made it yourself.' And he tried to tease a laugh out of her, clowning, pretending to put a banana skin or an egg shell between his bits of bread.

He could search in Helga's house, find the money, stuff the house with petrol rags, set fire to it and no one would know about the theft.

'Here is a new car for you Natasha . . . Take Oriana. . . .' Pity it wasn't the old house. That one would have been easier to burn.

Refreshed with the thought he went home early. He was surprised that Natasha was already at home and in the shower. Then he remembered it was the staff welcome party at the university. Though he always said he did not belong with academics, he always went to this party. He believed it was right he should be Natasha's escort. So for her, he must make the effort this evening. He took a dose of sparkling liver salts from the sample tin in his case.

'Take off the badge,' Natasha said. 'It's a bit ridiculous and, in any case, it looks cheap.'

'But why Precious? I'm proud of the old firm, my love.'

The badge he wore on his lapel represented the firm's one hundred years of service. Morris had had to pay ten cents for

245

it as the firm was, with regret, unable to give them away. He had been pleased to buy the badge and wear it.

Natasha simply shrugged with one shoulder and examined her finger nails.

'You're looking very fit and sunburnt Mister Bernard.' It was Natasha's head of department. He always called Morris, Mister Bernard. Every year he said the same thing to Morris. 'Just had a holiday?' And Morris tried to explain it was because his work took him out of doors all day but, as in other years before, he realised no answer was needed to this question.

He was on the fringe of the party waiting for Natasha, who had been, as usual, obliged to look in at the department before coming across to the garden where a large group of people were quickly gathering. She would come in about half an hour, he guessed, with the tall fair-headed young man who had come lately, quite often, to their house. He had been a research student and was now on the staff of the department working with Natasha.

The size of the party was oppressive. Morris nodded and smiled hopefully to one or two people but they did not remember him. Someone near him was telling a joke, he tried to listen, to be in on it. . . .

'So when the two gynaecologists were introduced finally, he said *At your cervix m'dear,* and she replied, *Dilated to meet you.*' All around him were faces with the mouths wide open; the heads were thrown back and laughter flew out between pickets of teeth.

He could not understand the joke but he tried to join in the laughter.

It was the bath salts, suddenly he was burdened. Thirty-four plastic urns, some pink, some blue, of bath salts, his quota for the month. He knew he would not sell them. Already half the month had gone. And for the first time in all the years, because of this, he would not be invited to the business lunch, an event to which he had always looked forward for he was, or had been, with a modest smile of self depreciation, the life and soul of the whole affair.

As he stood there in the fringes of the evening, he felt again the ebbing of his energy. It was his work. It was the kind of work which took so much personal effort and energy, all day and every day. If he allowed himself to give up at all, then he failed, and there was nothing to support or sustain him in his failure.

He would have had another sherry but the steward went by too quickly, so he stood holding the empty glass waiting for Natasha to come.

Once he had had a pet monkey to entertain the children. It was only a puppet made of cloth, he had him on one hand and made him do all sorts of funny things. Every day he thought up fresh antics for the monkey.

'Where's Jacko today?' the children called. And he made them laugh while their mothers plundered the cases, their long fingers diving in between the jars and tins and packets as they chose perfumes, spices, and household things like polish and soap.

'Bring me, bring me two of these.'

'Put me down for half a dozen.'

'I'll have these please.'

'Bring . . . bring, bring, bring. . . .'

With one hand he entertained the children and with the other he scribbled down the orders in his docket book.

Sometimes he wore an elastic garter on his ankle. It had little bells sewn on to it and the bells tinkled out of sight as he walked from house to house.

'Here's the Ring-a-Ring Man.'

'Jingle, Jingle Man.'

'Where's Jacko today?'

'What have you brought for us today?'

'Where's Jacko, Jacko . . . Jacko. . . .'

'Echo Jacko . . . Jacko echoing!'

It must have been half an hour Morris waited for Natasha and then she came, crisp and cool and smiling at everyone. With her was the fair-haired young man. He stayed by Natasha as they mingled, Morris just behind them, with the other guests.

Morris managed to get beside Natasha a moment. He was tired.

'How about an early night, my Precious?' he asked in a low voice. A fragment of irritation flickered momentarily, spoiling Natasha's lovely face, but she changed it at once into a smile.

'Yes, yes of course you go Morris,' she said. 'Victor will bring me home. We have some work to do first.'

'You'll not be late?' Morris persisted, knowing he was losing. Again the flicker of annoyance, anger almost, spoiling the calm of her eyes.

'No, of course I'll not be late,' and she smiled again. 'You go on home. We shall not be long.'

At home Morris sat opposite Oriana and ate hurriedly. Oriana had prepared a massive meal. Natasha of course had not come in.

'Have we any old rag, my dear?' he asked Oriana. But though she sat still, thinking, she could not think of any rag. Morris couldn't think of any either, so he went and pulled some underwear out of his drawer.

'I may be a little late home, my dear,' he said to Oriana. He nearly explained, 'It's a sales lecture my dear, and I have been asked to demonstrate the products.' But he couldn't lie to Oriana, already she was leaning over the sink. So he just called, 'See you later alligator,' to her thick back.

He drove slowly towards his area. This was ladies' night at the bowls club. He drove slowly by the glass pavilion. The floodlights were on and a great number of ladies, in their white hats and dresses, were already there. Helga was there. He saw her car badly parked, taking up two spaces, one wheel up on the footpath. So like Helga, completely unaware of anyone else.

He was pleased to have seen her car there parked like that;

he was pleased to feel anger and resentment towards her. He drove quickly and was soon outside her place.

'Better stop round the corner.' His own voice and clear thinking were a pleasant surprise.

Oriana's meal was a nuisance; he felt sick. Really, he always had to eat more than he wanted. Tuna mornay and creamed sweet corn rose with the rising pain in his chest. In the darkness he prowled all round Helga's neat house. Helga had had far more than her share of good fortune, but he softened. 'I won't burn the whole house, only the room where that box is,' he said to himself. And then he thought he would leave her the remaining thirty-two urns of bath salts. It would be a kind of sale.

He went back down to the car and sat in the fragrance of the bath salts, with the light on, and wrote a docket for Helga: '32 plastic urns bath crystals + two free gifts,' and underneath he wrote, 'Paid,' and scrawled his initials in the appropriate square.

The sale was a tremendous load off his mind. Scenes from the business lunch floated agreeably. Perhaps they would ask him to make a speech. 'Mr Manager, distinguished visitors, ladies and gentlemen. Unaccustomed as I am, I would like to say a few words. . . .' He was one of the salesmen with the most years of service to the firm. He would make a speech full of laughter and happiness.

He went up Helga's path carrying the cartons of bath salts. He had to go four times as he could only carry one at a time. He stacked them in the front porch.

'Hurry! Hurry!' he urged himself. 'Bowls don't go on all night. So hurry! Hurry!'

He went several times round the dark house. Of course there was no way in.

'Oh hurry! She may come back.' He began to panic. He cut the fly wire door and tried to force the front door but it would not yield. Every window was locked, even the louvres of the laundry. In the end he broke the kitchen window and stood appalled in the silence after the noise of breaking glass. He ran down again to the car, sweating, and fetched the bundle of underwear and his can of petrol. Panting and excited he cut his hand on the broken window while reaching through to unlock the kitchen door. Blood was on his trousers and he dabbed at himself with the underclothes. The look of his hand frightened him but he was grateful to be in the kitchen at last. He hurried to the front door and unlocked it and dragged the cartons into the sitting room, one after the other, pushing them behind the studio couch, as quickly as he could.

He laughed as he thought of Helga buying so many bath salts but stopped laughing because, of course, she hadn't paid yet.

He must find the money quickly.

In the old house the box had been in her bedroom. He sighed for the old house, not only because it was so burnable, but because he had known there where to stretch his hand out to touch the box. This house was different; it was all concrete, all sealed up with carpet and vinyl tiles. Where should he look? He supposed the bedroom. She would sleep with the box near her.

In a panic again for time, with his cut hand, clumsy, wrapped in some underpants, he pulled things out of the wardrobes and from the dressing table. He tore up the cushions of the window seat and, pulling off the candlewick bedspread, he then heaved the mattress off the bed. In a sudden fear he switched off the light. How could he have been so stupid? He let down the blind, drew the curtains and groped again for the light switch, moaning and gasping softly like a child in a nightmare, his hands crawling and feeling along the strange wall.

It was better with the curtains drawn. In the drawer in the side of the bed he found some money; bundles of notes, folded in with stockings and scarves and jumpers. He nearly wept with relief. He stuffed the money into his trouser pockets. He poured petrol onto the singlets and pants. It was not nearly enough rag. He put the petrol-soaked clothes round the room. Of course he could soak the bedclothes with the rest of the petrol and then set fire to the whole lot.

He was afraid the place would not burn enough. Best to set it on fire quickly and go. Helga might be back any minute.

It was quite a lot of money but not enough for a car. Never mind about the car.

'Here Natasha, take this. Take Oriana to town and buy yourselves nice new clothes. You know . . . pretty things. . . .'

Suppose Natasha were to thank him, 'Thank you, thank you Gingerbread Daddy.' In all the years she never called him by that private name. It was such a private thing, the Ginger; a secret joke once because his body hairs were so surprisingly ginger coloured.

He wondered how much money.

'Helga's coming! Helga's coming!' he chanted, while he searched in her all-electric kitchen for matches. The money was better to have than the silver and jewels, so never mind about finding the box. What could he do with the jewels in any case?

Searching had an undesired effect on his bowels and he had to retire hurriedly to the toilet.

'Helga's coming! Helga's coming!'

Of course he could switch on the hot plate on the stove and carry a bit of burning paper to the bedroom. He was waiting, engrossed in the slow processes of the electric stove, for the hot plate to redden, when he heard the front door being opened. He peered into the sitting room.

'Why Morris!' Helga said. 'What are you doing here? How did you get in? . . . Oh! You've hurt your hand. You're all over blood. Is this your blood too all over my lounge?'

'I thought I saw a light. Someone breaking in. I knew you were out. So I came up . . . surprised him. . . .' Morris was amazed at the way his own voice slipped on and on explaining. All the same he was trembling. Helga was formidable; he knew this.

251

She hurried forward. She took his hand. It was all stuck inside the blood-stained underpants.

'My,' she said. 'That'll make a good story! Look at your trousers, they're all blood too,' she said. 'Take them off. I'll sponge them when I've seen to your hand.' Morris clutched at his trousers.

'It's all right Helga. I'll be all right directly. I must be going.'

'Take off your trousers.' Helga's voice was a command. She fished about in the kitchen cupboard and found cotton wool and bandages. Either she had not seen the broken window and the cartons of bath salts, or else chose not to mention them.

A terrible fear seized Morris, his trembling became violent. He wanted, more than anything, to be at home in bed. 'I must go home to Natasha,' he said, his voice crumbling.

'Take off your trousers,' commanded Helga. Morris did so and was ridiculous in his underpants.

Helga stalked off across the hall to the laundry. She was away a long time. Perhaps she had discovered the bedroom in its terrible state, and of course the money. Suppose Helga put her hand in the trouser pockets and found the money. Oh he hoped she would not. Morris sat in an easy chair groaning to himself. He felt cold; he shivered in his underpants.

'I've been a fool. I should have taken the money straight to the car and not bothered about the fire.'

A thousand times, as he sat waiting for Helga to come back with the cleaned trousers, he went through the motions of finding the money and going straight off out to the car with it.

He felt dreadfully tired.

He thought he heard the murmuring of voices in the hall. Helga came into the room and immediately behind her was a policeman.

'Now then,' he said to Morris. 'Come along quietly with me.'

'You can't prove anything against me,' Morris said.

'Well, mate, you seem to be in this lady's lounge-room, if I may say so, indecently exposed,' said the officer.

'But Helga has known me for years.' Morris was indignant.

'Yes, but apparently not in the lounge-room in your under-wear, though I'm told this isn't the first time.'

'Oh that other time I had been stung by a bee,' Morris said. 'Hadn't I Helga?'

'Oh I'm sure I don't remember any bees,' Helga said.

'Now get up mate and get dressed. We'll have to go along.'

Morris thought the officer spoke in quite a kindly manner and he wanted to allow himself to be soothed but the sight of Helga seemed to infuriate him.

'She made me take my trousers off,' he shouted. 'She took them!'

Helga stood there like someone seen in a dream. She shook her head slowly and pointed to the studio couch; the trousers lay in a little crumpled heap beside it. So they had been there all the time, and the money, so she couldn't have found it in his pockets. It was still there. Morris began hastily, but care-fully, to dress himself. He could feel the money still in his pockets and he felt comforted. If only he had noticed his trou-sers before, he could have gone away while Helga was out of the room.

'Anyway those are mine,' Morris bleated, indicating the car-tons. The policeman bent over them.

'There's a docket with them,' he said. 'It appears the lady has paid.' And Morris wanted to scream, Helga looked so smug.

'That was clever of you Helga to get my trousers off me,' Morris said in a low voice.

'It seemed the best way, at the time, to pin something on you, Lover Boy, till I was absolutely sure,' Helga replied, in an even lower voice.

'Can I go home first and explain everything to my wife?' Morris asked the officer.

'I'm afraid not.'

As they left the house and walked down to the gate, Morris thought he heard Helga singing as she walked round her house, scratching herself and inspecting it all. 'Oh you . . . you make my heart go ticketty boo.'

He was glad some of his blood had dirtied her white frock. No harm could ever really come to Helga. She would enjoy doing up her bedroom again. She would have everything just as she wanted it, and get it all done before leaving to go up to her son-in-law's property in time for the new baby. Helga was like that.

'My underwear is all in that house,' Morris explained, hanging back from the night and what lay ahead. Helga's house seemed so secure and comfortable in comparison.

'Never mind that, we'll get it later. I've no doubt there's a fair bit of sorting out to do.'

The night seemed cool and unconcerned and Morris walked uncertainly beside his new companion.

The first visiting time passed uneventfully. Natasha came with Oriana just a few minutes before the end of the time allowed. Oriana had made a marble cake to bring. Morris tried to eat some.

'Daddy am I pretty?' Oriana asked him when she was thirteen. Already then she was too solid, her face too big and her complexion pasty and white.

'To me you are always Daddy's prettiest little girl,' he replied. He would have liked to tell her how much he loved her, but he couldn't find the words.

'I mean pretty to other people,' she persisted. And Morris, searching for comforting things to say, tried to amuse her. He waddled, like a duck, to the door and spread himself out, wedged across it.

'Even if you get too fat to get through this door, I'll always think you're the prettiest.'

'Well I think I'm ugly,' she said, the tears beginning to come into her eyes.

'There's no such thing as an ugly girl,' Morris said gently.

He wished Natasha was at home, he felt suddenly quite unable to reach Oriana in the mysteriousness of her adolescence.

'But look at me!' he said laughing, and he pulled a face. 'I'm the ugly one!'

And he watched in dismay as she slowly left the room, her shoulders shaking with her quiet sobbing.

Morris wished he could eat Oriana's cake.

'Don't eat the brown part. It's bad!' He tried to make Oriana laugh, as she used to when he said this about the chocolate pattern of the cake.

Morris raised his bandaged hand.

'I must have had a bee sting,' he said to Natasha.

'Do you think so?' Natasha looked out of the window as if she was thinking about something else.

Oriana ate most of her cake. She sat comfortably regarding the other little tables, where other visitors sat close together unpacking and sharing out food with those they had come to visit.

After Natasha and Oriana had gone he tried to remember the quiet fragrance of his area and the soft laughter of the doves. He tried, in his mind, to feel the fresh air and to picture the sun-washed streets, detail upon detail, the houses and verandahs, the lawns spotted all over with yellow weed, the hibiscus hedges and splashes of poinsettias and, of course, the glimpses of the sea.

But for some reason he kept thinking, instead, of the way in which Oriana, every night, put her slipper in her bedroom door to keep it from slamming shut. As he sat there he seemed to see the slipper so clearly in the dark doorway and he felt he couldn't bear anything any longer.

In spite of the heaviness of his thoughts he went along to the Sunday evening concert. Many of the prisoners in the rehabilitation centre performed, either singing or dancing or reciting. He thought if he tried hard, he also might think of something entertaining to do.

Grasshoppers

Also when they shall be afraid of that which is high, and the fears shall be in the way, and the almond tree shall flourish, and the grasshopper shall be a burden, and desire shall fail because man goeth to his long home, and the mourners go about the streets.

Ecclesiastes 12, verse 5

Jetzt wird mein Elend voll, und namenlos
erfüllt es mich. . . .

Jetzt liegst du quer durch meinen Schoss,
jetzt kann ich dich nicht mehr
gebären.

'Pieta', Rainer Maria Rilke

Now is my alienation full, and without name
it floods me. . . .

Now you lie hard across my lap,
now can I no longer
carry you.

The long hot afternoon was coming to an end, the only sound in the stillness was from the endless energetic imagination of the grasshoppers. Their sound was so monotonous it was possible not to notice it unless some persisting thought or sorrow caused the noise to become an intrusion, a nuisance. The old woman, surprised to hear a car turning slowly on the gravel, peered through the window to see who was coming.

'Mother, this is Bettina,' Peg said as she stepped into the neat kitchen.

'Pleased to meet you,' the old woman said to Peg's friend. 'I wasn't expecting you for another week Peg,' she said with the nervous little laugh which belongs to people who live alone.

Outside there was a noise, the geese and the ducks had taken fright and the hens were cackling and squawking, the strident voices of the children could be heard as they ran, making the most of the chase, scattering the disturbed poultry.

'Kerry! Kerry!' Peg shrilled from the porch, 'Kerree—come along and see Grandma,' she laughed. 'They've been right down the paddock, here they come, they're like grasshoppers in that long grass. Oh Mother, your grass is high this year, and dry!'

As the two small girls came indoors, the old woman bent to kiss her grandchild but Kerry drew back staring at her with cold blue eyes.

'I don't like you,' she said. She had never said that before.

The old woman tried again,

'Let me see,' she said. 'How old are you now, dearie?'

'I'm not dearie,' Kerry said. 'I'm five,' she said. 'And Miranda's five and her Billy's gone away like our Lucien's gone.' Both the children raced off through the living room onto the verandah, banging the door and the fly-screen door.

The old woman noticed that they had little bunches of feathers tight in their hands. She had always had the feeling that the discarded poultry feathers were dirty things, that they might even carry some sort of illness or disease. She would have liked to tell the children to throw the feathers away, that they were not clean and that they must wash their hands now because they might have picked up something nasty.

'Billy's my little girl's father,' Bettina said. 'He's an ex., he's left me.'

'Oh, I'm sorry,' the old woman said.

'There's no need to be sorry,' Bettina said. 'I'm better off without him, eh Peg?' And it seemed to the old woman that the two young women smiled at each other in an intimate way which was more than a little sly.

'It's very quiet and lonely here,' the old woman said. 'I hope you'll be comfortable. I expect you both need a rest and it'll be a change for the children.' She was wondering if she was saying the right things. She noticed her daughter's friend was restlessly taking stock of the cottage; her hair was cut long over her greedy eyes and the skirt she wore, instead of being tied round the waist, was tied high under her armpits and looked as if it would slip down any minute. She felt she must do her best but, straight away, she had not taken to Peg's friend; for one thing, why didn't the girl wear a blouse like other people. She had been looking forward to having her daughter and little granddaughter come to stay. Nothing had been said about this, what was her name, Betty, Bettina and this Miranda coming too.

'I've never seen such a small house with so many beds in it,' Bettina said, hitching up her garment. The old woman felt sure she had nothing on under it.

The old woman laughed her nervous laugh, 'Oh we were quite a big family once upon a time,' she said. Peg brought in a case from the car.

'We'll have tea directly,' the old woman said. 'And I'll make up the beds when you've made up your minds where you want to sleep.'

The children rushed through the cottage again banging the doors and shrieking. Peg said comfortably, 'They slept all the long way up here. They get on so very well together, Mother, they react with each other perfectly.'

As they drank their tea the old woman tried to make conversation with the silent young women.

'Are you a teacher too?' she asked Bettina.

'Lord no!' Bettina said, and she laughed with Peg as if over some private joke. 'I've just been overseas,' she explained.

'Bettina is a faith healer,' said Peg.

'Oh, I see,' said her mother. 'Kerry! Kerry!' She poked her head out of the door, she had a little parcel all ready. 'Kerry!' she called. 'Come and see what Grandma's got for you! Come and see what I made for you!'

'Not now I'm busy,' came the childish voice from the lean-to shed which was the bathroom.

'Perhaps they're playing medicals,' Peg said.

'I think they're having a bath,' Bettina said and laughed. 'I could do with one myself. I might just get under the cold hose,' she added. 'It's killingly hot!'

'Oh you can have a nice shower later,' the old woman said. 'I'm not all that short of water.'

'I'm afraid we shan't have time,' Peg said. The old woman was surprised, she hesitated, her thin arms hugging folded sheets.

'Not have time?' she said. 'You going out then? Tonight?' she asked. 'You've only just got here, won't you be too tired?'

'No, we'll be all right Mother,' Peg said slowly and deliberately. 'We were wondering if you would watch the children for us.'

'You are going out then,' the old woman said. 'Of course I'll look after the children if you want me to. But where can you go tonight from here?'

'Well, Mother,' Peg said. 'It's not just for tonight, it's for a week. Bettina and I want to go away for a few days.'

'Oh I see,' the old woman tried to hide her disappointment. 'It's a little holiday you're having?' She thought Peg was looking very worn and tired; she had a lot to do with her school work and housekeeping in the flat and looking after Kerry with no one to help her. It was lonely being a woman on your own, she had known that herself for a good many years.

The two young women stood smiling at each other. 'We'll have to leave at once, more or less, to get to the airport in time,' Peg said to her mother.

'And not have a meal?' the old woman cried out. She wanted to say, 'Airport, so you're going somewhere far away.' But she did not say it. She tried not to show that she had had a shock.

'I'm afraid so Mother,' Peg said. 'But we'll be sure to get something on the way. I'm sure the children will be good,' she added.

While Bettina went to get the children to come and say good-bye to their mothers, Peg said in a low voice, 'You know, Mother, Bettina's very brave, she had Miranda on purpose, all on her own, because she felt she ought to experience mother-hood to be a more complete person.'

'I'd say that was very foolish, not brave,' her mother replied.

'There's some clothes and things in that case, Mother, and here's some money.'

'Oh there's no need . . .' the old woman started to say, but Peg pushed some notes into her hand.

It was dusk and the large moon climbed quickly. The old woman, standing on the gravel clutching a child on either side, watched her daughter's car turn slowly and drive off. In the moonlight she saw that Bettina sat right up close to Peg and that Peg was driving with one hand on the steering wheel and one arm round the bare shoulders of her friend. For a moment she remembered Lucien and his handsome fair face and how he had come rather late into their quiet lives with his poetry and his songs, and with such tenderness. He had turned the car and driven up the track with his arm just like that, round Peg's shoulders. Then, not all that long ago, they had driven off after a visit and the next time Peg had come alone, paler and thinner but brave, even seeming not to care. The old woman often wondered how much Peg cared. She would have liked to ask her how she really was, and she would have liked to help her.

She was not sure that having these two children for a week would be a help.

Back inside the cottage the little girls took off all their clothes and tickled each other with the feathers they had picked up in the yard.

'I'm Bettina,' Miranda explained giggling and squirming. 'She's Peg. In a minute we're going to have a cuddle.'

'I see,' said the old woman. She finished making the beds and then could not find the children. The cottage was so small it did not take long to look in the corners and under the beds.

The old woman called to the little girls. She was suddenly frightened. She never thought that they would go outside alone in the dark. She knew they could not be far away, but when she went outside it was so quiet. The moonlight lay in silent patches over her land and sheds. Her almond trees stood dark and indifferent. There were shadows moving over the long dry grass in the paddock and a sweet smell came up as the night air touched the grass. Softly she called their names, trying not to frighten them, and trying not to be afraid herself. It was hardly half an hour since Peg and Bettina had driven off and she had lost their children. She thought of the dam, steep clay, slippery down to the summer-lowered water and, in spite of the warm night, she shivered.

Close by in the yard the geese were talking softly to one another, helping each other with the burden of their lives, softly comforting each other in the dark. To and fro they talked first one and then the other. They would talk like this for hours and only cry out in alarm if something startled them. Sometimes during the day they whispered at the back door, standing, stretching first one leg and then the other, their long necks outstretched and their feathers preened and softly ruffling like the frills of petticoats put on to attract. It seemed to the old woman then that they forgot that they were widowed geese as they paraded and danced, pirouetting and eyeing her and all the time, singing their little whispering song of flirtation. A young rooster, cheated by the moon, flapped his wings and crowed close by and the old woman, in the shock, trembled as if she had never heard a cock crow before. And, as if she had forgotten that they crow at odd times, she was sure it was unlucky.

Stumbling, she twisted and hurt her foot and it was painful. Not able to see what it was that had caused her to fall she limped back into the house. Both the children were there dressed up now in different clothes taken from the case. They must have come in at the other door while she was across the yard, searching the sheds in the dark. Somehow, noiselessly, they had managed to pull the fly-screen door off its hinges so that it would not open properly or close. It was incredible that two such small girls could break something as strong as the door. Later on in the evening they did the same thing to the other door swinging out across the porch on it chasing each other with pretend spiders and screaming with a terrified joy.

They ate steadily from a supply of jelly babies and chewing gum.

The old woman felt they should not have taken fresh clothes without asking, and she said so, but Miranda said that Bettina let her wear what she liked, and that Peg said Kerry could wear what she liked too. With tiny capable hands she folded and unfolded clothes, she shared the clothes into two heaps and then put them away again. The old woman was sure that all the clothes belonged to Kerry really, she saw things she had sewn and knitted herself for her little granddaughter.

Miranda shared the sweets in the same way, restlessly dividing them into little portions and then, with hot sticky fingers, gathering them in again.

'These are for you Kerry to eat in the morning and these are

262

for me and these are for you Kerry not to eat now.' She hopped from one foot to the other.

'If you need the toilet, Miranda, don't put off going.' The old woman, in her pain, was irritable. Something spoiled children. The spoiling seemed in some way connected with cheap frilly nylon under-clothes, and the ugly colours of toffee papers, and the crunching of boiled sweets, and the unnatural green and yellow of the different lemonades. The children smelled of the things they were chewing, she would have liked to say something about it.

The children were sucking their thumbs, hardly able to keep their eyes open, and the old woman told them to go to bed. She wanted to lie down herself, her foot was bleeding and painful. She needed to see to it.

'We don't go to bed yet,' Miranda said, but she lay down and tucked her little hand between her little thighs. Before the old woman had time to feel relief, Miranda was up again.

'Mrs Mercer, I want something to eat and drink,' she said. 'Kerry wants icing sugar, have you got icing sugar?' and, unable to open the cupboard, she pulled at the knob till it broke. The children took turns dipping their fingers in the sugar and licking them. The old woman hovered with a sponge and a cloth trying to clear up the mess they made.

While the children coloured in each other's finger and toe nails with green and purple crayons, the old woman took off her stocking and bathed the blood off the hurt foot. She was afraid she had broken open a vein where there was a discoloured patch on her ankle. Something had spiked into her when she fell. It was very painful and she tied it up with clean rag.

The children had a new game. They were dancing on the beds with cushions on their heads.

'We're widows,' they told the old woman. 'This is how you have to be a widow,' they said. The old woman told them she did not need to be told how to be a widow. She thought how pale and tired they looked. She longed to put them to bed. They had such dark rings round their eyes. She said she thought children should not dance on beds.

'Oh, we won't fall,' Miranda said and, overbalancing, she broke the lamp.

The old woman did her best to clear up the broken glass but she was hardly able to put her foot to the floor. She thought a bit of rusty metal must have gone in under the skin. Her eyesight was not good, in daylight it would be easier to see.

'Mrs Mercer, Kerry wants a paper hat, will you make paper hats for us. Kerry wants a nurse's hat, Mrs Mercer make us hats!'

The children said the paper hats were no good and they tore them up.

'Let's dance,' Miranda said. 'Let's have some music.' So the old woman sang for them. Perhaps they would sleep if she sang. She chose a hymn,

All things bright and beautiful,
All creatures great and small,
All things wise and wonderful,
The Lord God made them all.

She liked the hymn she said, she told them to look out for the mountain and the river,

The purple headed mountain,
The river running by,
The sunset, and the morning
That brightens up the sky.

'Do you know any Disco Mrs Mercer?' Miranda called. 'Kerry wants Disco.' The old woman said she did not know what Disco was. So the little girls danced to the hymn. They danced across the room and back, they danced with their mouths open, they rolled their eyes and their hips and they nodded their heads and shook their shoulders, they swayed and kicked and wriggled.

The old woman could not understand the children. In spite of the long soak in the bath, they seemed grimy as if they were soiled in some way which she did not know about. Suddenly she knew she could not trust them at all. It was dreadful, horrible to know this. She searched crazily along the mantlepiece.

'Miranda! Kerry! Where are the matches! Where's my purse and my keys!' The children looked up at her with clear blue eyes.

'Mrs Mercer, perhaps they've fallen in the dam.'

'Yes Grandma, we saw them fall in the dam.'

The old woman would not believe them. Tomorrow she told them they would find the things. She told them she would have to slap them both. It was a long time she said since she had slapped anyone.

Sometime after midnight Miranda was sick and the old woman, badly in pain, had to change all the bed covers and wash the child's long hair. As she sat by the child she longed to go to sleep herself. The pain in her foot and leg was worse. However would she manage the whole week. Peg should never have done this. Her other daughters would never have done something like this.

'Oh Peg,' she moaned softly. 'What's happened?'

There seemed to be someone in the kitchen, there was the noise of teaspoons being put on cups and saucers. The old woman was pleased.

'Are you there Mary? If you're making tea I'd love some it's such a hot night is that you Mary thank God you've come my good girl my foot's so painful it's not really I just fell in the yard really silly of me it's just a nuisance that's all I'll be better directly but oh Mary I'm so glad you're here silly of me to cry.' The old woman woke with tears on her cheeks. The child was asleep and she lay down on her own bed. She was thirsty. Of course Mary was not there, how could she be, she'd gone to Canada years ago.

'Oh Mary I wish you were here.' The old woman was surprised at her easy tears, she must try to sleep.

'Mary it's lovely to see your kind face like this I remember when I was so ill after Peg was born and you stayed off from school and looked after me and then later on when poor Dora died I was thinking Dora would be home for Christmas but of course I was forgetting it's my silly leg and it was only a little fall out there by the shed Mary I'm so glad. . . .'

A plate broke in the kitchen. It was bright daylight. The old woman heard the children, some more crockery was dropped and broken. She must have overslept. She could not get up, her leg was swollen and stiff.

'Kerry! Come to Grandma, Grandma wants you Kerry!' It was Miranda who came, her hair was knotted and sour in spite of being washed.

'Where's Kerry?' the old woman asked. 'Tell Kerry I want her to find my keys and my money purse.' It was hard to talk, her mouth was so dry.

'I've got a pain Mrs Mercer and I feel sick can I come in bed with you?' The little girl scrambled up on to the bed beside the old woman.

'Why you naughty girl, there's clay all over your feet.' The old woman tried to move away from the clumsy child. Mind my leg,' she moaned. She struggled off the bed.

In the kitchen there was a pool of milk on the table and the water jug was broken. Kerry was not there.

'The matches!' the old woman suddenly remembered. She thought of her paddock, neglected, and the children like grasshoppers hidden in the long grass; they were like grasshoppers coming up through the dry grass.

'Mrs Mercer! Mrs Mercer! I'm going to be sick again!'

'Wait if you can, dearie, while I find the pail.' The old woman could hardly cross the small kitchen. It was strange that she minded the children so much, she had always loved children. She supposed it was because she was old now, and that made looking after the children such a burden.

'I'll find the matches and put them away,' she muttered. 'I'll get some water. I need some water.'

The children must have turned on the tap and left it on all night. She never thought to look, she was unaccustomed now to children. Her own children, and other children she had known, would never have let the water tank run out.

She knew she might faint and she struggled back to the bed and lay down gratefully. If Kerry would come she could remind her about the other tank.

'Miranda,' she said to the sleeping child beside her. 'Fetch Kerry, tell her Grandma needs a drink of water. Please go and fetch Kerry.'

The old woman and the child slept.

'Miranda!' the old woman tried to rouse the child. 'Tell Kerry not to go down to the dam, it's dangerous down there, there's water by the fowls, Miranda, please find Kerry and tell her, there's a good girl.'

In spite of the severe pain it seemed to the old woman that she was having refreshing little sleeps and that she would be better soon.

It was better to sleep as she had no real wish to wake up.

Peg was on her way home. She could hardly wait to be back with her mother and her little girl. The tedious journey would have been unbearable if she had not raced ahead in her thoughts to the peaceful farm. She kept thinking, with pleasure, how she would have time at last to play with Kerry. She always went home to her mother's for holidays and it was a relief to be going there after all in spite of the other arrangements she had made. She longed to feel the soft cool flesh of her little girl and she longed to hear her voice.

There was something about Bettina, during the short time

she had known her, that made her not notice Kerry. Perhaps it was something in herself, not just in Bettina, which made her find Kerry a nuisance at those times when she so urgently wanted to be alone with her new friend.

It was easier just now not to think about Bettina.

She wanted to be with her mother too. Her mother could comfort without appearing to be doing anything other than the work in hand. Looking forward to going home, she was even able to smile to herself during the long journey back.

'What's Miss Moles been up to this term?' Her mother liked to hear what was going on at the school. Deep in her comfortable seat Peg thought of her mother's question.

The Head Mistress, Miss Moles, though concerning herself chiefly with the necessary ugliness of the girls' summer uniforms, repeatedly made opportunities for calling Peg into her office, or she would wait at staff tea time to be alone with Peg at the end of the afternoon. She liked to talk with Peg, she regarded her as one of her more mature and senior mistresses. She liked to talk, among other things, about poetry, and how poems should be introduced in the class room.

'You know, Pegeen.' She was always breathless over poetry. 'Before I left England I had the kids in the East End absolutely bonkers over Keats. They lapped him up! Ectually.' She had an accent which put an affectation into everything she said. Peg knew this haughtiness was not intentional. 'Ectually,' Miss Moles was in earnest. 'You can get the kids to love Keats. We've got to get through to the little morons,' she said. 'And Pegeen, I know you can do it!'

It was a strange thing to think, but Miss Moles and Bettina, though so completely different, had a similarity. Peg felt vague about this and let the thought go. If worthwhile it would be sure to return. She smiled comfortably, that was what her mother would have said.

Miss Moles wanted the students to be encouraged to write,

especially the seniors. The Muse had, she admitted with the gleam of inspiration in her eyes, visited her. Gazing towards further inspiration somewhere beyond the top of Peg's head, she confessed,

'I'm afraid Peglette, I do suffer from literary pretensions, it's unavoidable. I belong to the minority of the literati, I am myself a compulsive poet!'

In an embarrassed way she pushed some sheets of paper into Peg's unwilling hands.

'The Children of my Muse. He visits me frequently,' she breathed and left the staff tea room quickly, saying awkwardly over her shoulder, 'You can keep them, I have other copies.'

Unable to say to Miss Moles that she did not look upon the children in her classes as morons, she was equally unable to say one word about the poems to the writer of them who, it was clear, from quick nervous looks and raised eyebrows, was waiting from day to day for appreciation and comment.

A few days later Miss Moles, recovering herself, continued with her request. Writing she said was cultivated all too easily in the young who had no difficulty in self expression. It was the older ones who locked away, she said, and these senior students were to be encouraged to unlock themselves, and made to hand in three or four complete stories in a term.

Peg, burdened with so much extra reading, most of it in illegible handwriting, took the manuscripts home when she visited her mother. With mounting despair she sat with the exercise books in her lap making shy comments here and there in pencil. Her mother, with pursed lips, folded clothes and ironed them on the other side of the table. All the students were handing in writing which contained characters, plots, themes and adequate symbolism, perhaps too many symbols really. They achieved a suitable balance between narrative and dialogue, in fact the stories contained all the qualities of the art and were incredibly dull. It seemed as though, in the effort of contrivance, the real art was lost or destroyed. Not one writer seemed able to present a living character. Peg said something about it to her mother.

'Well, Peg,' her mother replied. 'I look at it this way, it's like a percentage of the harvest, if one out of the twenty-five achieves something then all your work isn't wasted. And as for the other twenty-four, who's to know what they'll make out of it later. Nothing's ever a waste unless you look at it as a waste,' she said.

Peg had known all along that her mother counted only the survivors among the chickens and that she took pleasure in picking whole fruit and did not pine over bird-pecked peaches. She dismissed failure of any kind, it was a waste of time to think about it. She was able to ignore completely the little piles of peach and nectarine stones left by the midnight-feasting possums. It was her mother's way to reckon on the sound thing, anything else was of no account.

Peg, on her return journey, would have liked to regard Bettina like this, but it was not so easy. It would be better not to think about Bettina till she was safely home and comforted, and then perhaps there would be some sort of perspective.

Peg had lived on the farm for quite a lot of her life and, whenever she could, she went back there even though it was really too far for an ordinary week-end visit.

When she was staying there, there were times of the day which she knew without any clock. It was the constantly changing light as the day wore on. And it was the changing movement and noise of the poultry, the sheep and the calves. Towards the end of the afternoon a transfiguration of the trees took place as the sun, dropping down, sent a last golden light up into the highest branches. Long shadows began to reach up the slope and there were sharper contrasts in the light and shade of the varying greens. The sun sinking lower and lower wrapped glowing colour round bark and, softening the outlines of rocks and old tin cans, made the rubbish heap mysterious and beautiful.

At that time the few sheep and calves came up into the yard filling the silence with their noise. They even came into the porch if her mother was slow in coming out. The poultry gathered too and even the cockatoos, in their enchanted flocks, had some knowledge of the farm routine, for, when the old woman appeared in her blue overall, these birds came flying low, screaming, over the long paddock.

It was her custom to cross to the shed followed by her subjects and she would fling several measures of oats at them and stand watching their trust with reverence.

'I'm always so touched at their dependence and their faith,' she would say to Peg. 'It doesn't always do for humans like it does for them.'

It often comforted Peg in her life away from home to know that this ritual continued, especially at times when her own life, for inexplicable reasons, seemed to have no shape, or when it began to take an unexpected turn.

Sitting with Lucien on their last evening together while he read aloud a poem which had turned out not to be for her, she remembered clearly the bewildered expressions on the soft but strong faces of the calves when they looked up at her and stared, with the oats stuck all round their gently moving black mouths. She had laughed with her mother at their perplexed expressions, but while Lucien read she began to cry.

'Darling!' he said in his tender way. He had just explained very gently and kindly about the change that was to be a part of their lives, and that the poem, with the little rhyming refrain repeated in the middle of every stanza, would help them both to understand the change. He said she would know from the poem who it was he had loved and who it was he loved now. He said she could keep the copy of the poem. He thought the tears were for him so she never explained about the calves.

As she helped him to pack, the dark blue silkiness of his body shirts seemed to slip quickly through her fingers into the new case. Carefully she folded the white trousers he always wore, a bit like a sailor, she thought, who wears the right clothes but never goes to sea. His love poems resembled this sailor. Handling his fresh clean clothes made her aware, perhaps for the first time, that it was possible that she did not mind that he was leaving, that she might manage to live without him. The thought, like the seriousness of the poem, made her smile while the calf tears were still wet on her cheeks.

They shared a chicken and a bottle of Moselle, and Lucien put on a record and moved towards her.

'Lucien must dance,' he said somewhere down in his throat. 'Lucien feels like dancing.' Slowly he turned round and round, he seemed to move without lifting his feet from the floor.

'Dance, Maria,' his name for her. 'Dance!' He raised his long-fingered hands above his fair head and smiled at her. Bewitchingly and gracefully he tilted his head and looked at her over one shoulder as he turned. He twitched his hips, first the left one and then wickedly, though she knew without any feeling for her, the right.

'One last dance Maria,' he said. When he smiled like this it was impossible to imagine that his jaw could exchange the smile for an obstinate, cold, cruel look.

Clumsily, because she was unwilling as well as big, Peg danced and caught her hip on the edge of the table. Long after he was gone she still felt the ache, there was quite a bruise, as if the last thing he had done was to hit her.

'Where's my daddy gone?' Kerry asked the next morning.

'Daddy's gone to America to find a nice house for Kerry and mommy,' Peg said.

'Are we going there?'

'Some time. But not for ages yet.'

'When we go, can Doossa come too?'

'Of course.'

'Doossa's got white lacey stockings, can I have some like Doossa's, can I?'

'Yes of course.'

272

'This week, can I? can I? can I?'

'No, next week.'

A few days later she moved with Kerry into a much smaller flat very close to the school. This closeness she supposed would make up for the ugliness.

With Bettina's last words she had almost cried but at the time there were people on all sides enjoying their curry.

She was not absolutely sure, at the time, that Bettina's little phrase was final, though it was Bettina's way to make sure that whatever she wanted could never be misunderstood. In the crowded restaurant she made an effort to return, in her thoughts, to that time of the transfiguration, when the long afternoon began to change to the evening. This gathering and noise of the animals belonged to the times when her mother had been out and was returning. She drove an old and battered car, and when this car, covered in dust, rattled into the yard it did not matter what time of day it was, all the life of the farm responded as if the return signified that special time of serenity with the setting sun, the long shadows, the extra light on leaves and bark, and the contrast of deepening, spreading shade, together with the hospitable scattering of oats from a tin basin. It would be the same for anyone returning.

On these occasions, when the creatures discovered their mistake, which they did quite soon, they would disperse shyly as hotel guests do when they have mistaken the time for dinner and arrived at the dining room while it is still locked.

Peg understood on the return journey that Bettina had not confided in her to protect her but it was simply in desperation.

'I must get to a cold tub,' Bettina burdened Peg suddenly with the mysterious pain. 'I can't stick it any longer.' Her pain intruded so much that Peg, already tired with travelling, was worn out for her friend. Bettina kept longing for a cold bath to sit in, even though it was cold in India. She was quite unable to stand the discomfort of her very unpleasant condition.

273

'All you have to do is to open the door and clap your hands, and someone will come.' She was restless and irritable. Peg longed for her to lie down and rest, she wanted to sleep herself.

'Up all those terrible stairs at this time of night?'

'Yes, why not, the hotel offers room service, it says so here on the back of the door, but there's no 'phone and Indians clap their hands for things. They'll expect other people to do the same. Go on!' Bettina's hoarse voice was persistent, she looked at Peg with her head lowered so that her eyes seemed to threaten from under the long fringe. The first time Bettina had looked at Peg, in the flat on the first evening, like this, both of them had laughed aloud. And for Peg, who had some time before stopped laughing, this laughter brought deep refreshment.

In the hotel bedroom neither of them laughed. They were both exhausted with the long journey. The covers on the beds were not clean and the light bulb, without any shade round it, was fly specked and mournfully dim.

'Perhaps they'll give us a better light tomorrow,' Peg said.

'They'd better give us a better room,' Bettina said. 'And we want something now.' Peg had to agree they were cold and hungry and it was that dreadful hour of arrival in the night when it seems impossible to get anything, though they could have had a dozen taxi drivers, there were so many of them falling over each other to take passengers.

Peg opened the door to the cold draught which rushed up the stair-well. The hotel was built round a narrow courtyard, they had crossed the cracked cement to reach the stairs. Beyond the bannister, immediately outside their door, it was all blackness.

Peg clapped her hands. Unaccustomed to clapping she made a soft sound. She waited with uneasy wretchedness.

'Is there a bell anywhere, by the beds or by that little table?' She re-entered the room, closing the door quickly as if to shut out her feeling on the landing.

'No of course there isn't, Dilly!' Bettina said. Together they inspected their bathroom, the towels looked thick and seemed clean. Somehow, for a moment, Peg was reminded of her mother. It was the towels; she knew how her mother would take Kerry laughing from her bath and put her, wrapped in the soft towel, on the kitchen table and pat her dry. Her old capable hands would have everything ready, clean night-gown, bread and butter and warmed milk.

'The bath looks all right,' Bettina said. The brass taps, well polished, were reassuring. She turned on the taps, they hardly trickled.

'Oh damn and blast! Shit!' Bettina said. 'Bloody hell!'

'We'll have to go all the way back down if we want anything, even water,' Peg said. So they went groping down the dark stairs. Peg, who was so much older, felt responsible. And she loved Bettina, this made her all the more responsible. She loved Bettina. That was why they had made the journey.

Back in the flat they had talked about it.

'I'd do anything in the world for you,' Peg said to Bettina. She had cried a little when she said it. It was a silly thing to do, to cry, she had said laughing through the tears. It was a rare thing in her lonely world to have found someone to love, she told Bettina.

'You've got Kerry, you love her,' Bettina said in her hoarse whisper. They had to be quiet because of the children.

'Yes, I know, dearest Bettina, of course I love Kerry,' Peg replied. 'But loving a child and loving an adult are two different things. Thank you for letting me love you.'

'What I want to do in this world,' Bettina said, stretching and yawning in Peg's bed, 'is to be able to cure people.'

'Why that's wonderful!' Peg was pleased. 'Oh little Bettina, that's wonderful.'

'I've got quite a reputation,' Bettina said yawning again. 'Overseas,' she stretched. 'For the laying on of hands.'

'I don't quite know what that is,' Peg said, feeling that she ought to know.

'Faith healing, Silly Dilly!' Bettina said. 'Faith healing, I want to be a faith healer. I want a mission in my life, the only trouble is I haven't any money, not a bean.' She frowned and looked up at Peg from under her long fringe. 'I'm flat broke! I'm on the rocks!'

Bettina, naked in Peg's dreary flat, transformed the small rooms. Even the light seemed different when she was there. Sometimes Bettina seemed smooth and radiant and her body glowed. At other times her restless vitality made every word and movement urgent and mysterious, and it was like being in the presence of a fierce unpredictable little animal. An unnamed one.

She had an entirely unselfconscious way of being naked while she fried an egg or read a magazine. As people often kick off their shoes when they come home Bettina shed her few clothes. Peg, on the edge of this liberation, could not help telling Bettina,

'I think you're beautiful, Bettina, really I do, you're really beautiful.'

'Aw, there's spare tyres all over me!' Bettina laughed. 'I'm fat and skinny in all the wrong place.' Peg could tell that, though she laughed, Bettina was pleased to be admired.

Peg had not known Bettina very long. It was strange, she reflected, that it seemed as if Bettina and Miranda had been a part of their lives for a long time. Before Bettina had come there, the flat was a place where she looked after Kerry and prepared her school work. It was a place she left every day when she went to school, and then came back to try to recover from her work, and once more prepare for it.

In her loneliness she attempted to recapture the days of her childhood and she chose poems which carried, in their words, the sounds of the earth and the countryside. She described the grasshoppers and she read to her class,

276

The poetry of earth is never dead:
When all the birds are faint with the hot sun,
And hide in cooling trees, a voice will run
From hedge to hedge about the new-mown mead,
That is the grasshopper's . . .

She avoided poems which reminded her of the pain of loneliness; and she avoided the obscure. Obscurity was a form of
loneliness, or so it seemed to her when she remembered Lucien
and his friends. Instead, she reminded her pupils of the sound
of a baby crying and of a baby laughing. She read to them,

My baby has a mottled fist,
My baby has a neck in creases
My baby kisses and is kissed
For she's the very thing for kisses.

She suggested that they might like to write poems about
grasshoppers and babies, perhaps even to write a poem to a
baby.

There were times when she longed to give up school work.
Every day it was the effort required and the draining of her
energy. Often she tried to avoid Miss Moles who, with bright
new ideas, lay in waiting for her at the end of the afternoon.
Just when Peg was trying to slip away from school Miss Moles
would come out of the staff tea room holding out a cup of tea
to her.

'Pegeen! I've saved you a cake bravely rescued from the jaws
of the Crimp, here you are, pink icing! Miss Crimp, dear, you
shall have two cakes on the morrow.'

Sometimes Peg felt quite unfit to be teaching and, because
she needed to have work, she hoped Miss Moles would not
notice.

Miss Moles often put her head round the classroom door.

'May I come in?' She was coy. 'The word of the day is creative,' she would say, smiling at Peg and at the class. Once she stayed sitting at one of the empty desks. 'Take absolutely no notice of the fact that I am here,' she said.

Uncomfortably Peg continued to read, '. . . "trees, rocks and flowers send back the echo man desires." It's from Beethoven,' she told the girls. 'Beethoven wrote it in his diary when he was composing the Symphony Number Six, the *Pastoral Symphony*.'

Miss Moles interrupted, 'Peg, didn't you know that Beethoven was not the gentle creature you are making him out to be, he didn't love the country and he used to beat his wife!'

A sigh of soft laughter went through the girls.

'Beethoven never married,' Peg said quickly and, too late, understood her mistake. She should have waited. The roomful of girls saw Miss Moles blush painfully all down her neck. And in the open front of her white blouse the red colour spread, giving more than a hint of embarrassment. Peg ached with the knowledge of what must have seemed like unkindness, the ache lasted for some days.

She was tired all the time. Some days she seemed only able to think about the end of the afternoon when she could leave and fetch Kerry from the kindergarten, and get home as quickly as possible.

For some reason, however much the sun might be shining, no sun came into the flat. The opposite wall came towards her as soon as she opened the front door. Because of the way the flats were built, there was no view from the window. Though the sea was so close, its sighing could be heard all night, it was not possible to look out across the sea. The windows of the flats faced each other. Often she tried to recall the pleasure of looking at the narrow paddock directly outside her mother's window. It was possible to sit in the small living room there and look right down the long slope to the willow trees overhanging the dam. Sitting in that room was almost the same as being out in the paddock. Because of the grass and the trees and the water there were birds. So near to these it was impossible to feel alone.

All the tiredness and the depression of the day, and of the days following one another, fell on her as soon as she was inside the tiny flat. Any food she prepared tasted of the flat. Kerry was discontented and white faced and always wanting things she could not have.

Often they went, the two of them, down in the lift and out on to the grass at the side of the flats. The tall buildings blocked out the sun. Kerry, too near her mother, pretended to play with a ball, talking in a silly voice to Doossa, while Peg tried to mark compositions and read the forced stories handed in by the seniors. The wind, bringing dust and grit, caught at the pages.

'Tell Doossa it's my turn,' Kerry insisted.

'Doossa it's Kerry's turn.'

'Tell her again, she didn't listen. Go on tell her, tell Doossa again.'

'Oh Kerry I must get my marking done.'

'Doossa's going to wear her second party dress tomorrow, can I wear my second party dress, can I? Can I? like Doossa?'

'Yes, yes but be quiet just now, play with your ball, there's a good girl.'

'Doossa's good too, tell Doossa she's good.'

'Yes, yes two good girls, now be quiet do!'

And Kerry skipped and chattered and stared shamelessly at anyone who went by.

It was all different when Bettina came. Everything changed when she came. She came by mistake. She said she was looking for someone, Peg could not now even remember the name she had said. It turned out to be the wrong address. She had a little girl with her.

'What's your name?' Kerry asked her, from Peg's side, at the door.

'Miranda,' said the other child.

'Mommy, can Miranda have tea with us?' Kerry asked, her voice rising with excitement.

'Oh well, I'm afraid not . . .' Peg began, and then she hesitated, she had just told the young woman that she must have made a mistake with the address.

'Oh please!' Kerry said.

Peg looked awkwardly at Bettina who appeared to be clothed from head to foot in sunshine though there was no sun on the concrete stairways and landings. So often she had explained to Kerry that little girls did not ask people to tea like this, not in front of them, but only privately so that mothers would not be forced to invite. Her blue and white frock was like a uniform confronted in this way.

Bettina, audacious, smiled at Peg.

'Would you like to come in?' Peg asked Bettina shyly. The two little girls rushed through the flat shrieking and banging the doors. The two women followed slowly, smiling slowly at one another.

With some makeshift arrangements Bettina and Miranda stayed the night.

The place was full of sunlight with Bettina there. She had ideas, and she had ways of moving things so that with four people instead of two, the flat actually seemed to have more space. She pulled the rug from Peg's bed and flung it over the shabby settee. Peg had never imagined such a transformation possible.

The next day at school she thought all the time, with pleasure, of going home to Bettina. Towards the end of the afternoon two girls in the music room were practising the duet from Orpheus, the young voices carried the pleading and the refusal along the empty corridors. Peg, hurrying to her poetry class, was moved by the two voices singing with so much feeling. She had never noticed before how the perfection of the harmony enhanced the feeling. To accompany her poetry reading she chose music with drums and a song with a throbbing beat. In the class room suddenly there seemed a sharing of anticipation and pleasure. She told her girls how to find the pulse which was the heart beat.

'Put your right forefinger on your left wrist, inside, in line with the thumb and feel your own hearts beating,' she said. And, feeling the steady beat of her own heart, she thought of Bettina and read

But hark my pulse
like a soft drum
Beats my approach
tells thee I come.

'Now listen again to the music,' she said. 'Listen to the music of the drums and listen to the beating of the heart in the poem,

But hark my pulse
like a soft drum
Beats my approach
tells thee I come.'

The little flat was so close to the school, it would take only a few minutes to be back there with Bettina.

Downstairs in the hotel the young English man was still at the reception desk. He was pale with bluish rings round his eyes. He could not do anything for them he said. 'No food is served during the night,' he said.

'That's no way to treat hotel guests!' Peg was angry. For herself it did not really matter, but there was Bettina. 'My friend is very tired,' she said. She was tall, taller than the young man. In her awkwardness and anger she was more unkind in her voice than she meant to be. They were both extremely tired after their journey.

'Tomorrow I shall see the hotel manager. I shall report you and we shall move somewhere else.'

A deep colour spread over the young man's haggard face. As if it hurt him to blush, his eyes looked as if they would burst in tears out of his face. Looking down at his feet he said, 'Just a minute, I'll see what I can do.' He slipped away through a small door curtained off behind the desk.

At once Peg felt incredibly unhappy. She had made an unbearable mistake in speaking to him as she had. His pale eyes looked at her in disbelief as the little veins and capillaries, misplaced on his crooked boyish face, slowly reddened. She had not imagined that she could strip him of covering and dignity. It was as if she had peeled him and left him raw without his skin. It wasn't his fault, she thought.

'What a perfect drip!' Bettina said. She walked restlessly in the poorly lit foyer. The hotel was not one which reminded of better or more glorious days. It seemed as if it had never known much of anything.

'What I need,' Bettina said, 'is a nice bath, now!'

It was not possible to put on the hot water during the night the young man explained when he came back.

'It will be on at six o'clock sharp,' he promised them, almost sharing the tones of an Indian as though, having discussed with the person in charge, he had taken on the voice. Peg had for a moment, in her mind, a picture of the Indian proprietress, glossy and fat, propping herself on her elbow in bed to speak to the young man, uneasy at disturbing her, half in the doorway of her stuffy room. She imagined the voice.

'Tell them it will be on at six o'clock sharp.'

The young man brought with him a handsome little tray of beaten metal with cracker biscuits, some sort of sweets in silver foil, a banana and an orange, two small glasses and a small bottle of soda water.

The young women, not pleased, carried their supper upstairs, looking up anxiously to the square of yellow light which came from their open door.

'I should have chosen a better hotel, dearest,' Peg apologized while they examined the sweets. The bath water trickling made Bettina very impatient.

'It's going to take ages to fill that great big bath,' she complained.

'It will be cold,' Peg said, and shivered.

'I must get to a cold tub.' It seemed to Peg that Bettina was obsessed in some way, or ill. Peg longed to comfort Bettina but felt awkward and foolish in the strange surroundings, and Bettina had lost her happy carelessness in her present trouble. Peg, on her own, could not achieve carelessness.

Though Bettina had borrowed five hundred dollars from Peg, it was Peg who paid their fares. She was the one earning money. Because of this she carried money and she paid. As many generous people do, Peg suffered from moments of knowing that she was behaving stupidly with her hard-earned money. She disliked, not Bettina, she loved her, she found herself disliking the moments when she knew how foolish she was over the money and the giving of presents. The money was not lent to Bettina, it was given because Peg could never, and did not, expect it to be returned. Thinking of this made her feel huge and stupid. She disliked, if it was possible to dislike, and perhaps it was just possible, more so in India, to hear Bettina's ways of asking for money, the particular note in her voice, the false half-swallowed words in her special language when describing her moneyless plight.

'It's terrible to be without money darling,' Peg agreed and soothed. 'But you've no need to worry, honestly, there's no need.'

'That's just where you're so wrong,' Bettina said, her hoarse voice, which normally attracted, becoming rough. 'I'm right down on the rocks, though I hate to talk about it I simply don't know how I'll manage. Everything costs so much. I don't like saying this, but it's . . . it's all very well for you, you've got it, but when you haven't it's serious. You see I haven't a soul in the world I can ask, no one at all to help me.'

Peg was touched deeply. She kissed Bettina on her wet hair.

'Come out of that miserable bath,' she said softly. 'We ought to get to bed, d'you know it's nearly three and we'll have to get up quite early.'

'I really need money badly,' Bettina said. 'I hate asking favours of anyone, specially you.'

Peg, even more touched, put her arms round Bettina. She did not allow herself even a moment's thought about the five hundred dollars and its apparent disappearance.

'You're sweet, really sweet,' she said tenderly. 'Come on, let's try to forget all the sad things, it's so sweet to be alone together,' she said. 'Come to bed.'

Peg tried and Bettina tried.

'How can I set up as a faith healer when I'm scratching myself to ribbons,' Bettina complained. She sat bouncing angrily away to the side of the bed, her eyes red rimmed and sore with lack of sleep and infection.

'Bettina, darling, you must not scratch!' Peg, appalled, tried to comfort her. 'And really you shouldn't rub your eyes, you'll make them much worse.'

'Oh, what's the use!' Bettina said. 'I feel every minute as if I could bring it off but I can't. I just can't get there!'

She got up and moved restlessly all round the room, she picked up Peg's hair brush. 'Perhaps this'd do the trick.' She put it down. 'Oh! I could scream,' she almost screamed.

'Perhaps you should see a doctor,' Peg suggested gently. She felt the disappointment too, with the failure of their first night really alone together; the disappointment of being sleepless and having to understand that sensations from disease can easily be confused with other sensations, but do not respond and bring about the desired relief and satisfaction.

'Perhaps you should see a doctor,' Peg suggested again, just as gently as before.

'Me see one of the crummy doctors here!' Bettina was scornful. 'I can handle this myself,' she went into their bathroom and, as there was now water in plenty, she mixed herself another bath.

'Some Indian doctors are very good,' Peg said from the doorway. Bettina lay back in the water.

'Good at fleecing,' Bettina said. 'I'd have to pay through the nose,' she said. 'Who'd pay,' she said. 'You know I haven't got a bean.'

'I'll pay,' Peg said quietly.

'If they're so good why don't you go!'

'Me?' Peg said. 'Why should I go?'

'Because,' Bettina said, 'because you're sure to need to soon.'

Before setting out for the house in the hills where the faith healer was known to give classes in his art, Peg and Bettina went together to shops in Madras and bought scented lotions and medicinal oils. Bettina would try them all she said.

The two hundred dollar taxi ride was frightening, partly because of the loneliness and wildness of the countryside, but mainly because of Bettina's frantic need for another bath, and her inability to be comfortable sitting still. She was not comfortable walking either, and when the driver stopped the car on the particularly steep and nasty little road, Peg suffered severe misgivings for Bettina.

'Here we have to walk only this last part,' their driver said. 'Follow me, is not in the least difficult to walk, but for car is not possible!' He set off rapidly.

The two young women, Peg with raised eyebrows, and carrying a case, and Bettina with her tiny picturesque bundle slung over her shoulder, slowly followed.

It was soon clear why the car had to remain so dangerously parked on the steep bend. The rains had washed deep gullies across and into the road. These gullies gaped so horribly Peg did not trust herself to step or jump from one crumbling edge to the other. The first one was so deep it was not possible to see to the bottom of it; it was wide enough for a man to fall down, and narrow enough to make it impossible to rescue him. Peg felt dizzy on the edge of it. The road too made her feel dizzy. On one side the hill went up solidly like a wall and on the other side there was nothing; the slope fell away so steeply she could not bear to look over. A long way down this steep hillside were dark ugly scars of earth and rock, where the water, during the rains, like an infection taking the line of least resistance, found a way out from these bottomless holes.

The driver, as if aware of their fear, for they were afraid, straddled the first gully, his thin feet, in the unsuitable patent leather shoes, hardly planted in either edge. His undernourished body swayed backwards, dangerously, but quite faithfully unconcerned that death was certain with one clumsy movement. He held out his hand to Peg.

'Trust me,' he said simply. She thought his hand too small and too incompetent but she was wrong. As she made her first jump she knew he felt safe because it simply did not matter to him whether he stood there helping the ladies or whether he fell like a little cloth doll, head over heels, all the way down to the bottom of the hill. His life and their lives, so it seemed to Peg as she made her landing, were all to him as only a small part of something much greater. His own life was of little consequence to him. She wondered perhaps if she would ever be able to cultivate and keep this thought for herself, and living on it, give this same impression.

The last day of the term came into her mind, the last tea time in the staff room where Miss Moles was waiting for her when the other teachers had gone. Peg had been anxious to slip off quickly to Bettina. Miss Moles had saved a cream cake for her.

'Pegeen!' Miss Moles was excited. 'In so far as being head

mistress is concerned I am at last joining the ranks of the liberated! For the first time in my life, and not too soon either.' She paused. 'Pegeen, I am at last a whole complete woman, fulfilled at last! I am myself pregnant!'

Peg was shocked, though she did not say so. She would have liked to say how lonely it was being a mother on your own. She said nothing, even though she knew Miss Moles would regard what she said as being important. Miss Moles discussed all kinds of things with her. They were usually the last for afternoon tea and the time was suitable for conversation, or so Miss Moles thought.

'Let me see.' Miss Moles hurried on as if to cover up the unexpected silence from Peg. 'We don't seem to have one pregnant girl in the school,' she said sounding disappointed. 'When I was teaching in the East End some years ago a number of the school girls were preggers. Some were already mothers, their babies were in the school creche. The girls, you know Peg, were encouraged to feed and bath their babies there, and to attend their lessons as usual.' Miss Moles paused thoughtfully, her keen eyes searching Peg's. 'Some of the boys went to the nursery quite unselfconsciously, you know, and nursed the babies or watched the young mothers. Really quite touching and lovely,' Miss Moles sighed. 'It doesn't seem to happen like that now,' she said and then, squaring her shoulders, she said, 'I shall of course remain at the school as long as possible, and later I hope to . . . or should I say, we hope to come back. We shall come back. Who was it who said, "The value of education is the knowledge of its worth." ' Miss Moles took a deep breath and looked hard at Peg, it was a moment of deep emotion for her, 'Well, Peg,' she said. 'Have a splendid holiday. Ad astra per arduam and all the rest of it.'

Peg had very little imagination, and so her thoughts hardly ever intruded but, in the moment of relief at being on firm ground, she laughed. Suddenly she was wondering about the moment of conception. Miss Moles in charge of all those girls was herself an eternal school girl. Peg laughed again, Miss Moles awkwardly undressing? Or had someone undressed her?

'Miss Moles!' she said aloud.

Bettina, making her jump with the little Indian, did not notice Peg laughing and talking to herself. Bettina would never be interested in Miss Moles, but Peg's mother would be sure to ask, 'What's Miss Moles been up to now?'

Bettina cleared the gully safely. And slowly, gully by gully, they made their way up to the house, which was almost hidden by the steepness of the hill and an overgrown garden which had been planned for the kind of leisure enjoyed by those who do not have to work.

Even when they could see the house they still had a long way to walk to it. The secluded garden hinted at secret meetings. Voluptuous but broken curves of marble and fragmented white balustrade, moss covered and hidden by leaves and branches, achieved a desolation which seemed to come towards them as they approached. It was impossible not to notice the dirty arms and legs of once admired statues, and they turned back quickly from a flight of steps which led down through the damp earth to broken marble baths of enormous size and filled with rubbish. Clearly, the garden held all the fallen-down summer hiding places of lovers long since forgotten.

No one came out to meet them.

The house was double storeyed with balconies. It was white, stained and crusted from the weather and from birds. All the windows were boarded and no sound of any kind came from within.

Peg felt very cold and she was frightened too.

'The front door's open,' Bettina cried in triumph. 'It's wedged, it only needs a shove.' She kicked off her shoes. 'Come on Peg!' Together they pushed the door open a little way.

'I don't think we ought to just barge in,' Peg said. 'Perhaps we should knock.' She wondered what sort of person would answer the door.

288

'I'm so hot and thirsty Peg. Ring the bell Peg. Can you see a bell Peg?' Bettina was excited. 'Thank God we're here at last!'

Peg shivered. She wondered again about Bettina being so hot, and her ever-present thirst. It was as if she burned inside and could not cool this burning. She wished she could persuade Bettina to go to a doctor.

'You know, Bettina dear,' Peg had renewed her attempts at persuasion during the taxi ride. 'I always go to the doctor if I think I've got something wrong with me.'

'Oh yes, sure!' Bettina had scoffed. 'I can just see you taking every blemish on your body to show to the doctor; doctor,' she mimicked, 'see here doctor, I've got a freckle on my bum, is it dangerous?'

As Peg looked at the house, and thought of the need for a doctor when there was no hope of finding one, she felt more and more hopeless. How stupid she'd been to come.

'Come on Peg, don't be so wet!' Bettina was impatient.

'Is a very nice house,' the driver said. 'But is empty, quite empty.'

'It can't be!' Bettina's voice was high pitched and sharp.

'Oh yes,' he said simply. 'I can see at once it is empty,' he shrugged. 'It has all the signs of an empty house, do you not see for yourselves, it has not people.'

'But the faith healer wrote that he lived here,' Peg explained gently and firmly as if her explanation could place him at once in the house and cause him to come out to welcome them.

'Madam,' the driver said. 'I should think no longer.' And there was no reply to this.

They did not walk far into the deserted house. The once noble staircase was melancholy. Their footsteps and voices made too much noise so they crept rather than walked, and they talked in whispers.

'It's a lovely house,' Bettina's hoarse voice reached Peg. 'But just look at the dreadful plastic lampshades, and here's a packet of custard powder!' Disappointment in her laugh made Peg sorrier than ever. Restlessly Bettina peered into rooms.

'There's only a few dirty old mats,' she complained. 'It's such a shame! I love the stairs. The house could be so lovely, it is lovely!'

'Yes, very nice house, but is quite empty,' their driver insisted.

Bettina stood by the partly open door. 'I love it here,' she said, 'I think it's glorious here, look at the view. I shall sleep in one of the rooms looking out this way, a room with a window looking out down there. Think of waking up every morning to see that view.'

But Peg could not see any beauty, she could not look for any mountain, purple in the distance, and she had no idea if any river was close by. She could not look at beauty there however much it may have been at her feet.

'Bettina dearest, we can't stay,' she said.

'He may come back at any moment.' Bettina did not seem worried at all by the isolation or the deserted appearance of the house. 'He's sure to come soon,' she said.

'But where on earth could he come from?' Peg asked uneasily. Bettina, she thought, did not seem to notice that it would be dark soon.

'Wonnerful ride back, for you, very cheap.' The taxi driver had the immediate solution for his own problem.

How comfortable an aeroplane was, Peg thought on her return journey. It was better to travel alone. Most of her present exhaustion had come from Bettina's ambition and the trouble of her sudden symptoms. This illness she was sure had not come about from dirtiness. Bettina looked dirty, especially when she went round the supermarket dressed in an old towel knotted high up under her armpits, but she was really very clean and very fresh in her youth and her wish for life. It was something in life which had spoiled her. It was an infection from living.

A little extra tenderness for Bettina welled up in Peg. She was fifteen years older, that in itself was an indication; the fifteen years, or some of them, should bear the responsibility. Mixed with the tenderness was envy too, not for the illness which was too horrible, but because she had to admit to herself that she had none of Bettina's ability to turn experience into moments of pure happiness.

Though she longed for Kerry it was a relief to be travelling without her. Kerry was ambitious and wanted things, so that there was never any real rest in her company either, or with the imaginary Doossa who was always even more in need than Kerry of every dress, every toy, every sweet, and all the other unnameable never ending wants. Doossa had, through the years of being Kerry's ever present companion, been an equal destroyer of rest.

There were similarities between Miranda and Doossa, Miranda, perhaps more explicit in her needs and, of course, since her arrival Doossa had disappeared.

It really was better to travel alone. To travel with Lucien, Peg discovered at once that she needed tremendous energy, and personal discipline, to keep up with his cleanliness.

'Your young man looks so clean,' her mother said after seeing him for the first time. 'He looks as if you could safely eat your dinner off him! If you marry him, Peg my girl, you'll spend your days in the laundry tub.'

Peg told her mother, 'He's got such a terrible landlady, Mother, at the place where he lives. Every time he uses the toilet she rushes in straight after and cleans it with a brush.'

'Well,' her mother replied, 'I suppose if he'd seen to it himself she wouldn't have needed to.'

Peg never discussed Lucien with her mother after that except once, at the beginning, when they read his first poems together, *Come live with me and be my love/And we will all the pleasures prove,* and there the discussion really only took the form of a pause at the two lines. Knowing that they were not the young

291

poet's but, as if by an unspoken agreement about the possibilities for the future, neither of the women said anything. Though later Peg's mother said to Peg, when they were alone, 'I like those two lines, Peg, and what's said in them. All Lucy's got to do is put a couple of inverted commas and it doesn't matter then who's written them.'

'His name's Lucien, Mother, not Lucy.'

'Of course, Lucien,' her mother said.

Peg knew too that Lucien's cleanliness and freshness was more an appearance of both these qualities. This was a shock. But even so, keeping up appearance was a lot of work. She guessed too that with other people there were appearances and shocks, and that the other people managed to live in spite of them. It did not occur to her then that Lucien may have experienced some sort of shock too, but was either too well mannered or too unconcerned to mention it.

There was nothing of shock in his final poem. But by then he had passed on to other experience.

Bettina slept most of the way back on the ride down from the hills. She slept sweetly and Peg, feeling her body so innocently and so trustingly against her own as the car swung and jolted, experienced fresh tenderness and desire for her friend. Perhaps she would be better soon. Peg felt she must get Bettina cured quickly. Perhaps they would find another faith healer anxious to pass on his art to those with the gift in their finger tips, or wherever it was the gift concealed itself. Faith healing, Peg told herself in the dark car, could do so much for mankind. Lovingly she steadied the sleeping Bettina. She pictured her walking lightly between rows of sufferers putting her soft hands on a stomach here and on a stomach there and, for a moment, she smiled as she saw the tortured faces of those who had been in such pain looking up at their little healer with gratitude.

But pain was pain and came from a cause, tooth ache, appendicitis, gall stones, any kind of pain had to be regarded with truth and Peg, in her heart, knew she had to put aside Bettina's skill. Bettina, she thought, should be encouraged to sit at a desk and study, she should give up the idea of the feet of the faith healer. Rattling along in the taxi Peg acknowledged the necessity of having doctors and nurses and dentists. In the morning she would gently and firmly tell Bettina,

'Bettina darling, listen to me, if something is bad and has to be removed from the body then nothing will do but to remove it. It's no use, Bettina, to cover a splinter of wood, or glass, or metal with a clean rag or a bandage. Bettina, however much a person might care for another person, love them and observe them, if something needs to be taken out from the body, it has to be taken out. If there is an infection in the body it has to be identified and treated. Bettina, faith and belief are good but by themselves they are not enough.'

Peg fidgetted in the car and smoothed her knee-length blue and white dress. Sometimes the good quality of her clothes worried her, she felt she was not casual enough about them.

Straight away on that first evening Bettina had examined Peg's wardrobe. She needed to wash out her skirt, she said, and laughing she thought Peg might have something she could borrow. She had not been in the flat an hour.

'Why ever don't you get some long things, dresses or skirts— instead of these, I never saw such boring colours!' she said, tossing through Peg's dresses and suits.

'I've never worn anything long,' Peg said shyly.

'There's always a first time,' Bettina said.

Bettina was probably right about her clothes. She was so used to dressing suitably for school.

'I feel absolutely huge in this,' Peg said to Bettina in the hotel bedroom. They had needed to rest after the long drive down from the house in the hills. She turned round slowly in the cramped space. 'It's just not me!' she said plaintively. Awkwardly she peeled off the prickly cotton caftan bought hastily during the early morning hunt for the scented and medicinal oils for Bettina. 'It's such a gorgeous colour, this orange,' she sighed. 'You try it on.' She passed the garment to Bettina. 'Perhaps we could make it smaller for you, it's your colour.' She patted herself, regretting her height and the size of her creamy thighs. Carefully she shook out her dress and hung it up. The heavy silky material would endure. The blobs of blue and white reassured her, the pattern was so meaningless and safe.

'I'm starving!' Bettina ignored Peg's clothes. 'Let's go out to an expensive restaurant and have some really good food.' She was feeling a lot better she said. Peg laughed and quickly tucked her nightdress back under the pillow. She kissed her friend's round wet head.

'Of course, darling,' she said. 'That's a wonderful idea.'

In the busy restaurant in Madras, Peg started to think of her home-coming. She ate the large and expensive meal alone. On the table were dishes of curried meat and fish and vegetables. There were small dishes among the larger ones which looked as if children, playing, had arranged fragments of fruit and ginger, generously covered with shredded coconut. There were platters of rice patted into balls. Some balls were coloured and stuffed with prunes and sultanas. On a side table were a dozen tiny plates, as if put there for a dolls' tea party. The little plates were filled with various Indian sweets and puddings which shivered when they were moved. She hardly noticed the food. She thought she would cry. But to cry in a place where people have come to enjoy themselves, and particularly to enjoy food, is hardly acceptable, so Peg did not cry. She ate the unwanted food quickly, glancing shyly from time to time at all the different people and their different ways of eating. The restaurant was crowded.

Bettina, as soon as they had chosen their meal and ordered it, thought she saw someone she knew sitting at a table on the far side of the room.

'I must just go over,' she said. 'See you around Peg.'

Thinking about going home while she ate alone in the restaurant was just the right thing for Peg to do. She needed to be comforted and looked after, and the best place for these needs was the farm, so far away but so close in her thoughts.

Her holiday time was all before her. She would take her mother and Kerry to the sea. They could manage a trip in one day so that the animals need not be left uncared for. Peg remembered going with her mother years ago. Her mother drove the car, a crazy carload of girls, a neighbour had once described them, with beach towels and food to the sea. They always went to the same place, to an estuary where the river widened till the banks were hardly visible. On one side there was a wooden structure known as the baths. There it was possible to swim safely protected from waves, hidden currents and sharks, inside grey splitboard fences supported by enormous grey weathered piles. The lively water lapped to and fro through the spaces between the boards. Only small harmless things moved with the freedom of the water, in and out of the boards.

Out of their depths Peg and her sisters clung to the piles and peered at the expanse of swelling river through the wide cracks. The water, outside the fence, shone and rippled and the swell, as it came and went, lifted them up and dragged them down so that their screams and laughter were a mixture of high-pitched joy and a choking and gasping tor breath. Sometimes one of them pretended to sink, crying for help, one arm raised high, and then disappearing with only thin white fingers above the water,

'Hep! Hep! I'm drowning. Hep! Hep!' And the others, splashing and kicking, pretended to rescue.

The angry old man, the attendant, said no one should ever pretend to drown. He gave swimming lessons to the children of the well-to-do. He stood up to his chest in water, hour after hour, giving private tuition to individual children. Their rich mothers sat nearby on the solid boards round the baths to make sure their children were having their money's worth. He said he taught every child separately, but it was clear he was shouting to at least twenty children at once.

Peg and her sisters threw jelly fish at one another and the old man said they must move away, and keep away from the serious swimmers. Peg's mother told him to hold his tongue or else she'd report him and his open pan lavatories. Peg smiled as she remembered the days in the river and she smiled even more as she thought how she would take Kerry and her mother there as soon as possible.

There was no doubt that air travel was very comfortable, quite mindless in a sense, because it was not possible to do anything about anything, however much you might want to.

She suspected she had been dozing instead of reading, she had a book open on her lap, like an old woman, she thought, but the last few days had been too much. Among other things, Bettina had a sore on her lip. It was not there one day and then the next day there it was broken and painful.

'You should eat fresh fruit,' Peg was gentle and quick with advice. 'Bettina dear, fresh oranges. I'll get you some.'

'I'll hit the roof with them,' Bettina said and refused the fruit. Peg had the extra sorrow of knowing that Bettina was in more pain, the sight of the dry cracked painful lip was more than Peg could stand. She suffered dreadfully for every one of Bettina's symptoms. She admitted, for she was always honest with herself, silently, that more than a small part of her suffering was intense disappointment for, in knowing Bettina, Peg had come to know passion and desire for the first time in her life.

She had never imagined that travelling could be so dream like. It was strange to be purring like a cat through the sky, with clouds on either side looking like soft mountains which could be walked on quite easily.

Soon it would get dark, and be dark before she could reach home.

Perhaps because of the sense of being not responsible during the journey, Peg remembered the times of mounting and heightened feeling between Lucien and his friend, a pretty young man with prematurely white hair and clean childish clothes. Taking no part in her aeroplane journey was like being on the edge of the rising laughter of the two young men. She took no part in that either but moved on in her life, rather as if on a quiet journey. She was not discontented.

'Sit! Sit for me Maria, Marienchen,' Jaffa would say to Peg. He imitated Lucien in saying she was Mary, Maria the Madonna. 'You are a nice plain one,' he said. 'With your smooth face, it is an oval! And your smooth neat hair and this—your big big belly. Let me feel,' he said, placing his delicate hand where he thought the baby's feet would kick. Peg smiled.

'Ah!' Jaffa said. 'You must sit for me, just like this, you must sit,' and he described circles in the air with an imaginary camel hair brush. And then he ran back a little and, after a little pause, ran forward in a nimble little dance squinting at her, his head on one side, screwing up his eyes, measuring the proportions of her body, seeing where her shadows lay, noticing her stillness.

'One day I am going to paint you,' he said every time he went through this amusing little ritual. 'I'll paint you with your baby at your fine breast,' he promised. 'You will be the Madonna del Jaffa!'

But by the time Kerry was born Jaffa did not come to visit them any more and Lucien had a new friend. It happened that one night Jaffa and Lucien had a quarrel. Peg heard them from where she lay in the next room reading herself to sleep. Jaffa stabbed Lucien with Peg's embroidery scissors, it was not serious in itself.

'But it's the idea!' Lucien sobbed his startled grief and pain onto Peg's big stomach and she stroked his soft fair hair, and comforted him. When Jaffa called the next day to say he was sorry Peg answered the door and, towering over the frightened young man, she sent him away.

'I'll come back and paint you when you know your misery,' Jaffa said over his shoulder. 'I'll paint you when your lap is full, I'll paint you in a Pietà!' It was a threat. Peg felt it then, in spite of it being uttered chokingly through rising tears. She never forgot how he looked at her, though in her comfortable way, she did not spend much time later wondering about his words.

Lucien and his friends laughed and laughed, and often spent hours teasing and sulking in turns. When they were melancholy it was impossible to rouse them. Peg knew better than to try. She did not laugh with them, but neither did she waste time sharing in any of their unhappiness.

When Peg sat holding Bettina close between her strong naked thighs they did not speak. It was serious and they did not laugh. Peg thought it was sweet and tender to cherish this young Bettina, so very sweet and special. She would have liked to say more to Bettina about her happiness; perhaps to say that all the time she was at school she was looking forward to the times when they could forget everything except the excitement of their kisses and the pleasure of caressing each other. She would have liked to ask Bettina exactly how she felt, perhaps to ask too if Bettina loved her as she loved Bettina. There was not much use in thinking about any of it since it had come to an end.

Years ago at the baths a little girl pushed her foot through the split fence and then was unable to pull it out. Peg's older sister tried to help the child. The water, slapping and tossing, came up too high, and Peg saw them struggling, almost fighting in the water. As she watched, trying to keep herself afloat, she felt herself choking. The water seemed to rise in a tower, there was nothing under her feet, and she had to struggle up, up in the tower of water.

From the bank and the entrance to the baths the water always looked smooth and peaceful. It had a vigorous life of its own, which did not show from the bank. Perhaps all water was secretive.

In spite of praise and comfort from the people, Peg's sister cried and cried in the car on the way home.

'Hold your noise or you'll get something to cry about.' It was not often their mother slapped anyone, but sometimes she said there were times when she needed to slap someone.

Lucien's new friend, the one in the final poem, was called Helen. Peg had never seen her.

'I really ought to have married a gynaecologist,' Lucien used to say at parties.

'Why, Lucien darling,' people laughed, their elegant fingers clutching their drinks, their beads and each other.

'Because,' Lucien said with his arm resting lightly round Peg's thick shoulder, 'they earn so much more than teachers, eh Peg?'

Peg did not mind, it was one of Lucien's little party jokes. Perhaps Helen was the longed-for gynaecologist. Because she was on her way home it did not seem to matter.

It was dark when Peg at last reached the little farm. There were no lights on in the house. She had difficulty getting in because both doors were hanging broken and wedged.

'Mother!' she called in a frightened voice. It seemed as if she was returning after being away for years instead of a few days. There was a different smell about the house. She thought it might be because of all the strange smells of India she had forgotten the smell of home. Perhaps too it was the severe change from excitement and anticipation, as well as the very long journeys, which helped to give this impression of being away for such a long time.

'Mother! Mother! What's happened? Mother are you there?' She stood quite still in the dark. All the anxiety of the last few hours seemed gathered in this one spot. She had waited and waited for Bettina in the hotel room. The night seemed impossibly long and lonely as she, half sleeping, waited for Bettina to come.

Bettina did not return that night nor the next day, and Peg, afraid of being all alone in the strange city, and with no reason to go on staying there, packed her few things, paid the bill, and set off for home. Now here she was at home at last. Standing in the dark kitchen; without really wanting to, she found herself thinking of Lucien, and she remembered the first time she had brought him to the farm. It was after one of Miss Moles' poetry evenings. She quite often had small performances as she called them, intimate evenings of music and poetry at her own house. Miss Moles unselfishly never read her own poems, but simply invited others to read, while she busied herself even more unselfishly in the kitchen bringing out sandwiches and cups of coffee at the right moments.

Peg first met Lucien at Miss Moles' house. Lucien was so fair, his hair was cream coloured like Peg's. He was young and tender like a sapling. While the other poets read he sat with his eyes closed, deep in concentration and, when it was his turn to read, he repeatedly looked up from the pages, looking straight at Peg till it seemed he was reading only for her. When the others applauded, they clapped for them both, as though Peg was a part of the poetry. She felt she was.

Lucien sat down gracefully beside her. He was grateful to her, for some reason he thanked her. Peg was touched. She was going home that night to the farm she told him, and Lucien said how wonderful to be going out to the country on a summer night.

'You can come with me,' Peg said to him quite simply.

'Oh could I,' the young man said. 'Oh could I!'

'Yes, of course, but it's a long drive.' She was laughing.

'But would it be all right if I came?' he asked.

'Oh yes, of course, Mother would love to have you come.'

They arrived during the hay-filled night, the moonlight lay in silent patches over the land and the sheds. A sweet smell came up as the night air touched the grass. Peg took Lucien by the hand to lead him into the dark kitchen.

'Mother!' she called. 'Mother it's me, Peg, are you awake?'

The old woman roused herself and welcomed the young poet and made up a bed for him in the living room. The next morning he sat up in his bed and saw the long narrow paddock which came right up to the window. He looked down the slope to the willow trees overhanging the dam.

'It's enchanting,' he said to Peg later that day, and he asked her to marry him, and he wrote a poem about it.

'Mother!' Peg, alone in the dark kitchen, called softly. 'Mother it's me, Peg, are you awake?' In the dark she was unable to find any matches on the mantlepiece.

'Mother? Kerry? it's me Peg, I've come home.' She thought she heard a moaning from the bedroom and then a slight rustling.

'Here's matches,' Miranda burrowed in the case. Peg lit the lamp. The kitchen smelled of sour milk. The children must have been playing with the dishes and saucepans, they were all over the table with spoons in them and bits of bread and broken-up biscuits. Some dishes were broken on the floor. Miranda, very sleepy, rubbed her eyes.

'Where's Bettina? Where's my mommy?' She began to cry.

'She's coming later, pet, now hush your crying.' Peg took the lamp into the disordered bedroom.

'Mother!'

The old woman moved slightly, she moaned and she did not know her daughter. Peg could smell the infection and, when she saw the swollen angry leg, she knew she must do something quickly.

'Where's Kerry?' she asked Miranda. 'Is she asleep?'

Together they went down through the sweet-smelling dry grass and stood at the edge of the ugly dam. The willow trees were dark and motionless at the edge of the secretive water.

Something moved lightly on the water, a shadow crossing that light which water holds in the night.

Peg called, 'Kerry?' knowing it was stupid. 'Kerry?' she called softly.

'It's the gooses,' Miranda, clutching Peg's skirt, explained. The geese slowly floated from the black shadows of the willows and circled slowly in the shining unmoving water. They made no noise and they were without blame. The only sound in the stillness was from the grasshoppers. They kept up their monotonous sound all night, it was not possible not to notice it.

In the narrow space at the side of her mother's bed Peg crouched and cried and cried as she had never cried before. It did not need imagination to know this grief would be there for the rest of her life.

'These sweets are for you Kerry and these sweets are for me Kerry these are for you to eat now and these are for you to eat later . . . Peg tell Kerry not to eat her sweets the ones for later I mean Peg tell Kerry it's my turn to wear the party dress . . . these are my clothes Kerry and these clothes are yours Kerry . . .'

Peg heard the weary voice of the child somewhere behind and inside her own weariness. Miranda, too near to Peg, pretended to play, talking in a silly voice almost falling asleep and then waking in an endless energetic imagination. Peg at last stopped crying and set about what she had to do. Because of what she already carried there, she knew it would be some time before she would be able to take this other child on her lap.

Self
Portrait

A Child Went Forth

There was a child went forth every day,
And the first object he looked upon and
received with wonder or pity
or love or dread, that object he became . . .

Whitman

When I was seventeen I sold my doll and all her little frocks and coloured knitted things. At the time I thought I ought to sell her, it seemed important to have some extra money. She was advertised for one pound. It was near Christmas, a good time for selling.

A woman came and I saw her alone with the doll in the front room where my mother had made a fire as she did only on Christmas Day and other holidays.

The parting with the doll made an unexpected dark space all round me. I never admitted to anyone that I gave the doll to the woman whose sharp, unfriendly eyes intimidated me and whose tale of a little girl who had never had a doll filled me with shame.

My mother and sister were waiting in the early dusk of the winter afternoon.

'Where is the money?' my sister said to my empty heart.

305

'In my purse of course,' I lied.

Byron wrote to Murray, his publisher:

all reading either praise or censure of myself has done me harm—when I was in Switzerland I was out of the way of hearing either—AND HOW I WROTE THERE!

But Byron was very willing to write about himself, not only in his poems and journals but in twelve volumes of letters. He, clearly, often wrote a self portrait.

It is flattering to be asked to follow this precedent established long before and continued long after Byron's time. But what should go into a self portrait if it is to hold a reader's attention, let alone convey something of understanding?

Perhaps a writer's self portrait should concentrate on those aspects of life which appear to influence the writing. Looking over my own work I have been surprised to find how important is the theme of exile.

It is not given to the child either to know or to understand the happiness or the sadness of the parent. Clytemnestra speaks of this to her daughter, Electra, when she arrives at the dirty hut where the banished Electra lives:

. . . I agree, one should not speak
Bitterly. But when people judge someone,
*   they ought*
To learn the facts, and then hate, if they've
*   reason to*
And if they find no reason, then they should
*   not hate.*

My mother and father were married in Vienna soon after the Great War which ended in defeat and destruction of the Hapsburg Empire. Vienna was no longer the administrative centre of a large Empire. Filled with almost destitute inhabitants, it became an overlarge capital of a small nation. My grandfather, who had been a General in the Imperial Army, belonged now to that large class whose reason for existence disappeared with the Emperor.

It is not surprising that my mother saw in the young Englishman not merely an acceptable husband but a way back to prosperity and social status. An understandable but disastrous error. My mother found herself in an England which was not made up of castles and country estates but which was urban, industrial, dirty and mean. An England and a people which were beyond her understanding. She responded to her new surrounding with imitation and contempt. My father must have made great efforts to compensate.

'Your mother has such pretty arms,' he often said. He defended her from the world and from herself. Perhaps my vicarious experience of homesickness and exile starts, without any knowledge or understanding, from the early memories of incomprehensible unhappiness.

My mother and father always spoke German together and I spoke German till I was six when I started school and then, surrendering to my surroundings, I stopped speaking German.

My father was an exile of a different kind. During the Great War he suffered brutal imprisonment as a conscientious objector. His father, my other grandfather, disowned him because of his beliefs and the disgrace of being in prison. He went to Vienna as a relief worker with the Quakers. His position in his father's house was not improved by his bringing back, as a bride, an impoverished aristocrat from an enemy country. When speaking of this, once in later years, he was not bitter about his father but he did say that he felt that for many years, because of the experience, he had been 'warped'. In an embarrassed way he was, at the time, trying to make some sort of explanation and apology to me.

307

When I was a child we lived in a neighbourhood where foreigners were regarded with curiosity if not outright distrust.
Opinions were those of George Eliot's villagers;

In that far-off time superstition clung easily round every
person or thing that was at all unwonted . . . and how was
a man to be explained unless you at least knew somebody
who knew his father and mother?

'My mam's bakin' yo' a cake,' a little boy I played with said,
' 'er says yor mam can't cook.' The cake was never delivered
but it's the thought that counts.

My father was a science teacher. In him were contained all
the conflicts between science, human effort and feeling and what
is called, in a lump, religion. Thinking that children lost their
innocence at school he took my sister and me away from school.
I was eight years old then and my sister was seven. My father
and mother and a rapid succession of French and German gov-
ernesses provided what education we received. Perhaps we
learned most from the BBC school programmes. Images sprang
at once from quality and tone of voice whether the voice was
describing the plight of the Flying Dutchman, the remarks made
in Parliament or the necessity of taking off one's vest every
night to shake out the germs gathered during the day.

Children who do not go to school and whose family speak a
foreign language are exiles in their own street. Like all lonely
children we retreated into the fantasy and imagination. The
people who lived in our dolls' houses are still alive. One of my
characters, Weekly in the novel *The Newspaper of Claremont*
Street, though I did not realise this for some time, comes, in
part, from the tiny, well-cleaned kitchen of my sister's dolls'
house. On bus and train journeys we drew pencil people in
what we called Day Books and we shouted their dialogue and
their actions across the other passengers to one another. This
game lasted for years; perhaps in our letter writing we still

continue it. It is continued on bits of paper, in solitude, at my own table now.

My mother never allowed us to have long hair. Some may recall the haircut called a shingle. An old lady, passing the dusty hedge in front of our house, paused to ask us:

'Are you two girls or boys?'

'I'm Monica Elizabeth,' I explained, 'she's Madelaine Winifred. We're boys.'

At the age of eleven I was sent with my father's reluctant permission to a Quaker boarding school in rural Oxfordshire. Being brought up as a Quaker is not the same as being a Quaker by Birth. I was an exile on the edge of the Birth Right Quakers. Unaccustomed to being with other children and missing the smell of the bone and glue factory and the heave and roar of the blast furnaces, I cried. Between autumn-berried hedge rows I cried in the middle of a road which seemed to be leading nowhere. Brown, ploughed fields sloped in all directions, there were no houses, shops or trams, and there were no people, only the rooks gathering, unconcerned, in the leafless trees at the side of an empty life-less barn.

The pain of home-sickness has to be cured in some way. I wrote stories, mainly about rabbits which were rather like people I knew, and sent them home to my sister. I made up stories to tell in the dormitory at night. I made for myself a picture of a longed-for cosy home life which never existed but which, in thought, comforted.

Another edge of exile; the daughter of a teacher nursing in a hospital at a time when probationer nurses needed a well-to-do background in order to survive on twenty-eight shillings a month and frugal 'keep'. As with the Quakers there was the feeling of being excluded from an establishment and its members. This time it was a layer of society called *county* in which tweeds and twin sets and pearls were not just a joke.

Perhaps the writer, in writing, overcomes and accepts feelings of exclusion.

'Are these tomatoes English?' I asked a Scottish green-grocer. 'Madam! They are Scotch!' and I discovered at once that to move to Scotland was to move to another country.

Being a stranger is not to reject one's environment. I store the images of coal mines, brick works and slag heaps. I can never forget the smooth hills of the Cotswolds and the wet tough grass and heather of the Scottish moors. I store too the regional sounds of voices, accents and dialects and the contemporary idiom of every place and of every decade.

Perhaps, for me, encountering and accepting strange territory is a necessary part of learning to be a writer.

I came to Western Australia in the middle of my life. I realise that the freshness of my observation can distort as well as illuminate. The impact of the new country does not obliterate the previous one but sharpens memory, thought and feeling thus providing a contrasting theme or setting.

I am always being asked, 'Do you write from your own experience?' Obviously any author must write from experience, but if the question means do I write accounts of people I have known or of a sequence of events I have witnessed the answer is decidedly 'no'.

The experience from which I write is created by things seen or heard or read about or imagined. I use small fragments, hints, suggestions of experience. The landscape of my writing is not to be found clearly on any map. A particular aspect of a tree or a paddock at a particular moment may be used. All my life since the earnest, hopeful prayers written in my diaries during the first real miseries of boarding school life I have kept journals in which I write about people and places; dwelling on, perhaps, some detail of human effort or the way in which a tree might change in the changing light of an afternoon.

The character of Miss Hailey in the novel *Mr Scobie's Riddle* is based on the sight of a woman in an unusual straw hat. That is all I noticed about her as I passed her in the street. But as I passed I imagined how pleased she would be to be able to tell someone the way.

A picture of the sea or even the sharp rise from the coastal plain which is characteristic of the southern part of Western Australia, as well as many other regions, is based on something seen but not seen in a sharply defined geographical location.

I explain, when asked, that my stories start with a character and not with a plot but I know that this distinction is unreal. Perhaps I start with a feeling for a character and then try to develop this in a number of situations. Most of these situations will never be related in the final work. In any writing it is only what is actually written that counts but all these exploratory studies contribute to the character which is finally offered. I can use material only when it can be imaginatively transformed. Some personal experience, the nursing of soldiers sent back from Europe during the war, had to be accepted but I have not yet been able to write from this experience.

Some years ago I was offered teaching work at the Western Australian Institute of Technology and at the Fremantle Arts Centre as well as workshops in the country districts of Western Australia. I think that teaching helps my writing, certainly it does not hamper it. I have never ventured into the principles of criticism. With my students I look at a text and try to make clear what the writer is trying to achieve and how this achievement is brought about. This is of great value to me and I hope it is of value to my students.

I read a great deal. I realise that however much time I spend in reading I shall not be able to read as much as I would like to. It is necessary to distinguish between writers who have made a great impression on me and those who may have influenced my writing. I often re-read the *Elective Affinities* and *Rasselas* but I do not imagine that I write in any way like Goethe or Johnson. I suppose both have shown me ways of using words

311

and ways of looking at people. This may be all that is meant by a writer's influence on another writer.

I am unable to name a book which has been a model for me. I read the same stories, plays and novels over and over again. When I am writing I find I have to avoid reading some of the 'strong' writers, Henry James and Patrick White, for example, because they intrude with the power of their words.

In times when I am unable to write I re-read a wide range of authors, Cervantes, Chekhov, Ibsen, James, Hardy, Thomas Mann, E. M. Forster, and I read as many contemporary poets and fiction writers. Apart from the pleasure of reading, I find it is better to read than to simply fret in despair about being unable to write.

I have to disagree with the often made remark that the short story is unpopular. Before writing or while I am writing a story I never consider whether it will be published or not, whether it will be saleable or not. I am drawn towards short stories both in reading and in writing and I continued to write them during years when I was not being published. I would have gone on writing even if nothing was published.

V. S. Pritchett in his preface to his *Collected Stories* has written about the short story:

> *thousands of addicts still delight in it because it is above all memorable and is not simply read but reread again and again. It is the glancing form of fiction that seems to be right for the nervousness and the restlessness of contemporary life.*

The same can be said of the short novel as it is written at the present time.